"Clever and witty. Wilde artfully portrays Regency London, from its ballrooms to Bow Street, in all its glory and hypocrisy, and provides readers with a heroine worthy of our attention. With its colorful cast and scandalous intrigue, *A Useful Woman* would surely have set the famed patronesses of Almack's atwitter."

—Anna Lee Huber, national bestselling author of
the Lady Darby Mysteries

"Well-drawn characters and a perfect plot make this historical mystery a winner."

—Nancy Haddock, national bestselling author of *Paint the Town Dead*

"[A] wonderfully entertaining Regency mystery romance, and I really enjoyed it. With a cleverly cunning plot and characters that are engaging and witty, I was easily enfolded in the dangers and subterfuge of the ton. Rosalind is a strong, determined character who knows what it is like to carry the world on her shoulders—very intelligent and savvy . . . With plenty of twists and turns, and romance thrown in to boot, *A Useful Woman* by Darcie Wilde is a delight to read, and I look forward to the next in the series."

—Fresh Fiction

"Wilde brings the haut monde of early nineteenth-century London to vivid life, and the characters she peoples it with are complex individuals whose basic decency, or lack of it, is carefully hidden behind a facade of manners and propriety."

—*Publishers Weekly*

TITLES BY DARCIE WILDE

Lord of the Rakes
The Accidental Abduction

REGENCY MAKEOVER SERIES

Part I: The Bride Behind the Curtain
Part II: The Stepsister's Triumph
Part III: An Exquisite Marriage

ROSALIND THORNE MYSTERIES

A Useful Woman
A Purely Private Matter

A
Purely
PRIVATE
Matter

A ROSALIND THORNE MYSTERY

DARCIE WILDE

BERKLEY PRIME CRIME
NEW YORK

BERKLEY PRIME CRIME
Published by Berkley
An imprint of Penguin Random House LLC
375 Hudson Street, New York, New York 10014

Copyright © 2017 by Sarah Zettel
Penguin Random House supports copyright. Copyright fuels creativity, encourages
diverse voices, promotes free speech, and creates a vibrant culture. Thank you for
buying an authorized edition of this book and for complying with copyright laws
by not reproducing, scanning, or distributing any part of it in any form without
permission. You are supporting writers and allowing Penguin Random
House to continue to publish books for every reader.

BERKLEY is a registered trademark and BERKLEY PRIME CRIME and the
B colophon are trademarks of Penguin Random House LLC.

Library of Congress Cataloging-in-Publication Data

Names: Wilde, Darcie, author.
Title: A purely private matter / Darcie Wilde.
Description: First Edition. | New York : Berkley Prime Crime, 2017. | Series:
Rosalind Thorne mystery ; [2]
Identifiers: LCCN 2016043580 (print) | LCCN 2016050440 (ebook) | ISBN
9780425282380 (paperback) | ISBN 9780698404298 (ebook)
Subjects: LCSH: Women detectives—England—Fiction. | Private
investigators—England—Fiction. | Murder—Investigation—Fiction. |
London (England)—Social life and customs—19th century—Fiction. | BISAC:
FICTION / Mystery & Detective / Historical. | FICTION / Mystery &
Detective / Women Sleuths. | GSAFD: Mystery fiction. | Historical fiction.
Classification: LCC PS3623.I5353 P87 2017 (print) | LCC PS3623.I5353 (ebook)
| DDC 813/.6—dc23
LC record available at https://lccn.loc.gov/2016043580

First Edition: May 2017

Printed in the United States of America
1   3   5   7   9   10   8   6   4   2

Cover art by Matthieu Forichon
Book design by Laura K. Corless

CHAPTER 1

The Art of Obtaining Discreet Entry

Avoid as much as possible going out in the evening, especially on frivolous errands.
— Samuel and Sarah Adams, *The Complete Servant*

How will you get inside? Mrs. Devery's question echoed in the back of Rosalind Thorne's mind as she climbed out of the hired carriage. *They do not admit women at Graham's.*

That was the first problem. Had Rosalind needed to get inside a respectable house, she could have followed the daisy chain of her acquaintance to find a plausible reason for visiting. There were, however, limits to even Rosalind's carefully cultivated connections. Fashioning an anonymous admission to one of the most exclusive gaming clubs in Pall Mall had proved beyond her powers, until tonight.

Tonight Graham's was holding its Selenite Ball. Once a year, the club members welcomed London society's richest and most riotous inhabitants. Champagne and brandy would flow and tables would groan under the weight of the food prepared by the club's French chef, and most important for Rosalind's purposes, women would be welcomed into the club's exclusively masculine preserve.

Rosalind clutched her blue silk cloak closed with one hand

and held her white and silver face mask with the other as she shouldered her way through the opulent crowd. Ladies and gentlemen done up in enough colors to outfit a hundred stained glass windows jammed the steps. Precious stones, some of which were surely genuine, sparkled on every throat, bosom, and brow. Rosalind was not the only woman to affect a mask. Creations of gold lace and peacock feathers adorned the faces of some who did not scruple to expose their shoulders, arms, bosoms, and most daringly, their ankles.

Graham's Club had three sets of doors facing St. James's Street, and all of them stood wide open in an attempt to accommodate the flood of fashionable visitors. Rosalind selected the doors farthest to the right, and inserted herself into the particolored current with the efficient yet unobtrusive sidestep she'd perfected for navigating crowded ballrooms.

When she reached the golden doorway, the liveried footman shook his head at her until all his chins wagged. "Now, then, ma'am, I will need to see your invitation."

Rosalind was as devoid of invitation as she was of any intention to join the festivities. She stepped closer to the footman and, in a familiar manner that would have shocked any respectable house or manservant, took his hand.

"I am here to meet a friend," she breathed as she pressed the coin into his palm.

The man looked at her mask, and closed his hand around the coin. He also stepped back, and bowed deeply. Rosalind gathered her hems and sailed past him with a straight back and smooth step that would have made her old deportment master smile.

How will you know where to go? Mrs. Devery had asked. *You will not know what the place looks like inside.*

This much, at least, was easy to solve. The circulating library kept a number of guidebooks describing the more notorious sights and haunts of London. The article in *Clubs of the Metropolis: A Comprehensive Guide* had proved most detailed. Rosalind looked about her now, matching that description to what she saw.

Dozens of flambeaux and beeswax candles lit Graham's marble entrance hall. A pair of brightly rouged women in low-cut gowns of pale green silk glanced curiously at Rosalind, but did not pause as they joined the shining river that flowed up the famous (according to the guidebook) marble and gilt stairs. On either side of that sweeping stairway stood a pair of poorly executed, larger-than-life gilded statues of naked women. They were crowned in stars and holding aloft fans of playing cards in one hand while the other beckoned the members to come try their luck. These were meant to be representations of the goddess of fortune. Privately, Rosalind thought the goddess of fortune should have a word with her solicitor.

But surely you'll be recognized.

That had been a genuine worry. Graham's counted many sons of aristocratic families among its members. Rosalind could not risk being seen unescorted in a place she had no business even entering. That meant not one, but two, disguises became necessary, the first to get her through the door, and the second to render her invisible once she was inside. It also meant that she could not make use of the attended cloak room or retiring room to effect her transformation. But as she had hoped, behind each of the great, gilded statues, there was a narrow, shadowed space that was simple enough for Rosalind to fade into.

Keeping her motions small and quick, Rosalind drew off her mask and unfastened her cape. Underneath, she wore a plain black dress. The addition of a white collar and plain cuffs made the garment originally designed for mourning into a passing imitation of a lady's maid's severe dress. She had pulled her golden hair into a simple knot at the back of her neck, and left off even the most modest pins or jewels. Instead of a reticule, she carried a plain work bag for holding thread and scissors, scraps of lace, and other needlework.

Presto! thought Rosalind to herself as she smoothed the cloak over her arm.

It was not as easy to imitate a servant as one might be led to believe from stage plays and three-volume novels. In addition to the thousand highly specialized forms and skills that a life in service demanded, there were habits of motion and attitude that were as difficult to assume without training and continual practice. Therefore, Rosalind had waited until after midnight to make her attempt. By now, the majority of the guests were quite drunk. The rest were concentrating on getting drunk, or taking advantage of others' drunkenness. Under these circumstances, the finer details of her dress and demeanor ought to pass unnoticed.

Rosalind slipped into the very edge of the crowd and let herself be carried by mutual motion up the stairs. If anyone asked what she did here, which was unlikely, she could say she was taking the silk cloak to her mistress, who wished to leave without delay.

Rosalind reached the first floor. Clarence blue carpets softened the floors. More gilded statues in the style of those downstairs guarded the entrance to a hive of galleries and salons. Music and laughter filled the whole building as men and women danced and drank and crowded around the tables. The new game of *la roulette* was also on full display and, to judge by the cheers thundering through the gaming rooms, was proving a magnificent success.

Rosalind turned her face away from that gaudy door. Fortunes would be lost tonight. Women as well as men would be swept up by the excitement, and they would commit sin and folly to be allowed to continue to play. It was that sort of folly which brought her here tonight, and what she needed was not to be found on this floor. Rosalind breezed past the gaming rooms, making her way to the plainer stair at the end of the passageway.

I am at my wits' end, Miss Thorne. You must help me. Mrs. Percival Devery, née Lucille Allenby, had cried as she sat in Rosalind's small parlor and poured out her story.

Rosalind Thorne had a reputation as what society called "a useful woman." Usually, this referred to some gently bred woman in distressed circumstances who managed to keep a kind of position in the fashionable world by helping her better-off sisters organize their visiting lists and entertainments, as well as running those errands that these more fortunate women found too fatiguing.

But recently and singularly, Rosalind had enlarged upon her occupation. She had begun to help women with their more serious problems. The problems that could affect lives, marriages, and families.

Rosalind listened to Mrs. Devery's halting description of how she had come to this city as a new bride and how her husband had introduced her to society. Society, in its turn, had introduced Mrs. Devery to cards. She quickly took to the games, and enjoyed them enough that she found herself playing deeper than her income allowed. In order to keep playing, she had borrowed money from a man named Russell Fullerton.

He was so charming. So understanding, Mrs. Devery told Rosalind miserably. *If I had known what kind of man he was, if I had any idea . . .*

But no one among her new acquaintances had thought to warn her. Not even when Mr. Fullerton had asked her to give him her cameo brooch as a promise that she would repay his loan. But although she did repay him, the brooch had not been returned. Then, the letters had started to come, and the demands for more money began.

And you have been paying?

I have, or at least I have tried, but he wants so much, Miss Thorne.

Rosalind mounted the narrower, quieter stair that led to the club's second floor with a firm step.

My advice, Mrs. Devery, is that you tell your husband the truth. If he cares for you, he will forgive you.

Mr. Fullerton has threatened to take the story to the papers. My husband is in the House of Commons, Miss Thorne. The scandal would destroy his career. He would not forgive that.

The hallway of the second floor was deep in shadow. The windows at either end admitted some flickering light from the street outside, but no candles had been lit here to alleviate the dark or the cold, because no one was expected to be up here this early.

Like most clubs of its kind, Graham's kept rooms that could be reserved by those who had no wish to bother traveling London's streets to get to their tables. Some gentlemen, in fact, lived almost exclusively at their clubs, either for the convenience of the location, or to avoid the entanglements of hearth and home. Mr. Fullerton was one of these. Rosalind had bribed Graham's servants for information well before she ever set foot in the club. A glass of gin and a few coins had enabled her to discover that Mr. Fullerton occupied the corner suite on the second floor.

Rosalind kept her gait steady as she moved down the darkened and silent corridor. To look furtive would be the greatest folly. She must act as if she was under orders to be in this exact spot.

She reached the door that should lead to the corner apartment, and stopped in the puddle of orange light that flickered through the arched window.

This point had always been the weakness of the plan and the question for which there was no answer. Was the door locked? It might not be. Mr. Fullerton was in the club, after all, down in the gaming rooms, enjoying the rout and riot. But then, he was a blackmailer and therefore not a trusting soul. If he'd locked his door, then Rosalind would need to find where the housekeepers stored the keys. That would take her into the realm of the servants, which would be risky beyond measure. The masters might all be drunk and distracted tonight, but their attendants most certainly were not.

But she glanced at the floor and saw a bright line of light gleaming at the level of the carpet. There was a fire in the room. That might mean the door was open, but it also might mean that there was someone in the rooms. Rosalind's heart thumped once, but she did not permit herself to hesitate. She knocked softly, as a servant alerting those within she was about to enter.

There was no answer.

Rosalind's heart thumped again. She closed her hand around the doorknob. It turned, and the door opened quietly. Rosalind resisted the urge to dart inside, and kept her movements sedate, at least until she closed the door behind herself, and drew the bolt.

He told me he keeps my cameo in the drawer of his bedside table, so that he has it near him always.

Mr. Fullerton would have had no fear of divulging this little detail to Mrs. Devery. A young lady of her class would never be admitted into a gentlemen's club, much less his private rooms. Except for one reason, of course, and Mrs. Devery had been painfully aware of this.

I think . . . I think he may eventually demand more from me than money.

Mr. Fullerton clearly reveled in his high living, and Rosalind felt certain he must have had these apartments privately furnished. Despite the display of gilt and excess downstairs, Rosalind could not believe that the club provided all its members with such a profusion of silks and velvet, marble tops and painted enamel handles.

A beautiful little marquetry table waited beside a luxuriously curtained bed. Rosalind put her hand to the ornate drawer, and held her breath.

The drawer didn't budge. Mr. Fullerton, it seemed, was not entirely careless.

Rosalind bit her lip and quickly reached into her work bag to pull out the sandalwood letter opener she'd brought against this possibility. Rosalind had been gently reared, but some of that gentle upbringing had included a girls' boarding school, a place where one might gain experience with all manner of petty larcenies.

Rosalind's hands had not lost their touch, and Mr. Fullerton's drawer proved no more difficult than the headmistress's desk had. When she slid it open, she found half a dozen articles of jewelry in that drawer. Rosalind saw a garnet ring, a pearl collar, and a figured brooch. Mrs. Devery had clearly not been Fullerton's only victim.

There were also several packets of letters tied in silk ribbon.

Did you send him any letters? Rosalind had asked Mrs. Devery. *Any at all, even a brief note?*

No. I did not. Everything was communicated through my old nurse. She is still as sharp as she ever was, and . . . is sincerely attached to me.

It would seem, however, that there were other ladies who were not so careful. Still, those letters were not Rosalind's business. She was here for the white and sepia cameo that was a portrait of Mrs. Devery's grandmother, framed in gold and tiny diamonds.

Before she began to plot her entry into the club, Rosalind had visited Mrs. Devery's jeweler. That careful artisan had kept the description and pattern of the cameo. Many ladies had copies of their jewels made so that the originals could be stored for safekeeping, or sold without their families being the wiser. The jeweler was quite happy to duplicate the cameo in paste and resin, and did not demur at the alterations Rosalind requested.

Now Rosalind claimed the original cameo and, in its place, dropped the copy from her work bag into the drawer. She looked again at the packets of correspondence, and hesitated. Then, she took up the letters and tucked them away as well. She closed the drawer. There would be no way to relock it, but that could not be helped. Hopefully, Mr. Fullerton would think his thief had just been after the letters, and not consider the jewels left behind.

There. Done. As long as she could manage her exit.

Rosalind slipped once more into the hallway. She strained her ears for the sounds of bells or the cry of the watch for some indication as to the time, but heard neither. It was a far different sound that broke the cool silence.

"You there!" The woman's voice stopped Rosalind in her tracks. "Come here and help me fix this thing!"

Rosalind stood paralyzed for a handful of frantic heartbeats before she gathered herself. It was not the command that held her frozen. It was that she recognized the woman's voice.

Charlotte? she thought, but immediately caught herself. *No. It is not possible.*

"I must get my mistress her wrap," she murmured without turning around.

"Never mind your mistress. Come and help me."

No. It is not her. This voice is too low. The accents are wrong.

Rosalind turned to face the woman who stood at the top of the stairs. The flickering torchlight glimmered on a dress of pale silk and netting. In one hand, the woman held a swath of gauze that had clearly been torn at the shoulder.

Rosalind gathered her nerve, but her answer was cut off by the sound of footsteps on the stairs.

"There you are, my dear Cynthia!" A slim man with his hair

swept back from his forehead trotted up the stairs. "I thought I'd lost you!"

"Ferdinand!" The woman in silver turned at once. Rosalind was so quickly dismissed from all consideration, she might as well have dropped through the floor.

"You frightened me. Feel how my heart beats!" The woman lifted the man's hand to her breast and laid it there.

Rosalind dropped her gaze. She knew she should retire. If she had been a real servant, she would have known how to retreat and where the back stairs were located. But she was not, and these two blocked her only exit.

"Ah, a thousand curses upon me as a fool," murmured Ferdinand, stepping closer to the woman, and lacing his arm tightly through hers. "Come, let me find you some champagne. You will drink until you are quite calm again."

"But my dress!" The woman pulled the torn gauze from her shoulder. "I cannot be seen like this."

Tenderly, the man took the netting and draped it around her throat, arranging it with great care. "Then I shall take you where you cannot be seen."

The woman lifted her face to his. They linked arms at once and hurried down the corridor, away from the stairs, and Rosalind, leaving her alone, forgotten, and entirely safe from all risk of exposure.

This fact barely touched her. In her mind Rosalind was miles and years away. She stood in another darkened hallway, watching another young woman—slimmer, more plainly dressed—run through another door. Despair, confusion, and betrayal washed through Rosalind, as clear and sharp as if she were still a girl, on the night when she watched her sister, Charlotte, disappear.

CHAPTER 2

A New Acquaintance

Gentlemen, if we are to regard our friends with such constant suspicion—if we are to be jealous of the wives of our bosom, we had infinitely better close our doors against society altogether.

—*The Trial of Birch vs. Neal for Criminal Conversation*

It was early in the gray, grim, grimy London morning, and Rosalind Thorne was entirely exhausted. She hadn't even been to bed. After leaving Graham's, she'd been able to return home just long enough to change out of her lady's maid costume. She'd promised to return the cameo to Mrs. Devery before her household was awake. Once there, she'd needed to stay long enough to make sure the young woman not only heard but retained her instructions. Mrs. Devery was to confess her debts to her husband. She was to face Mr. Fullerton calmly when she produced the original of the cameo, but to speak to him no more than was strictly necessary and on no account to allow herself to be alone with him. If Fullerton made any additional threats or demands, Mrs. Devery was to write to Rosalind at once.

Mrs. Devery was also to make sure she gave her old nurse a token of gratitude to help ensure the loyal woman remained loyal, despite any additional provocations, or bribes, that might be offered.

On the long, jostling ride back through the morning traffic of vans, carts, and sheep flocks, Rosalind kept herself awake by considering what to do with the letters she had stolen from Fullerton's drawer. Probably, they were additional fuel for his blackmail. Therefore, the wisest, simplest, and most honorable course of action was to burn them all unopened. This firm and sensible thought warred with the image of the woman retreating into the darkness with her lover. It raised in her the unworthy idea that Mr. Fullerton might be someone she needed to speak with in the near future, and if she did, she would need to have some way to encourage him to answer her.

With all that ringing through her head, and her conscience, Rosalind entirely forgot she'd agreed to receive her friend, Alice Littlefield, until the moment she walked back into her house.

"Oh, Rosalind, at last!" Alice darted out of the parlor just at the moment Rosalind entered the cramped front hall. Mrs. Kendricks, the housekeeper, was caught with her mouth open. "I was beginning to think we'd miss you altogether." Alice gave Rosalind a quick kiss on the cheek. "I've brought Mrs. Seymore, as I told you, and I have promised her faithfully you will not turn her away." She paused. "What is the matter? Are you unwell?"

"No, I'm perfectly well, thank you," Rosalind replied. "I'm sorry I was so long. The appointment this morning turned out to be more complicated than I had hoped."

Rosalind left her coat, bonnet, and a request for coffee with Mrs. Kendricks and allowed Alice to seize her hand to draw her into the tiny, tidy parlor.

"Rosalind," said Alice. "This is my friend, Mrs. William Seymore. Margaretta, may I introduce Miss Rosalind Thorne?"

Mrs. Seymore stood, and she and Rosalind both made their curtsies.

"How do you do, Miss Thorne?" Mrs. Seymore's voice was unusually low for a woman's, and held a distinct musical tone. "Thank you for agreeing to see me, especially at such an hour."

Had Alice been alone, or with her brother George, Rosalind might have just confessed to her midnight adventure and asked to be excused. But this Mrs. Seymore was a stranger. Therefore, etiquette must take precedence over exhaustion.

"A pleasure to meet you, Mrs. Seymore," said Rosalind. "Won't you please sit down?"

Mrs. Seymore settled onto Rosalind's sofa beside Alice, while Rosalind took her usual chair by the fireplace. Mrs. Seymore was a striking woman. She had left the flush of youth behind, but she was one of those ladies whom time had bloomed rather than withered. She had a wealth of dark hair that was dressed simply. Her eyes were likewise dark, and wide-set. Her matron's summer gown was cream and apricot, without lace or ribbon. Its simplicity spoke not only of excellent taste, but of the easy poise so prized by members of the *haut ton*.

Mrs. Seymore took Rosalind in with a glance of those dark eyes, assessing her quickly, and showing Rosalind there was a sharp mind behind that beauty.

"Mrs. Seymore is a poetess," said Alice. "And a ballad writer."

Mrs. Seymore inclined her head with studied modesty. This explained how she came to know Alice. Like Rosalind, tiny, quick, dark Alice Littlefield had been born into the aristocracy. But her father had squandered his fortune, and his children were left to make shift for themselves. Now, Alice kept house with her brother, George, and made her living as a writer for newspapers and annuals. This change of station had gained Alice a large and eccentric acquaintance throughout London's literary world.

"Do you want me to begin, Margaretta?" Alice asked Mrs. Seymore.

"No. This once I will tell my own story, even if I never do so again." Mrs. Seymore straightened her shoulders, and Rosalind had the distinct sensation of an actress striking a pose. "You have before you, Miss Thorne, a woman on the edge of public disgrace."

Mrs. Seymore paused, possibly expecting a gasp of horror or pity. Rosalind did not oblige. "I am sorry to hear it, Mrs. Seymore. What form of disgrace are we speaking of?"

Mrs. Seymore looked to Alice, a little disappointed. Alice shrugged. "I did warn you, Margaretta. Rosalind is not easily shaken."

"I see that," said Mrs. Seymore. "I can be direct then. My husband, Miss Thorne, is threatening to file suit for criminal conversation."

"Ah."

English law had many complexities and strange aspects. One of the strangest, and most frustrating from Rosalind's point of view, was the tort of "criminal conversation." According to the law, a man and wife were considered a single body (his, naturally). The act of unsanctioned intercourse between a married woman and a man other than her lawfully wedded husband was, therefore, considered something akin to property damage. As a result, if a husband believed his wife to have been sharing her favors with another man, he could sue that other man for monetary recompense.

Mrs. Kendricks entered the parlor carrying the silver coffee tray. Only some of the Thorne family plate had survived the family's various adventures, but the coffee service was still intact and

Mrs. Kendricks insisted on it when there was company, even though the tray dwarfed the round table where she placed it.

"Thank you, Mrs. Kendricks," Rosalind said. She did not miss the way Mrs. Kendricks kept her eyes lowered, or the tight frown of disapproval on the housekeeper's normally placid face. A pool of disquiet formed in the pit of Rosalind's stomach. She covered the unwelcome emotion with the business of pouring out and inquiring how her guests preferred their coffee (with a bit of milk, if you please, no sugar, thank you).

Once they all had their cups in their hands, Rosalind asked the next, and the most important, question. "Against whom is your husband bringing suit?"

Mrs. Seymore stared at the cup in her hands but made no move to drink. "Fletcher Cavendish," she said.

Finally, Mrs. Seymore had said something that startled Rosalind, and she could not help looking to Alice for confirmation.

Alice nodded. "*The* Fletcher Cavendish. The first man of the English stage. The greatest Shakespearian since Garrick, the man who holds more hearts in thrall than even Lord Byron . . . but you've read the columns."

"Has your husband any evidence to support his suspicions?" Rosalind did not ask if the accusations were true. That hardly mattered. What mattered was whether they might be believed.

Mrs. Seymore cocked her head and regarded Rosalind with a fresh, and much cooler, gaze. "Captain Seymore has been questioning—perhaps I should say badgering—the servants. So far they have remained loyal and steadfast. That may change. But he says he has letters."

"Between you and Mr. Cavendish?"

"No. He says they are from a third party, one, and here I am using his words, 'fully informed upon the gross and indecent nature of this act of treachery.'" For the first time, Mrs. Seymore's musical voice faltered. "I was very young when I married Captain Seymore, Miss Thorne. I was an orphaned girl and desired nothing so much as a home and family to call my own." Rosalind inclined her head in encouragement and understanding.

"Seymore's family connections admitted me to society of a better class than I had previously known," Mrs. Seymore went on. "I gained some popularity for my work, and some for what were considered my personal attributes." Meaning her beauty. Probably her conversation as well, but mostly her beauty. "I think Seymore liked having such a woman on his arm. He enjoys being the object of men's envy and admiration. He always encouraged me to write and to keep myself active in society while he was away with his ship."

"But matters changed when he came home?" The final defeat of Napoleon had left many an officer facing the complications of a life on reduced pay with no chance of action, or advancement.

"Profoundly. Where once he encouraged me to mix in society, now he accuses me of flirtation, and disloyalty. Before, he praised my efforts. Now, I am slothful and a disgrace because I do not work hard enough." Mrs. Seymore sniffed. "I have borne it as best I can. But now when we argue, he tells me about the suit. He tells me he has engaged an attorney. He tells me . . . he tells me many things, some of them might be true. I know he is working up the nerve to do the thing, and that it will come to him very soon." She paused and repeated, "Very soon."

"Are you even acquainted with Mr. Cavendish?" It happened sometimes that men, especially men in straitened circumstances, simply picked out a rich target for their accusations.

Mrs. Seymore turned her head away. Her face had flushed bright red, not in embarrassment, but in anger. "As it happens, Mr. Cavendish and I are well acquainted. We met almost twenty years ago. He was the one who saw my talent for verse and urged me to try for publication. We have always corresponded and I've never concealed the connection. Mr. Cavendish has visited our house and dined with us. We have accepted invitations to his performances and supper afterwards. That this accusation should come so suddenly . . . I am bewildered."

You're not, thought Rosalind. *You're hurt and you're angry, but you understand this all too well.*

"The fact of the matter is, Miss Thorne, I would not care whether Seymore brings his ridiculous suit or no, except for one thing." She fumbled in her bag for a handkerchief to press against her eyes. "I am with child, Miss Thorne."

Rosalind made no answer. Felicitations did not seem appropriate, given that Mrs. Seymore was struggling against tears that had much more to do with outrage than with sorrow.

"Seymore insists the child is not his. If he says this publicly, if he divorces me, then I am not the only one ruined. My child, my son or—God forbid!—my daughter, will be labeled a bastard and must carry the taint of the accusation, and their mother's disgrace, through their life."

"But how is it you wish me to help you?" asked Rosalind. "I am unacquainted with Captain Seymore. I do not believe he would be dissuaded by another woman—"

"He would laugh in your face," Mrs. Seymore said grimly. "No. What I wish is to be proved innocent. Obviously, I am not allowed to appear on my own behalf in court, but if I have some solid evidence of my innocence, perhaps I can persuade Seymore that he will only make himself ridiculous by pursuing the case. I could even plead my case in the newspapers if I must." She nodded toward Alice. "But I cannot sit idle and helpless while my future, and my child's future, is decided by my enemies."

It was a strong word, and it pricked Rosalind's curiosity. "Who is advising the captain?" she asked.

"His brother, Sir Bertram, primarily. Sir and Lady Bertram dislike me for failing to be humble enough for my unsatisfactory origins, and yet they are quick enough take the money I make when it comes in."

Alice nodded once in confirmation and agreement.

Despite this, Rosalind felt there was something wrong in Mrs. Seymore's story and the manner of her address. She could not put a definite name to this kernel of suspicion, but Rosalind was inclined to trust her own instincts.

"Have you seen these letters Captain Seymore is threatening you with?" Rosalind asked.

"I have one." Mrs. Seymore pulled out the folded paper. "Seymore has hidden them, but I was able to snare this one from his desk." She handed it to Rosalind.

Rosalind opened the letter and read:

Sir,

I strive only to warn you. Last night again, the woman who calls herself your wife was seen at the Theatre Royal, and at the King's Arms. She entered the establishment brazenly and alone at such times as she could have had no legitimate business being there. She stayed in both places at least an hour and left again, quite smug and satisfied with herself. Mr. Cavendish himself was not so far behind. Indeed, when she left the hotel, he was with her and they strolled openly arm in arm, quite comfortable together.

I leave it to you to decide what your honor as an officer and a gentleman requires to be done.

There was, of course, no signature.

"Could Seymore's brother—you said his name was Sir Bertram?—could he be the one writing the letters?"

"It is possible, but I could not say for certain."

"And may I keep this?" Rosalind held up the paper.

"Of course, if it will be of use. If Seymore missed it, he would have said something by now."

Rosalind folded the letter and made up her mind. "I will make some preliminary inquiries into the matter, Mrs. Seymore. I will not, however, be able to promise anything until I have explored the situation further."

Disappointment flickered behind Mrs. Seymore's dark, expressive eyes, but she rallied quickly. "Of course," she said. "We are strangers, you and I. You require assurance that I am speaking the truth. Women do lie at such times, even to their sisters in misfortune."

The words stung. Not because of the accusation, but because of the blatant attempt at manipulation. If Alice had not been there, Rosalind might well have shown the woman to the door.

"I do not make promises I cannot keep, Mrs. Seymore. Such matters can be made simple or complex by the nature of the persons around whom the circumstances gather. I must discover for myself the range of personalities involved here. That is the only way in which a practical and complete resolution may be discovered. If this is not acceptable, you must seek help elsewhere."

"I ask your forgiveness for my hasty words," Mrs. Seymore said. "I have been under a great strain lately, and have become used to being called everything from hysterical to dishonest. You will let me know your decision?" She paused. "I don't wish to be indelicate, but Alice mentioned that there would be a fee. Perhaps you may write and let me know your requirements."

"If I feel I will be able to help, I will do so." Rosalind took a deep breath. "Now, if I agree to look into this matter, I will be seen with you and out on your business. Therefore, we will need a plausible reason for our acquaintance. I believe Alice said you are a poetess?"

Mrs. Seymore nodded. "Very good," said Rosalind. "We may say that you are engaged in compiling a new volume and that I, as a friend, am assisting you with the project. You have, I'm afraid, been suffering somewhat from eye strain of late."

"Indeed, I have," Mrs. Seymore replied promptly. "How good of you to agree to help, Miss Thorne. I cannot thank you enough. And now I must go." Mrs. Seymore got to her feet. She also held out her hand for Rosalind to take. "I hope and I pray that you will see your way toward helping me." She squeezed Rosalind's fingertips for just a moment, before she let go and glided out of the parlor. Alice glanced back at Rosalind hastily and followed her friend to the foyer so Mrs. Kendricks could help them with their bonnets and gloves.

Rosalind stood staring at the parlor door for a long moment.

"Well, Alice," she murmured. "What have you gotten us into?"

CHAPTER 3

A Meeting of Like Minds

It is most unwise on the part of any woman to allow her husband to discover of what shreds and patches women are composed.

—Catherine Gore, *Pin Money*

"I'm not certain your friend likes me," Mrs. Seymore said as she and Alice Littlefield descended the steps from Miss Thorne's house into the clamor and bustle of Little Russell Street. It was a straight but cramped thoroughfare. Its buildings crowded shoulder to shoulder, and practically nose to nose. This forced the traffic and the pedestrians to jostle together on the muddy cobbles. Margaretta happened to know this street had once held several houses of a much lower reputation than the cramped but decorous parlor where she'd spent her morning. But fashions in neighborhoods, as in all other things, were subject to change, and this one had begun to attract a more respectable sort of resident. Still, its reputation lingered like a faint malaise. Mrs. Seymore supposed that was among the reasons Miss Thorne had chosen to make her home here after her own disgrace. It was, above all things, cheap.

Oh, Margaretta, what a snob you've become.

"Don't worry about Rosalind, Margaretta," Alice was saying. "She's simply very guarded."

"I suppose she would have to be." Margaretta let herself muse. "I expect in her life she must come into contact with all manner of persons."

Alice smiled at this, as Margaretta hoped she would. "If that's an invitation to gossip, I'm going to have to disappoint."

"Would I ever ask you to do such a thing?" Which of course made Alice look down her snub nose at Margaretta, in an attitude that sent them both into peals of laughter. "All right, all right. But you cannot blame me for trying. Even a writer of sentimental ballads must have some fodder for her work."

"I understand. I confess I've tried to winkle a story or three out of her myself. But Rosalind is entirely closemouthed about those she assists. A fact that you should be glad of."

"Oh, I am."

The women both pulled their hems back to avoid being splashed by the ragman's barrow as he shoved his way past them. A stout and harassed woman signaled him from behind the area railing and he bumped his barrow across the way.

Alice pulled herself and Margaretta through a gap in the traffic between a pair of serving women and an oyster seller with his basket. When they'd hit on a clear path again, she cocked her head toward her friend. "You are telling me the truth about your situation, aren't you, Margaretta?" she asked bluntly.

Margaretta felt her spirits sag. This was what it had all come to. Even her friends and colleagues had begun to distrust her. She should have known, she supposed. She should have taken more care, planned better . . .

Stop this. Regrets will not serve.

"I promise, Alice, every word I have said to you is true."

"What about the ones you haven't said?"

Clever dear. Margaretta felt herself smile. "Those as well."

"Margaretta . . ."

"No, Alice. No more. My nerves are gone. We must talk of something else." Margaretta slipped her arm through the newspaperwoman's. "Will you come home with me? We could take a dish of tea, and afterwards I'll have my man take you wherever you need to go."

Alice hesitated. "I'm sorry, Margaretta, but I've got A. E. Littlefield's *Society Notes* to write out, and if I'm late, the major will have my head." The major was the publisher of *The London Chronicle*, chief among the various papers and periodicals that Alice wrote for.

"I understand," said Margaretta. "I should be working myself. I've promised Mrs. Duncan six new poems for her annual and I'm woefully behind. Well, at least let me pay for your carriage home."

"There's no need. It's a fine day. I can walk."

"I insist," Margaretta told her. "You've done me a good turn this morning, you must allow me to repay the favor."

Despite her irrevocable change to a workingwoman of the middling classes, Alice's genteel pride was still liable to show itself in the odd corners of her life. *That's the difference when you've fallen rather than risen*, thought Margaretta. *One I will soon become familiar with, if I am not very careful.*

This time, however, Alice's pride surrendered after only a brief struggle. "In that case I accept. Thank you."

There was a cab stand where Little Russell and Great Russell Streets met. Alice climbed into the hackney carriage while Margaretta gave the appropriate fee and a tip to the man who sat on the box and looked only slightly less dispirited than his horse.

Alice leaned out the window, her little face quite grave. "Margaretta? If you've misrepresented any part of this, Rosalind will find you out."

"Are you saying her powers are superior to yours, a trained woman of the newspapers?" Margaretta gave the words her finest drawing room lilt, but the effect was quite lost on Alice.

"She can see through a brick wall," Alice said grimly. "Don't try parlor games on her, Margaretta."

Or on me. But Alice did not say that. She just nodded and Margaretta stepped back so the hackney driver could touch up his horse. The animal shook itself once in annoyance and walked on.

So. That is that.

Satisfied that Alice was not looking back toward her, Margaretta strode swiftly along the length of Great Russell until it crossed Drury Lane, and hurried toward the Theatre Royal.

By daylight, the great, pale Theatre Royal, commonly called just "Drury Lane," showed itself as an oddly graceless building, with its arched windows blanked out by dark draperies and its doors securely shut. Men and women in smocks and aprons scrubbed the steps, and polished the glass in the doors. It was all mundane beyond description. Magic was a property of darkness.

Margaretta smiled at the turn of phrase, and tucked it away in the tidy drawer of her mind. Surely, she would find a use for it somewhere.

The grand entrances at front of the theater might be shut up tight, but the doors at the back were flung open wide. Carters and porters hauled crates or canvas-wrapped bundles or sacks of coffee, and rolled barrels of beer. Women toted great baskets of fruit or sweetmeats or linens. Margaretta sidestepped them all and took herself up to the principal stage door, where a broad-faced man wearing a striped waistcoat stood, watching all the chaos with a sharp eye.

"Is Mr. Cavendish in yet, Paulling?" Margaretta asked.

"He is, Mrs. Seymore," answered the doorman without

taking his eye off the swarm of activity. "An' he asked me to keep an eye out for you. Get yourself right in. Hi, there!" he shouted to a pair of carters manhandling a wooden crate. "Have a care with that, you . . ."

Margaretta took herself through the door before she could hear the complete recital of the carters' ancestries and personal predilections.

To hear Fletcher tell it, the back of the Drury Lane theater was the height of luxury, modern order, and cleanliness. Margaretta had always taken his word for it. It was more common to hear the theater's bowels described as a warren. Privately, Margaretta thought this was giving warrens too much credit. Surely no rabbit had ever dug such a bewildering maze. Even the new gas lighting failed to lift the gloom of passageways that reeked of dust, paint, hemp, and tar. No carpeting had been laid here to deaden the echo of tromping boots, shouting voices, or the ring of hammers and saws in the scenery shop.

Two flights of stairs took Margaretta to the surface of the theater's churning workaday ocean. The corridor here had the benefit of both matting on the floor and windows to let in light and air. Margaretta nodded to the principal mantua maker as that man bustled past, followed by a tiny boy clutching a bolt of blue cloth to his chest. Once they were gone, she was able to cross the passage and knock on the door of Fletcher's dressing room.

"Enter!" came the booming reply.

Margaretta did, leaving the door open behind her a scant inch for propriety's sake.

Fletcher's position as a principal actor earned him an airy dressing room he had to share only with Edmund Kean. It was furnished with chairs and wardrobes and folding screens, a broad vanity table where he could apply his makeup by the light of good oil and gas lamps, and a broader window to admit the daylight and, Margaretta had reason to know, the occasional cries of silly, lovesick females.

When she walked in, Fletcher was kneeling by the window with a book held up to the light and his free hand pointing at a hapless coat stand. His shirt hung open, almost to the waist.

". . . dare your worst, sir! I will not yield!" he told the hat stand and paused. "Why do you hesitate? My hands are bound, my breast bared for your blow . . . No. Softer, I think." He dropped his voice to a grim stage whisper. "My hands are bound, my breast bared for your blow."

"I like that better," said Margaretta.

"Yes, you would. But it might be too subtle for our theater-going public." Fletcher laid a red ribbon in place to mark his page before he closed the book. "Hello, Margaretta. How did your appointment go?"

Margaretta shook her head, moved the dressing gown off the tapestry chair, and sat down. "Alice's Miss Thorne is not at all what I expected."

"Oh?" Fletcher tossed the book aside, got to his feet, and set about closing his shirt. "What was she?"

"Tired, for one thing. Clearly a lady in reduced circumstances. But clearly very intelligent and Alice respects her abilities, which is an important recommendation."

"Will she take up your cause?"

"I think she will look into me first."

He was quiet at this. "You don't have to go through with this, Margaretta."

"Are you going to give me the money, Fletcher?"

He hesitated and she waved her hand. "No, of course you are not. I have never asked anything of you but this, but you never do like your women when they begin to make demands."

"That is unfair."

"Is it? I am reduced to begging for money, I am about to have my name dragged out for the amusement of the public, my marriage destroyed, and you will not lift a *finger!*"

"Margaretta, I do not *have* the money! According to my man, your captain wants ten thousand pounds in damages!"

Margaretta felt the blood drain from her cheeks. "So much? I had no idea."

"I simply don't have that much." He spread his hands. "Even if I did, he'll only be back for more and we both know it." Fletcher paused for a long time. Margaretta watched how his eyes cleared. "Now, there's a thought."

"What?"

Fletcher tapped his chin. "It is possible that we may yet find a way out of this. I have a . . . potential source of funds yet untapped."

"One of your women?"

Fletcher's mobile face fell. "I haven't had to crawl that low in years." He picked up his play manuscript and leafed through a few pages. "This may work, Margaretta, but it will only be buying time. Whatever I can raise, Seymore will run through it in a very short time."

"I know," she said again. "But even a little silence will give Alice's Miss Thorne time to work."

Fletcher closed the book and turned it over in his hands, running his well-kept fingertips over the leather binding. "Perhaps we should have married when we had the chance."

"No. Our friendship would not have survived such a marriage as you and I would have made. If I lost that, I would have far more regrets than any I carry now. No," she said again. "We must trust that Miss Thorne can find a way to make this suit more trouble and expense to the Seymores than it's worth."

"And after that?"

"After that is after that. All I care about is that the matter is dropped before Lord Weyland dies." She laid her hand on her belly. "Because I know what this is. This is Sir Bertram trying to remove the competition for the title." The Seymores were first cousins to the Marquis of Weyland. Neither the marquis nor his brother had yet produced legitimate sons. This fact caused the Seymore family to eye the title, and the estate that came with it, rather like wolves eyeing lambs. "If the criminal conversation trial goes forward, I am sure my husband will publicly deny the paternity of my child. Then, if it is a boy, it can never inherit the title, which eliminates a potential bar to Sir Bertram inheriting." Sir Bertram was the younger of the Seymore brothers. That put him decidedly down the line for the marquisate. If Margaretta had a son, he was pushed back that much farther.

"You really believe Bertram's thought this through that coldly?"

"You've met him, and his wife—what do you think?"

"He may be doomed to disappointment. Lord Weyland has rallied before."

"I've been listening to the little birds and they are all gathering around Lord Adolphus now, in preparation for Weyland's death." Fletcher just shook his head at the name of the younger Weyland. "I'm sure that's why my brother-in-law is urging this suit on now."

"Lord Adolphus is still a young man," Fletcher reminded her. "He could marry and produce an heir of his own."

"A fact which Sir and Lady Bertram will certainly address themselves to next."

Fletcher faced the window that looked out across the broad, cobbled street. "Perhaps I should just walk over to the magistrate's court and tell them all," he said softly. "It might be simpler."

"If you make that threat again, Fletcher, I will go over and tell them myself. I am not the little girl in the boardinghouse anymore. I do not believe your gestures of self-sacrifice. You said nothing then, you will say nothing now." She laid her hand on his sleeve, so that he turned and met her gaze. "Please, Fletcher. Get me the money. Let me buy the captain off until I have my proof of Sir Bertram's duplicity to show him."

"And then?"

"I don't know," she admitted. "But I can at least shift the balance."

Fletcher cupped her chin in his broad, soft hand. Margaretta waited for the shiver of warmth that had once passed between them, but that was long gone.

"I'll do what I can," Fletcher promised, and Margaretta willed her heart and her mind to believe him, just once more.

CHAPTER 4

The Usefulness of the Circulating Library

He gazed on her with admiration and flattered her with attention; and for a long time mutual civilities and favors passed between her husband and the defendant.
—The Trial of William Henry Hall vs. Major George Barrow
for Criminal Conversation

On another day, Rosalind might have set straight to work considering the person and the problem presented to her. Her sleepless night, however, had left her muddled and impatient. She could not in good conscience embark upon a new solution in such a state. Neither could she fairly and accurately judge the person of Mrs. Seymore.

Therefore, Rosalind set the whole matter aside for a day while she rested, and caught up with her accounts, correspondence, and other such household matters. The following day, much more refreshed and clear in her mind, Rosalind was able to consider a starting point on her path toward a solution for Mrs. Seymore. As always, that path depended upon Rosalind making discreet use of her connections. In London society, connection was a great, tortured, largely invisible net thrown over the lives of thousands of persons. Whom did one know? Who knew one's family and under what circumstances? This determined one's status, whom one could visit, and whom one could ask for favors.

Rosalind Thorne had been born into the *haut ton*. Her father, Sir Reginald Thorne, had in his day been possessed of enormous charm and wit, not to mention taste and that ineffable quality called *ton*. He'd been a sought-after houseguest, and his daughters, Rosalind and Charlotte, had been feted and petted on this account.

But like so many young men of his caste and class, Sir Reginald had regarded money like water. It flowed in rivers from his hands, and when it failed to come in as easily, he simply borrowed more. When he could no longer borrow, he listened to the stories of fortunes to be made in the markets and invested. When the investments failed, he took to forgery to create the notes of credit that would allow him to keep living a life of leisure and grace.

But when Sir Reginald was caught signing the name of a friend to a bill, he packed up and left his wife and younger daughter to make what they could of out of the ruins.

The punishment of social disgrace was immediate, and it would have been total, had it not been for Rosalind's godmother, Lady Blanchard, who provided both home and a social lifeline that allowed Rosalind to be received in the great houses by the prominent hostesses, although not quite on the same footing as formerly. The acceptance of one of their number allowed the others to be charitable, and to congratulate themselves for being so.

But while it might be a tight net and an inescapable one, caution had to be used when tugging on the threads of connection. To society, the only thing more important than connection was appearance. If one was seen using connection in a way that might be interpreted as brazen or forward, it could spell disaster. Therefore, matters must be arranged with a delicate hand.

Fortunately, this was Rosalind's specialty, and once she had finished her morning roll and coffee, it took her to Mr. Clements's Circulating Library.

"Good morning, Mr. Clements," Rosalind said as she pushed through the door.

"Miss Thorne!" cried the little man behind the counter. "How delightful to see you!"

Mr. Clements had been born Ernesto Javier Garcia Mendoza Clemente in Argentina. By what route he had come to London, Rosalind had not yet been able to ascertain. But the straight, red scar that showed through his thinning hair spoke of an active past, as did the firm and definite way he spoke when saying the greatest felicity a man could know was a perfectly quiet life.

"May I ask how you do this morning?" Mr. Clements's English was impeccable, as was his Latin, his Greek, his Italian, and, of course, his Spanish. A slight hint of lilt and lisp was all that betrayed him as not being a native of London.

"I am very well, thank you."

"Excellent, excellent. How is it I can help you? I have a new memoir that might interest you, very fine . . ."

"Thank you, Mr. Clements, but today I am in search of poetry."

"Excellent!" He clapped his hands together. "Of what sort? Classical? Romantic? Devotional?"

"Have you anything by Mrs. William Seymore?"

A pained look came across Mr. Clements's mobile features. "Oh, Miss Thorne. I should not think she would suit your tastes at all."

"I am sorry to disappoint, Mr. Clements, but it is specifically Mrs. Seymore's work I am come to find."

He sighed. "Oh, very well. She is most popular, I will not deny that, but I think we may have one volume left on the shelves. If you will just give me a moment." He wrote down a note on his pad, tore off the leaf, then let himself through the door behind the counter that led to the stacks.

While Rosalind waited for the librarian's return, the bell jangled as the door was pushed open. A plump, open-faced woman in a dark blue Spenser jacket and bonnet bustled into the library.

"Why, Mrs. Buckland!" exclaimed Rosalind. "How lovely to see you this morning."

"Is that Miss Thorne?" Mrs. Buckland fumbled for a moment with the spectacles she wore on a gold chain about her neck. "Why, it is! Good morning, Miss Thorne!"

Mrs. Buckland was an amiable woman, of newer money but good repute, as long as one did not cross any of her particularly cherished opinions. Among her exemplary qualities was that she believed in the importance of routine. Whether this was the result of being married to a naval officer, and having sailed with him for several years during the early days of their marriage, or if it was some inborn quality, Rosalind could not say, but it was established fact that Mrs. Buckland ran her house, and her life, according to schedule and rule.

For example, at ten o'clock on Wednesdays, having seen her girls settled at their lessons with their governess, reviewed the day's menus with the housekeeper, and assembled her assorted lists, Mrs. Buckland could without fail be found at Clements's Circulating Library.

"How are the children?" asked Rosalind. "And the admiral?"

This polite inquiry elicited a fountain of domestic concerns and triumphs: Angelica was turning into a madcap, Hortense had the croup. Thomas was called up twice for good at Eton. A letter had come from Brendan's commander aboard the *Boniface* that he was excelling in navigation.

"As for the admiral, why, we hardly ever see him these days." Mrs. Buckland shook her head, causing the curled fringe on her forehead to swing dramatically. "I would have thought with the peace he would be home more often, but heavens no! There's always something that must be done in that great, gray building, and it seems none of it can be done without him! Still, at least he is able to dine with us three or four times in the week, and I need no longer worry about some French cannonball removing his dear head."

Rosalind smiled at this pronouncement. At that same time, Mr. Clements reappeared from the stacks with two books in his hands. These he gave to Rosalind before he turned to greet Mrs. Buckland.

"I'm returning these." Mrs. Buckland gave the librarian several slim volumes. "Have you anything new?"

Mr. Clements did. He'd set it aside especially, in fact, the first volume of a new novel by Mrs. Cuthbertson. If Mrs. Buckland would wait just a moment . . . Mr. Clements retreated once more into the bookroom.

"And what is it for you today, Miss Thorne?" Mrs. Buckland gestured toward the books Rosalind had received from Mr. Clements.

"I was in the mood for some poetry today, and a friend recommended Mrs. Seymore."

A troubled look crossed Mrs. Buckland's mobile features. "Well. Yes. She is reckoned to be very good, in her way. A trifle mawkish for my tastes, but then, not everyone enjoys Mrs. Cuthbertson."

"I believe she is married to a naval man. Mrs. Seymore, that is, not Mrs. Cuthbertson."

"Yes," said Mrs. Buckland flatly. "That she is. Captain William Seymore."

"Oh?" Rosalind permitted her brows to arch. "Are you acquainted with the Seymores? I suppose your husband must know so many officers."

Mrs. Buckland sniffed. "Some of them rather more than he would wish to. Oh, thank you, Mr. Clements. This looks marvelous. Now, let me check my book." Mrs. Buckland pulled a small notebook from her reticule, opened it, and held it up so close to her eyes that her face was nearly obscured. "Yes, yes. I'm sorry to send you back, but Hortense has been plaguing me for *Glenarvon*." Mr. Clements bowed in acknowledgment and trotted away again. "I really can't say I approve," Mrs. Buckland sighed to Rosalind. "But she'll only get it from someplace else, and I do think girls must read bad books to learn to recognize the good, don't you?" Rosalind agreed this was probably true. "Now what were we . . . Oh yes, Captain Seymore. Well, it's all too bad, really, and I feel for his family, of course. You have to understand, with the peace and everything still in an uproar on the Continent, and no one quite sure where everything will settle, great changes are afoot in the Navy. While the blockade and the fighting were going on, every single hand was needed. Many faults might be overlooked, particularly among the officers. That is no longer the case. Half the admiral's business these days is reading letters from men begging for position or consideration, and turning them down."

"May I take it then that Captain Seymore has been looking for a new position?"

Mrs. Buckland suddenly became very engaged in smoothing down her sleeves. "William Seymore has been demanding one.

Impertinent man. Presumes heavily on his family's connection to the Marquis of Weyland. We've had to quite strike him off our list for dinner invitations."

"Oh, dear," murmured Rosalind. The Marquis of Weyland must be the high connection Mrs. Seymore had alluded to.

"Now, that connection may have been enough to get him his commission," Mrs. Buckland went on. "But it's up to him to keep it, isn't it?"

"Naturally." Rosalind nodded. "And of course, it speaks volumes that the marquis is not intervening for his cousin now."

"That's just what I was saying to the admiral, and *he* remarked it was very telling that neither the marquis nor his brother Lord Adolphus had spoken up at all for such a close cousin. In fact . . ." But Mrs. Buckland stopped, and she regarded Rosalind over the rims of her spectacles. "Miss Thorne, are you up to something?"

Rosalind raised her chin and assumed a lofty air. "Mrs. Buckland, you can hardly expect me to own such a thing."

"You are then. Hmm."

Further remarks were delayed, however, by Mr. Clements's return with the three green morocco-bound volumes of *Glenarvon*. Mrs. Buckland accepted these and stowed them in her copious carrying bag.

"Well. If you are determined to indulge your curiosity about that family, I happen to know that my friend Mrs. Oldman will have Seymore's younger brother, Sir Bertram, and his wife to dine with her on Thursday. I believe Lord Adolphus may be there as well. It may be that I can procure you an invitation."

"I admit that would be most welcome. I only wish I could return the favor."

"It may be you can," said Mrs. Buckland. "Angelica is making her come-out next season, you know. We've been taking her around a bit now, getting her used to things. Lady Thompkins has arranged a private concert to close out her season, Dolcenetti is singing, and Angel is mad to go, but I have been unable to procure a ticket for love or money. You are so clever at such things, perhaps you might be able to manage?"

"I hardly like to promise, but there are one or two people I could ask."

"Then I'm very glad I happened to run into you. Now, however, I must be off, Miss Thorne. I will have a card sent round to you for Thursday. Good-bye. Good-bye, Mr. Clements."

Satisfied with the conclusion of her morning's business, Rosalind returned to Little Russell Street. There were, as always, a great number of letters to be answered. There were few things as necessary to maintaining sources of information about the currents of society as the maintenance of an active and varied correspondence.

In fact, this morning would not be too soon to begin writing to her various acquaintances who might know something about the Marquis of Weyland, and what difficulties existed between him and his cousin, the beleaguered Captain Seymore.

Rosalind spent a good hour opening, reading, and sorting the morning's mail, arranging her piles according to whether the letters were personal or business, and the urgency of each. At the bottom of the pile, however, she discovered a letter closed with a seal she'd never seen before. It was an ornate medieval letter *C* surrounded by a wreath of laurels.

Rosalind broke the seal, and unfolded the paper to discover two tickets to the evening's performance at the Theatre Royal, Drury Lane.

She stared at the tickets, and then at the letter, which was written in a bold, neat, and flowing script, and read:

Dear Miss Thorne,

It is my very great hope that you will excuse the impertinence of this letter. I was recently informed of your efforts on behalf of Mrs. Seymore, and wish to take this opportunity to fully acquaint you with my perspective on the matter. I sincerely hope I will be able to make it clear that the lady is in no way to blame for the fulminations and errors in judgment currently being pursued by that man to whom she is espoused.

I hope you will find yourself able to accept the gift of these two tickets to the Theatre Royal, and that you and the companion of your choosing might be willing to accept my invitation to dine afterwards.

Yours, with humility and respect,
Fletcher Cavendish

"Well," murmured Rosalind as she laid aside the tickets and the letter. "Now, I wonder, Mr. Cavendish, just what has Mrs. Seymore told you of this business?"

CHAPTER 5

A Pleasant Evening at the Theater

Among the principal objects which call for reform in the Theaters of London, no one appears to me to be more important than that of protecting the more rational and respectable class of Spectators from those nuisances to which they have long been exposed.

—Benjamin Dean Wyatt,
Observations on the Design for the Theatre Royal, Drury Lane

"Well," announced Alice as she and Rosalind climbed down from their hired carriage. "This is quite the most gorgeous mess."

There were few locations where one could see the entire panoply of London life crammed together, but the entrance to the Theatre Royal was one of them. Unfortunately, that panoply made it almost impossible to actually get into the theater itself. The line of grand private carriages stretched down the block, causing Rosalind and Alice to agree the thing to do was to get out and walk. Mrs. Kendricks, who had accompanied them to perform the offices of chaperone and lady's maid, looked pained, but did not argue.

"*Allons-y, mes amies,*" murmured Alice to Rosalind. They linked arms, gathered hems, and thus united, plunged into the crowd with Mrs. Kendricks following close behind.

Rosalind had chosen Alice Littlefield as her companion for this momentous evening. Of course, Alice was her dearest friend, but she would also be very slow to forgive if Rosalind denied her the opportunity of dining in the company of a renowned actor, especially one on the cusp of what promised to be a splendid criminal conversation trial. It was to Alice's credit that she did not even attempt to deny this.

Despite the fact it was frequently called just the Drury Lane, the Theatre Royal was in reality situated on a corner of Russell and Broad Streets. That corner was at the moment filled to over-flowing with all manner of traffic. Idlers stood and gawped at the grandly dressed men and women as they exited their carriages. Hawkers of goods, programs, oranges, and other tidbits shouted to be heard above the din and brandished their wares overhead as they pushed through the crowd. A number of women displayed their personal wares just as openly. Mounte-banks and musicians played and danced and sang, hoping for the possibility of a few pennies in return for their efforts. No doubt there were others looking for coin as well, sliding unseen through the crowds, hoping to lift a wallet, watch, or reticule.

"Rosalind." Alice clutched at her sleeve. "I think that's Mr. Harkness!"

Rosalind's head whipped around. There, in the shadow of the public house, she saw a tall man. Torchlight glinted on his fair hair. He was dressed far more soberly than the majority of the crowd, but the most remarkable thing about that man was how very still he stood. Indeed, if he took but half a step back, he would be invisible in the shadows.

"One wonders what brings the Bow Street runners to the theater tonight," said Alice.

"I expect it is a combination of the worthies' jewels and those who would have them change ownership." Rosalind had only recently met the principal officer, but the encounter had been eventful, and unsettling. Now she made herself turn away. She had other business tonight, and there was no reason for her to be standing and staring at a man who did not want to be seen.

The Theatre Royal itself was a low, square building with the liveried ushers standing in strict attendance by every door. Its most outstanding feature, however, was the brightness of its illumination. The theater was the first in London to be lit entirely by gas. The resulting hard, brilliant light took the eye some time to get used to. Many complained of the smell, and decried the jets as unsafe and lacking the friendly warmth of lamps and candles. But once her eyes adjusted, Rosalind found she rather liked it. For one thing, it produced far less smoke than more homelike lights. For another, it was singularly steady and reliable in a way no candle could be.

The gilded entrance hall was every bit as crowded as the lane outside. A steady stream of persons in silk and jewels made their way up the two massive stone staircases, each one comprised of three separate flights. Mrs. Kendricks took charge of their cloaks and handed over their shawls. Rosalind handed their tickets to a liveried attendant, who examined them minutely. He was in the act of bowing the two women toward the right hand stair when a man's voice stopped them all where they were.

"Miss Thorne. I thought that must be you."

Rosalind turned, slowly, in order to be sure her face was completely composed when she looked up to see Devon Winterbourne, Duke of Casselmain, approach and make his bow.

"Lord Casselmain," Rosalind murmured. "How lovely to see you." She curtsied, as did Alice.

Devon Winterbourne, the eighth Duke of Casselmain, was a

tall man, rather lean for his height, but neatly made. His hair was very black and his eyes a striking pale gray. His black coat and white silk breeches fit his well-knit frame exactly. Rosalind ruthlessly suppressed the urge to adjust her cashmere shawl to cover her burgundy and lace gown a little more. The dress had belonged to Rosalind's mother, and she was torn by a sudden fear that Devon would recognize it.

But Devon wasn't looking at the dress—he was looking directly into her eyes, and that was even more unsettling. Devon Winterbourne had been Rosalind's first love. She had once confidently and eagerly expected he would ask her to marry him. But then Rosalind's father had deserted his family, taking her older sister with him. Her mother had lost her wits, and Rosalind had been forced to find ways to support them both. Even that might not have been enough to end things, but then Devon's profligate older brother, Hugh, fell from his horse and broke his neck. Suddenly, Devon was no longer the solemn younger brother of the Winterbourne family. He was the Duke of Casselmain.

Alice's helpful kick against her ankle reminded Rosalind she was staring.

"I did not realize you'd be here this evening," Rosalind remembered to say.

"He's with me," announced a young girl who came up to take Lord Casselmain's arm. "I nagged him until he agreed. I could not miss the chance of seeing Mr. Cavendish onstage."

"Hello, Louisa," said Rosalind. Louisa Winterbourne was Devon's cousin. A cheerful, petite girl, she shared his black hair, sharp features, and gray eyes. Louisa was also the oldest of four daughters of a branch of the family that was rather less than well off. Devon was allowing her to stay in his town house for the season, with her firm aunt, Mrs. Showell, for a chaperone. He provided the use of his carriage, and his wallet, to allow Louisa to try her chances on the marriage mart. Word had reached Rosalind that there had been offers, spurred by the fact that Devon was also supplementing the vivacious girl's dowry. Louisa, though, did not appear to be in any hurry to relinquish the fun of being a debutante just yet.

"Are you one of Mr. Cavendish's admirers, then, Louisa?" Rosalind asked. "Is he as good as they say?"

"Is he . . ." Louisa fairly gawped at her. "Have you not seen him yet? Oh, Miss Thorne! How I envy you! You have so much to discover!" With this, Louisa launched into full-throated, if high-pitched, praise of the handsomeness, the sensitivity, the perfection of Mr. Cavendish's performance. Louisa had seen his Romeo, his Hamlet, his Faustus, his Jack Absolute, and seemingly, a score of other interpretations, including of course, the dashing Montgomery Fitzhugh in *Stand and Deliver*.

"And did you faint?" inquired Rosalind.

"Don't be ridiculous." Louisa sniffed. "I might have missed the performance. Oh, I see you smile at me, Miss Thorne!" the girl added loftily. "But I am certain the moment you hear him speak, you'll be lost yourself. You'll join us, won't you?" The lofty attitude dissolved in an instant. "You and Miss Littlefield both. I want to be there when you see him for the first time. Say that you will. Devon, she must, mustn't she?"

"That is for Miss Thorne to decide." Devon did not turn his attention from Rosalind even for a heartbeat. "She and Miss Littlefield are of course entirely welcome."

Louisa was not above the occasional social deception, nor was she ignorant of the relationship that had formerly existed between Devon and Rosalind. Rosalind, though, detected no hint of matchmaking here, just the enthusiasm of a young girl for a favored performer.

The same could not be said for Alice, who regarded Rosalind

with a shrewd gaze, nor Mrs. Kendricks, who was quite openly bestowing a fond and longing look upon the duke.

Then there was Devon himself. He'd returned to her life during a recent interval of chaos and confusion. It had raised all manner of feelings, not all of them complimentary to herself, or him. Rosalind told herself she needed time to sort out all those warring emotions and so was justified in avoiding him. But she knew the truth was much simpler. She was afraid of what she might come to feel if she spent too much time near him.

As Devon looked at her now, she saw the old longing in his gray eyes, but something else as well. There was a tinge of desperation, and Rosalind had to suppress a smile at her own vanity. Of course Devon wanted her and Alice to join him. It would give Louisa someone else to talk to about the magnificent Mr. Cavendish.

"We would be glad to join you, wouldn't we, Alice? That is, if you're certain, Lord Casselmain . . ."

At this addition, Alice suddenly had to cover a cough.

Devon bowed, and held out his arm. Rosalind did not permit herself to hesitate as she took it. The usher and Mrs. Kendricks were both informed of the change of plan and location. The one bowed. The other fairly glowed with delight.

The Duke of Casselmain quite naturally kept a private box in the dress circle on the first floor. A gilded half wall separated their designated area from the neighboring box, and an ornamented rail kept them from toppling over onto the heads of those crowding themselves into the "pit" in front of the stage.

Somehow, Alice managed to slide into place next to Louisa, ensuring that Rosalind would have to take the seat closest to Devon. Rosalind glowered at her friend, who turned away quite casually, as if nothing at all could possibly be the matter.

"I hope you've been well," ventured Devon to Rosalind.

"Yes. Perfectly well, thank you."

"Louisa had hoped to hear from you before this," he added.

Rosalind glanced at Louisa. At the moment, the girl was engaged in a further detailed recitation of the perfections of Mr. Cavendish. Rosalind was going to have to find some way to make it up to Alice for this.

"Do we really need to play the game of polite conversation?" she murmured to Devon.

"That's for you to say," he answered. "I'm happy to talk about whatever you wish."

Rosalind made the mistake of looking into his eyes as he said this. She felt her hand tremble, and her heart strain at the seams. She remembered the sick, sad days when she finally realized that her family's disgrace and his inheritance meant that she would never marry Devon Winterbourne after all. She remembered how she felt when they danced, and yes, when they had kissed. And now here they were, side by side, making proper conversation.

Or improper conversation. Whichever she wanted.

Which do I want?

Before she could answer this most dangerous question, a merry laugh lifted out of the crowd and Rosalind's head snapped around.

The term "private box" was a misleading one. The theater's tiers had been deliberately designed to eliminate shadowed spaces where improper or riotous behavior might be indulged. With the exception of the royal boxes, all portions of the seating area were in full view of all the others. Therefore, nothing prevented Rosalind from seeing straight into the well-filled boxes nearest theirs. What she saw was a crowd of white and pink faces, set off by the flash of jewels and the glitter of gowns and white shirt fronts. There was not one thing to truly differentiate one member of the grand gathering from any other.

But there it was again, the sound of a laugh. A golden head tossed merrily, and Rosalind saw a particular face in the box a quarter turn of the great curve from theirs. Rosalind started to her feet. The motion made heads turn, made eyes widen.

There. A slender woman with an oval face and wide-set eyes wearing a gown of spring green figured satin. She sat beside another woman, this one in a gaudy dress of gold net and cloud white silk.

The woman in green stared, startled at Rosalind.

Alice was saying something behind her, possibly calling her name. Rosalind neither knew nor cared. She blundered out the door and into the passageway. The hall curved and the doors to the general seating areas opened to her right. She tore open the one nearest and ran down the aisle. Now everyone was looking, as well as hissing and groaning at the intrusion. Rosalind still did not care. All she saw was the woman in the green satin, sailing as graceful as a swan up the farther aisle.

Rosalind grabbed her hems up to an almost indecent height and ran up the aisle, barging through the door, and back into the corridor. A pair of drunken dandies laughed at her. A dowager lifted her quizzing glass.

Rosalind ran for the stairs, and down them, and out into the entranceway and through the doors.

The lane out front of the theater remained as crowded as ever. The carriages still jostled each other. The mountebanks and their audiences still sang and cheered and passed their jugs and bottles back and forth.

There was no sign of her. It was as if the earth had opened to swallow her whole.

"Miss Thorne?"

The words were very quiet, but they turned Rosalind around as if pulled by invisible reins. There stood Mr. Harkness, looking down at her with concern in his blue eyes. He kept an entirely polite distance, with his hands behind himself. She saw the edge of his badge gleaming beneath the lapel of his coat.

"I thought that was you. Is anything amiss?"

"No, no, nothing. I . . . Did you see a woman come this way? She would have been wearing green satin, cut very low . . ."

"Rosalind, for heaven's sake, what is it?" Devon was behind her and then beside her, taking her arm in his so that it would be seen she had protection, of course. He saw the other man, and recognized him. "Harkness."

"Lord Casselmain." Mr. Harkness bowed. "I saw Miss Thorne here and was concerned something might be amiss. Now I see that she is with you, I bid you both good evening."

Mr. Harkness walked away. A particular crowd of rowdies saw him coming and abruptly scattered.

"What's the matter, Rosalind?" demanded Devon. "Come inside, you'll catch your death of cold."

He turned her and began walking, so she had no choice but to stumble along with him.

"I saw . . ." she gasped. "I thought I saw . . ."

"Who? What?"

Tell him. No. I can't tell him. I don't know. It can't be. It would mean . . .

"Nothing, Devon," she whispered. "It was no one."

CHAPTER 6

The Presence of Mr. Cavendish

Decorum among the several Orders and Classes of Visitants to the Theater, [is] as essential to the accommodation of the more respectable part of the Visitants.
—Benjamin Dean Wyatt,
Observations on the Design for the Theatre Royal, Drury Lane

The performance was probably excellent. Rosalind was aware of bursts of applause and laughter at frequent intervals. These were punctuated by sighs, and rapturous callings out, and one or two wordless screams. Once, the play halted completely when one screaming woman fainted dead away, and had to be carried out.

But had Rosalind been asked, she would have had to confess she could not have described the events onstage that caused these demonstrations. She might not have even been able to remember which play she was watching. Her mind was fully occupied by the sight of the woman in the green silk, the shape of her face, the sound of her voice.

Was it possible? Could it be that her sister, Charlotte, had really returned to London after all this time?

Rosalind told herself that her imagination had been excited at the masquerade at Graham's. She told herself, firmly and repeatedly, that the woman she had seen in the darkened corridor had no more been Charlotte than this woman in green had. She reminded herself of the first months after Charlotte had disappeared with their father. Then, every fair-haired woman on the street or in a drawing room made Rosalind blink and look twice. Each one of those hopes had been false. Rosalind had learned to gather up her grief and carry it with her, quietly concealed in the corners of her heart. Charlotte was gone, and would not return. Rosalind would never know why her sister had vanished with their father. She came to accept this as an irrevocable fact.

What, then, could have revived those old hopes for the second time in as many days? If that woman was not Charlotte, who could she be?

Rosalind had no answer.

The audience was applauding again. Rosalind blinked and tried to focus on the stage, only to realize the curtain was being rung down and the interval had begun. Around them people were getting up to go in search of the water closets or to meet their friends in other boxes or the great salons, or to make room for the waiters bearing the trays of supper.

"Rosalind?" murmured Devon. "Are you well?"

"Yes, yes, I'm just fine."

"Yes, of course," said Alice tartly. "You always turn white as a new-washed sheet when you're just fine."

"I often observed this when we were children," remarked Devon blandly. "Especially after she'd seen some stranger in a crowd and given chase."

"Oh, leave off, the pair of you," said Louisa. "If Miss Thorne does not wish to talk of it, she does not. Now, tell me, Miss Thorne, what do you think of Mr. Cavendish? Is he not divine? Oh, I thought I would die . . ."

Rosalind made herself smile and turn toward Louisa. She

had seldom been so grateful for a young woman's enthusiasm. Louisa's raptures did not require active participation, only murmured affirmations at regular intervals. Listening to Louisa delayed the moment when she had to tell Devon or Alice who she thought she'd seen.

Devon had arranged for refreshment, and the waiters duly brought in the table along with cheese, fruits, cakes and jellies, and a bottle of champagne. It was a menu, Rosalind thought, more calculated toward Louisa's taste than Devon's. Having seen the effect fashionable gluttony had worked on his older brother, Devon tended to eat and drink in a restrained manner that many of his acquaintances found astonishing, if not positively Quakerish.

One of the waiters bowed to Devon. "Lord Winterbourne? A note has arrived for Miss Thorne."

"Thank you." Devon took the note, and handed it to Rosalind.

Rosalind looked at the handwriting and her mouth went dry. The hand was smooth and flowing and delicate. She was aware of her heart pounding at the base of her throat. She unfolded the paper.

And all her spirits sank into acute disappointment. She read:

Miss Thorne,

I trust you and your companion have not forgotten we are engaged to dine after the performance this evening. You may send word by Hunter and he will escort you to the King's Arms Hotel. If your friends wish to join us, please do invite them.

Fletcher Cavendish

Rosalind quickly folded the letter before Louisa could glimpse the signature.

"Not more bad news?" said Alice.

"Oh, no," Rosalind replied casually. "Simply a reminder that you and I are engaged to dine after the performance."

"You are?" said Devon, and Rosalind knew she did not imagine the note of disappointment in his voice.

Louisa was more demonstrative. "Oh! How provoking! I wanted someone to talk to, and Devon is hopeless. He knows nothing of acting and only wants to maunder on about the play and its meaning and its place in history and such piffle."

"Ah, yes, Devon's bent toward piffle." Rosalind smiled. "That is something I remember from our childhood."

"You would not break your engagement?" asked Devon. "For Louisa's sake?"

Rosalind's heart was pounding again. The gaslight showed her Devon's face with perfect clarity. She saw the rather stern, mature man he was, the man who had restored the pride to his title and family. But she also saw the boy she'd known—kind, quiet, awkward, and angry in the shadow of his raucous brother. But that was before her father's disgrace, before her mother's long and terrible ending. Before the thousand other things that had driven a wedge between them.

No, they did not drive a wedge. They built a wall.

"I'm sorry," she told him. "I promised that I would do this. It is for a friend."

Devon's eyes shifted from Rosalind to Alice. Alice, unusually, maintained her silence. Rosalind suspected she was biting the inside of her cheek to do so.

"Of course," Devon said. "I would not ask you to break your word." He turned to his cousin. "There we are, Louisa. You will have to make do with me. I promise that I will pay particularly close attention to the acting in the second half so I can say something intelligent."

Alice decided that this was the moment to come to Rosalind's rescue, and began directing Louisa's attention toward the audience and the various lights of the *haut ton* she recognized within it. In short order, the two of them were engaged in a rapid exchange of gossip, much of which Rosalind suspected would be repeated in the column *Society Notes*, which Alice wrote under the byline of A. E. Littlefield.

Devon remarked about the weather.

Rosalind inquired after his mother's health.

Devon asked after a mutual acquaintance of theirs.

Rosalind remarked that the Cheshire cheese was excellent.

Devon agreed.

Both were relieved beyond measure when the gong sounded the end of the interval and they could turn their attention to the stage again and have an excuse to stop trying to make polite conversation.

The performance concluded with no fewer than seven curtain calls. Flowers showered from all directions to land at Fletcher Cavendish's feet as he bowed to the audience, to his leading lady, to the musicians in the orchestra, to the ladies leaning over the box rails and holding clasped hands out to him. Rosalind suspected it was only Devon's presence that kept Louisa from behaving in a similar fashion.

She had no opera glasses with her, so all Rosalind could see of Mr. Cavendish was a broad man in a flowing cloak. He towered over his fellow actors, so she must assume him to be built on the grand scale. His hair was a sandy brown and his nose prominent. More than that she could not say.

At last, the curtain lowered itself a final time and the crowd began its slow but inexorable press toward the passageways and stairs. Mrs. Kendricks arrived with Louisa's maid and Devon's manservant, and a withered, white-haired man in a plain green coat who bowed deeply.

"Miss Thorne?" he murmured so low that Rosalind could barely hear him over the rustle and laughter of the departing crowd. "I am sent to escort you to the King's Arms. If you would be so good as to come with me?"

"Are you sure you can't break your engagement, Rosalind?" asked Devon.

"It's impossible," she answered, and she tried not to see how Mrs. Kendricks's face fell at this. "But thank you for allowing us to join you and Louisa. It was a delightful evening."

Devon, though, lacked the will or the capacity for one more polite lie. He simply bowed, then turned to take Louisa's arm and shepherd her away.

"Well, I don't know when I've enjoyed such a free and unrestrained evening," announced Alice as she stood still to allow Mrs. Kendricks to fasten her simple gray cloak around her shoulders.

"I'm sorry, Alice." Rosalind smoothed down her own cloak and checked to make sure she still had her fan, gloves, and reticule.

"What's worrying you, Rosalind?" asked Alice as they signaled to the servant they were quite ready to accompany him. He led them down the grand staircase and across the lobby.

"I don't know for certain." The night had remained fine, thankfully, and they were able to make their way through the crush of people and carriages with only the usual fuss.

"All right," Alice said. "We'll try something simpler. Who was it you saw that sent you running out of the box?"

Rosalind bit her lip and considered lying, but she dismissed that thought almost as soon as it formed. Alice would be alert to any attempt to put her off. "I thought . . . I thought it was Charlotte."

"Oh, Rosalind!" Alice seized her hand. "After all this time?"

"I know, I know. It was most likely my imagination. But this was the second time in the past two days."

"Do you want me to ask some questions at the theater? Or George could. There's several ushers who are willing to talk more than a little. The major keeps a fund for encouraging them."

Rosalind smiled. "Thank you, but I think we may save you and George for more important work. If Charlotte wants to find me, she will." She tried to put at least some conviction into her voice as she said this, but from the expression on Alice's face, and even more from that on Mrs. Kendricks's, she knew she did not succeed.

CHAPTER 7

Dining in Private and Comfort

A man of fascinating manners and accomplishments, of enticing habits and appearance; but I fear of unchaste and vicious passions.
—*The Trial of William Henry Hall vs. Major George Barrow for Criminal Conversation*

The valet conducted Rosalind, Alice, and Mrs. Kendricks through the ladies' entrance of the King's Arms, and from there through the ladies' parlor, up the narrow and enclosed stairs that led to the private dining rooms and sheltered them from the view of the gentlemen dining in the open front room.

Rosalind had heard that in Paris it was considered quite unexceptionable for respectable women to dine in public quite casually in all manner of *cafés* and places called "restaurants," which were a sort of public eating house. She wished heartily for the day this sensible custom might be adopted in London. Until then, the dance of gentility must be danced, whether the dining rooms were in grand hotels or public houses.

They were admitted at last to a tidy little parlor room. While Mrs. Kendricks helped them off with cloaks and bonnets, the valet adjusted the lamps.

"Mr. Cavendish sends his compliments and hopes you will

find the room quite comfortable," he told them. "He requests you make yourselves entirely at home and hopes you will accept an offer of tea or sherry wine."

This little speech was delivered without any perceptible shift of his features, or lifting his eyes above the level of the floor. Rosalind presumed that discretion was a prime attribute of anyone in the employ of such a man as Fletcher Cavendish.

Tea was duly requested and delivered, and while Rosalind settled on the sofa to sip hers, Alice wandered about the room. Rosalind could tell her friend was missing her notebook and focused entirely on memorizing every detail of the parlor to reproduce later in one of her columns.

She had not yet finished with this absorbing occupation when the door was thrown open and their host strode through.

"At last! Miss Rosalind Thorne? Permit me to introduce myself. I am Fletcher Cavendish and I do most humbly apologize for taking so long to come to you." The actor took her hand and bowed crisply over it.

"There is no need for apology, Mr. Cavendish. I understand an actor has many people to speak to after a performance."

"Too true, too true, but none I wished to speak with more than yourself, and . . ." He turned his deep and shining eyes to Alice.

"May I present Miss Alice Littlefield?" said Rosalind.

"Miss Littlefield, I am delighted." Mr. Cavendish bowed over Alice's hand as well, and Rosalind was treated to the unusual sight of Alice being disconcerted by the gesture. Mr. Cavendish did not linger, but turned at once to his valet.

"Hunter, help me with this coat. Our dinner should be arriving momentarily . . ." Just then there was a soft knocking at the door. "On cue! Splendid! Enter!"

The manager and a small army of servants in the hotel's blue livery flooded the room, bearing table and chairs, cloth and a stream of covered dishes, both silver and porcelain. Much to Rosalind's relief, when the covers were lifted, they revealed a feast far more substantial than fruit and cakes. When the final server bore in the enormous country ham, her stomach made a most unladylike sound.

"Excellent!" announced Mr. Cavendish. "My heartiest thanks, Mr. Beers. You have outdone yourself. Ladies, pray, will you join me?"

The ladies would. Mrs. Kendricks, of course, assumed her station in the corner, where she could be ready if her mistress or Alice required anything more personal than a second helping. Rosalind used the fuss of having her seat drawn in and accepting the napkin and answering inquiries as to what dainty she preferred to begin with to observe the actor who presided over the table with such skill and evident relish.

Up close, Mr. Fletcher Cavendish was shorter than she'd expected, but that did not lessen the impact of his presence. He was dressed plainly, in a black coat and burgundy waistcoat and a simply tied cravat. The only ostentation about him was the outsized double-cut diamond ring on his right hand, and the pearl stick pin in his lapel. His face, though, was molded and sculpted into a state of patrician perfection that would have dropped Michelangelo to his knees. Seldom had Rosalind been in the presence of a man where good looks combined so forcefully with ease and confidence. Mr. Cavendish engaged in nothing beyond the simple actions of directing the servants, carving the ham, and laying the slices on the platter, and yet Rosalind found it impossible to look away from him. *I believe I may owe Louisa an apology.*

"There now, Miss Thorne." Mr. Cavendish handed a plate of ham, potatoes, and greens, all laced with parsley sauce, to his man, who in turn placed it in front of her. "I trust this will be to your liking. Miss Littlefield, what may I help you to?"

"Oh, just the same if you please, Mr. Cavendish," said Alice cheerfully. "May I ask if one of the people who delayed you so was Lord Sawbridge? I noticed him and a large party in his box tonight."

"Indeed, his lordship was kind enough to say a few words in praise of our efforts tonight." Mr. Fletcher added greens and sauce to Alice's plate.

"They say he's very interested in the theater. There's even some talk, I'm sure it's flummery, that he might be opening his own."

Mr. Cavendish finally seated himself and filled his glass from the bottle of red wine before handing it to his man to serve the ladies.

"Miss Littlefield, you will forgive me if I say I know when I am being prodded. Our director does it often enough. I also am a habituated reader of the society columns. Therefore, confess it." He pointed one well-kept finger at Alice. "You are the infamous A. E. Littlefield of *The London Chronicle.*"

Alice shrugged. "You've caught me out. What will you do?"

Mr. Cavendish's deep gaze slipped sideways to linger on Alice.

"First of all, I will be very careful with my words." Mr. Cavendish raised his glass just far enough that he was looking at her from over the rim. For the first time in many years, Rosalind watched a flush creep across her friend's fair cheeks, and absurdly, she felt the better for it. If Mr. Cavendish's charm could affect Alice, she had less reason to be ashamed of her own response.

"I will also congratulate Miss Thorne on her intelligent choice of companion. I could not now dare do any ungentlemanly thing, lest it be proclaimed across London in the pages of your newspaper."

"It was Miss Littlefield who introduced me to Mrs. Sey-more," Rosalind informed him, at least partly to take his formidable attention off Alice, who was showing distinct signs of becoming badly overheated. "You may be assured of her discretion on this matter."

"On this matter," Mr. Cavendish said with only a hint of a drawl. "But this matter may touch on many others. Still, as I invited you to bring the companion of your choosing, I must accept the consequences. To business then." He saluted them both with his glass and took a gulp of the wine. "You are, Miss Thorne, aware that Mrs. Seymore's odious little husband has decided to bring suit against me for criminal conversation."

Rosalind felt her eyebrows arch. "You state this quite matter-of-factly, Mr. Cavendish."

Mr. Cavendish laughed. The hearty sound sent a shiver up Rosalind's spine. She decided all at once she did not like the free and easy charm which he spread so lavishly about him. It smacked of a personal carelessness.

Which was ridiculous.

"Miss Thorne," said Mr. Cavendish. "For me, being threatened with criminal conversation is a matter of routine. Captain Seymore's suit will not be the first of this season, let alone this year. Of course, most of them are attempts to extort money or gain notoriety, and my attorneys make short work of them. Occasionally, there is an injured party." Here he paused and smiled into the distance, so that they could see him reliving some pleasant, private memory. "But those men are generally willing to accept a settlement along with my hand on my heart that I will never trouble their hearth or home again." He laid that hand upon that heart, and all at once his face was as set and solemn as any man called to swear upon the Holy Bible.

"But it is not for you to actually regret such injuries?" murmured

Rosalind. She supposed it was refreshing that this man was willing to speak openly, and was a little disappointed at her own immediate urge to stiffen her spine and purse her mouth in disapproval.

Mr. Cavendish laughed again, and again the warm and annoying shiver traveled up Rosalind's spine. "If a man cannot keep his wife's affections or attentions, he has only himself to blame for what happens."

That dislike Rosalind had felt before suddenly seemed to be upon firmer foundation.

"Did Captain Seymore have reason for his particular complaint?" prompted Alice.

"If he did, Miss Littlefield, it was not my doing."

"But you do know Mrs. Seymore?"

"Very well," he said amiably, but without any detectible hint of deeper meaning. "We met, as she may have told you, when we were both much younger, before I became the Great Fletcher Cavendish." He raised his hand in dramatic pose. "I was an actor in a traveling troupe, marching up and down the length of England. We played at every country fair and cow barn that was willing to have us, and I counted myself lucky that I was being paid rather than having to pay for the privilege. A friendship was formed, and Seymore knew of it when he swooped in to marry Margaretta."

"What did you think of the marriage?" asked Rosalind.

Cavendish considered this, and as he did, Rosalind saw the actor's confident mask slip to show the man beneath. That man, she decided, was uneasy. "I think it is no surprise Seymore is having troubles," he said. "He has bound to himself a gracious muse, but he has neither the temperament nor the skill to keep her."

"Then why did she marry him?"

The mask slipped again, and this time Rosalind saw a flash

of anger, bright and hard as the flash of the diamond on his ring, and just as quickly gone.

"He promised her all manner of things. Security and honor, to begin with. He was on the rise in the Navy then, and looked fair to prosper. He was older as well, with very good connections, which is always attractive."

"Have you seen the accusatory letters sent to the captain?"

"Only one. Seymore has the rest under lock and key somewhere."

"And what do you think of that one?" asked Rosalind.

Mr. Cavendish shrugged again. "It would do for the provinces but would never play in the capital. Whoever this aspiring troublemaker is, he's a rank amateur."

Rosalind thought of Mr. Fullerton and his drawer of correspondence and keepsakes, and found herself in agreement with this assessment.

"Mr. Cavendish," she said. "If you are not concerned about the suit, or the potential for scandal or blackmail against yourself, then may I ask why you extended us this most kind invitation?"

Mr. Cavendish smiled in acknowledgment of her pointedly polite turn of phrase. "I wished to satisfy myself that you were the genuine coin of the realm, Miss Thorne. I may not be on such a footing with Mrs. Seymore as her husband believes, but Margaretta is dear to me. She is in a bad situation, and I do not want to see it made worse."

"I understand."

"I'm glad that you do." Mr. Cavendish shifted himself in his chair, his voice falling soft and low, almost a lover's tone. "Because we all have secrets, Miss Thorne, and connections that might surprise our friends if they were made publicly known. If I suspect that you are playing Margaretta false in any way, I will do everything in my power to blacken your name from here to the Antipodes and back again."

Fear lanced through Rosalind, but only for a moment before it was blotted out by anger. She bit both emotions back. The threat was real. This man could say whatever he wanted and it would be repeated across the length and breadth of London. Alice, whom she'd brought to be her witness, would become her accomplice. She might be a member of the club of the journalists, but her voice would be no match for Cavendish's and they all knew it.

Cavendish settled back in his chair and saluted them once more with the wineglass. "Now, I do apologize for speaking to you so frankly." The conciliation in his voice did nothing but grate against Rosalind's nerves. "But I wanted you to know that I am serious in this matter."

Whatever Mr. Cavendish meant to add, however, was interrupted by a sudden, tremendous banging against the door.

"Where is he!" shouted a voice in the passage outside. "Where is that blaggard Cavendish?"

CHAPTER 8

The Arrival of the Captain

The plaintiff himself being at this time, in a highly respect-
able situation in a military department cultivated and
perhaps encouraged, but innocently, an intimacy with the
defendant.
　　　　—*The Trial of William Henry Hall vs. Major George Barrow*
　　　　　　　　　　　　　　　　for Criminal Conversation

Mr. Cavendish uttered an oath, and was on his feet in the next instant.

"Cavendish!" Something slammed hard against the door, rattling it in its frame. "Cavendish!" A fist pounded furiously. "Come out, you dog!"

The actor put himself between the table and the door. At the same time he gestured for Rosalind and Alice to stay where they were. Behind his back, Alice and Rosalind exchanged swift glances. Alice calmly plucked the fish knife from her place setting and tucked it underneath her napkin. Rosalind moved the heavy wine bottle a bit closer to hand.

Mr. Cavendish threw back his shoulders, and at once, his attitude shifted entirely from a gentleman of leisure to a soldier marching into battle. In one strong but fluid motion, he threw open the door. The abrupt motion caused the beefy red-faced man on the other side to stumble into the room, despite the pair of liveried footmen hanging off his shoulders.

Rosalind glanced at Alice, and Alice nodded. This then was Captain Seymore.

"I'm so sorry, Mr. Cavendish," gasped one of the men who was attempting to get his arms around the captain's shoulders. "We tried . . ."

"It's all right, Davies." Mr. Cavendish waved both footmen back with a single grand gesture.

Freed from the extra weight, Captain Seymore did his best to straighten up. Even under normal circumstances, he was not such a figure of a man as would impress anyone. Next to such a lion as Mr. Cavendish, he appeared little more than ridiculous. He was short, red-faced, pockmarked, and puffy. The top of his head was bald and shining and the remaining fringe of pale hair was pulled into a sailor's queue. Judging by the way his blue striped waistcoat strained, his paunch was new, and growing. The only aspect of him that was truly impressive was his voice.

"Where's my wife, you great gilded son of a whore?" the captain roared.

"Have a care, Seymore." Mr. Cavendish spoke in an entirely conversational tone, and yet managed to sound ten times more dangerous than the swollen man in front of him. "These ladies are my guests."

"Ha! Ladies. Yes. If you say so." But then the captain stopped, and took a second look at Alice. "Wait. You're that Littlefield woman."

"Good evening, Captain Seymore," replied Alice. "How delightful to see you again."

"I might have known you'd be in on this thing. Another woman who doesn't know her place is at home. And who might you be?" he demanded of Rosalind.

"This is Miss Rosalind Thorne." Cavendish folded his arms. "There, Seymore, you've met the whole of the company. If you are indeed searching for Mrs. Seymore, she is not here."

Seymore started backward, his eyes darting in all directions, as if he expected to see his wife lurking in some shadowed corner. But as he did not find her, the bluster bled away. He drew his shoulders back, and Rosalind thought she could see something of the proud man he must have once been.

"She's been here, though," Seymore tried. "Here, and with you."

"I'd give you my word she has not, but since I know you won't believe me, I'll save my breath."

"Better you should," Seymore retorted. "Liar and knave and thief that you are! You'll put nothing over on me, sir." Seymore pointed one fat finger at the impassive actor, and shook it. Alice clapped a hand over her mouth and looked away.

"May we take it Mrs. Seymore is not at home, Captain?" remarked Rosalind.

"Why would she be at home? There's no one there but her husband!" The despair in his voice was real, Rosalind would have sworn to it. It was also becoming very evident that this whole scene was fueled by copious amounts of brandy. "What command have I over the attentions of such a woman?"

"Perhaps she will be home when you return," suggested Alice.

"No, she will not be. It's all ruined. There's nothing left." The captain shook his head violently, as if to clear it. "And it's this man's fault." He didn't say this to Cavendish, as Rosalind would have expected, but softly, as if to himself.

She was not the only one who noticed either.

"Seymore, there's no reason for any of this," Cavendish said. "Mrs. Seymore has not been here. Surely she just had an engagement for the evening. Miss Littlefield said she mentioned a card party at the Hoffmans'." He looked across to Alice, who did not speak to confirm or deny this. "Let me send my man 'round to find out."

"No," said Seymore, his mood and demeanor sloshing from one extreme to the other on the tide of the alcohol in his belly. "I'll go. I . . . You're right, Cavendish, there's no need for this." He blinked up at the actor. "If only you'd *settle*, it would all be over in a heartbeat. Just say the thing was done and let it be. You can afford ten times what I'm asking!"

But Cavendish shook his head. "It's beside the point, Seymore. The suit means nothing to me, but it's everything in the world to Margaretta. I will not seal her doom to please your pride or your creditors."

"Then what comes is your fault. You're not king of the world, Cavendish! I will by God see you brought low!"

He stomped out of the room. Cavendish closed the door very softly.

"I'm sorry, Miss Thorne, Miss Littlefield. I would not have had you witness that scene."

"I do not expect it will receive a favorable notice in the *Times*." Alice casually replaced the knife beside her plate.

"It's of no consequence, Mr. Cavendish," said Rosalind. "Although I am very sorry to see any man reduced to such a display."

Cavendish grimaced. "Seymore's real sin is that he's weak, and he's ashamed. It's a bad combination for such a man, especially when he's got a whole family's worth of disappointments behind him."

"Then you also think his family is urging him on in this suit?" asked Alice.

Cavendish eyed her warily. "I forgot for a moment the newspapers were in the room."

"I'm asking only as Margaretta's friend," said Alice.

"Yes. Of course." But there was no conviction in his tone. He picked up his wineglass and downed the remainder of the liquid. "Well, as a matter of fact, I do believe it. Neither the captain nor his brother, Sir Bertram, has lived up to their expectations. While she lived, their mother has always blamed their aristocratic cousins for not helping enough. Sir Bertram at least took this as Gospel and has forever blamed them as well."

"Including the Marquis of Weyland?" said Rosalind.

"Especially the Marquis of Weyland," agreed Mr. Cavendish as he refilled his glass. "But the truth is, there's not enough help that could be given. That family's expectations will always exceed their realizations. I'm sure you know the sort."

Rosalind nodded. "It means they are doomed to failure, and must continually find someone to blame for it."

"Exactly, and the blame right now is falling on Mrs. Seymore, and me." Mr. Cavendish gestured to himself. "Again, I don't mind for my own sake, but Margaretta . . . this is killing her." He sighed, and took another sip of the wine. "So there we are. A sorry tale, filled with woe and avarice and the commonplace sins of a commonplace life. I wish I could have put on a better show for you, Miss Thorne."

"I believe I've seen quite enough for the evening."

Cavendish smiled, and once again, Rosalind felt the effects of his charm wash over her. "And thus am I dismissed. From my own table, no less, which is a neat trick, Miss Thorne. I salute you for it." He placed his hand on his breast and bowed. "Let me call for your carriage."

"May I take it then that you are satisfied that I am, as you say, the genuine article?"

"Miss Thorne, I am positively terrified that you may be all

you are reported and more. I feel I must now be very much upon my guard."

"Well," said Alice, as soon as the carriage was closed up and the driver had touched up the horses. "So that's what the married ladies are fainting over."

"He is certainly a powerful draught," said Rosalind. She and Alice were seated next to each other, with Mrs. Kendricks on the opposite bench. For form's sake, the housekeeper was busy with a piece of darning pulled from her work bag, but neither Rosalind nor Alice forgot her. Indeed, Rosalind saw the frown on her servant's face and her heart contracted just a little.

"I'm beginning to feel I should apologize for dragging you into this mess," said Alice. "I thought it was something . . . simpler."

"It's not your fault, Alice. You were helping your friend."

"I thought I was," she muttered. "Now I'm not so sure that I haven't been used."

"By whom?"

"Mrs. Seymore. She's . . . Well, I can see why she gets on so well with Mr. Cavendish."

"You mean you think she might be playing a part?"

"Do you?"

"I believe the threat to her reputation, and thus her livelihood, is very real. But the rest . . . that has yet to be seen."

"What do you intend to do, Rose?"

Mrs. Kendricks glanced up sharply at Rosalind, reminding her that Alice was not the only person waiting for her answer.

"Alice, those ushers of yours, do you think one of them might be willing to tell you which ladies have lately been seen visiting Fletcher Cavendish?"

"You think he and Mrs. Seymore are lying about the affair, don't you?"

"I don't know, but I do not like the tone of what we saw this evening."

"What do you suspect?"

"I don't know that either, and it worries me, Alice. It worries me a great deal."

CHAPTER 9

The Choices of a Woman Alone

*The husband very innocently, the wife most guiltily
became the wretched victims of his arts and intrigues.*
—The Trial of William Henry Hall vs. Major George Barrow
for Criminal Conversation

"Will you want to get ready for bed now, miss?" inquired Mrs. Kendricks as she helped Rosalind off with her cloak. The house around them was still and cool, the fire having been banked before they left. The only light was that which filtered through the window from the street, and the warm glow of the lamp Mrs. Kendricks had lit when they came in.

"Yes, please," said Rosalind. The frown that had settled on Mrs. Kendricks's face in the carriage had not shifted at all. Rosalind sighed. She was bone-weary and longed for nothing so much as to crawl into her bed and sleep until tomorrow. That, however, would only be delaying the problem.

"Is something wrong, Mrs. Kendricks?" she asked.

Her housekeeper folded Rosalind's good cloak carefully over her arm. "That's not for me to say."

"I do not agree. It is very much for you to say."

Mrs. Kendricks was silent for a long time, but Rosalind watched her face settle into deeper lines.

"Miss Thorne, I have stood by you," she said at last. "It was my duty to do so, but it was also something I was glad to do. I had hoped, however, after the difficulties with Lord and Lady Blanchard, and with Lord Casselmain returning, free . . ." She let the sentence trail away.

"You hoped that I would marry."

"I hoped that you would take the clear path to a good life. The life you deserve. I thought this"—she waved toward the parlor—"would prove a way to keep yourself occupied until you and his lordship could come to an understanding."

"I see."

"Oh, I'll grant you the money's been a blessing. It's wonderful not to have to slink in and out of the green grocer's, or wonder how we're going to make the coal and candles stretch, but . . ."

"Yes, Mrs. Kendricks? Please continue."

"You're not going to stop, are you, miss?"

"No, Mrs. Kendricks. I don't believe I am. Not for a while anyway."

"If it's not too much, may I ask why not, miss? You have such a chance in front of you. You're not a romantic girl. You know what it is for a woman to try to live on her own for any length of time. You could be a duchess. You could wipe your feet on the rest of the world, and never have to look at a bill again."

"Even duchesses fall down, Mrs. Kendricks. You and I know that."

"That's as may be, but a clever duchess has a much softer landing than a clever woman alone ever can."

Perhaps, if she'd had more sleep, or a head less full of what had occurred with Mr. Cavendish, Rosalind would have maintained her silence, at least until she had a better idea of what she should say.

"I'm not sure I have an answer for you, not a good one. It's only that, these past months, I've finally felt that I am doing something good." She laid her hand on her bosom. "Something that speaks to my heart. I think if I were a writer or a painter and I'd finally created a work that I knew to be beautiful, I would feel much the same. All these skills, all this organizing and arranging and learning how to act and to move and who to talk to and how, I can at last take all of that and make some kind of difference with it."

"Yes, and with it you've learned to lie, and to steal, and consort with all types."

"You're talking about Adam Harkness." Adam Harkness, who spent his nights watching the world from dark corners, was a principal officer of the Bow Street Police Office. "Or is it Mr. Cavendish who worries you?"

Mrs. Kendricks lifted her nose in the air. "I am talking of no one in particular, except you, Miss Thorne."

Of course not. Rosalind pushed aside a sudden burst of impatience. Still, she had started this conversation. She could not fairly complain she didn't like the results, and she most definitely did not. There was, however, one more thing that needed to be said.

"If you feel you cannot continue in service here, I of course respect that," she told Mrs. Kendricks. "You will have the finest reference I can provide, and always, always, you will have my most profound gratitude for all you have done for me. This is not the sort of life either of us bargained for. I understand that another woman of sense and feeling might find it appalling."

Another woman might have shown a hint of a quiver, or a gleam of unshed tears, if not actually wept, but not Mrs. Kendricks. She had begun this conversation and she would see it through.

"I will have to think on it, miss," said Mrs. Kendricks, and that was all she said for a long time.

The routine of closing up the house—of making sure the parlor fire remained properly banked, that the doors and windows were locked, and the candles and lamps were all extinguished—was carried on in silence. As was the business of changing for bed, of brushing out Rosalind's hair, and turning the bolsters. Mrs. Kendricks wished her good night, and Rosalind wished her housekeeper the same. She lay in her iron-framed bed and blinked up at the darkness. Faint lights flickered underneath the window curtains as the carriages rattled past outside.

She had learned to sleep through the noises, most nights. Some nights, like tonight, the agitation was too great, and she must lie awake, a silent and unacknowledged witness to the life that never stilled in the city streets.

What do I do? What have I done? The questions were not new, although the circumstances were. Mrs. Kendricks was right. Rosalind had seen the affection in Devon's eyes tonight, and her heart had yearned toward it. He would take her to him, if she gave him the chance. She knew that, just as she knew she could make him ask for her hand—with a word, with a smile, with the small confession that she missed him and missed the ease of their friendship. It would be easy.

Certainly it would be simpler than this odd path she had set herself on. Society was entirely about place and relative position. Life revolved around knowing to a nicety where one stood in relation to all of one's acquaintance. But Rosalind did not know where she stood in relation to herself, never mind anyone else. There was not even a proper name for what she was doing. The cache of her birth and her breeding would be steadily worn away by the money passing through her hands and the newer, lower company she moved among. And when that was gone, who would she be?

With these uncertainties ringing around her head, Rosalind slid into a doze. Uneasy dreams flickered through her like the passing carriage lanterns. All she was sure of was that she had missed something or forgotten something, and it was vital she find it. Even though she did not know its name.

Someone was pounding on the door. The noise was distant, but it would not stop. Rosalind struggled through the layers of uneasy dreams until she was able to push herself up on the bolsters and blink. The watch was calling three of the clock and all's well, but that was somewhere farther down the street. In her modest room, the door opened and Mrs. Kendricks, in housecoat and ruffled nightcap with a candle in her hand, hurried in.

"I'm sorry, Miss Thorne, but a messenger has come. It is from Mrs. Seymore, and the boy said it was most urgent."

Rosalind took the note and unfolded it. It was very brief, but it seemed to take a very long time to read:

Fletcher Cavendish is murdered.

CHAPTER 10

A Place Naturally Suited for Violence

Something more goes to the composition of a fine murder . . .
Design, gentlemen, grouping, light and shade, poetry and
sentiment are now deemed indispensable to attempts of
this nature.

—Thomas De Quincey,
On Murder Considered as One of the Fine Arts

The constable slammed hard against Adam Harkness, just as he
was about to enter the Bow Street Police Office.

"What the devil!" Harkness staggered against the area railing, reflexively clutching the man who'd collided with him.
Now that he could see clearly, Adam recognized Ned Barstow,
a member of the night patrol, panting, pale, and hatless, his coat
hanging open so it flapped in the morning breeze.

"Murder!" gasped Ned. "Murder, Mr. Harkness!"

Harkness felt himself go very still. "Where?"

"The theater, sir! Drury Lane!"

"Stand there." Adam strode through the station door and
into the ward room. The spare, musty chamber was filled with
a dozen or so men, a combination of the "emergency" patrol who
manned the office from midnight to dawn, and the early arrivals
of the day's foot patrols. Every man turned toward Harkness,

from Sampson Goutier to spindly Tommy Aitch, who cleaned the boots and lit the lamps.

"Mr. Townsend or Mr. Stafford in yet?" Harkness demanded of the boy.

"No, sir."

"Run to Townsend's house at once. Wake him up if you must, and tell him there may have been murder done at the Theatre Royal. Then you go to Mr. Stafford and say the same." Harkness didn't wait for the boy's reply but turned to the men. "All of you, with me!"

But the patrolmen were already on their feet, grabbing coats, hats, and truncheons, ready to follow the principal officer out into Bow Street's soot-smeared dawn.

The relief on Barstow's face as he saw the reinforcements pouring out the door was intense. To his credit, though, he wasted no time on thanks or oaths. He just turned and ran, and Adam Harkness followed close behind. He did not need to turn his head to know the patrol was right on his heels. Their boots thundered on the cobbles and their oaths split the sounds of traffic as they dodged the mud holes, carts, and barrows.

Harkness concentrated on forcing his own path through the crowded street. That, and the fact that there'd been murder done practically on the station's doorstep. Drury Lane was just one street over from the public offices which held the police station and the magistrate's court.

Mr. Townsend would not be pleased.

Harkness stretched his long legs to catch up with Ned. "Tell me what happened."

"I was headed back to the station, sir. All was quiet. Just passed the night watch. They'd no disturbances to report. All at once, the theater porter comes running out into the street shouting blue murder. I runs in, and they takes me to the room.

There's the man, right in the middle, stone dead and . . ." He swallowed and wiped the sweat from his brow. "Stabbed, sir. God bless us. Ain't never seen such a thing away from the docks."

Harkness made no answer. He'd know what to say when he saw the man for himself.

It was only a handful of minutes before Harkness and his hastily assembled patrol reached the broad, busy corner where the Theatre Royal sat like a great block. At night, the place was generally the focus of attention of one or two men from Bow Street. They'd be hired along with a cluster of special constables in an attempt to keep at least some of the sneak thieves, cut-purses, and dips from making off with the patrons' belongings. Harkness himself had taken part of the watch last night. But he seldom had reason to consider the massive building itself. Now that he did, Harkness had two thoughts.

This is going to be a damned nightmare, was the first. He became immediately and painfully aware he had a relative hand-ful of men at his back. Curious passersby on foot and horse, even if carrying heavy baskets or pushing barrows, had already stopped to stare. Mumbling and calling to each other, they began to bunch together, forming a crowd that would only get bigger and more aggressively curious with each passing minute.

"Spread out," Harkness ordered his men. "Goutier, take charge of this. I want two men on each side of the theater, and four in the yard behind. Find the doors and keep watch on them. Do what you can to keep the crowd back."

"Yes, sir." Sampson Goutier was an imposing figure of a man, far taller than average, with midnight black skin. He was also one of the best and most levelheaded among the night patrol, and he at once began issuing orders in a voice that could have been heard upwind in a freshening gale. Harkness paused just long enough to make sure the men were indeed listening to his orders, before he followed Barstow into the theater.

In the evening, the entrance hall of the Theatre Royal was a grand sight. This morning, it felt cold and cavernous. Harkness's boots echoed as he and Barstow crossed the marble floor toward a little man with a large head and a shock of dark hair who stood at the foot of the right hand staircase. A spindly and nervous boy all but hopped from foot to foot beside him.

"Dr. Arnold, sir," Ned told Harkness. "The theater manager."

"Dr. Arnold, I am Adam Harkness, principal officer of—"

Harkness got no further. "Thank God!" The manager clasped both his hands and shook them like he meant to wring them right of Harkness's wrists. "Come in, sir, come in! My office, at once!"

But Harkness resisted Dr. Arnold's firm tug. "We'll come to that, sir. Where is the dead man?"

"The dead man? The dead *man!*" Arnold cried. "Great God, sir! It's no man! It's a disaster! It's Fletcher Cavendish, sir! My principal actor, the heart's blood of my theater!"

"But where is he?" persisted Harkness. "Has he been moved yet?" Generally, so much time passed between the commission of violence and someone getting word to Bow Street, there was no chance to see the thing as it had actually been done. Harkness was determined not to let this one be wasted.

"He's in his dressing room," said Arnold. "Never such a thing, not in all my days. Not even—"

"Will you show me?" Harkness cut him off. "And if you have a man you trust absolutely, send for him to meet us there."

Thankfully, while Dr. Arnold might be voluble, he was a man used to a crisis. He nodded once, and grabbed the boy. "Michaels, fetch me Park, and tell him to get up to the main dressing room. Now! Now! Now!" He shoved the boy roughly on his way. The lad stumbled, but took off at such a speed, he might have been one of Harkness's own runners.

"Barstow, stay here," said Harkness. "If anyone comes looking for me, tell them we've gone—"

"To the main dressing room, yes, sir."

With that, Harkness plunged after Dr. Arnold into the theater's depths.

It quickly became clear to Harkness that the Theatre Royal was a place where it would be easy to quietly kill a man. There seemed to be a thousand staircases and private rooms. He'd been in rookeries that admitted more light than these hallways. Hammers, awls, and lengths of stout rope, not to mention bags of sand, sharp-edged trowels, and lead weights, had been stacked in every other corner.

Harkness was in no way surprised to see a mob clogging the passage at the top of the narrow stairs. People exclaimed and craned their necks and tried to cram themselves into what must have been the dressing room's doorway. Not that Adam could see it through the wall of backs and shoulders. "Here now! Clear out!" shouted Dr. Arnold, bouncing up and down on his toes. "Clear out! Martin! James! You! And you!" He jabbed his fingers at men in smocks and leather breeches. "Clear these people out of here!"

"Allow me, Dr. Arnold. All right!" Harkness bellowed. "Bow Street's here! Make way! Make way!"

Harkness began grabbing shoulders and pushing the spectators toward the men Dr. Arnold had named. This raised a ruckus, of course, but Arnold's men were a rough and ready bunch, and a path was cleared to the dressing room in fairly short order.

Dr. Arnold dove forward through the open doorway, but in the next instant reeled back.

"I'm sorry," he gasped, clutching at Harkness's sleeve. "I'm sorry. I . . ."

Harkness pushed past the man, and saw at once the reason for his distress. He was used to scenes of violence, and had caused more than one himself, but this was a grim sight. There was blood, in quantity. It fouled the walls as well as the floor. In the middle of this grim setting, a half-dressed man lay on his back. One hand was flung out, the other clutched at the dagger in his chest. It was so horrible and so dramatic that for a brief and unworthy moment, Harkness wondered if it had been staged.

"Close the door behind me," he said to Arnold. "Get your man Park to stand there. No one who is not a patrolman is to come in."

With that, Adam stepped into the dressing room. The smell was already bad, but Harkness ignored that. He crouched down beside the dead man, and gently closed his still, startled eyes.

Cavendish had not been long dead. There was still some slight warmth to the corpse and Harkness was able to move his hand from the weapon that killed him. It seemed Mr. Cavendish had either been in the act of dressing or undressing. His collar and laces were loose, and his shirt opened almost to the waist. The linen strip of his cravat lay nearby. There was no sign that Harkness could see of any bruises on his face or his hands. It was difficult to tell, but it looked like it was a single blow that had dispatched him, straight to the heart.

Harkness pulled his handkerchief from his pocket and freed the knife from the corpse's chest.

It was an incongruously pretty thing. A thin, double-edged blade. Not a kitchen knife, nor yet such a knife as a ruffian would carry for mischief or defense. It was more delicate than a Scotsman's dirk. Almost flimsy. The handle was chased silver and enamel. This was a decoration, not a tool. But for all that, the tip and the edges were quite sharp.

Expensive tastes or expensive friends? Harkness wrapped the knife carefully and stowed it in the interior pocket of his coat.

Someone—possibly the murderer, but possibly the constable or someone else—had stepped in some of the blood while it was wet. None of the streaks and splotches, unfortunately, was so clear as to be recognizable as a footprint. Harkness looked at these unhelpful smudges and muttered several equally unhelpful oaths.

He straightened up then and surveyed the room. There were no immediate indications of robbery. The place was disordered, but it was only the natural disorder of a much-used room. The two mirrored dressing tables were notable for the sort of perfect organization usually found in the room of a woman with a very persnickety lady's maid. The two wardrobes were closed up. No drawers hung open, no boxes or papers lay on the floor. The remainder of the furniture was upright and in its places.

No struggle then. No fight for the knife. Cavendish had either known his murderer, or had been taken entirely by surprise.

Or both.

There was a knock at the door. "A Ned Barstow here, sir," called a voice, presumably belonging to Arnold's fellow Parks. "Says he's one of yours."

"He is," agreed Harkness. "Come in, Barstow. Carefully."

Barstow opened the door slowly. Harkness put himself between the constable and the dead man, but Barstow clearly had gotten hold of himself and was able to speak fairly steadily.

"Word's come from the coroner, sir. They want us to bring the body to the Brown Bear. Sir David Royce will meet it, us, there."

"All right." It was the usual practice to hold both the examination and the inquest at a public house. "Tell Goutier to find us a cart and a sheet and another fellow with a stout stomach."

"Yessir." Barstow retreated, and closed the door again.

Unfortunately, a more thorough search of the room revealed nothing helpful. If anything had been removed, it was nothing that left a trace. There was a purse with several bank notes and some coins. There was a watch and chain, and Cavendish's diamond ring still glimmered on his bloody hand.

"Well, Mr. Cavendish, what is it you've done?" muttered Harkness. "Because it looks to me like someone came here with the sole aim of seeing you dead."

CHAPTER 11

The Consequences of Staying Out Late

I would earnestly implore all who are anxious to form an impartial judgment not only to note minutely the precise time of every incident, but to consider its importance to him who is a villain of no ordinary stamp.
— *The Trial of Birch vs. Neal for Criminal Conversation*

"Miss Thorne." Mrs. Seymore rose from her sofa, her hands alternately twisting together and smoothing her hair down. "I . . . Thank you so much for coming. I didn't know who else to call."

Dawn was breaking over the rooftops as Rosalind and Mrs. Kendricks entered Mrs. Seymore's parlor. Though elegantly appointed, the room was dark and cold. Only one lamp had been lit and the coals were still banked in the hearth. But that poor light was enough to show Rosalind that Mrs. Seymore's strength and poise had both dissolved and left her trembling.

"Sit down, Mrs. Seymore. You are not well." Rosalind hurried to the other woman's side. Mrs. Seymore was white as milk and her ringlets hung randomly about her ears and shoulders. She was still dressed in an evening gown of embroidered blue silk and Italian glass beads. That dress was ruined now, its hems splashed with mud and worse. Rosalind indulged in several unhelpful and impolite thoughts regarding the servants of the house who had left their mistress in such a state. Indeed, the only maid in evidence was a thin, pale girl with dark rings under her eyes and her cap perched crookedly on her disordered hair.

Mrs. Kendricks, of course, took in the situation with a single glance. "You," she said to the little maid. "Where is the house-keeper? Your mistress needs tea, and food. And another lamp, and someone must get that fire lit."

The orders startled the girl into life, or at least into a hurried curtsy. "Yes, ma'am," she yelped. "And Mrs. Nott's just come, miss, she don't live in . . . an' . . . I didn't know . . ."

"Take me to the kitchen." Mrs. Kendricks put firm hands on the girl's shoulder and steered her out the side door.

There was a silk shawl discarded across the sofa's back. Rosalind grabbed this up to wrap around Mrs. Seymore's shoulders.

"Thank you. I . . . thank you," Margaretta murmured as she clutched at the shawl's ends. "I'm sorry, there's nothing to offer, there's nothing to . . ." Her words broke off and she gazed instead at her hands. "I can't stop shaking."

"You've had a shock." Rosalind gently pressed Mrs. Seymore to sit back down. "We'll have you warm in a minute. But you must tell me what's happened."

Another spasm shook Margaretta, and for a moment Rosalind feared she might descend into active hysterics. *Perhaps a simpler question.*

"Where is Captain Seymore?" she tried, but Mrs. Seymore shook her head violently.

"I don't know. I have not seen him since . . . since . . . Dear God." She pressed her hand against her mouth. "Since after dinner."

"But how did you find out Mr. Cavendish had died?"

Mrs. Seymore swallowed again. "I was . . . I went there. I saw him."

Their conversation was interrupted by a flotilla of servants. A great, grim-faced housekeeper in impeccable black, her hair braided into a coronet around her head, carried in a huge silver tray, heavily loaded with rolls, cheeses, a cold pork pie, and most welcome of all, a pot of tea. While Mrs. Kendricks relieved her of this burden, the Seymores' housekeeper at once sent her troops scurrying to fetch blankets and light the fire. Rosalind lit the lamps to drive back the darkness and then went to throw open the curtains.

In short order, Mrs. Seymore was wrapped in stout wool with a hot cup of tea in her hands and seated in front of the fresh hearth. Rosalind nodded thanks to her own servant, and received in return only a look of resignation.

Mrs. Seymore gulped the tea down and shuddered, but this time it was from the scalding heat. "Do you think . . . you think someone will be sent? The constables? B-bailiffs? I can't, I won't, I . . . the scandal . . ."

"Until I have more information from you, I cannot say what will happen," Rosalind told her firmly. "You must try to speak calmly of what you saw, or I can do nothing."

"Yes. Of course. Forgive me. I . . . just . . ." Margaretta shuddered again.

Rosalind was relieved to see someone had put a bottle of brandy on the tray and she used it now to liberally dose Mrs. Seymore's tea. That, and a roll thickly spread with butter and jam, seemed to be having some good effect. At least Margaretta's color improved.

"Start from the beginning," said Rosalind. "What was the first thing that occurred this evening?"

"The captain's brother came to supper," said Mrs. Seymore promptly.

Rosalind nodded. "This would be Sir Bertram Seymore? The one you said might be writing the insinuating letters?"

Mrs. Seymore nodded. "We ate. Turbot, roasted pheasant, and apple pie for dessert. The captain and his brother retired for port and cigars. I took my tea alone in the parlor, and then went up to dress. We had an invitation out." Margaretta's hands trembled, sloshing the remains of the tea in her cup. "When I came down to inquire if the captain was ready to go, I found his brother had departed, and the captain was beginning to get drunk. This was not a surprise. Neither was the way he spoke to me." The weight of her domestic troubles leveled Mrs. Seymore's voice, and returned some color to her faded cheeks. "He was lurching between protestations that he loved me and wanted all to be right between us, and complaints of my various faults and promising he would be revenged.

"This, Miss Thorne, was his brother's influence. I knew from experience the best thing to do was to simply pretend I heard and understood none of it. I asked Captain Seymore if he meant to come out with me. He laughed and said he'd surely meet me later. I left him in the company of his bottle and his bile."

Rosalind thought of how Captain Seymore had hammered on Fletcher Cavendish's door and how clearly he'd expected his wife to be there. Who had told him where to look for her? Was it his brother? If Sir Bertram was a frequent guest, he could have easily bribed a servant to gain information about Mrs. Seymore's movements.

"So you went alone to . . ."

"A card party and late supper at the Ralph Hoffmans'. I was there for some little while. Then . . ."

Hoffmans. Cavendish had mentioned that name during their dinner. "Then what? Then where?"

Mrs. Seymore set her cup and plate aside on the table at her elbow. Those hands were steady now, Rosalind noted. "I admit, it had been arranged I should meet Fletcher, but not at the theater," she said. "He was supposed to come to the Hoffmans' after his own supper, to tell me his impressions of you." She glanced sideways, but Rosalind kept her face impassive.

"But Fletcher, Mr. Cavendish that is, did not arrive at the Hoffmans'," Mrs. Seymore went on. "And as it was nearly two in the morning, I confess, I was concerned. So I decided I would go to his hotel and find out what delayed him."

Alone at night, you went to the hotel of a man who was not a relation, but whom you swear was not your paramour. That portion of Rosalind which still regarded propriety to be as necessary as breathing shuddered.

"I waited in the ladies' parlor at the hotel while one of the staff took up a note," Mrs. Seymore went on. "But although he knocked and called at Mr. Cavendish's door, there had been no answer. Ordinarily, I would have simply gone home, but the manager knows me and he told me he had seen Fletcher go back to the theater."

"Was it usual for him to return to the theater so late?" Rosalind asked.

"Not terribly." Mrs. Seymore reclaimed her teacup and drained the contents. "But he sometimes left behind some book or manuscript or letter only to discover he needed it. So I went there after him."

"You went to the theater? Alone at night?"

"I have done it so many times and I did not particularly think of it," said Mrs. Seymore, her tone almost daring Rosalind to be shocked. "And yes, I am aware of how it might appear to those less familiar with the peculiar customs of the theater world."

Rosalind busied herself with pouring out more tea for Mrs. Seymore, and for herself. Rosalind knew that those who dwelt in the tribes of the artists, theater dwellers, and pen wielders had their own courtesies and their own rituals. They could forget how their habits might look to those more straightened and correct foreigners who gazed upon their shores. But what concerned Rosalind was how each word Margaretta spoke indicated her familiarity with the routine of the theater, and the particular habits of Fletcher Cavendish.

"Paulling, the day porter, had gone off duty by then, but I remember I spoke with Ulbrecht, the night porter." Mrs. Seymore's eyes had gone distant, and she drummed her fingers against the rim of her cup, trying to recall each detail. "He told me he'd seen Mr. Cavendish go up to his dressing room. That's on the first floor, so I went up the house stairs, and knocked. I may have called as well . . . But there was no answer. I then returned and asked Ulbrecht if he had seen Mr. Cavendish leave, but he said he had not. Some presentiment reached me, and I asked Ulbrecht to unlock the door."

"It was locked?"

"No, as it turned out," she admitted. "But while I am somewhat casual in my habits, I could not quite bring myself to enter a man's dressing room without some witness. Not with . . . all that is hanging over my head right now."

And yet you went to him alone at night. You proceeded from hotel to theater, all alone. You only took care for your reputation once you understood something might be amiss.

"Of course. Go on."

"Fletcher was on the floor. He was on his back. He was . . . There was blood everywhere, Miss Thorne. Ulbrecht started howling and I ran to Fletcher . . . I . . . He was dead. His hands . . . I tried to pry them free." She held up her own hand, as if, like Lady Macbeth, she would see the stains still there. "They were warm and soft and . . ."

Mrs. Seymore reclaimed her teacup and took another large swallow. It was clear she was determined to stiffen her spine against all she had seen, which was just as well. Rosalind was keenly aware of the ticking of the clock, the brightening of the room, and the continued absence of the captain.

She wondered what was happening in the dressing room now, and if the officers from Bow Street had been summoned yet. Would Adam Harkness be set on this work? In her own mind, Rosalind saw Mr. Harkness as she had the previous night in front of the theater; a figure lost in the shadows, calmly watching all that occurred.

"I became aware of a terrible commotion," Mrs. Seymore was saying. "Ulbrecht kept shouting and people were running and . . . I am very ashamed to admit it, Miss Thorne, but I lost my head. I ran away."

Rosalind said nothing. She looked again at Mrs. Seymore's ruined skirts.

"I couldn't think," Mrs. Seymore protested softly, even though Rosalind hadn't said a word. "I couldn't see anything except . . . Oh, my dear lord, Fletcher. What have I done?" Her hands trembled again.

Rosalind snatched the cup from her hands before she spilled it. "Mrs. Seymore, you must remain strong. Tell me, was the house empty when you returned?"

"Yes, and quite dark," she whispered. "Much as it was when you arrived. Only Eustace and little Margie were here, and I had to send Eustace for you. After that, I was in rather a fog until you arrived."

"Did anyone say when the captain left?"

"Yes. Eustace did. It was about ten o'clock."

Ten o'clock. That would have given the captain more than enough time to polish off another bottle somewhere, in company or alone, and then to travel to the King's Arms and climb to the private dining room in the hopes of catching his wife with Mr. Cavendish. Where had he gone after that?

"Mrs. Nott," said Rosalind to the housekeeper, who had taken up an unobtrusive post in the corner. "Could you go ask Eustace if the master possibly came back and went out again? Very early?" It was a forlorn hope, for the captain would have had to go before daybreak.

"No," whispered Mrs. Seymore before Mrs. Nott could make an answer, or a movement. "Oh, merciful heavens, Miss Thorne, you cannot think *William* did this. I will believe a great deal of my husband, but I tell you flatly, he hasn't the heart to kill a man in cold blood."

"No, of course not," said Rosalind hastily. "But it is important that he be found. You were seen at the theater. There will be questions about all the things that happened last night. He must be here to help answer them."

"Oh. Yes. Of course."

But Rosalind could tell that despite her protestations, all manner of unpleasant ideas were forming in Mrs. Seymore's mind. "He may have gone to his club," Margaretta said. "He has spent the night there before. Or perhaps he met Sir Bertram and returned to his house? He does that sometimes."

"Very good," said Rosalind. "We can send your man to either place."

Mrs. Seymore closed her eyes. "But . . . once we find the captain, then what? I must know what to do and what to expect."

It was difficult to think of the correct answer. Rosalind knew too little of the forms and procedures. This was not her world.

One thing she could say with certainty, however.

"You must come forward at once," said Rosalind firmly. "If you try to hide your connection to this thing, it will go the worse for everyone. You must let me send to the Bow Street Police Office. There is a man there, Adam Harkness. He is one of the principal officers and you may trust him to hear your story with disinterest."

And that disinterest would be needed, as would all the shrewd and careful insight Mr. Harkness possessed, and not a little of the friendship Rosalind knew he felt for her.

Because Mrs. Seymore at this moment might be telling a terrible truth, or a terrible lie. As soon as the lights had been brought, Rosalind was able to see that not all the stains on Mrs. Seymore's pale skirts were street dirt.

Several were very clearly dried blood.

CHAPTER 12

The Supporting Cast

[He] may, and ought, to inquire of all circumstances of the
party's death, and also of all things which occasioned it.
　　　　　　　　　—John Impey of the Inner Temple,
　　　　　　　　　　　The Practice of the Office of Coroner

"And you knew Mrs. Seymore on sight?" Harkness asked the night porter.

Harkness sat in Dr. Arnold's office with a glass of brandy in his hand to help wash away the iron tang that being in the room with a dead man left in the back of his throat. As he drank, he listened to the night porter relate how the body had been found.

"I did know her that plain, sir." Stanislas Ulbrecht was a weathered man who seemed to be composed entirely of bones and knobby joints held together by sinew. Despite his name, his accent was that of a native Londoner born within sight of Covent Garden. "She been at my door many's a time."

"But you had not seen her last night, before she came asking if Mr. Cavendish was there?"

"Not she, sir. Nossir." Unlike some Harkness talked to, Ulbrecht did not seem to relish his chance to stand before one of the famous Bow Street "runners." But neither did he look worried, like a man with something to hide. Ulbrecht just seemed put out, like a man who wanted to finish his work and be off to his breakfast, and his bed.

Harkness had a great deal of sympathy for Mr. Ulbrecht, but unfortunately there were other things he needed to know. "Did any others come asking for Mr. Cavendish?"

"Ha! Everybody wants to see Mr. Cavendish. Or they did." For the first time, unease crept into Ulbrecht's manner. "Damme, sirs, I must get back to my door, or we'll have the whole of London pouring through trying for a peek."

"You stand there, Ulbrecht," said Dr. Arnold. "I've put Selby outside, he'll see to it. You answer Mr. Harkness. Who else asked after Mr. Cavendish last night?"

"Well." Ulbrecht's keen eyes darted this way and that, as if he was looking for answers in the corners of the office. "It weren't Mr. Cavendish he asked for . . ."

"Who is this?" Harkness set his glass down and met the man's gaze, making it perfectly plain he was ready to wait as long as necessary for the answer.

"Cap'n Seymore, sir. Dead drunk and bellowing, but it weren't for Mr. Cavendish. He wanted Mrs. Seymore. But that was 'afore I seed her."

"And who is Mrs. Seymore?" Harkness asked.

"You don't know Mrs. Seymore, the poetess?" exclaimed Dr. Arnold. "A very famous lady of letters, and a friend of Mr. Cavendish's."

"And Captain Seymore is . . ."

Dr. Arnold's face twisted. "The lady's rather less famous and much drunker husband, I'm afraid."

"What time did the captain make his appearance?" Harkness took care to keep his voice and manner calm.

"Well, now, let me think." The porter scratched his nose, and his ear, and his stubbled chin. "Curtain'd come down. Good run, good house, quite the crowd there was, but that'd cleared away . . . aye. Morgan cut his hand . . . aye . . . Cordington got into a fight with Betty Lucas . . . aye . . ."

"Go *on*, man!" Dr. Arnold slammed his hand against his desk.

Ulbrecht didn't even flinch. He did tug at his ear. "Half two!" he cried triumphantly. "I was opening the door for Mrs. West. Her carriage had just come, and the watch was calling out, and Seymore comes rolling up himself, you know that walk that sailors have." He showed signs of being willing to demonstrate, but Harkness held up a hand to stop him.

"You could swear it was Captain Seymore?"

"As easy as I'd swear to me own name. He'd come to my door 'afore, just like his missus. Well, not just like. Alwus glad to see her. Grand lady, alwus quiet and polite with a please and a thank-you and . . ."

And probably a shilling or three. "Was the captain here before or after Mrs. Seymore came?"

"Oh, 'afore, sir. An hour maybe, maybe a bit more, but not so much, or I would not a' been here, you see, but Mrs. West was late an' wanted her carriage brought 'round then and somebody 'ad to get between Cordington an' Betty Lucas 'afore they tears themselves to bits. It was—"

"Did you let Seymore up to the dressing room?" interrupted Harkness. Maybe Cordington and Betty would become important later, but he could not let Ulbrecht go chasing down that road just now.

"When he could state no proper business?" Ulbrecht drew himself up indignantly, and with a worried glance toward Dr. Arnold. "Not I, sirs. Not the lord mayor himself. Not the king!"

But you did let the lady up, an hour and maybe a bit more later.

Harkness thought about the warren of passages and stairways

that made up the back of the theater; about all the people going about their own work, or thinking to get home to their own beds and families. With the porter sending for carriages and breaking up fights, it would be simple enough for a man to slip through any one of the dozen open doors, find a place to hide, and wait.

"Thank you, Mr. Ulbrecht," said Harkness. "You can go, but we'll be wanting to ask you more questions soon, and you should know you may be called to give testimony at the coroner's inquest."

"At yer service, sir," Ulbrecht said, although he did look to Dr. Arnold to confirm it. Arnold nodded and waved in dismissal. As soon as the office door shut, he got up and went to the sideboard to pour himself a fresh brandy.

"What is it we're to do next, Mr. Harkness?" Dr. Arnold asked as he stared at the fresh spirit in his glass. "Cavendish has no family that I know of."

As if the question were some cue upon the stage, the door burst open and a short, bandy-legged man all but tumbled into the office and fetched up against the manager's desk.

"Arnold!" the man cried. "Is it true?"

"Ah, Mr. Kean." Dr. Arnold settled himself back into his chair. "You weren't long in coming."

"Did you think this could be kept a secret from me! Did you think—"

"And you are, sir?" asked Harkness.

The new arrival, Mr. Kean, pivoted toward Harkness, his dark eyes flashing fire and daggers and all the rest that an insulted man might think to throw into such a glance. "Arnold, who is *this*?" Kean demanded.

With a sigh, Dr. Arnold put down his brandy. He also swept out his arm in a grand gesture. "Mr. Kean, I present to you Adam Harkness, principal officer of the Bow Street Police

Office. Mr. Harkness, I present to you Edmund Kean, one of the greatest actors ever to grace the stage of the Theatre Royal."

Harkness made his bow. One of the greatest actors ever to grace the stage inclined his head without any trace of modesty. Edmund Kean was a short man with a rugged, horsey face and dark hair that he wore a bit longer than current fashion. His legs were both a little crooked, and Harkness wondered if he had suffered some accident.

The small man looked up at Harkness with dark and searching eyes. "Not the famous Watchdog Harkness, scourge of the highways!" he exclaimed in a voice trained to carry in a much larger space. Harkness acknowledged the cant name, and the title. "Then it is true! Cavendish is dead?"

"He is," said Harkness.

To his surprise, Kean barked out a harsh laugh. "Well, well. I would have thought the pox would get him first. Which husband was it?"

"Husband?"

"Of course, husband!" Kean grabbed Dr. Arnold's brandy off the sideboard and drank it down. Arnold neither flinched nor complained, he just got out a fresh glass and unstoppered the bottle, taking care to fill Kean's glass first. "There's not a bed in London that our Mr. Cavendish hadn't made himself comfortable in. Half of old Ulbrecht's business is turning sputtering spouses and other such righteous relations away from the door after a show." It might well have been jealousy that colored the actor's words, along with contempt. But whether it was or not, nothing was going to keep Kean from his main objective. "Arnold, they're talking nonsense outside that we're closing down for tonight."

"We have to. Mob's already gathering out there." Arnold

gestured toward the window with his glass. "If we open again too soon, they'll pour in and tear the place down."

"But you're missing the best take of all our careers!"

"No, I'm not. You'll have to trust me, Kean."

"And what about our pay, eh?"

"I tell you to trust me." Arnold put his arm about the man's shoulders. He also poured some more brandy in his glass. "You get your eulogy ready and brush up your doleful sobs. As for the public"—Arnold winked as he stepped back—"let's just let them stew a little, shall we? Let the anticipation grow and the word spread itself out properly. Why should we bother our heads with a buildup when the newspapers will create one for us? We'll reopen in three nights, and I swear to you, Mr. Kean, you'll have the entire house in the palm of your hand and a bigger profit than you've seen in your life. We'll be giving Cavendish farewell performances for a month and all be rich as Croesus when we're done."

Kean threw back his head and roared with laughter. "Now, that is the way I like to hear a theater manager talk! I'll go convey the good news to Mrs. West. She's quite beside herself. Mr. Harkness." Kean bowed and breezed out with a considerably more lighthearted air than he'd brought in.

Harkness looked at Dr. Arnold with raised brows. Arnold met his gaze calmly. "I know what you're thinking, sir. He's a callow, heartless money-grubber."

"No, Dr. Arnold, that is not at all what I was thinking." Actually, he was thinking about the jealousy he'd heard under Kean's words, and wondering what the man might know about Cavendish's friends, acquaintances, and affairs.

"Well, you should have been, because I am." Arnold slumped down in his chair. He considered his brandy glass, but pushed both it and the bottle away. "Damme if I can do anything else with this, though. Cavendish was the biggest draw we've had since Garrick, and we've no choice but to wring the last bit out of him we can get."

"Who is Mrs. West?" Harkness asked.

"I see you are not one of our regular patrons. Mrs. West is an actress. As great a leading lady as that"—he raised his glass toward the closed door—"is a leading man."

"Then it was her carriage Ulbrecht said he was calling for about the time Captain Seymore tried to get into the theater?" Which meant she might have seen or heard something of the encounter in the dressing room, or its aftermath.

"We have no other Mrs. West here, you may be sure," Arnold said. "If you need to talk with her, I'll see it's arranged."

"Thank you, Dr. Arnold," Harkness said. "May I ask where you were last night?"

Arnold spread his hands. "Where wasn't I? Mostly I was in the strong room, counting the receipts and going over the accounts. I was here in my office for a bit with the cash box and the ledger, settling with our fruit sellers and a few others. But all that was finished before two o'clock and then I was in my own carriage and on my way home."

"And you saw nothing missing and noticed nothing wrong?"

"Our treasurer and all his clerks are counting every ha'penny and farthing now, you may be sure. We'll let you know if any turn up missing." He shook his head. "Damme, I almost wish it would turn out to be a robbery or something of the kind. It's too bad when a man's life just gets the better of him." He looked bleakly up at Harkness. "Mr. Kean interrupted us before you could answer me, Mr. Harkness. What happens now?"

"The coroner is waiting to receive Mr. Cavendish. He'll begin

his inquiries and there will be a formal inquest within a day or two."
Harkness paused. "You said Mr. Cavendish had no family?"

"None that I know about. He lived over at the King's Arms
when he was in town. They might know of someone."

Harkness climbed to his feet and held his hand out. "Thank
you, Dr. Arnold. This has all been very helpful."

Dr. Arnold's own hand was soft, but surprisingly strong.
"Catch the blaggard, Mr. Harkness," he said flatly. "If there's a
reward to be posted, the theater will subscribe. Cavendish was
a braggart and a swaggerer, and I'd lock up my daughter before
I let her near him, but there was no real bad in him, and my
God, never did I see a man who could seize a house by its heart
as he could."

"We'll do all we can, Dr. Arnold. You may be sure."

And the first thing after the body's safe with the coroner, thought
Harkness as he walked out of the office, *is to find out exactly
where this Captain and Mrs. Seymore have got themselves to.*

CHAPTER 13

The Master's Return

*Whatever demands secrecy, you may be sure it is wrong
for you to do, or suffer to be done.*
—Samuel and Sarah Adams, *The Complete Servant*

Mrs. Seymore's lady's maid had arrived at last, and had hustled
her mistress up to be changed from her ruined dress. This left
Rosalind alone in the parlor for several long minutes. Rosalind
found she was grateful for the interruption, because it gave her
time to think.

What should she say? What should she do? She was certain
that was blood on Mrs. Seymore's skirt. It could have got there
quite innocently when Margaretta knelt beside Mr. Cavendish's
body. She need not have struck whatever blow had killed the
actor. That could have been done by other, stronger hands.

The hands of a drunken man, for instance, who was schooled
in the ways and uses of violence.

*Do not think it. Do not tell yourself tales. You have no real infor-
mation. You know nothing at all.*

This was excellent advice, but it changed nothing. Events had
shifted so abruptly that Rosalind felt seasick. She looked help-
lessly around the parlor and, in the end, settled for pouring
herself another cup of tea, not because she wanted it, but because

the familiar motions might calm her disordered thoughts. Those thoughts, however, were determined to stray back to her dinner with Alice and Mr. Cavendish. Mr. Cavendish, who last night had been a presence to reckon with, and who could move young girls to excesses of love and grand devotion.

Oh, poor Louisa. She'll be heartbroken when she hears.

Rosalind tapped the strainer twice against the rim of her cup and returned it to its place. She opened the sugar bowl, extracted one lump with the tongs, and dropped it into the amber liquid. She replaced the tongs, and the lid. She lifted her spoon.

A single loud bang exploded from the hallway. Rosalind jumped, dropping the spoon into the tea and spilling the whole across her dress.

"Ah! Careful, you bastard son of a mongrel bitch!" roared a man's voice.

Blushing furiously, more at her clumsiness than at the oaths, Rosalind nonetheless hurried to open the parlor door. Captain Seymore staggered into the front hall, leaning heavily on a second man, who by his boots and coat Rosalind knew must be the coachman.

That poor man alternately dragged his master and stumbled with him toward the staircase. The captain's face was mottled gray and green and he cursed the floor underneath him as roundly as he did the man who supported him.

"William!" Mrs. Seymore, now clad in a fresh morning dress of claret and white, came hurrying down the stairs. "Where have you been!"

"Where have I been?" the captain roared. He also lurched toward Margaretta so that the coachman almost lost both hold and balance. "What right have you to question me, madam?"

"Have a care, sir!" cried the beleaguered coachman.

"I'll have a care with you!" The captain tore his arm free of his servant's grip and staggered forward under his own power.

The drink and his temper had wiped away what little nobility Rosalind had seen in William Seymore's profile. The captain sagged and slouched, rumpled and thoroughly ruined. Rosalind could not help but notice Mrs. Nott standing in the doorway to the kitchen, but the housekeeper did not move forward to assist. She just watched her master with an expression of ice and stone. Mrs. Kendricks was there, too, hovering beside her sister house-keeper, waiting for some signal from Rosalind as to how to intervene. Rosalind, though, gave none, because truly she did not know what they could, or should, do.

Unfortunately, Rosalind was not allowed to continue in the role of mute witness to this private scene. The captain had caught sight of her.

"*You!*" he bellowed. "What are you doing here?"

Mrs. Kendricks made as if to move between them, but Rosalind waved her back. "Mrs. Seymore asked me here as her friend," she told him evenly as she could.

"*This* is one of your friends?" Captain Seymore staggered backward until he banged against the wall. "God in heaven, Margaretta! You're laying traps for me now! You knew I'd go looking for you, at Hoffman's, at the theater, at the goddamned *hotel* . . ."

"William, what are you talking about?" Mrs. Seymore's voice rang low and dangerous through the spacious foyer.

"Captain Seymore came to Mr. Cavendish's rooms when Alice and I were having supper there," Rosalind told her.

"I meant to catch you, Margaretta." The captain pushed him-self away from the wall, or at least he tried to. "But I only snared your proxy. Been having a good laugh, have you two?" He pressed his hand to his eyes. "All about how you so cleverly deceived the one who should be your lord and master? Made me parade myself about the town, let as many people see the cuckold raging as . . ."

"You had no right to spy on me!" cried Margaretta.

"I have every right!" the captain snapped. "No one has more right than I!"

"Captain Seymore," began Rosalind. "Allow me to explain . . ."

"I'll allow you to leave, madam!" He threw his hand out, pointing toward the door, but he misjudged the gesture and slammed it against the wall. "Damnation! Leave! Now! Or, by God, I'll throw you out into the street with my own hands."

But at this, Margaretta strode forward and seized both those hardened hands.

"Will you stop being a fool and a brute for one instant and *listen!*"

"To what?" sneered the captain. "Another recital of lies? Where were you, madam? Not at your sister's and not at Hoffman's." He did not pull away, though, probably because some part of him knew he would fall if he did. "Then where, hmm?" The captain leaned forward, a sly leer spreading across his face.

"Never mind where I was. Where were you?" cried Mrs. Seymore. "Fletcher Cavendish is dead, sir! He is murdered!"

Rosalind expected oaths or, considering how very drunk the man was, for him to be sick or fall down insensible. But the captain only swayed a little on his booted feet.

"How do you know this?" Captain Seymore whispered.

"I saw him," answered Margaretta. "I went to the theater, and I found him there."

"*You* went . . . *you* saw . . . Dear God." Seymore pulled free of his wife's grip and wiped at his face. A sheen of perspiration appeared on his face from the effort of thinking clearly. "What a bloody, damnable mess. You betray me, you shame me, and now you . . . you . . ."

"William, stop." Mrs. Seymore took the captain's face between both her palms and turned him toward her. "William, please. I need you."

The captain clasped his wife's hands, and Rosalind saw Mrs. Seymore's face spasm. But the gesture worked. The sagging, shamed anger in the captain's manner dissolved slowly under his wife's familiar touch. His face creased in an effort to right the thoughts pitching on that internal sea of distress and drunkenness.

"How has this happened to us?" cried Seymore.

"I don't know," Margaretta answered. "But I need you, William. I need your help. Please. Speak to me. Have you been with your brother?"

"I was at my club. I was . . . the worse for drink. I . . ." The captain swallowed and it became clear to Rosalind that the enormity of what had happened was beginning to rise up from the stew of drink and jealousy that filled his fevered mind. "Margaretta . . . Margaretta . . . you cannot . . . you did not . . . I would not have hurt you, I swear, I swear." He clutched at his wife's sleeve. "I never gave a damn about what Bertram wanted. All I wanted was for you to stop. For you to be all mine again."

Margaretta did not answer, at least not directly. "The deed has been done," she said softly, fatally. "All that is left is to face the facts and try to survive it." She gently disengaged his rough fingers from the fine fabric of her sleeve, and still holding her husband's hand, Mrs. Seymore turned to her servants. "Let us get you upstairs, William. John, come and help the captain. Mrs. Nott, send for Drummond."

At last the servants moved, the coachman again took his master's arms, and the housekeeper took herself and her silent disapproval off below stairs. Only Mrs. Kendricks remained in the doorway, waiting for Rosalind's instructions.

As soon as her husband and the coachman were out of sight, Mrs. Seymore faced Rosalind. "As little as I like it, Miss Thorne,

I think we had best follow your advice and write to Bow Street. But not to this man, Harkness. A note must be sent directly to John Townsend."

"Mr. Townsend?" Rosalind was not surprised Mrs. Seymore knew the name. Mr. John Townsend was the most senior, and the most celebrated, of the officers at Bow Street.

"While I am sure this man Harkness is reliable, I am personally acquainted with Mr. Townsend. We must use all the influences we have in this matter."

"Yes, of course," said Rosalind because this was no time to argue the point, and because she could as easily write a second, private note to Mr. Harkness. In fact, she would be very surprised if he did not already know what had happened. He might even be on his way.

Rosalind's heart lurched a little at this thought. *You have enough troubles*, she scolded the unruly organ, and the memories that caused it to falter momentarily.

"Will you do me the very great favor of writing in my name?" Mrs. Seymore asked. "I must go see that the captain is being attended to properly."

"I'm glad to be of assistance," said Rosalind.

"Thank you. You can use my desk. It's in the side parlor, and Mrs. Nott can summon a messenger."

Mrs. Seymore retreated up the stairs. Slowly, Rosalind walked into the small, secondary parlor. It was as clean and elegant as the front room. The desk beside the window was broad and stacked with books, all of which had little slips of paper sticking out of them marking points or passages to be reviewed.

"What will you do, miss?"

Mrs. Kendricks had followed her and closed the door

soundlessly. Rosalind sat down in the straight-backed chair and took a sheet of writing paper and one of the quills from the center drawer. She unstoppered the crystal inkwell and found it filled.

"Please give me a minute, Mrs. Kendricks," she said. Rosalind dipped her pen, faced the page, and made several different decisions all at once.

She wrote quickly, but it was not the requested letter she set down. Instead, she wrote out all she could remember of the captain's rambling speech to his wife. She blotted this and folded it up so that it was simply an anonymous piece of paper lying at her left hand.

When she had finished, her mind felt clearer, and she knew what she must do.

"Mrs. Kendricks, I need you to take a message to Miss Littlefield," said Rosalind. "If she is not at home, she will surely be at her paper's offices." She might already be on her way here. Fletcher Cavendish was murdered. A murder was reason enough for the papers to be at their work, but Fletcher Cavendish was hardly some anonymous citizen of the metropolis. The clock on the mantle showed it was past ten already. The whole world would know what had happened before too much longer, and the whole world would run absolutely mad. "You may return home afterwards. I will be there as soon as I can."

But her housekeeper neither moved, nor assented to these instructions. "Miss Thorne, you cannot stay here," said Mrs. Kendricks. "You cannot allow yourself to be drawn into this."

"I'm already in it." Rosalind looked up at the woman who had stood by her in all her troubles for so many years. "You were right. I should have listened to you, but it is too late now, and we must go from where we are."

Mrs. Kendricks sighed. "Yes, miss," she said, all obedience and resignation. Rosalind felt a stab of shame and not a little of loss. She forced herself to concentrate on the page in front of her and wrote quickly:

Alice,

You know by now Fletcher Cavendish is murdered. I'm with the Seymores. Bow Street is being summoned here. Send an answer by Mrs. Kendricks saying where you are and what is happening.

R.

Mrs. Kendricks accepted the note without comment and left Rosalind alone. The parlor was cold, and she shivered as she took out yet another sheet of paper. She stared at it a moment, trying to gather her thoughts and understanding. It was more difficult than it should have been. A face kept intruding on her thoughts. Somewhat to her surprise, it was Devon's, and she did not understand why. Then she did. Devon represented safety and steadiness, the exact opposite of everything she had seen and was about to do. And she missed him.

Rosalind set her jaw and began writing two more letters. There was something yet to be accomplished here and she could not do it if she was distracted.

When she'd finished sealing the letters, she rang the bell and waited until Mrs. Nott appeared.

"Yes, miss?" The housekeeper folded her hands in front of her. Her face and demeanor were faultlessly correct, but Rosalind remembered the cold way she'd watched her master, and how very different that was from the way she'd helped her mistress.

"I was told there would be a messenger to take these." Rosalind held out the letters she had just finished. "Both are to go to the Bow Street Police Office. This one"—she held up the one sealed in red—"is from your mistress for Mr. John Townsend. This one"—she handed across the letter sealed in blue—"is to go directly into the hands of Mr. Adam Harkness. No other."

"Yes, miss." The housekeeper took both letters.

"It is a dreadful thing, Mrs. Nott," said Rosalind softly.

The woman lifted her chin. "God shall judge."

"He shall," Rosalind agreed soberly. "Your mistress must be suffering most cruelly."

"My mistress bears her sufferings with patience. She is a true lady." This last was spoken with absolute certainty and not a little defensive pride. Rosalind nodded in agreement. Then, she looked the woman in the eye, and lied.

"I am also instructed to write to Captain Seymore's brother, Sir Bertram, but I do not have the direction. I did not wish to disturb your mistress as she is attending her husband . . ." Mrs. Nott's face puckered more tightly. She did not approve of the captain, or his drunkenness, possibly both. "I thought perhaps if there was a letter or some such on his desk, I might simply copy the direction from that?"

The housekeeper looked dubious, as well she should. It was a terrible excuse, but then it was a terrible morning.

Mrs. Nott looked down at the pair of letters she held. "Miss, is it true? Is Mr. Cavendish dead?"

"Yes, he is."

"We reap what we sow," she sighed. "But the mistress will be heartbroken."

"All her friends can do now is help see her through this tragedy." Rosalind laid careful emphasis on those last words. "Both the captain and Mrs. Seymore will be under siege from the papers and the public very soon. All manner of gossip and slanderous speculation will be raised. If we cannot clear this trouble away quickly, everyone in the house will suffer."

Mrs. Nott said nothing, but understanding flickered across her severe features.

"I need to let the captain's brother know what's happened," said Rosalind. "Will you help me find the direction? All I need is one letter, any that happens to be to hand. I would not ask at all, but I do not wish to trouble your mistress at this time."

Mrs. Nott nodded once. "Let me see what can be found."

The housekeeper left, and Rosalind, with one ear open for any sound from the passage, proceeded methodically to search the desk's drawers. She found more books, more paper, and stacks of neatly ordered correspondence. None of it, though, looked to be set aside especially. None was bound in ribbons of red or pink or tied with flowers or any other such token that a sentimental woman might use for letters from a lover. Rosalind had not expected it. Mrs. Seymore's poetry might be sentimental, but Rosalind was beginning to understand that the authoress herself was ruthlessly practical. She would not have let Rosalind near her desk if there was a chance Rosalind might easily uncover anything that could be used against her.

Rosalind had just slid the last drawer shut when Mrs. Nott returned with a folded paper in her hand.

"Here you are, miss."

"Thank you."

"Is there anything else?"

"Not at this time. I'll ring when I'm ready for you."

The housekeeper curtsied and glided away. Rosalind waited until the parlor door was completely closed to unfold the letter.

Brother,

I've read your letter, and what you call your "proofs." I know how badly you wish your wife to be innocent, but you must face facts. If you do not want to petition parliament for divorce, then you must draw up the deed of separation. Once Margaretta proves herself to be thoroughly repentant, and that blaggard has paid for his violations, you may take her back, if you choose. What you will do with her bastard is up to you. But it is for you to examine your conscience and ask whether you can allow her continued humiliation of you and still call yourself a man. She has by her actions with this actor, and the Devil knows how many others, dragged the whole of our family into the mud. She must be made to smart for it.

    Bertram Seymore

Rosalind laid this ugly missive onto the desk and opened the other note, the one she had written to herself, recalling the captain's speech.

> *You're laying traps for me now! You knew I'd go looking for you, at Hoffman's, at the theater, at the . . . hotel . . .*
>
> *I meant to catch you there. But I only snared your proxy. Been having a good laugh, have you two? All about how you so cleverly deceived the one who should be your lord and master? Made me parade myself about the town, let as many people see the cuckold raging as . . .*
>
> *You went . . . you saw . . .*
>
> *You betray me, you shame me, and now you . . . you . . .*
>
> *You cannot . . . you did not . . . I would not have hurt you, I swear, I swear. I never gave a damn about what Bertram wanted. All I wanted was for you to stop. For you to be all mine again.*

Rosalind sat at the pretty, useful, organized desk, reading and rereading both pages for a long, cold time.

CHAPTER 14

A Careful Inquiry

All wounds ought to be viewed, the length, breadth and
deepness, and with what weapons, and in what part of
the body the wound or hurt is and how many be culpable
and how many wounds there be.

—John Impey of the Inner Temple,
The Practice of the Office of Coroner

When Adam Harkness was still a boy, a house on his street had caught fire. He'd lined up with the rest of the neighborhood, passing buckets of water from hand to hand to try to douse the flames. He remembered looking up through the stinging smoke to see a flurry of sparks shower down, seemingly from the clouds, onto the next house. Before he could blink, the whole roof went up in flame. It was that fast.

It was nothing compared to the speed of rumor through the streets of London.

By the time Harkness emerged from the Theatre Royal, the cobbles were clogged with staring idlers. The few men he'd brought with him were shouting over the heads of the mass of persons, waving their arms and ordering them to keep back, to move along, to clear the streets. The battle was not lost yet, but it wouldn't be long. Adam cursed himself for not thinking to order a couple of the men to bring the horses here to help keep the mob back. He just had to hope Goutier had gotten the cart with Cavendish's body away safe.

"Park," Harkness said to Dr. Arnold's man. "Tell your employer he better lock his doors."

"Too right, sir," said the young man as he retreated back into the theater. Harkness stood beside Ned, who glanced at him nervously.

"Do your best, Barstow, but no brave last stands. I'll get a patrol of special constables over as quick as may be."

"Goutier's already sent word ahead," answered Barstow. "Hope they hurry."

Harkness patted his arm and privately hoped so, too. "All right, all right," he bellowed to the spectators. "Clear the way! Clear the way! You've no business here! Clear the way!"

Not one of them budged.

"Oy! You're Watchdog Harkness, ain' cha?" shouted some man. "Is it true then? 'As Fletcher Cavendish been done for?"

"Clear the streets!" Harkness called in answer. "The papers'll have all the news soon enough!"

"True then!" called somebody else.

"No! No!" wailed a woman's voice. "It can't be!"

"Who done it?" shouted another. "Who's the fiend!"

The crowd gathered itself to surge forward. Harkness grabbed Barstow, prepared to link arms either to try to form some kind of barricade, or drag the younger man out of the way. Before he had to decide, though, the theater doors flew open, and Edmund Kean emerged into the watery sunlight.

"Good people of London!" Kean threw up his hands and moved forward slowly. "I beg you stand silent and hear what I have to say!" He'd gotten a black cloak from somewhere and the wind caused it to billow like a sail about his shoulders.

"'At's Edmund Kean!" cried somebody at the front of the crowd and the name rippled out among them.

"Mr. Kean! Is it true? Is it?" called half a dozen voices. Someone was sobbing already.

Kean had put on a black doublet with the black cloak. Both were probably dug out from the theater's costume warehouse. He should have looked ridiculous, but somehow did not. In fact, Harkness's first instinct was to fall back a respectful step and let the man pass.

"Silence!" Kean boomed. "Silence, good people, pray you! Hark and hear me!"

That pose and that voice ringing out without shame or irony mingled with the vivid presence radiating from this single man. The combined effect did what a host of Bow Street runners could not do. Stillness spread across the agitated crowd.

"My friends, for all of you here today are my friends." Kean spread both arms as if to embrace the gathering. "It is with a broken heart that I must speak these words. Fletcher Cavendish, the best and greatest man to ever grace the English stage, is dead."

Kean clapped his hands over his face as a howl went up from the crowd. Harkness cursed inwardly and got ready to yank the actor and Barstow both back inside before they were trampled in the surge of the mob, but Kean already had his hands raised again.

"Hark now! Hear me! We must stand together in awe, not in anger. Each of us must examine his conscience and ask, am *I* ready to meet my Maker should the dreadful hour befall me? Friends!" Kean's voice dropped low, and the crowd leaned forward as a single body, intent on catching each word. "Let us bow our heads and thank God in His infinite wisdom for allowing such a great man as Fletcher Cavendish to have walked among us. Let us pray that Our Lord receives him in such kindness and divine mercy as we—knowing ourselves to be so much less worthy—would hope to be received in our turn." Kean lifted his face toward the heavens, and Harkness could see the tears streaming down the man's face.

To Harkness's surprise, the people transformed from a crowd to an audience, to a congregation. There was no surge, no breaking for the stairs or the doors. Hats were removed, eyes closed, and palms pressed together as voices murmured the Lord's Prayer. A few persons knelt on the cobbles, and then a few more, and still more.

Harkness, who no one would accuse of being slow on the uptake, removed his hat. Barstow stared for a minute, but took his off as well.

Kean glanced sideways at Harkness and winked. "Make your exit, sir," the actor murmured. "Stage left is your best chance."

Hat in hand, Harkness slipped down the steps with Ned right beside him. "Hold the line as best you can, I'm sending reinforcements." He slapped Ned on the shoulder, sending him back to his fellow patrolmen.

But it wasn't until he'd got a good ways down the street that Harkness jammed his hat back on his head and took off at a run.

Behind him, he heard the faint echo of Edmund Kean calling, "Amen!"

Harkness first went to the station. There, he found Stafford, Bow Street's chief clerk, surrounded by a clutch of patrolmen and constables and a few hale but gray-haired fellows Harkness recognized from the night watch. Stafford was briefly and briskly issuing orders for them to get to the theater. Satisfied all was in hand, Harkness only tipped his hat to the clerk and took himself off across the street to the Brown Bear.

The Brown Bear public house held an unusual status. Situated directly opposite the public offices, the low, venerable house had functioned as a sort of adjunct to the police office since Bow Street first opened. The officers and runners who wished for a quiet drink found it over at the Staff and Bell, but they did business at the Brown Bear—whether it was arranging for a chance for a witness to pick out a wanted man from a crowd without being observed or holding an inquest. Because of this long tradition, the pub's cellar had a table where the coroner could have a look at a body in case of sudden death.

When Harkness reached the bottom of the stairs, it was to see Sir David Royce folding a stained sheet back across the corpse. Light slanted through the barred windows, and three lamps burned on the shelves behind him, rendering the cellar bright enough to make Harkness blink.

"Harkness," Sir David hailed him. "I was told to expect you."

Sir David was a portly, unflappable man. Unlike some coroners, he had training as a physician to go with the family connections that got him his position. He was coatless, with his shirtsleeves rolled up to the elbows, exposing his hairy, brawny forearms.

"It was a straightforward business at any rate." Sir David caught up a towel and rubbed his hands vigorously with it. "I could only see the one blow, straight to the heart. He would have barely felt a thing, poor devil. They tell me he was found with his shirt open to the waist and his coat off?"

Harkness confirmed this, and Sir David sighed. "So either he felt the need for a sudden change of costume, or more likely, our Mr. Cavendish was thinking to engage in a little private entertainment."

"Perhaps the lady was not willing," suggested Harkness.

"*Pshaw.* He was Fletcher Cavendish. They were falling at his feet. Did you ever see him onstage? Took Lady David once." Sir

David shook his head. "Never again. Thought she was going to faint on the spot, and my wife's as steady a woman as you'll find."

"I took this from him." Harkness pulled the blade from his pocket and handed it to Sir David. The coroner unwrapped it, and whistled.

"Well now, well now, that's a pretty little thing, isn't it?" He held up the knife to examine its chased silver hilt. Then he tested the edge and the tip of the blade with his thumb. "Sharp as a razor. Go right through him, if whoever held it were lucky and missed the ribs. But it would not be a clean deed. They'd be covered in blood afterwards."

Harkness, unwillingly, remembered the state of the dressing room and nodded his agreement. If either the captain or Mrs. Seymore had been close enough to commit the murder, they'd have been badly stained by it. A fact which would surely have been remarked on by Stanislas Ulbrecht, or anyone else in the theater at the time.

"Have his family been told?" asked Sir David.

"Dr. Arnold, from the theater, says there is none. I need to interview the manager of the hotel where he took his rooms. He might know more. That is, assuming you'll want Bow Street in on the chase?" In a case of sudden death, it was the business of the coroner's office to conduct the inquiry. It was not, however, unusual for Bow Street to be called to assist, especially when murder was suspected.

"Oh, to be sure. This looks like a nasty piece of work, and given who our man is, it's better it be cleared up quickly. I'll speak with Conant and Townsend."

"No need, no need!" cried a man's cheerful voice.

A stout man stomped down the cellar stairs. He wore a white coat and a broad-brimmed white hat more suited to the garden than the street. He took in the scene at once and clapped his meaty hands together. "Well now, Mr. Harkness, what have you fallen into this time?"

John Townsend was the chief among the principal officers at Bow Street. He was the darling of the *haut ton*, dined out on his friendship with the Prince Regent, and was widely consulted by wealthy families desirous of keeping themselves and their belongings secure. In addition to all these honors, he had been given oversight of those special patrols that kept watch over the palaces of London whenever the royal family was in residence. All these matters were of the greatest importance to him, something his fellow officers learned quickly, and took seriously.

While Sir David and Adam explained all that had occurred, Townsend lifted up the corner of the sheet that wrapped the corpse. He whistled long and low, and promptly covered the dead man over again.

"A most unfortunate business, and no mistake. No question, I suppose, about the blow that killed him, Sir David?"

"None, Mr. Townsend. And Mr. Harkness secured the weapon for us." Sir David handed Townsend the elegant little knife.

"Well, well." Townsend turned the slender weapon over in his fat fingers. "Harkness, you'll circulate the description of this, of course. Check with the dealers in antiquities. In the meantime . . ." He pulled a letter from out of his pocket. "I've had a note from Mrs. William Seymore. You know the name, of course?"

"The poetess?" said Sir David before Harkness had to confess he did not. "You don't mean to say she had a connection to Cavendish?"

"Now, Sir David, you will not infer any impropriety. Mrs. Seymore is a lady of grace, intelligence, and tact. And of course, she moves in literary circles, so it should be of no surprise that she might form an acquaintance among the theatricals as well."

"Of course," said Sir David blandly. "I wouldn't suggest

otherwise. Since you have some acquaintance with the lady, Mr. Townsend, perhaps you'd do me the favor of conducting the interview to hear what she has to say."

"Thank you, Sir David, that was just what I was going to suggest." Townsend replaced the letter in his coat pocket. "Don't want to step over the bounds, of course, but if she should know something of the matter, we must treat it delicately. Harkness, the same hand brought something for you as well." Townsend pulled a second letter from his pocket. "Fellow was extremely reluctant to let go of it, but I swore I'd see it delivered safely and he eventually did believe me."

Harkness broke the seal on the letter and read:

Dear Mr. Harkness,

I must ask you to come at once. I am at the home of Captain William Seymore, and you will want to speak with us all about the death of Fletcher Cavendish.

Yrs.
Rosalind Thorne

Rosalind Thorne. Harkness felt himself go still as he remembered the tall, golden woman he'd met only a few months before. He'd been impressed then by her intelligence, her humor, and her sheer nerve. All had struck him again when he'd seen her last night at the theater. She'd been pale and distraught, and he had not wanted to let her go until he found out what was the matter. In the end, though, she'd walked away from him on the arm of a lordly gentleman who looked at her with longing in his eyes.

It could not possibly be jealousy that welled up in him now,

Harkness told himself. Neither could it be a vague anticipation at the possibility of looking into Miss Thorne's clear blue eyes again. Except he was also remembering a moment in a darkened room, when he'd almost kissed her, and she'd almost allowed it.

"What do we have, Harkness, eh?" Townsend clapped him on the shoulder. "Something from one of your lady loves?"

"No, sir." Harkness hastily folded the note. "But it is from Miss Thorne. She writes she is at the Seymores' house and says she also has some information to communicate."

"Miss Thorne, eh?" Townsend rubbed the side of his nose. "I remember the woman, I think. Well, well. Since she writes to you so particularly, Harkness, you'd better come along, hadn't you?"

Townsend was watching him closely, waiting for him to betray any partiality. "Of course, sir," said Harkness. "I'm assuming we'll go at once?" Townsend affirmed this and Harkness turned to the coroner. "Do you want to keep the knife, Sir David, or shall I?"

"You keep it. You'll need to circulate those descriptions and the rest of it. I'll be calling on you as soon as we're ready for the inquest." Sir David wiped his hands on his towel once more. "Sad thing, all that fame and here he is alone."

"Ashes to ashes, dust to dust." Townsend cocked his head toward Harkness. "Something for us all to remember, eh, Mr. Harkness?"

"Yes, sir," Harkness agreed, and he followed his superior out of the cellar and into the public room and wondered about that look in Townsend's eye, the knife he carried, and the notes they'd both received.

He also remembered that when he had seen Rosalind Thorne rush from the theater the night before, she had very clearly been looking for somebody she could not find.

CHAPTER 15

An Entirely New Story

*It has sometimes happened, on occasion of a murder not
sufficiently accounted for, that . . . some person has forged
and the public accredited a story representing the murderer as having moved under some loftier excitement . . .*
                                        —Thomas De Quincey,
                           On Murder Considered as One of the Fine Arts

As it transpired, Rosalind was left to her own devices in Mrs.
Seymore's study for some little time. Servants went to and fro
in the hallway outside, bearing trays and bottles and cloths.
Mrs. Nott came into the room once to ask if Rosalind needed
anything. Mrs. Kendricks came in to deliver Alice's reply to
Rosalind's note and say she would return home and tend to matters there, if Miss Thorne preferred. Miss Thorne did.

Alice's letter was brief.

Major has me writing up the details. Come as soon as you can.

AWFUL!!
A.L.

"Yes," murmured Rosalind. "I have to agree."
No note arrived from Mr. Harkness.

Rosalind took the time to make a more thorough perusal of the desk, and the books on it, but she found nothing she recognized to be of immediate use or interest. She noted that the servants were diligent in the general way at least, and that the grate had been recently swept and polished, so there were no convenient traces of papers or letters having been burnt.

This much accomplished, Rosalind found herself reduced to pacing, until she heard the doorbell ring.

As she was a guest, propriety dictated that Rosalind remain in the parlor unless and until asked for. Impatience, worry, and the events of this truly extraordinary morning, however, dictated that she step into the corridor, and the front hall.

Therefore, she was in time to see Mr. John Townsend handing his stick, his coat, and his famous white hat to the footman, Eustace, and to see that Mr. Adam Harkness had followed him through the door.

Mr. Harkness removed his old-fashioned tricorn hat and his great coat and handed them to Eustace without any sign of having noticed Rosalind standing in the doorway. But she knew he had not missed her. He had seen her, and as clearly as she saw him now.

Mr. Harkness looked much as he had when Rosalind had first passed him on a grand staircase. Now, as then, he wore the red waistcoat and black cravat that marked him as one of the officers of Bow Street. The men never referred to themselves as "runners." That was a cant name bestowed by the papers and the public.

All the times they had been together seemed to flash through Rosalind's mind: that grand stair, her small parlor, him diving to her rescue in another woman's boudoir. In a private study in the dark, where the light had caught in the depths of his eyes as he stood far too close to her.

Saying good-bye with a deep bow and a sweep of that same unfashionable hat.

Here they were again, only this time, she could not speak to him, and he could not even acknowledge that he had seen her because it was not proper to do so until their hosts and superiors had spoken first. The absurdity of it cut deep.

Fortunately, it was only a brief moment before the captain and Mrs. Seymore appeared. Now Rosalind saw what had kept them secluded in their own rooms for so long. The captain had not only put on fresh clothing, but his color was much revived. His gait was straight and steady, and his eyes clear, as he descended the stairs beside his wife to greet their new arrivals.

Mr. Townsend, however, did not seem much disposed to notice the captain.

"Mrs. Seymore!" Townsend took up both of Margaretta's hands and kissed them. "Can I say how very sorry I am to see you under such circumstances?"

"Whereas I am so very glad to see you here, my dear Mr. Townsend!" The low, musical note had returned to Mrs. Seymore's voice. "I know now that everything will be all right."

Unacknowledged, Rosalind hovered in the doorway. She watched Captain Seymore's shoulders slump in resignation. She watched Mr. Harkness taking in the entire scene, including herself. Their eyes met, and he nodded once. Rosalind inclined her head minutely in return.

Absurd. Ridiculous. Required.

Mr. Townsend smiled in warm reassurance at the poetess. Only then did he turn to the captain to make his bow. "A bad business, Seymore, very bad," Mr. Townsend said. "But you must not worry yourself, sir. I am certain a very little careful inquiry will clear the matter up."

"Yes, of course." The captain's voice sounded thick and

graceless after his wife's musical tones. "So good of you to come in person."

"And this is Miss Thorne, is it not?" Mr. Townsend turned to Rosalind. "Mr. Harkness told me you would be here as well."

Mr. Townsend's eyes raked over her, and she could tell that he did not like what he saw. He did not like that this was the second time their paths had crossed. She was not genteel in the ways he appreciated, and yet he could not dismiss her. Therefore, he slotted her into the column of his mental ledger marked UNSATISFACTORY.

Rosalind stiffened her spine and composed herself. There was only one defense against such a reception, and that was to wrap herself in every single iota of her deportment. Manners might make the man, but they armored the woman.

"I admit," Mr. Townsend went on, pleasantly, of course, "it is a surprise to find you here at such an early hour."

"I am Mrs. Seymore's friend," she replied coolly. "And have been assisting her with her new poetry collection."

It was not precisely an answer, something Mr. Harkness noticed, and he signaled this with a lift of his brows.

"Mr. Harkness," said Mrs. Seymore before Rosalind could say anything. "Thank you for coming as well. Miss Thorne has spoken of you and now I feel quite confident that everything will be handled directly and discreetly." Mr. Harkness bowed but made no reply. Rosalind thought Mrs. Seymore looked a little perplexed at his silence. "Shall we all go sit down? There is coffee in the front parlor."

There was indeed coffee, and cake and sandwiches and a number of other savory items all neatly laid out for the reception of the gentlemen. While the Seymores and Rosalind seated themselves, Mr. Townsend commanded a cup of coffee with plenty of sugar from the waiting girl and took it to stand in front of the fire.

Mr. Harkness did not help himself to anything, but he did settle into the wing-backed chair by the window. It was, Rosalind realized, the place that would command the best view of the entire room, and all its occupants. She lifted an eyebrow toward him. He curled the corner of his mouth up at her.

No one else in the room paid them the least attention.

"Now, Captain, Mrs. Seymore." Mr. Townsend took a swallow of coffee and set the cup on the mantelpiece. "You will forgive me if I get straight to the business?"

"You must proceed exactly as you see fit, of course, Mr. Townsend," said Mrs. Seymore.

"Of course," agreed the captain dully.

Mr. Townsend bowed. "Well, well. Now, the great thing, Captain, is that you give us the exact details of that night, of what you did and all that occurred, just as if you were writing your ship's log, eh?"

Rosalind flickered her gaze toward Mr. Harkness. He had pressed his fingertips together, getting ready to hear and to judge whatever it was Captain Seymore had to say.

But again, it was Mrs. Seymore who spoke.

"I am sorry, Mr. Townsend, but you must hear this first. You will find it out soon enough in any case, as I know very well nothing can be hidden from you."

Which was, apparently, the right thing to say. Mr. Townsend smiled upon Margaretta, entirely pleased to find before him a lady who understood the correct forms of address toward a man such as himself. "That's right, Mrs. Seymore. You must regard me in the capacity of an uncle, or an attorney—ha-ha!—and speak quite truthfully."

Rosalind found she was holding her breath. Mr. Harkness did not move. Mrs. Seymore reached out to take her husband's hand and pulled it unresisting toward her.

"*I* went to the theater last night, Mr. Townsend," said Mrs. Seymore softly. "Quite late and quite on my own. I . . . I found . . . Mr. Cavendish."

With this, Mrs. Seymore began to cry. These were not the cold shuddering sobs Rosalind had seen before. These were decorous tears that would have been easily blotted by a handkerchief, if she had one. The captain stared.

Mr. Townsend came forward at once and pulled a handkerchief out of his pocket to press into her hand. "There, now, Mrs. Seymore. You must compose yourself."

And smile in thanks, thought Rosalind, a moment before Margaretta did just that. Margaretta also nodded, and sniffed once.

Rosalind felt the urge to salute Margaretta. For all her years in ballrooms and drawing rooms, she had seldom seen a woman who raised the public display of femininity to such a height. Rosalind looked toward Mr. Harkness. She could tell he drank down every word, and each show of emotion. She wished for some hint of what he thought of this little tableau. Absurdly but desperately, she wanted to know that he could see it for the performance it was.

"I blame myself," Mrs. Seymore was saying to Mr. Townsend. "I should not have been there. It was not right. But Mr. Cavendish was so old and dear a friend of ours . . ." "*Ours*," noted Rosalind, *not* "*mine*." "And the misunderstanding between us so grave . . . that I felt, I hoped, that there was some way I could make it right."

Mr. Townsend leaned forward, all attention. Mrs. Seymore lowered her eyes decorously. "Fletcher . . . Mr. Cavendish was in love with me."

The captain turned his face away. Rosalind, who had so recently seen him drunk and berating his wife for her supposed infidelities, suddenly felt oddly sorry for the man. Whatever he had or had not done, right now, he was clearly out of his depth.

"Cavendish told you he loved you?" asked Mr. Townsend incredulously.

"I had been aware of his feelings for some time. I tried to pretend ignorance, but, well, a woman always knows. But as I said, Mr. Cavendish was so old a friend of the captain's . . ." She pressed her husband's limp hand. "I did not wish to believe his emotions had carried him so far beyond his reason."

"Actors may be fairly easily carried away," murmured Mr. Townsend.

Mrs. Seymore nodded in agreement. "My husband saw more clearly than I did. He tried to warn me away from Fletcher, but I would not listen. I will regret that to the end of my days." Her voice dropped to a trembling whisper. "But matters had reached the point where I could ignore them no longer, for I discovered that I had committed a wife's worst fault. I had given my husband cause to believe I might be disloyal."

Where had Margaretta learned to comport herself like this? To be so dignified and so fragile at the same time? She was not a gentlewoman. She had never been drilled in deportment as Rosalind had. Did Fletcher Cavendish give her acting lessons? Now, that was an interesting idea.

Captain Seymore slowly drew his hand away to rest on his own thigh, where it curled into a fist. Mrs. Seymore did not seem to notice. She just blotted the corner of her eye with her borrowed handkerchief.

"When my husband spoke to me, my shock was very grave, as you can imagine." Mrs. Seymore glanced toward Mr. Harkness, judging the effect her performance was having on him. The principal officer did not even nod, and Mrs. Seymore turned quickly back to Mr. Townsend. "I protested my innocence, but it was too late. Therefore, rather than cause my husband a moment's more discomfort, I resolved I must at once break off all contact with Mr. Cavendish. I wrote a letter explaining my reasons and asking him to cease to attempt to communicate, except when we might see each other in public.

"But he wrote back, and begged me to come see him, just once more."

"Have you kept the letter?" inquired Mr. Harkness. Mr. Townsend shot him a warning look.

"I . . . don't know," murmured Mrs. Seymore, and the hesitation might have been genuine. *She truly did not expect the question*, thought Rosalind. "I may have."

"That's fine, Mrs. Seymore," said Mr. Townsend firmly. "We will worry about that later. Go on."

"What happened next . . . my only defense is that Mr. Cavendish was truly an old friend. When I was still a young girl, he encouraged me to submit my little poems for publication and he was the means of introducing me to my husband." Margaretta looked to the captain again. Captain Seymore was still studying the coffee tray and the wallpaper. Rosalind thought she saw a flash of annoyance in Mrs. Seymore's eyes. "I felt I owed Mr. Cavendish something," she went on. "Therefore, I honored his request, and I went to see him."

When would the captain speak? Mrs. Seymore kept casting him little glances, like she was expecting him to say his lines, but he remained mute and sullen. *Embarrassed*, Rosalind thought. *No. Humiliated.*

"I must apologize to Miss Thorne as well," Mrs. Seymore said weakly. At the mention of her name, Rosalind's head turned and she was too slow to wipe the startled expression from her face. Margaretta saw it, and so did Mr. Townsend. "She comes to me as a friend and yet I have not been honest with her.

But the matter was so close to my heart, so grave, and so private, I felt I could not."

"Which speaks to your natural delicacy, Mrs. Seymore," Mr. Townsend assured her. "But the time for such discretion is past. Surely you see this?"

"I do. I do." *She is going to shed another tear any moment now*, thought Rosalind. "When I went to the theater, at first, my only intention was to say my good-bye to Mr. Cavendish. I was wholly unprepared for what would happen." She trembled. "Fletcher told me he loved me. He told me he could not live without me. He . . . declared he would die before he lost me. I told him that there was no choice. I must break off all contact with him because I was a loyal and loving wife. I bid him fare-well and I begged him never to write to me again, and to burn those letters he had of me.

"I left him then. I believed that would be the end of it. I was so ashamed of the scene I had been part of, I could not bring myself to speak of it, not to my friend Miss Thorne, nor, I am sorry to say, to my husband."

"That was very wrong of you, Mrs. Seymore." Townsend wagged his head heavily, as if to a naughty child, which was probably the response Mrs. Seymore had been hoping for. Children were guilty of mischief, not murder.

"I know it was wrong," she answered. "I tried to go on as normal. We had been invited to a card party and I went but . . . I was in agony, so I left early." She slipped a sideways glance toward her husband. "That was why I was not there when you, William, went to meet me. I came home, hoping to speak to you privately. But there . . . there was another letter from Fletcher."

The room was absolutely still. She had them all spellbound.

"It was a letter of farewell. He said when the curtain came down, it came down on his life as well. I could not bear the thought of him harming himself. I went again to the theater. I wanted only to remonstrate with him. To remind him what a horrible sin . . . but I was too late."

With this, she buried her face against her husband's shoulder. Finally, he seemed moved. He wrapped his arm around her. "There, there," he whispered. "It will all come out all right."

Mr. Townsend turned away, displaying his delicacy of feeling. He left it to Mr. Harkness to ask the question.

"Mrs. Seymore, are you telling us that Fletcher Cavendish stabbed *himself* through the heart?"

CHAPTER 16

Suitable Drawing Room Conversation

*She is, despite all talents and sweetness, a London lady ...
well do I know the London* ton.

— Mary Wollstonecraft Shelly, *from private correspondence*

"Fletcher told me he would kill himself," Mrs. Seymore murmured, her face still pressed against her husband's shoulder. "He had shown me the dagger . . . before. He said it would be through the heart, because I had already wounded him there so badly."

Rosalind waited. She felt certain if Mr. Townsend pressed any question, Mrs. Seymore would find it necessary to faint. At the same time she was aware of a tightening of her own shoulders. Surely, Mr. Townsend would turn to her next. He would ask her where she had been and what she had seen, and if there was anything she could add to confirm Mrs. Seymore's extraordinary tale.

What would she say when he did?

The captain tightened his arm about his wife's shoulders. "I am sure." He cleared his throat and tried again. "I am sure that will do, Margaretta. You see, Townsend, my wife is deeply distressed, and you can in no way blame her."

He's relieved, thought Rosalind. *He wasn't sure she'd go through with it.*

Whose idea was this story? She'd been certain it was Margaretta's concoction, but that tiny note of relief in the captain's voice gave her a moment's pause.

"No, no, no one is blaming your wife, sir," Mr. Townsend was saying. "But Mrs. Seymore did act very foolishly, putting her trust in this man more than in her husband."

"I know it." Mrs. Seymore lifted her face away from the captain's sloping shoulder. "I do know."

Mr. Townsend sighed heavily. He also drank a long swallow of cooling coffee. "Well, Harkness," he said as he handed cup and saucer back to the maid. "I think we have heard all we need to from Mrs. Seymore. I'm afraid, however, Captain, that you will have to come with us. Sir David will want to hear from you directly, and the magistrate, Mr. Conant, may want a word as well."

"Of course." The captain got to his feet steadily enough, but his back and shoulders were bowed like those of a much older man.

Mrs. Seymore rose as well. "Then let me at least see you to the door. Please." She took her husband's arm, and he looked surprised, and grateful.

Mr. Harkness also got to his feet. He bowed to Rosalind and she curtsied. He met her gaze, and he maintained his silence.

Why? Why aren't you asking me all the questions I can see behind your eyes?

But that was not something she could say, not here and now. The four of them exited the parlor, and Rosalind dropped back down to her seat, stunned.

What just happened here?

She glanced about the room as if seeking escape. Surely she

should be doing something. Her heart was racing, her mind was spinning. She prided herself on her calm and her ability to think clearly in any crisis, and now she could not even remain standing because of the weight of her confusion.

But Rosalind was conscious of something else beyond that confusion—a scalding anger. She had been used. That was bad enough. Worse, however, was the fact that Adam Harkness must be wondering if this gross and dramatic falsehood Mrs. Seymore spoke was the creation of Rosalind Thorne.

She knew that anger must have been showing in her face when Mrs. Seymore re-entered the parlor. Thankfully, she was entirely alone.

"That was a dangerous mistake, Mrs. Seymore," said Rosalind as soon as the door closed.

Mrs. Seymore did not even blink. She sat gracefully on the sofa. She had kept Mr. Townsend's handkerchief and she touched it to the corner of her eye.

"I had no choice but to tell what happened, Miss Thorne," she said, her musical voice absolutely smooth and steady.

Rosalind's temper blazed. *Do you really think I will be taken in by such a show?*

"There are a thousand ways that story could be contradicted. A half a dozen questions will give it the lie."

"But now there won't be any questions, will there?" Mrs. Seymore laid aside the borrowed kerchief. Her manner was so entirely flawless that Rosalind suddenly felt herself to be gauche and clumsy. "At least, not as many. And if those strays do come home, I will tell the story again, exactly as I told it here."

"I hope that you are certain you will be able to do so." Rosalind struggled to gather the shreds of her temper. "Just as I hope you are certain of what your husband will say at the police office and at the coroner's inquest." *If you are not there to charm the gentlemen, mistakes might be made.* "You must be aware that if this tale of self-harm is exposed, suspicion for Fletcher's death will fall on Captain Seymore and his jealousies."

Mrs. Seymore looked shaken at this, but only for a moment. "My husband has only one thing to confess. He remembers very little of what he did or said on the night Fletcher was killed because he was so much the worse for drink. If it is necessary to verify this, then I'm sure his brother and the coachman will swear it." She paused. "As could you, Miss Thorne. You were here when he came home."

Of course. Mrs. Seymore must have questioned her husband closely while they were alone upstairs together. Mrs. Seymore knew all the captain's answers before she came down to greet the officers. He had been jealous. He had believed there was a liaison. He had confronted her with the fact, repeatedly. He had been drunk. It was around this that Mrs. Seymore had woven the story of desperate love and the threat of suicide. Captain Seymore safely could tell the truth. All the lies belonged to Mrs. Seymore.

Again, Rosalind felt the surge of bitter admiration. She had underestimated this woman. Perhaps not quite as badly as Mr. Townsend, or Captain Seymore, but badly enough.

And Margaretta was not done yet.

"There is something you should know, Miss Thorne," said Mrs. Seymore quietly. "As we were leaving, Mr. Townsend took me aside. He warned me away from you."

Rosalind felt the blood drain from her cheeks. "Did he say why?"

"He said you had been involved in some unsavory business at the beginning of the season. You are not entirely delicate, he said, and he fears association with you might leave a blemish." She paused, giving this time to sink in. "As you are my friend,

I, of course, told him I knew all about the other matter, and that I held you entirely blameless. You were unlucky, that is all, and should not be held answerable for the sins of another."

"Well," said Rosalind. "It would seem you have matters well in hand. I am sure Mr. Townsend will ensure you have no difficulties at the inquest. Therefore, you can have no more need of such assistance as I could offer."

She moved to get to her feet, but Mrs. Seymore stopped her.

"That is not so, Miss Thorne," she said. "I need you more than ever."

Rosalind drew herself up, her cold retort ready. But as she met Mrs. Seymore's gaze, Rosalind saw the fear behind her melting eyes. She paused. A new thought tumbled heavily into place.

"There is another reason Fletcher Cavendish might be lying dead," Rosalind murmured. "Someone might be trying to place the blame for his murder on you."

"Yes," said Margaretta, and this time the tremor in her voice was real.

"But *why?* If you are right, there are already plans in place to disgrace you and declare your child illegitimate. Mrs. Seymore, can you possibly have that many enemies?"

"I don't know, Miss Thorne, and that is why I still need you." The facade Mrs. Seymore had been able to maintain for the gentlemen slipped, turning the warmth of her distress to cold exhaustion. "I have managed to divert suspicion from my husband for the time being, but it may soon fall on me instead. That may have been the murderer's ultimate plan. You must find out who really did this thing and how it truly happened. You must urge your man Mr. Harkness on. If there's a fee, I'll find the money."

Could it be true? It might. Rosalind knew. She knew this

was a matter of families, of money, and of station. Those things could drive people to dare their absolute worst. But she knew next to nothing about the people involved. It might be that Mrs. Seymore's fear was genuine, and well founded. But Rosalind had just watched this woman spin an elegant and dramatic lie out of thin air. That lie had been about the cruel death of a man she had known for years, and had declared the deepest friendship for. Such a woman would surely be ready to tear down the reputation of a relative stranger if she did not get what she wanted.

Rosalind forced herself to concentrate on the situation in front of her. "You have put yourself into a precarious position, Mrs. Seymore," she said. "You are correct. After your husband, you are the next person the officers will suspect. You cannot depend on your story being left unexamined, even by Mr. Townsend."

Because there was a hole in Mrs. Seymore's tidy story, a detail she had forgotten, and without it, the whole structure of her story would collapse in an instant. Margaretta had not told Mr. Townsend about the accusing letters. Those letters changed the tone and nature of the trouble existing between Mrs. Seymore, the captain, and Mr. Cavendish. Used properly, they could reinforce the story of unrequited love, suspicion, and self-harm.

So, why hadn't Mrs. Seymore mentioned the letters while the Bow Street men were here?

A soft scratching sounded on the door, and a footman entered. "A letter for you by hand, Mrs. Seymore. I thought it best . . ."

"Yes, give it here."

The servant obeyed and departed. Mrs. Seymore opened the missive and read it.

"Well, Miss Thorne," she sighed. "The business will begin sooner than I expected."

"What is it?"

"It is from my sister-in-law. We are summoned to the house, or at least, I am." She paused. "Will you consent to come with me?"

There were many reasons not to, and very few reasons to do it. But those few were strong as iron bands and shackled Rosalind to this woman just as securely. Because if Rosalind disappointed Mrs. Seymore, Mrs. Seymore was in a position to destroy Rosalind's reputation.

"When are we expected?" Rosalind asked her.

"Tomorrow," replied Mrs. Seymore, folding the letter back in crisp lines. "She is giving us a day's grace to examine the state of our souls. Then, Miss Thorne, you will see for yourself exactly how much I have to fear."

CHAPTER 17

The Nature of the Inquiry

Likewise it is to be inquired who were culpable, either of the act or of the force: and who were present, either men or women.

—John Impey of the Inner Temple,
The Practice of the Office of Coroner

"And that's all you can tell us, sir?" Townsend asked Captain Seymore. "Nothing else?"

Captain Seymore had ridden with Harkness and Townsend back to Bow Street. Now they all sat together in Mr. Townsend's well-furnished private office. Mr. Stafford had been pressed into service, and was stationed at one of the side tables with his book open to write down the captain's account of what had happened.

Not that the account was lengthy, or detailed. Captain Seymore, by his own repeated, red-faced admission, had spent the night of Fletcher Cavendish's death, blind drunk. This condition had persisted from about ten of the clock that night until the next morning when he was brought home, where his wife demanded to know where he'd been. That, he told them, was when he learned that Cavendish was dead.

"And was this also when you learned Cavendish had threatened to harm himself?" Mr. Townsend's inquiry sounded a great deal like a suggestion.

Seymore scratched at his face. He hadn't shaved that morning, and the patchy stubble gave his chin a soiled look. "Probably. I was still trying to get my head above it then." Seymore scowled at Stafford, who sat with his pen poised over the book. "Believe me, sirs, if I had known the blaggard was planning to kill himself that particular night, I'd have drunk less."

"You were seen at the theater more than once," Harkness said. He hadn't had a chance to speak with the staff at the hotel yet, but he was sure he'd hear something similar. Whatever else he was, Captain Seymore was not subtle, or thoughtful. Those talents belonged entirely to Mrs. Seymore. "A repeated quarrel, or a worry, such as a lawsuit, may prey on a man's mind."

"The scoundrel was making advances to my wife. I warned him off, but he persisted. I had to keep after them. Him," he corrected himself.

"Mrs. Seymore says she quite properly rejected those advances," Mr. Townsend reminded him.

The captain looked at the wall, and at the door. *Looking for his way out*, thought Harkness. "She did. After the thing became known, at least. She . . . Margaretta's a beautiful woman, and everybody thinks she married beneath her. They swarm around her every night, and every night, I'm made more of a laughing-stock. No, no." He held up his hand. "Don't. I know what I am and I know what you are, sir." He favored Mr. Townsend with a tight, unpleasant smile. "You're another of Margaretta's oh-so-dear friends looking to protect her from her fool of a husband."

"We are investigating what might be a breach of the king's peace," said Mr. Townsend firmly. "And I should think a husband would be concerned whether any part of the matter could touch upon his wife's reputation."

"Yes. You would, wouldn't you? But it's your reputation you should care about, Mr. Townsend. It's one thing to admire the silken goddess and pity her for being saddled with her boorish husband. But it's not so much fun to think you've been taken in by a garden-variety coquette, is it?" Seymore leaned across the desk. "She's using you, Mr. John Townsend, just like she's using me, and you'd do well to remember that."

Time to put a stop to this. "Captain Seymore," said Harkness. "From what you tell us, your wife had a wide range of acquaintance. Why did you suspect a liaison with Mr. Cavendish above any of the others?"

"Because he was Fletcher Cavendish!" Seymore shouted. "He just had to crook his little finger and the women hiked their skirts! And for all her pretty little flirtations, Margaretta was no different. She'd met her match in him. It would have been funny, but she . . ." He stopped, seemingly suddenly aware of what he'd just said about his wife. "I just wanted it to end," he said softly. "I wanted him to leave her alone. I wanted my wife in my home, and things to be as they should."

"Of course, of course," said Mr. Townsend, but coldly. Captain Seymore's vacillations and slurs had worn his patience away. "Quite right and natural. I think we have what we need. Mr. Stafford? If you'll just read over what's written there, Captain Seymore, and sign it as being true and correct." The captain stared at the page for a moment, then plucked the quill from the ink stand and scrawled his name across the bottom.

"Are you done with me?"

"We are. Mr. Stafford, have Tommy call a carriage for the captain. Thank you."

Stafford closed the book, and escorted the captain out without comment.

Mr. Townsend sighed and sank back into his chair. He peered

around the edge of the draperies at the street beyond, and the clot of people trying to squeeze into the Brown Bear. "I wonder what old Selby is charging for a look at the corpse," he murmured and shook his head. "Well, Harkness, what do you think?"

"I think, sir, that if we don't clear this up quickly, there will be a breach of the peace over it."

"Just so. You need to find Cavendish's family to claim the body as quick as may be, and if they can't, or won't, the theater manager must be made to do it. That is the first thing. The second . . ." Townsend tapped his broad fingers against the edge of his fine desk. "The second is that Sir David must hold the inquest as soon as possible so that the correct story is made public and those most concerned are spared the worst of the idle speculation."

"Then, you believe Mrs. Seymore?" said Harkness.

Townsend shot him a narrow glance. "Have you reason to doubt her?"

Harkness thought back to the Seymores' elegant parlor, and how Miss Thorne had watched Mrs. Seymore so closely. He was certain Rosalind had been unaware of the range of emotions that played across the features she normally kept under such rigid control. Surprise had deepened to shock, and finally, fleetingly but unmistakably, to disgust. Miss Thorne quite clearly could not believe what she was hearing. Therefore, yes, Harkness found he had reason to doubt Mrs. Seymore.

Unfortunately, it was not a reason he could give to Townsend. Especially not since the captain had been right about one thing: Mr. Townsend was far more concerned about protecting Mrs. Seymore's reputation than her husband seemed to be.

Harkness found himself wondering what else the degraded captain might be right about. Now, however, was not the time to ask that question. "Sir David's a thorough man," he said instead.

"When he calls the inquest, he'll be rigorous in his questioning. If we're to close the matter quickly, we'll need every possible fact in our hands, so there can be no question as to whether the verdict is correct. Along with Captain Seymore's sworn testimony, and the affidavit from Mrs. Seymore, we should at least know if the knife belonged to Cavendish, or the theater."

"Yes. That's sound. With that in hand, as it were, there can be no doubt as to the truth." Townsend glanced at the clock on his mantle. "See to it, Harkness. I have an appointment at Carleton House and cannot keep His Royal Highness waiting. He was very much an admirer of Mr. Cavendish's," Townsend added significantly. "I am sure he will be glad to hear the matter is in safe hands."

Thus dismissed, and put on notice, Harkness left Townsend's office.

Mr. Townsend's private office opened onto the patrol room— the place of business and intelligence for Bow Street's principal officers. Where the walls were not covered in maps of London and Westminster and the network of roads and turnpikes that surrounded them, they were covered in shelves full of bound volumes of newspapers and clippings. More recent newspapers from across England hung on racks or were stacked on the tables, including Bow Street's own publication, *Hue & Cry*. This broadsheet circulated among the policing offices and its pages were given over to descriptions of crimes and criminals, as well as descriptions of stolen property that was either still missing or had been discovered in pawn, or some other such place outside the home of the rightful owner. Such as with a fresh corpse in a theater dressing room.

"Fine business this, eh, Harkness?" cried Samuel Tauton, who sat at one of the reading tables. Tauton was older than Harkness by at least ten years. He was also shrewd as any fox and possessed a memory for faces that was second to none. At the moment, he was in his shirtsleeves, engaged in the surprisingly domestic task of sewing the pocket of one of his plain coats. At least, it seemed domestic until one looked closer and saw Tauton was attaching a series of fishhooks to the pocket lining.

Harkness knew what Tauton was doing. He'd wear the coat, with its pockets padded out by handkerchiefs, and go walking by the theaters, making an easy mark of himself. But the thief who tried to relieve this particular gentleman of his purse was in for a rude and painful surprise.

"Damnable business." Harkness settled himself at one of the writing desks and pulled paper, pen, and ink out of the drawer.

"Can I be of any help?" Tauton bit his thread in two.

"Not yet, but thank you." Harkness dipped the pen and wiped it carefully. "I've got to get a description of the weapon out for *Hue & Cry* and the other papers. After that . . ." Harkness shook his head. "After that, it's a matter of asking questions and trying to have the facts lined up for the inquest."

"I'll leave you to it, then." Tauton carefully drew his coat on and gathered up his thread and packet of needles. "I'm to go help keep the crowd by the Drury Lane orderly."

"I think I'd rather have that job," muttered Adam.

Tauton laughed. "I think I would, too. Uneasy lies the head that wears the crown, my boy. Good luck."

"Good hunting," replied Adam. Tauton clapped him on the shoulder and left him. Harkness turned back to his blank page, and began writing. But even while his hands went through the motions of writing out the notice, his mind was occupied by other thoughts. Chiefly of a proud, golden-haired woman with a pair of unsettlingly direct blue eyes.

Rosalind Thorne.

Adam had first met Miss Thorne when they'd both become involved in the affair of a young man named Jasper Aimesworth. Aimesworth had the bad luck to be killed in the famous ballroom at Almack's Assembly Rooms. That Miss Thorne was a beauty had been immediately apparent. But Harkness had quickly discovered she was also highly intelligent and possessed of a dry and ready wit. They'd soon formed a strange and informal, but highly effective, sort of partnership.

The world of gentility frowned upon men such as himself. The Bow Street "runners" might be celebrated and feted in the abstract, but in particular, they were sneered at as thief takers and moneygrubbing busybodies. They had no writ, warrant, subpoena, or any other means that could compel the members of the upper classes to speak with them, no matter how grave the matter might be.

Miss Thorne, on the other hand, had been born among those who closed their doors in Harkness's face. She inspired all manner of confidences and, indeed, made a living for herself assisting those genteel and aristocratic ladies who found themselves tangled in matters beyond their personal scope.

Therefore, it was not entirely surprising to find her involved with a woman on the verge of a criminal conversation suit, and possibly a divorce. And now the death of the man accused.

But Rosalind had not been happy to be in the Seymores' parlor as Mrs. Seymore unfurled her operatic tale of unrequited love and tragic suicide. Harkness had watched Rosalind's cool poise crack, broken apart first by surprise, and then by anger. This wasn't just because she sensed Mr. Townsend's dislike of her. Something had been wrong before he and Townsend had walked into the house.

Miss Thorne had also been at the Theatre Royal the night before.

And Harkness hadn't asked Miss Thorne a single question. Not one. His mind slowly turned this fact over, and turned it over again.

He was in the act of signing his notice when Tommy Aitch darted in. "Sir, there's a Mr. Littlefield out front, and he's asking for you, personally."

"He would," murmured Harkness. "All right, Tommy, let him in."

Adam tucked his notice under a blank sheet, and stood to meet the new arrival, slightly relieved. He didn't want to have to continue to think about his conduct toward Miss Thorne.

George Littlefield was a dark, slender, neatly made man. He'd never lost the casual, slouching stance he'd learned at the boarding schools he'd attended as the son of a minor aristocrat. Had fortune been kinder and his father been less profligate, George would have been sitting in Parliament rather than at a desk at the twice-weekly paper, *The London Chronicle*. As it was, Harkness knew Littlefield to be good at his trade, and as honest as newspapermen came.

This time, though, Littlefield looked distinctly uneasy as he walked into the patrol room. "What's doing then, Littlefield?" asked Harkness. "Something's wrong?"

George laughed, a little. "Trust you to see it right off, Harkness. Yes. I've been bunged straight in the middle of this Cavendish business, just like you, I hear," he added, because he was a newspaperman, and he was not about to miss a chance to confirm a rumor.

"Who'd you hear that from?"

George waved his ink-stained hand. "The major keeps a fund to help encourage people to talk, just like your lot do. But . . . this isn't the usual, Harkness." In fact it was so unusual that Littlefield was digging his hands into his pockets without bringing out notebook or pencil.

"What's the matter?" Harkness gestured for George to take a chair. George perched on the edge, the heel of his boot hooked over the rung.

"It's my sister, Alice." George's crooked leg jigged restlessly up and down. "She had dinner with Fletcher Cavendish last night."

Harkness leaned back, taking care not to show how startled he felt. "Why was Alice dining with Cavendish?"

"She was invited, but not by him," George added quickly. "By Rosalind Thorne."

Adam opened his mouth. He closed it again.

"And why was Miss Thorne dining with Mr. Cavendish?"

"Well, that I'm afraid was Alice's fault."

Harkness steepled his fingers and looked over the tips at Littlefield, assuming an air of very obvious patience. George ducked his head.

"Sorry. Telling it all the wrong way round. Major'd read me the riot act for it, but it's my sister . . ." He scrubbed at the back of his neck, and started again. "Alice has a friend, a Mrs. Seymore. And since I saw Captain Seymore taking his leave"—George jerked his chin toward the door—"I expect by now you know all about the pair of them?"

"We're starting to."

"Right. Well, as Captain Seymore was filing against Cavendish for criminal conversation—"

"Wait. Stop right there," said Harkness. "Seymore was suing Cavendish?" Neither of the Seymores had thought to mention that. Not once.

"Well, I don't know if he'd gone so far as to hire an attorney, but he threatened it any number of times. Mrs. Seymore swears she's innocent, and when she said it to Alice, Alice introduced her to Rosalind. You know how Rosalind helps women with their problems?"

Harkness nodded. Rosalind had not mentioned the potential lawsuit either. But then, doing so would have directly contradicted what Mrs. Seymore said.

"And that, apparently, led to the dinner invitation from Cavendish. He invited Rosalind and a friend to dine, and talk over the matter of Mrs. Seymore. Rosalind, in turn, invited Alice."

"Was Mrs. Seymore there?"

"Not she, but Alice says Captain Seymore put in an appearance. Drunk and demanding to know where his wife was."

Harkness remained silent for a moment, letting George's words settle in among the ideas and images he already carried in his mind. The picture there shifted, and shifted again.

"Where is Alice now?" Adam asked.

"She's home. She's supposed to be writing up the details." George made a wry face. "The major's turning cartwheels. Says she's made all our fortunes." Harkness felt his mouth twist, but he kept his feelings to himself. Expecting a newspaper not to make what it could from the murder of a famous man was like asking a cow not to give milk. It was against the order of nature.

But George wasn't looking too happy about the prospect of increased circulation, or more inches in the columns. "To tell you the truth, Alice has gone a bit green around the gills about it all. I told her I'd come to you to find out what should be done. That, long and roundabout as it is, is why I'm here."

"It's fairly simple, actually," Harkness told him. "Sir David Royce, the coroner, is going to need to talk to Alice. All she'll have to do is tell her story clearly and simply and that will be that. She might not even have to speak at the inquest."

"So there will be an inquest?" prompted Littlefield. "They're saying Cavendish was murdered."

Harkness met the newspaperman's gaze. He liked George. They'd exchanged information in the past, but now was not the time. He had too much to find out on his own before he started telling the paper tales of murder, or suicide. Especially now that he knew that Captain and Mrs. Seymore were holding back important information. Captain and Mrs. Seymore, and Rosalind Thorne.

"Alice doesn't have to worry," Adam said. "Sir David's fair and levelheaded, and he won't be distracted by circumstances."

Disappointment flickered across George's face, but he rallied quickly. "That's good to know. When a man's sister is dining in company with one of the most notorious womanizers in the city . . . well . . . not that I think anybody could make Alice do anything she didn't want to . . . but . . . people talk enough nonsense about women who write as it is."

Harkness agreed that they did. "No one's going to talk nonsense about Alice on my watch. Or, I expect, on the major's."

That actually got a laugh out of him. "You're right there. He knows that A. E. Littlefield's *Society Notes* is what keeps the paper going." George got to his feet. "Still, thank you for saying it, Harkness."

"Bring Alice down here," said Harkness as they shook hands. "I'll take her to Sir David myself."

George agreed he would, and took himself out the door. Harkness watched him go, partly because he was worried about the man, and partly to make sure none of the patrolmen or others of the station's staff stopped to have a quick word with him. Because everybody in the station knew about that fund the major kept to encourage people to talk.

When George was gone, Harkness closed the door to the patrol room and dropped into his chair. He stared at the map of London without seeing it.

Harkness had known Miss Thorne was at the theater just before Mr. Cavendish had died.

That was not so strange. There were, after all, at least a thousand others who were there at the same time. But that she had been there, and then with the Seymores, was something to raise a man's curiosity.

But he'd said nothing. He had not asked a single question of her. The worst part was, he knew precisely why he'd held back. He wanted to give Rosalind a chance to speak with him first, privately, so he could decide how to best present the story to Townsend, and to Sir David and whoever else might need to hear it. He wanted to protect her, just like Townsend wanted to protect Mrs. Seymore.

No, not just like, he told himself irritably. *It wasn't about reputation and appearance. It was about Miss Thorne.*

But now George brought him this. Rosalind hadn't just been at the theater. She'd had an appointment to meet the dead man. She'd been engaged to act in her own particular way, for the woman most closely connected to this crime, if crime it proved to be. And if he hadn't asked her any questions, neither had she volunteered any information, including about this criminal conversation suit.

Which made Harkness wonder just what Rosalind was doing with and for the beautiful and clever Mrs. Seymore.

CHAPTER 18

What Reasons Must Come to Light

You think with horror of murder . . . but perhaps you little reflect that evil practices or habits may lead you, and that by no very long or winding path to these atrocious crimes.
—Samuel and Sarah Adams, *The Complete Servant*

"She did *what?*" cried Alice. "Oh, the *idiot!*"

Rosalind's morning at Mrs. Seymore's house had left her exhausted, confused, and not a little bit angry. None of this, however, had so overwhelmed her that she was ready to neglect her friend. As soon as Rosalind was able to leave Mrs. Seymore, she went to the cab stand and took a carriage to George and Alice's little flat. There, she found Alice sitting on her own at the table that served her and her brother both for dining and for working. Alice sat there with her portable writing desk in front of her. She looked pale and disheveled, and the sheets of crossed-out and cross-written paper scattered around spoke to the serious disorder of her nerves.

Rosalind's story of what happened that morning with Mrs. Seymore did nothing to calm her spirits.

"What is she doing, Rosalind, telling a tale like that to Bow Street?" Alice hurled her pencil to the table. "It can't *possibly* be true. Can it?"

"I was hoping you might be able to tell me, Alice. She's your friend."

"Yes, or so I believed. I . . ." Alice pressed her hand against her mouth. "I'm sorry, Rosalind, I don't think I'm very well right now."

"You look dreadful. Come lie down." Rosalind supported her friend to the sofa. Rosalind was familiar with the contents of George and Alice's small flat and she was shortly able to find the bottle of bad port wine they routinely kept on hand. There was water in the cracked pitcher to add to it, as well as to wet down a cloth for Alice's forehead.

"Oh, this is ridiculous!" Alice sniffed, accepting Rosalind's ministrations. "And it's my fault. I thought it was going to be so simple. You'd just talk to the right people, as you do, and find someone who could demonstrate proof of Margaretta's innocence. I didn't know . . . I never thought she might be lying!"

"How could you possibly have known?"

"Because it's my business to know things!" Alice shouted to the ceiling. "It's how I make my living!"

"You were not a newspaperwoman when she came to you. You were a friend." In answer, Alice clapped her hands over her face and the damp cloth and muttered something Rosalind couldn't understand, and probably wouldn't want to repeat.

"Tell me about Margaretta, Alice," she said. "How do you know her?"

Alice sighed and let her hands drop away from her cloth. "The usual way. Mutual acquaintances. There are more women who write than one might think, and we are a chatty group. Margaretta holds salons at her home, and I visit her once a month or so. She's paid me for translation work, too. Her education was not the best, so sometimes there's things in French or Italian she needs put into plain English. Of course, she's a good source of gossip for *Society Notes*, too. And now the major wants me to write all about her," she added abruptly. "I'm to write up everything I know about the Celebrated Mrs. Seymore." Rosalind could hear the emphasis and the capital letters. "It's not fair. I don't want to air her secrets. She's been a friend."

"I know, Alice." Rosalind brought the plain stool to the sofa so she could sit beside her.

"He told me I didn't have to do anything I didn't want to. Of course, he knows that if he dismissed me for refusing, he'd lose George, too, but . . . oh *damn*, Rosalind. The *look* on the major's face. I swear he was counting the money right behind his eyes. I don't want any part of this!"

"I know that, too."

Something in her soft words caused Alice to sit up and look at her properly. "You're not going to tell me I should help? That it's right and proper and for my own good to know the truth?"

"Why should I tell you?" replied Rosalind. "You've just told me."

"Oh. I did, didn't I?" Alice flopped back down, and put her slippered feet up on the sofa arm in an attitude that would have had their old headmistress after her with a broom. "Is this how you felt with your godmother, Rosalind?" she asked. "And Jasper?"

"Yes. It is."

"Why did you keep going?"

"Because it *was* my godmother. It was personal and I didn't just want to know, I needed to." *Do not think of Charlotte now. Keep your mind on what is in front of you.* Rosalind took Alice's hand. "You do not have to make the same decision. You can choose to walk away at any moment."

For all the years Rosalind had known Alice, she'd seen the petite girl in real distress only a handful of times. The first was when they were at school together, and Rosalind had sat in her room while Alice packed her things. George had been waiting downstairs then. He'd come to tell Alice that their father was dead, and they were ruined. Alice had moved quickly, almost frantically, as if she would find something vital she'd lost underneath her dresses and handkerchiefs, until she'd toppled over, right on the bed, not in a faint, but to just lie and stare at the ceiling.

The fevered, haunted look in Alice's eyes now brought that other moment back in sharp relief.

And as at that other, distant time, Alice sat up very suddenly and very straight. She also thrust out her pointed chin in absolute defiance.

"Rosalind Thorne, I'm surprised at you!" Alice shook the cloth she clutched at her friend.

"At me?"

"Yes! How could you let me act like a coward? I'm not some fainting debutante. I am a woman of the world! Will Alice Littlefield be made mousy and missish by a bit of actor's blood! Certainly not! And as for *Margaretta!* Well! If she thinks she can play her little parlor games with me, she had best think again!"

"And very carefully," agreed Rosalind. She also removed the cloth from Alice's grip before it could start dripping on the floor.

"What do we do then?" asked Alice. "You should probably know that George is off at Bow Street, trying to talk to Adam Harkness. He's going to tell him about our dinner with Mr. Cavendish."

"Very good." Rosalind watched her hands carefully as they folded the cloth along fresh lines. They did not falter, even a little. "It is better he and Mr. Townsend have the whole of that story at once." *At least I hope it is.*

Rosalind walked over to the little hearth and hung the cloth on the rusty fire screen, where it could dry. "We should turn our attentions to Margaretta," she told Alice. "What does your writing circle say about her? Who are her particular friends? Are there rumors of . . . intimacies? Indiscretions?"

Alice shrugged heavily with both shoulders. "She's perfectly willing to lead a dozen men about by their noses, but no one's ever seriously linked her name with anybody in particular."

"Not even Fletcher Cavendish?"

"Not even Fletcher Cavendish. I used to think it was because Margaretta loved her husband, and then I met him." Alice pulled a face. "After that, I just assumed she did it because charming the gentlemen was good for keeping herself *à la mode*, and that was good for sales." She paused. "The story you said she told, suicide for love? Did Townsend and Harkness believe it?"

"Mr. Townsend wanted to," said Rosalind. "I would say Mr. Harkness has his doubts." She remembered him sitting still and quiet in his chair with the best view of the whole room, watching them all and saying nothing to anyone, not even to her. Not even to ask the questions he should have.

Her skin prickled and it was a long moment before she could force her thoughts back into their proper lines.

"Another possibility came up this morning, Alice. Cavendish might have been killed so that Margaretta would be blamed for it."

"What would that accomplish?"

"Well, it would hang her, for one."

"Rosalind, I don't mean to be brutal. Well, all right, I do, but a pregnant woman cannot be hanged. She'd just plead her belly."

"Whoever did this thing might not know she is pregnant."

"That doesn't make sense. Margaretta told us that it was Sir Bertram who was pushing the captain to go forward with the criminal conversation suit. Sir Bertram is the captain's younger brother. The whole point of the suit is to have her child declared a bastard, so it can't get in line for the title."

"Assuming it's a son."

"Assuming it's a son. If the legitimacy of Rosalind's child was at the back of the quarrel between the captain and Cavendish, there's no *reason* for Cavendish to be dead. He's absolutely necessary for the suit, and the publicity."

"Maybe the captain's temper overrode his brother's dynastic considerations. Or maybe there is something more going on here." Rosalind frowned. "We know that Cavendish and Mrs. Seymore were acquainted for a long time. Do we know how they met? Or who her people are?"

"No." Alice frowned. "That is to say, I don't know who her people are. Margaretta will talk about every subject under the sun, except her past."

"That is significant," said Rosalind. If Mrs. Seymore had been a member of the *haut ton* instead of merely welcomed to its festivities, her background would have been sniffed out and chewed over within five minutes of her first appearance. But as she was only a species of entertainer, no one would think it necessary to question any story she told about herself, as long as it was not too terribly shocking. "She spoke of the potential for her child's disgrace with great feeling."

"Hardly surprising," Alice said.

"True. But that feeling might come from personal experience."

"Ouch." Alice winced. "There's a thought. How would it relate to the death of Fletcher Cavendish, though?"

"It would mean Mrs. Seymore has a great deal to hide. We both know that a woman's ability to make her way in the world rests heavily on her personal reputation." Rosalind thought back to her initial meeting with Mrs. Seymore in her own little parlor and all that had been said there. "We do know—or at least Margaretta did say—that marriage to the captain moved her into a better class of society than she was used to."

"Being cousin to a marquis will do that. But it does hint at a humble origin for Margaretta." Alice leaned forward. Now that she had a riddle to solve, her earlier distress vanished entirely. The newswoman's blood was up in her veins and her eyes were shining. "And one that she might well want to keep hidden. It's one thing to be the natural daughter of Charles II or one of the royal dukes . . ."

"But quite another to be exposed as the natural daughter of a green grocer."

"And attorneys have been known to bribe all manner of persons for information, especially during a criminal conversation trial."

The women sat in silence for a long moment, turning these ideas over in their minds.

"The question is, Alice, what inspired Margaretta to tell that story of suicide?" said Rosalind at last. "Was she just trying to take advantage of circumstances, or did she have that story ready beforehand? If it is decided Cavendish killed himself, that's what everyone will want to talk about. Margaretta herself becomes a figure in that drama, which will limit speculation about her personally."

Alice nodded. "It's notorious drama, but it would be far more acceptable than being gossiped about as being an adulteress or a bastard."

"But was she cold enough to have thought all this through before she came to you?" Rosalind remembered the captain's rant. About his wife laying traps. About her making sure he was seen raging around the town.

"Rosalind," said Alice seriously. "Are you asking if Margaretta not only killed Cavendish, but planned it from the very beginning?"

"Yes, Alice. That is exactly what I'm asking."

CHAPTER 19

Of Matters to Be Held in Confidence

Little did the plaintiff anticipate the consequences. The husband very innocently, the wife most guiltily became the wretched victims of his arts and intrigues.
—The Trial of William Henry Hall vs. Major George Barrow
for Criminal Conversation

Rosalind returned to Little Russell Street on foot to save the cost of another carriage. Before she quitted Alice, though, the pair of them had together determined their own course of action.

"Could you find Margaretta's mother?" Rosalind had asked Alice. "If her background is important, that is where we should begin."

"Maybe," Alice had replied. "It would be of help to know when and where she was married, though." The church records would list the bride's maiden name, as well as the names and occupations of her parents. If Margaretta really was an orphan as she claimed, that would be listed, too.

"I am to visit Mrs. Seymore's sister-in-law with her tomorrow as her witness and sympathetic supporter," Rosalind said. "I'll see what I can find out."

"That's a visit that should prove interesting."

"Very. And perhaps I will also be able to learn some more about the captain himself."

The fact of having a practical and simple scheme had sustained Rosalind for much of her walk, but the effects of a near-sleepless night and an agitated morning soon caught up with her. By the time she entered her narrow front hall, she was bone-weary and half-starved. She stood passively while Mrs. Kendricks removed her coat and bonnet.

"I've laid a tray in the parlor, miss," Mrs. Kendricks said. "And the fire's nice and warm. I knew you would need something after the day you've had."

"You were very right, Mrs. Kendricks." *I need a stomach powder. A fresh past. A different decision.*

"I'll bring the tea in at once."

And a pot of tea, of course. Rosalind felt an absurd urge to laugh, but all she said was, "Thank you. In the meantime, I will write to . . ." She paused. She had made the determination somewhere between Covent Garden and Great Russell Street, but she was gripped by a sudden reluctance to say it out loud. "I will write to Lord Casselmain. He'll hear all that happened soon, and he will worry."

"An excellent idea, miss," said Mrs. Kendricks promptly.

"But should Mr. Harkness arrive, you may show him in at once," Rosalind said, and she took herself into the parlor without looking back. She did not want to see Mrs. Kendricks's expression just then.

The door closed and what strength Rosalind had found while she was helping bolster Alice's spirits deserted her. The events of the day were almost too much to be borne, let alone comprehended. For the first time in a very long time, Rosalind felt herself on the verge of tears.

Fortunately, she was provided with the basic, practical

remedy for any encroaching attack of hysteria. Rosalind sat in her comfortable chair by her comfortable hearth and helped herself to the supper tray Mrs. Kendricks had set out. The ragout, bread, and cheese quickly warmed her body and settled her mind, allowing her to think through all that she had seen and heard, as well as the very many things she had not. She brought out the note where she had written down the captain's disjointed distress, along with the letter from Sir Bertram which she had surreptitiously acquired. She laid these side by side so she could look at them both again while she ate stewed fruit and custard and drank the tea that Mrs. Kendricks brought.

Rosalind wondered what Captain Seymore told Mr. Harkness while they were at Bow Street. He might have torn Mrs. Seymore's story to shreds, simply because he hadn't his wife's quickness of thought, or her powers of persuasion.

What, wondered Rosalind, *will she do then?* The answer, of course, would depend entirely on whether Margaretta had committed the murder, or if she was trying to protect herself from the person who did.

Or if it was someone else who killed Fletcher Cavendish, for reasons none of them could yet see.

A cold shudder ran down Rosalind's spine. She laid aside her napkin and picked up her teacup to take to her writing desk. She got out a sheet of paper, dipped her quill in her ink, and began her letter to Devon. It was not a polished or a carefully considered letter, and Rosalind tried not to think too much as she sanded and sealed it. If she let herself hesitate, she might be tempted to throw the letter into the fire instead of ringing for Mrs. Kendricks to come take it away. She shouldn't even be writing to Devon directly. It wasn't proper. She should be writing to Louisa or Mrs. Showell and decorously asking them to mention whatever she wanted him to know.

Rosalind felt her patience fray that much further.

The church bells were sounding the hour in the distance. Much more closely, the doorbell jangled. Rosalind lifted her head. She heard a man's voice, and had just enough time to compose her expression before Mrs. Kendricks opened the door and announced Mr. Harkness.

"Miss Thorne." Mr. Harkness's bow was straight and correct, and rather compact. He was not an overly large man, but he still seemed to fill her small parlor. "I apologize for calling during your dinner hour."

"I was quite finished, Mr. Harkness." She curtsied. "How very good to see you again. Won't you please sit down?"

"Thank you."

"May I get you a cup of tea? Something to . . ." But as she gestured toward her tray, she saw it was entirely empty. "Oh."

He smiled. "Don't worry. I would have been here sooner, but I stopped off at home on my way and my mother insisted I eat before I left again."

"I did not realize you lived with your mother," said Rosalind as Mrs. Kendricks came in to bring a fresh cup and clear away all the unnecessary items.

"My mother, my widowed sister, her two children, and my three younger brothers," he told her while she fixed the new cup. She remembered exactly how he liked his tea, which was somehow quite disconcerting.

"It sounds like a very full house," she said before she could dwell on that for too long.

"Sometimes you cannot move for the sheer weight of Harknesses. I've threatened to arrest the lot of them on a rotating basis to create a little peace."

Rosalind smiled, and covered the silence that followed by filling her own cup.

"George Littlefield came to find me," said Mr. Harkness when she turned to face him again.

"Alice said he'd gone to the station." The tea had been sitting for a while and was quite strong. Rosalind found herself grateful for the bitter taste. It helped burn away some of her weariness.

"How is Miss Littlefield? Her brother was worried."

"She was much better when I left her. Righteous indignation has always done wonders for Alice's constitution." Rosalind paused until she was certain she could keep her voice even. "I trust George told you I was at supper with Mr. Cavendish, and that the captain burst in on us?"

"Yes, he did."

"Does Mr. Townsend know this?"

"He does, and he knows I am here speaking with you. Mr. Townsend is anxious that the correct story be established as soon as possible."

"The correct one?" Rosalind was conscious of a distinct disappointment. "Then he really does believe the tale Mrs. Seymore told you?"

"I don't know." Mr. Harkness frowned at his teacup as well as his thoughts. "I think he wants to believe it, but that might become more difficult once he learns about the criminal conversation suit. I do know he hasn't closed the books on this yet, and that should worry your friend."

"She is not my friend," said Rosalind at once.

Mr. Harkness nodded once, acknowledging this. "Leaving aside the lawsuit, how badly did Mrs. Seymore lie to Townsend?"

"It's difficult to say," admitted Rosalind. "She was careful to weave her story around things I could not have seen. That story, however, was very different from the one she told me when I first got to her house, or the one she told when she first came to see me."

Harkness leaned forward until his elbows rested on his knees. His eyes glittered with intensity.

"Tell me," he said.

Rosalind did. She told him about her first meeting with Mrs. Seymore, the dinner with Mr. Cavendish, and the captain's appearance. She told him how she received Mrs. Seymore's note at the first light of morning, and how Mrs. Seymore had appeared when Rosalind arrived at the house, and all she had said then.

Mr. Harkness listened, silently and intently. Rosalind found herself wanting to lean closer and pull away in equal measure. She found herself remembering the last time she'd been alone with this man, and how she had felt then. She wanted to close her eyes. She wanted not to feel half of what was inside her.

She wanted to remember she had written to Devon not above an hour ago, and how very badly she'd wished he was the one who could be with her now.

It wasn't until Rosalind finished her story that Mr. Harkness spoke again. "I assume from what you've said you did not know Mrs. Seymore planned to tell the story of Mr. Cavendish's despair and suicide?"

He spoke calmly, steadily, as was his usual manner. It was the words he chose that stirred Rosalind to a soft smile.

"Thank you, Mr. Harkness."

"For what?"

"For not asking whether I advised Mrs. Seymore to spin that tale."

"Miss Thorne," he said with mock sternness. "We've only known each other a short time, but I know you well enough to understand you would never advise one of your ladies to spin a story straight out of the Sunday serials. If for no other reason than I hope you have a higher opinion of my intelligence."

"Much higher, sir," she agreed seriously.

"Tell me more about Mr. Cavendish. You saw him before he died. Did he say or do anything that made you think he was a man in despair?"

"Hardly," replied Rosalind. "If I am sure of anything, it is that the Fletcher Cavendish I saw would never kill himself over a woman, or anything else."

Mr. Harkness turned his head so he regarded her from the corner of one eye. "I imagine you've kept this anonymous letter Mrs. Seymore gave you?"

Rosalind was already moving toward her desk to hand it to him. Mr. Harkness quirked an eyebrow at her but said nothing as he unfolded the paper. He took his time reading it, as Rosalind had been sure he would.

"It's short on details," he remarked at last.

"Mr. Cavendish said it would do for the provinces, but not the capital."

"I expect he was correct." He paused, scanning the lines yet again. "You said you showed this to Cavendish, but he did not recognize it. No one had sent a similar letter to him?"

"No. And I . . . looked for other letters when I was in the Seymores' house," Rosalind told him. "I did not find any more of this variety, but I did acquire this." She gave Mr. Harkness the second letter, the one she knew to be from Sir Bertram.

Mr. Harkness read this letter through as thoroughly as he had the first. "Taken together, these would be more than enough to enrage a jealous man." He folded both papers carefully and handed them back. "Do you believe the captain could have done it?"

Rosalind considered this. "I think Captain Seymore is a bully, but I think if it came to any kind of a fight, Cavendish would have the better of it, and him. I assume you will be obliged to tell the coroner about the letters and the suit when you give evidence at the inquest?"

"Not necessarily," he told her. "The inquest will mostly be limited to how Cavendish died, and who might have been there when it happened and whether they could have committed the act. Whys and wherefores, and evidence for and against, will all be saved for the trial, assuming there is one."

Rosalind felt her brow furrow. "I wonder if she knew that."

"I beg your pardon?"

"I wonder if Mrs. Seymore knew that the letters would only be brought up if there was a trial, and so she felt safe keeping them secret, because the rest of her scheme involved making sure there was no trial."

"You've said it, but you don't look like you agree with yourself," remarked her guest, and Rosalind suspected he was trying not to smile at her.

"I don't," she said flatly. "It's too convoluted, Mr. Harkness. I am confused, and I am angry, and I don't enjoy either state of being."

He picked up his cup again and frowned into the clouded depths.

"You do not look pleased," said Rosalind.

Mr. Harkness shook his head. "I'm confused as well, Miss Thorne. I saw the dressing room where Cavendish died. If a drunken man attacked him, there should have been signs of a struggle. But there were none. When he was killed, his coat was off and his shirt open. If he had been surprised in the act of dressing, or undressing, perhaps he would have died without struggle. But why would he be dressing or undressing at that time? It was late. If our information is accurate, he was planning to spend the night at his hotel. I spoke to the night manager of the King's Arms before I came here. He said Mr. Cavendish had only gone back to the theater to retrieve a book."

"That's what he told Mrs. Seymore, too." Rosalind considered this, and the way Mr. Harkness's jaw tightened. "Do you suspect an assignation?"

"It fits. It might not have been with Mrs. Seymore, but with someone. We know he enjoyed . . . the society of women."

"But why would he meet one in his dressing room, when the very comfortable hotel where he had an understanding with the management was a few minutes' walk away? Not to mention the fact that he'd specifically arranged to meet Mrs. Seymore that evening?"

"These things do happen."

"Then, what is it you think?" asked Rosalind. "Do you think that Mrs. Seymore surprised Mr. Fletcher and this theoretical other woman and killed him for it?"

"I will ask you the same question I asked about Captain Seymore. Do you think Mrs. Seymore could have killed him?"

"I was asking myself that this morning, Mr. Harkness, and I do not know. I will say this. No story she has told so far hints at hidden jealousies. Her concern has been entirely about her relationship with her husband and his family, and her fears for the future of her child."

For one of the few times in their eventful acquaintance, Mr. Harkness looked genuinely startled. "There's a child?"

"The captain did not mention it? Mrs. Seymore is with child."

"With child," Mr. Harkness repeated. "No, he did not mention it. And of course, if there's a question of an affair, there's a question of parentage."

Rosalind nodded and Harkness grimaced. "All right. We will set aside the question of jealousy on Mrs. Seymore's part, but not the possibility of a plan."

"But if Mrs. Seymore planned to kill Fletcher Cavendish, the simplest and safest thing to do would be to allow the captain to be blamed for it."

"Couldn't that be why she came to you? To try to make sure as many people as possible knew about the criminal conversation suit and the rest of the captain's jealous behaviors?"

You have been laying traps, Captain Seymore had said. "But if that was the plan, she didn't need me, or Alice. We are both unnecessary complications. Alice is angry at her, and I'm here talking with you. Mrs. Seymore also didn't need this story about Cavendish committing suicide. If she'd wanted to set a seal on the captain's fate, she would have simply turned to him in front of you and Mr. Townsend and demanded, 'What have you done?'"

"Yes." Harkness set his cup aside. "That would be the obvious course."

"The genius of the suicide story is that it shields Captain Seymore as well as Mrs. Seymore. So if she committed the murder, why tell a story that could help exonerate someone else?"

Mr. Harkness raised an eyebrow. "I can think of one possible reason."

"What is that?"

"Mrs. Seymore did not commit the murder, but she knows who did, or thinks she does. This is the person she is trying to shield."

"She thinks Captain Seymore killed Mr. Cavendish?"

"I did not say she thought it was Captain Seymore," said Mr. Harkness. "Think on it, Miss Thorne. Mrs. Seymore swears Fletcher Cavendish was not her lover, but that does not mean she didn't have one."

CHAPTER 20

The Paying of Necessary Calls

*It is one thing to disdain those whom one does not think
worthy of our acquaintance, and another to insult those
whom one has thought it proper to invite.*

—Captain Rees Howell Gronow,
Anecdotes of the Camp, the Court, and the Clubs

Sir and Lady Bertram Seymore kept their home in Soho Square, a neighborhood of Westminster that had once been fashionable but had more recently fallen out of favor. According to Mrs. Seymore, one Mrs. Cecil Seymore, the wife of the captain's late brother, and her two daughters lived with them.

"It's a fate that Virginia does not deserve," Mrs. Seymore told Rosalind. "She's strong-willed, but reasonable, and not malicious. Perhaps that's because she's only a Seymore by marriage. It does make deferring to Johanna—Lady Bertram, that is—exceedingly difficult for her."

They sat together in the Seymores' carriage, rattling across the bridge, on the way to Sir Bertram's. Mrs. Seymore had ordered her man to take the Blackfriars route to avoid the crowds and toll on the more recently opened Waterloo Bridge. Mrs. Seymore's tone was insouciant, almost bored, but she held herself stiffly. It was no secret what caused her tension. The newspaper hawkers sang and shouted out loud on every street corner they passed:

"Fletcher Cavendish is dead! Read it here! Fletcher Cavendish found stabbed through the heart in his own dressing room! Pictures of the deadly weapon, right here!"

"And this is only the beginning," murmured Mrs. Seymore. "I had imagined there would be at least a day's grace. Foolish of me, I suppose."

"It is difficult to comprehend the speed with which such news can travel," Rosalind murmured.

"I should ask Alice to call soon," Mrs. Seymore went on. "I suppose I must talk to someone from the press. It would be better if it was a friend, don't you agree?"

Are you trying to find out if Alice is still a friend? Rosalind wondered. She knew she should be putting more effort into making herself agreeable. If she was going to find out the truth of the events swirling around Mrs. Seymore, she needed to keep the woman's trust. But somehow those instincts of drawing room and parlor would not rise past the memory of the scene Mrs. Seymore had played yesterday, and the unpleasant possibilities that lay behind it.

"Fletcher Cavendish is dead! Read of the tragic death of England's greatest actor! Read it here!"

Mrs. Seymore drew the curtains more firmly closed, as if shutting out the sights could shut out the voices.

"Where is the captain this morning?" asked Rosalind.

"Oh." Mrs. Seymore sighed. "He left early with Sir Bertram to go see the Seymore family attorney, one Mr. H. Close, Esquire. I expect they will meet us at the square."

"Read it here! Read it here! Fletcher Cavendish, first man of the stage, is dead! Read about the bloody and murderous deed, right here!"

"Mrs. Seymore," said Rosalind, curiosity rising above both pique and suspicion. "It might be advisable for you to be elsewhere while the newspapers are out on the scent. Is there anywhere you could go? Perhaps to family of your own?"

Mrs. Seymore turned fully toward her, and for a moment Rosalind thought she was actually going to laugh.

"No, Miss Thorne. I have no family with whom I can stay. If I am driven out of Captain Seymore's, I shall have to make shift among my friends."

No family with which I can stay. Those words repeated themselves inside Rosalind's head, and she noted how this was very different from having no family at all. "And I suppose staying with the captain's family . . ."

"Oh, I am sure they would love to get me under lock and key," she replied bitterly. "Controlling me fully would be the next best thing to getting rid of me."

"You said you believe it is your brother-in-law who is driving the captain to get a divorce, or at least a deed of separation."

"And I still believe it. You'll understand better why when you meet them." She paused, her face softening slowly into a genuine sadness. "The most miserable part of all this is that I would have accepted the divorce up until a month ago. In fact, I had planned to. I was making provision for myself. But when I realized I was with child, everything changed." A tear dropped from her eye and this time there was nothing artificial about it. "I did not expect to conceive again, not at my age."

"You have been a mother before?"

"Oh yes, four times, as it happens. The first two died within three months of each other from some fever the doctors could not even put a name to. The third was stillborn. The fourth simply went to sleep and did not wake up." She turned her face away, but she could not disguise how her voice shook. "This last one, this final gift of Providence, this one will live, and I will make certain it has everything to live for."

Rosalind watched Mrs. Seymore's profile harden with the strength of maternal determination, and found she had no answer to give.

Rosalind and Mrs. Seymore were admitted to Sir Bertram's pleasantly situated house by a short, square maid in crisp black and white, and ushered at once into a back parlor.

Lady Bertram had clearly once been a woman of queenly proportions and she still carried herself with pomp and pride. Time and temper had withered her, though, and her skin hung loose about her hands and long, corded neck. Her slack cheeks pulled down the corners of her eyes, giving her a permanently sorrowful expression. Those same dark eyes, though, gleamed with sharp-edged intelligence.

Lady Bertram made no move to stand when Margaretta and Rosalind were ushered into her presence, nor did she offer any greeting beyond a blunt declaration.

"Margaretta! What on earth have you done!"

"Johanna—" began Mrs. Seymore, but she was not permitted to get any further.

"I have tried to make allowance, heaven knows I have!" Lady Bertram wrung her hands. "I have tried to put the best examples in front of you, to provide that instruction I know you did not receive in your youth. I know you ignored me. I am resigned to your preferring to find your own particular sort of tutors to guide your conduct. But this . . . *this*!" She spread her hands to indicate the room, or possibly the whole unsatisfactory world.

Mrs. Seymore sighed heavily. "Johanna, I promise you, I have done nothing except stand by the captain as best I can."

"If you would come to me . . . if you would *listen* to me . . . but no, no, why should you? Who am I? What is my family, this family you married into? We are to be improved by *your* example, not you by ours. And who is *this?*" she snapped abruptly, as if she'd just noticed Rosalind.

"Lady Bertram, may I introduce Miss Rosalind Thorne, my friend and, for the time, my confidential assistant. Miss Thorne, my sister-in-law, Lady Bertram Seymore."

"What possessed you to bring such a person here? You should . . . Oh, never mind it. You cannot be expected to know or care. You, Miss Thorne." Lady Bertram raked Rosalind over with her sharp eyes. "You look like you've had some teaching. Sit there, if you please, while I attempt to speak sensibly to my sister-in-law."

Rosalind sat, straight-spined and still. A number of uncomplimentary thoughts and unsatisfactory emotions ran through her, including a perverse feeling of gratitude at not having been ordered out of the room. Listening at doors in a strange house was a risky way to gather information, not to mention terribly inefficient.

"Now, please, Margaretta." Lady Bertram not only clasped her hands toward Mrs. Seymore, but shook them. "I beg you for all our sakes, tell me what happened, and why on earth you are involved at all."

Mrs. Seymore glanced sideways at Rosalind, clearly meaning to say, *I told you, did I not?* She began to speak, calmly and clearly.

The tale she told was the one she had given to Mr. Townsend, but this time stripped of its tears and protestations. While Mrs. Seymore spun the drama out again, Rosalind had a chance to observe Lady Bertram's surroundings. The house might have been in a less than fashionable district, but the room was laid in exquisite taste. It was light and airy, arrayed in yellow silks, with a Chinese carpet on the floor. Its bay window looked out over a small but beautiful London garden. Tasteful ornaments stood on the shelves, each given its proper pride of place rather than crammed together like in a shop window. Rosalind recognized porcelain plates from China as well as beautifully painted icons from both Rome and Russia. Lady Bertram's dress was an entirely new and beautiful creation of forest green muslin and wide ribbons of French silk. That lady's fretting and fidgeting, though, had the effect of making her seem like an inmate longing for escape from a prison cell. Each word of Margaretta's story seemed only to increase her alarm, until she fairly leapt to her feet and began to pace back and forth between the hearth, with its pierced brass screen, and the sunny window.

"I don't know what we are to do, I really don't," whispered Lady Bertram tremulously. "I've tried, Margaretta, I have tried, but you will not *listen*. If you had, if you would remain at home, keep your house as you ought, if you showed any *proper feeling* for your husband's family . . ."

"If I kept at home as you advise, Johanna, there would have been far less money to be gifted to my husband's family," replied Mrs. Seymore evenly.

"Oh, yes, of course, the money!" Lady Bertram drew herself up as straight as she was able. "We must never be permitted to forget the money!"

Rosalind glanced once more around the bright, new room. Mrs. Seymore had said that Sir and Lady Bertram had taken, or at least borrowed, her money in the past. Mrs. Seymore's home was likewise elegant, and that neighborhood, while not aristocratic, was certainly within the accepted range of fashionable. And the captain had wanted money from Fletcher Cavendish.

All of which suggested that one or more of the branches of the Seymore family were in debt. And debt, Rosalind knew, could make any family desperate.

But Mrs. Seymore had no chance to make a reply to Lady

Bertram's latest outburst, because the door opened again to admit another woman dressed in a subdued morning dress. She was of brisk and determined countenance and wore a widow's cap over her chestnut curls.

"Johanna, I heard . . . Oh, hello, Margaretta." The new arrival took Mrs. Seymore's hands and kissed her cheek. "How are you bearing up?"

"Hello, Virginia. I expect I will manage. Miss Thorne, this is my husband's sister-in-law, Mrs. Cecil Seymore. Virginia, my friend and confidential assistant, Miss Rosalind Thorne."

Mrs. Cecil Seymore, *née* Virginia Edmundson, was a plain, stout, square-built woman. She was only a little older than Rosalind. Where Lady Bertram projected an air of bitter and inexpressible weariness, Mrs. Cecil Seymore moved with decision, like someone who expected there to be an obstacle thrown before her at any moment but was determined not to be caught off guard.

"I just came in to tell you the luncheon is almost ready," said the second Mrs. Seymore. "Will you be staying, Margaretta?"

"I'm sorry, we have some other calls to pay after this one."

Lady Bertram shuddered, as if something indelicate had been mentioned. "Of course. Your social calls must take precedence over the return of your husband and his brother, not to mention this dreadful business you have laid at our door. You will not choose to stay and hear what your husband and his brother have to say about it."

"Of course I would stay," replied Mrs. Seymore. "But I had no notion we were invited."

Lady Bertram stared at her, her little dark eyes staring out of her nervous face. She looked to her sister-in-law, but Virginia remained as silent as Margaretta.

"Well, naturally, you and your . . . guest are invited, Margaretta," said Lady Bertram. "Virginia will simply tell Cook there are two more. I am sure she will be able to make things stretch. Virginia, you won't mind . . ."

"Oh, of course not," said Mrs. Cecil resignedly. Running her sister's housekeeping errands was evidently something she was used to.

"And has Lord Adolphus arrived yet?" Lady Bertram inquired, her clasped hands quivering where they rested in her lap. "He said he would come."

Virginia's jaw clenched. "I promise you, Johanna, I will not leave Lord Adolphus waiting in the hall. Now, if you will excuse me? It seems I must go speak to Cook."

"I had no idea Lord Adolphus was expected," remarked Margaretta as the younger Mrs. Seymore took her leave.

"He insisted," Lady Bertram said, and there was an odd ring of pride in her voice. "Of course, any such show of family feeling must be a surprise to you, Margaretta, but I do promise you, in a *proper* family—"

"May I ask who is Lord Adolphus?" interrupted Rosalind, violating decorum, but hopefully it was in the service of maintaining some semblance of peaceful conversation.

"Lord Adolphus Greaves is my husband's cousin, and the younger brother of the current Marquis of Weyland," Lady Bertram said with a lift of her chin and a lilt in her voice, and possibly with a little emphasis on "current." "A most kind and excellent man."

"You are very fortunate to have such a good cousin," said Rosalind.

"Oh, we are, we are. And you should see his devotion to his unfortunate brother, the marquis! And his mother! He has dedicated his life, his *life*, to them! Another man his age and fortune would be indulging in worldly pleasures. He would have married and produced a hundred children, but not Lord Adolphus! Entirely selfless, he has lived an upright life of service to his family."

Rosalind could not help but notice how tightly Lord Adolphus's exemplary behavior was linked to the fact that he had so far not sired any sons to lay claim to the Weyland marquisate.

"Tell me, Lady Bertram, have you and Sir Bertram any children of your own?" she asked.

Lady Bertram drew herself upright, and for the first time since Margaretta and Rosalind entered the room, she did not fuss or fidget. "We have not been blessed yet but naturally we hope that very soon . . ."

"Naturally," murmured Mrs. Seymore. "Because we all believe in miracles, do we not?"

"I would suggest you moderate your humor, Margaretta. Or shall we talk about you and your latest? Have you informed . . . Miss Thorne of your condition? Have you informed *her* . . ."

Mrs. Seymore rose, ready for the clash she had begun, but the battle royal was forestalled when the maid stepped timidly through the door.

"Lord Adolphus Greaves," she announced.

"Oh, thank *heavens!*" cried Lady Bertram, and Rosalind was inclined to agree.

CHAPTER 21

Of Heirs and Parents

Every man's first care is necessarily domestic.
—Samuel and Sarah Adams, *The Complete Servant*

Lord Adolphus Greaves was a fair, sandy-haired man with a smooth, round face and blue eyes that protruded on either side of a bulbous nose. He was, Rosalind thought, about Mrs. Cecil Seymore's age, but it was difficult to tell. He was one of those diffident men who seem to be overlooked by everyone and everything, including the passage of time.

"Lord Adolphus!" Mrs. Bertram held out her hands as if he were her last hope of salvation. "How very good of you to come to us! You must sit down. You must tell us, how is the dowager? Lord Weyland? Do they . . . have they . . ."

"Johanna, please." Lord Adolphus bent down to take both her hands in his. "You mustn't agitate yourself so. It is in no way good for you. My mother sends her regards and regrets that she could not come herself, but my brother is not well, and she felt she should stay home with him. So I am here as their representative." He smiled across at Mrs. Seymore. "Margaretta. I had hoped to find you here. How are you doing?"

"How is *she* doing!" cried Lady Bertram. "She! Lord Adolphus, you cannot know . . ."

"I know quite a bit, Johanna," answered his lordship calmly. "And I say again, you must not agitate yourself. You will have to retire to your room and I'm sure you do not want that?"

The prospect of missing her chance to further sigh, exclaim, and pointedly observe proved to have a remarkably calming effect on Lady Bertram, and Rosalind found herself saluting Lord Adolphus in her thoughts.

"You will, I hope, introduce me to your new friend?" His lordship blinked at Rosalind.

"She's Margaretta's friend," snapped Lady Bertram.

"Miss Rosalind Thorne," said Margaretta smoothly. "Who has agreed to act as my confidential assistant."

"Miss Thorne." Lord Adolphus bowed politely. "I am glad to see that Margaretta has her friends about her at this difficult time. Now, Johanna." Lord Adolphus sat himself beside Lady Bertram before she could offer her opinion of Margaretta's friends. "You must tell me, is there anything you need? Anything at all?"

"I don't know! I don't know!" Lady Bertram cried bitterly. "That is what makes it so impossible! I never in my worst nightmares expected such a thing to be visited upon my family. I have tried so *hard*, all my life I have *tried* . . ."

"Yes, yes, Johanna, everyone knows it," said Lord Adolphus with an admirably straight face. "Where are William and Bertram?"

"My husband and his brother chose to go to their lawyer rather than having the man come here, so we must all wait until they choose to return and share what has been decided."

"Lord Adolphus!" Virginia reentered the room, an open smile on her harassed face. "How very good to see you." She accepted his bow and returned a curtsy. "The luncheon is laid, Johanna," she told Lady Bertram. "I assumed Lord Adolphus would be welcomed. If you've no objection to being included in

a meal declared fit only for women and invalids, Lord Adolphus?" she added to him.

"Truth be told, Mrs. Seymore, I am famished. But you will
not mind an unbalanced table, Johanna?" he said to her.

"As if I could ever object to your presence!"

"Will your daughters be joining us, Virginia?" Margaretta
asked.

"Miss Riall has taken the girls out for the day."

Rosalind surmised that those daughters had been gotten out
of the way while the various scenes unfolded at the house. Given
what she'd seen already, she decided this was an entirely sensible
precaution on Virginia's part.

Like the sitting room, Lady Bertram's small dining room
was bright and newly furnished. A pair of heavy silver-gilt
candlesticks had pride of place on the mantle. Because the table
was small, Rosalind found herself seated next to Lord Adolphus. While Lady Bertram exclaimed at her footman about the
service and the dishes to be brought, his lordship turned to her,
and blinked.

"Miss Thorne. I think we have a mutual acquaintance. I
believe I've heard Mrs. Broadhurst mention your name."

"I was unaware your lordship knew Mrs. Broadhurst."

"The admiral and my brother, Weyland, share an interest in
the history of the Renaissance. Have you had a chance to view
Admiral Broadhurst's collection? Weyland says he has several
pieces of enormous interest and importance."

"And are you interested in antiquities?"

"Only of a literary kind. I do not find the vases and cutlery
and so forth that so enchant my brother very stimulating. Do
you read much, Miss Thorne?" he asked rather abruptly.

Rosalind acknowledged that she did, and the discussion
turned firmly to books and authors, especially once Rosalind let

it be known she had some Italian and a bit of Latin and had indeed read both Vasari and Petrarch. Virginia joined in the conversation, a little bashfully, declaring she had not read much or widely, but the questions she asked were intelligent, and Lord Adolphus clearly enjoyed the chance to hold forth about his favorite works.

Margaretta watched them from the corner of her eye as she wielded her knife and fork over the (admittedly very good) salads and jellies, cold soup and duck, and fresh fruits selected from the basket placed at the center of the table. For her part, Lady Bertram punctuated her share of the conversation with a series of hasty orders to the footman to bring this item and take away that, at which point she would sigh and exclaim about the impossibility of servants of all kinds and classes.

The meal was finished and the party returned to the sunny yellow parlor to take coffee. Rosalind found her admiration for Lord Adolphus growing by leaps and bounds. He handled the table with finesse, managing to keep the conversation progressing, and yet somehow preventing Margaretta and Lady Bertram from having to say more than the occasional word to each other.

But the interval of calm was at an end. While Lady Bertram was pouring Lord Adolphus a second cup and urging him to another caraway biscuit, Sir Bertram and Captain William at last returned.

"Oh, Bertram!" His wife set down the coffeepot and leapt to her feet to run to him like a schoolgirl to her beau. "Thank goodness you are here!"

Jack Sprat, thought Rosalind, and had to reproach herself for that reflexive unkindness. But it was true that the family's tendency to stoutness had passed Sir Bertram by without a second glance. Although only of middling height, Sir Bertram was rail-thin with a sharply sloped nose, only somewhat offset by his large brown eyes.

"Johanna." Sir Bertram took his wife's hand and held it. "I am here. Everything will be all right."

"Yes, yes, of course it will! Now that you and his lordship are both here!"

Captain Seymore strolled across the room to stand beside his wife. "Have you any welcome for me, Margaretta?"

"Hello, William," Margaretta replied evenly.

"You seem unscathed after your morning in the realm of the lawyers," Virginia said. "I am glad of that."

Captain Seymore glanced at her, and frowned. "I . . . thank you, Virginia."

The pair of them regarded each other with something of challenge and something of forlorn hope, as if each one wanted to find the other changed somehow. Rosalind saw this. She also saw Margaretta huddle in on herself a bit further.

"But what does Mr. Close say?" Lady Bertram wailed at her husband. "What hope does he give? What counsel?"

"Very little, I'm afraid," replied Sir Bertram. "He advises that the captain tell the truth and hope for the best. If there's any more to be done, it will be done at the trial, if there is one."

"Useless man!" Lady Bertram plopped back down onto her sofa and clasped her hands. "Does he have no thought for what this will mean? Our family name will be dragged before the public! We ourselves will be made objects of calumny and ridicule because of *that* woman . . ." She raised a trembling finger and leveled it at Mrs. Seymore, but let her hand quickly drop, as if she lacked the strength to go on.

"Surely that's enough, Johanna," said Virginia.

While his wife might be preparing for an attack of the vapors,

Sir Bertram appeared quite composed. "Margaretta, William says you told a story about Cavendish threatening to kill himself."

"I did, yes. I will be asked to swear to it at the inquest."

"Will you do it?" he asked.

"Can you give me any reason why I shouldn't?"

"Mrs. Seymore," murmured Lord Adolphus. "Perhaps another tack would be best."

Throughout the meal, Margaretta had allowed herself to be led by Lord Adolphus and at least somewhat by Rosalind, and maintained her patience. That patience was now very clearly at an end.

"I am doing what I must to protect *my* family, brother," Margaretta said to Sir William, her musical voice turning low and dangerous. "What else would you have me do? Perhaps I should conveniently drop dead, like the marquis will." Lord Adolphus started badly at this, but Margaretta ignored him. "But wait, that wouldn't answer. William might remarry some fertile young creature and produce not one son but a dozen to get in your way. Perhaps I could arrange for us both to be thrown from a carriage? Or lost in a boating accident? No, perhaps not with such a sailor as William aboard. Perhaps . . ."

"Bertram! Make the creature stop!" wailed Lady Bertram. "She means to ruin us all! She means scandal and blackmail and—"

"I'm sorry," replied Mrs. Seymore calmly. "I spoke in jest."

"An ill-timed jest, Margaretta," said Virginia. "You're only hurting yourself."

"Margaretta, you will be quiet this instant." Sir Bertram spoke in an ice-cold whisper.

"Enough!" thundered the captain. "By God, it is enough! Margaretta is *my* wife. Mine! Whatever may happen, Bertram, you will remember that!"

Silence fell, and the entire gathering stared at William Seymore. The captain turned slowly to Margaretta, and he advanced to stand in front of her, his feet planted firmly, his fists clenched tightly against his sides. She held herself still and dignified, but Rosalind saw the uncertainty in her.

"Margaretta," Captain Seymore breathed. "Margaretta, please, just admit what you have done. Admit it, and the whole matter will be at an end. I will forgive you," he added softly. "You have my word."

Beside Rosalind, Virginia sucked in a soft breath. She held her teacup in both hands, and Rosalind noticed her knuckles had gone white.

"William, I have laid the private sorrow of a man's despair before the public," Margaretta said. "Is that not proof enough of my regard for you?"

"William—" began Sir Bertram, but the captain cut him off.

"We have fought this action according to your plan, Bertram. And believe it or not, I see where it has got us. Please, Margaretta. For my honor and on my honor. Say what you have done. It's all I ask."

Slowly and with absolute poise, Margaretta rose to her feet. Captain Seymore stared at her, an expression very close to the hope of a drowning man in his eyes. "What you want is for me to tell the particular lie your family wants to hear," she said.

"No, Margaretta, not all of us," said Virginia, but Margaretta ignored her.

"You trust the word of your brother, and some anonymous letter writer, more than you trust mine. But I swear to you, William, I have done nothing to betray my vows as your wife."

Captain Seymore stepped back, and he staggered over nothing at all that Rosalind could see. Lord Adolphus jumped to his feet and clapped his hand on the captain's slumped shoulder. "It will do no good, sir. Come with me, let us go talk this matter over quietly."

"But Lord Adolphus, it—" began Lady Bertram.

The look Lord Adolphus shot her would have felled a grown man, and was sufficient to close Lady Bertram's mouth. Keeping his hand firmly on the captain's shoulder, he steered him out of the room.

"Well played, Margaretta," said Sir Bertram. "But perhaps overplayed."

"I've tried." Lady Bertram sniffed. "I've *tried* to tell you—"

"Oh, for heaven's sake!" snapped Virginia. "How can anyone be so determined to destroy a brother? I swear, I'm tempted to knock your fool skulls together! If I was Margaretta, I'd tell the coroner it was the pair of you who killed Cavendish, and put an end to my troubles!"

With that dire pronouncement, the younger Mrs. Seymore sailed out of the room.

"Oh, dear," murmured Margaretta. "Virginia seems most upset. Don't look so worried, Sir Bertram. I would never say any such thing. What reason would I have?" She also got to her feet. "Now, if you'll forgive me, I think I should go find my husband." She, too, swept from the room, leaving Sir and Lady Bertram staring after her.

"You will perhaps excuse me?" Rosalind made her curtsy and took her own leave before either Sir or Lady Bertram could so much as move.

CHAPTER 22

An Inquiry into the Various Causes

All that was wanting in brilliancy of talent was made up
by sterling principles of honor and honesty.
—Catherine Gore, *Pin Money*

Once in the passageway, Rosalind considered trying to find the Seymores. She was here at Mrs. Seymore's invitation, and she should not be roaming around the house unescorted. But Rosalind had no idea when she would be able to speak to Virginia again, and suddenly it seemed important that she did.

An inquiry of the maid led Rosalind to a small workroom. The widowed Mrs. Seymore sat at a large tapestry frame, jabbing her needle into the canvas and pulling the thread through with such force, Rosalind feared the rose-colored silk might snap.

"Mrs. Seymore," she said as she stepped through the door. "Am I intruding?"

"No, no. I'm sorry. My temper is not always what it should be."

"Your feelings do you credit."

"My feelings." The young widow snorted and jabbed the needle once more into the fabric. The pattern was an elaborate and sentimental garden scene centered around a blooming rose tree. "You have no idea. I don't know what you must think of us."

"I think you are a family going through a time of difficulty."

"Yes. It seems to be a permanent state with us." She pulled the thread tight, winding the slack around her fingers to keep it from knotting. "One calumny after another. One enemy after another. Always another reason to litigate and make us welcome nowhere but our attorney's office."

"Would you prefer if I left you?" said Rosalind. But Mrs. Seymore shook her head.

"No, please stay, and sit." Aside from the stool in front of the frame, there was one spindle-backed chair in the room. She tucked her needle more carefully into the tapestry. "And do call me Virginia. No one bothers to call me Mrs. Seymore, except Margaretta, and I think she just enjoys the joke."

"It is very hard when families quarrel," said Rosalind quietly.

"Hard? It is impossible! No matter what I might say, or what Lord Adolphus may suggest, none of it does any good. Bertram knows himself to be hard done by, and nothing will change his mind."

"What is the nature of Sir Bertram's grievance?"

"That his mother only married a brewer while her sister married a marquis." Virginia just shook her head. "That the dowager marchioness somehow produced two sons, and William might yet produce one that lives, while Bertram has yet to produce any at all. That the money is gone somehow, somewhere, and he and Lady Bertram are reduced to begging and scrounging to keep"—she waved her hand—"all this."

"Money troubles can so easily tear a family apart," said Rosalind.

But Virginia didn't answer this. Instead, she asked, "How does Margaretta?"

"At this very moment, obviously, I could not say. But I believe she is trying to do her best under the circumstances." It was a noncommittal answer, but it was the closest Rosalind could come to the truth.

"Poor woman. I do not envy her. As bad as things may be for me, they are worse for her."

"Lady Bertram certainly seems to take great exception to her. Or is it only her background?"

"Her background certainly doesn't help. An orphan, even a genteel one, is hardly going to recommend herself to Lady Bertram. After all, what are any of us good for if we can't provide useful connections?"

"If Mrs. Seymore is an orphan," said Rosalind, thinking back to their conversation in the carriage, "that would mean her husband's family is all she has."

"Yes, poor thing."

"I'm glad she has at least one friend among her relations."

"You mean me?" Mrs. Seymore sounded surprised. For a moment, Rosalind thought Virginia was actually going to laugh, and she wondered at that. "Well, I am as much of a friend as I am permitted to be, I suppose. When my husband died, he did not leave me enough to enable me to take care of my girls on my own. Therefore, I am dependent on the goodwill of my brother-in-law Bertram and his wife, which rather limits the amount of sympathy I am allowed to show such a rival." She stopped again. "You must forget what I have said. It is nothing but the maundering of a bored widow."

No, it's not. "You have no family of your own either?"

Virginia shook her head. "Some distant cousins in the north, but no one I can make a claim on, especially with two daughters to be provided for."

"Perhaps you should marry again," said Rosalind lightly.

"Perhaps I should." Virginia tried to laugh, but the cheery sound quickly fell flat. "Unfortunately, our various troubles have alienated enough of our acquaintance, I find myself with very few prospects." She ran her palm over her needlework, but Rosalind still saw the genuine pain in her eyes. Was it just her loneliness, Rosalind wondered, or was Virginia breaking her heart over someone in particular?

Mrs. Seymore shook herself. "And here I go from being the pining widow to the fretful debutante. Have mercy, Miss Thorne, introduce some topic of conversation so I can sound like myself for a bit."

Rosalind smiled. "Tell me, do your girls go to school?"

The mother smiled gratefully in return and the conversation changed at once to talk of the two growing girls, their lessons, their accomplishments, and the other details of motherhood. Rosalind listened patiently and with genuine interest. When Virginia talked of her children, her face lightened and Rosalind could see the pleasant, cheerful woman underneath the harried sister.

But Rosalind saw something else as well when Virginia paused in a description of the drawing master's praise of her daughters' watercolors. She gave Rosalind a hard and clear-eyed look. She also glanced at the door to make sure it was still firmly shut.

"I do not for a moment believe Margaretta dragged you with her because you are her confidential assistant," she said. "Exactly what are you to do here with us, Miss Thorne?"

How much do I tell her? Virginia was already more suspicious of Rosalind than either of the Seymore brothers, who were so distracted with their own concerns. There was also some undertone to her conversation with both Captain Seymore and Margaretta that Rosalind could not yet fathom. Virginia had a store of her own secrets, including some heartache all her own. Rosalind found herself reluctant to add to it. At the same time, she very much wanted to see how Virginia would react to the truth.

"There are serious questions surrounding the death of Fletcher Cavendish," Rosalind said. "I have in the past been able to help ladies with similarly difficult problems."

Virginia swayed where she sat. She curled her fingers around the edge of the tapestry frame to steady herself.

"William," she whispered. "He . . . did he lose his head? He's been so badly pressed. Did he . . . does she *believe* . . ." Virginia stopped herself. She also looked to the door again. "No," she whispered, to the door and to herself. "No, I'm glad she has taken this step. Margaretta always was immensely practical," Virginia added. "It does not appear so at first, but that is her defining characteristic."

"In that I think you two are alike," said Rosalind. She meant the words to be light and consoling, but Virginia only turned paler.

What is going on here? Rosalind wondered. *What is the matter between you and Margaretta?* Her thoughts froze. *Or is the matter between you and the captain?*

"Well," said Virginia. "You need not worry, Miss Thorne, I will not say anything to Bertram or Johanna. I don't even want to imagine how they would react to the revelation that Margaretta was asking questions of her own." She paused. "But can you promise me you will act without . . . favor? You say you are Margaretta's friend, but is it your business to make sure—"

"It is my business to find the truth," replied Rosalind. "I know I am a stranger to you, but I ask you to believe this."

Virginia met Rosalind's gaze for a long moment. A dozen thoughts and fears swirled around behind her deep, tired eyes. Rosalind could not discern any of them, except one. Virginia was thinking of her daughters, and how, no matter what happened next, these events must fall heavily upon them.

"I do believe you," Virginia said finally, and as she spoke, she released her grip on her tapestry frame. "And that, it seems, would make us fellow conspirators. How can I help you?"

Rosalind paused, considering the woman in front of her and all she had seen and heard so far. She could not help but think how Virginia was the only person in this house who seemed willing to help William. She wondered about that as well.

"Sir and Lady Bertram are very convinced that Margaretta had been conducting a love affair with Fletcher Cavendish," Rosalind said. "Do you know if they had any definite proof? Did . . . were there letters, perhaps, or anything of that kind?"

"Not that I heard of. It always seemed to me the possibility of an active love affair was wishful thinking." She shook her head at this. "But Bertram and Johanna repeated it to each other so many times that they decided it must be true."

"And repeated it after Mrs. Seymore announced she was with child again, I imagine?"

"You imagine correctly, Miss Thorne."

Because Captain Seymore was the older brother, any son he produced would be a further block on Sir Bertram's road to the marquisate. From the point of view of Sir and Lady Bertram, this matter had nothing to do with Margaretta personally. She could have been an empress or a beggar, and it would have been all the same. As long as there was a danger she might have a child, she must be their enemy.

"And yet Lord Adolphus must be equally in their way," mused Rosalind. "And he is a welcome guest."

"He is also very generous," Mrs. Seymore told her. "A lot of these worldly goods you see around you are made possible by loans from the Weyland coffers, which are managed by his lordship."

That certainly would explain it. "But Lady Bertram seemed very certain Lord Adolphus would not himself marry or have children. Is that more wishful thinking? Or is there some reason . . ."

"That I do not know," said Virginia. "I do know Lord Adolphus has never shown any sign of looking for a wife, although as near as he is to title and fortune, there have been plenty of opportunities presented to him."

Yet more questions, thought Rosalind ruefully.

"Tell me, how did the captain meet Margaretta?"

"You haven't heard?" Virginia's brows arched. "It was Fletcher Cavendish who introduced them."

Rosalind could not help but draw back in surprise. Virginia nodded. "The man had, among other things, a rather mischievous sense of humor. Cavendish brought Margaretta to a house party being given by Lady Weyland, who is now the dowager marchioness. He introduced her as a rising young poetess, although I'm not sure at that time she'd actually had anything published. William happened to be there, and he was very much captivated. Margaretta has that effect on men."

"Yes, I had noticed." Rosalind tried to picture the bluff Captain William Seymore being thunderstruck by a woman, and to her surprise, she found it rather easy. This must have showed in her expression, because Virginia laughed.

"When you live with so little glamour, the touch of it is enough to make you act like a moth before a candle flame." Virginia's fingers danced restlessly across the leaves and flowers of her tapestry, as if she were smoothing down memories as well as stitches. "William was different then. He was a man on the rise, not . . ." She gestured weakly toward the door. "At any rate, his fascination was not reciprocated. Margaretta ignored him, but he continued to pursue her like she was a Spanish treasure ship. He even turned to *me* for advice, although I had only just married Cecil then." Rosalind heard the regret plain in her voice. "I think Margaretta was rather more annoyed by his persistence than anything, at least for a while."

"What changed her mind?"

"I've never known. One day William just came home and announced that he'd proposed and she'd accepted, and they would be married as soon as the banns were read and that was the end of the discussion."

"When was this?"

Virginia tapped the edge of a neatly formed oak leaf. "'Ninety-eight," she said softly. "In the summer. Margaretta was a very young bride, but very decided even then. This caused William's mother to take an instant dislike to her. She would not have the two of them married out of *her* house, no matter how William bellowed. So it was St. Margaret's in the early morning, and off to their own home right after that."

"I imagine Lady Bertram was not pleased by the event. Or were she and Sir Bertram not married then?"

"She and Bertram were married, and Lady Bertram did not leave her room for three days. She'd been counting on William getting himself killed in action to clear the way toward the Weyland marquisate for them."

"What fate did she imagine for Lord Adolphus?"

Virginia smiled bitterly. "You have to understand that Johanna is not a terribly realistic woman. In that way, she and Bertram are well matched. They both believe so very firmly that they are entitled to the marquisate that somehow the Almighty cannot fail to provide it."

"And if Divine Providence does not make itself felt?"

"Then may that Divine Providence help us all," answered Virginia softly. "Because no one else will."

Rosalind regarded this plain, tired, determined woman for a long moment, and made up her mind. "Virginia, I have a favor to ask of you. You have no reason to grant it, of course. I am at best a stranger to you; at worst, I am an intruder."

"If I was being honest, Miss Thorne, I'd say this house could use a few more intruders. What is it I can do for you?"

"I would like an introduction to the dowager marchioness of Weyland."

The answer she got was not the answer she'd expected. Virginia drew her chin back in surprise. "What on earth for?"

"Because everything I have learned so far tells me that the matters around Mrs. Seymore are tied to the marquis, the marquisate, and money. I have seen something of the Seymores' side of that equation. I need to see the Weylands'." And possibly find some reason to talk with Lord Adolphus, who of all the persons she had seen so far, had unlocked the secret of staying friends with both branches of the family.

Why was Lord Adolphus unmarried? Rosalind wondered. And why was Lady Bertram so convinced he would remain so? There were in the world gentlemen who had no interest in women. Was Lord Adolphus one of that kind? Or was there something else at work?

Virginia regarded Rosalind for a long moment before she nodded. "Let me think." This she did, running her fingers gently across the stitching in her fine tapestry. "Are you involved in charity work at all, Miss Thorne?"

Rosalind smiled. "I am, of course, interested in all worthy causes."

"Lady Weyland donates heavily to charities dedicated to providing relief to consumptives, allowing them to take recuperative visits to the seaside and so forth. Perhaps you are connected . . ."

In her thoughts, Rosalind opened her visiting book and leafed through its contents. "I know that my good friend Mrs.

Lindsay would appreciate a donation to her Committee for the Relief of Consumptive Children."

"Then of course I would be willing to introduce you to Lady Weyland, Miss Thorne. I am sure she would be interested to hear about the committee's work."

"Thank you." Rosalind stood. "I have imposed on you more than enough, Virginia. I should find Margaretta and see if she has need of me, or is perhaps ready to leave."

"Miss Thorne." Mrs. Seymore stopped her. "There is something else you should know."

Rosalind turned, and she waited.

"A few days ago, Margaretta spoke to me in confidence." Virginia swallowed. "She told me that I should rest easier. She said she'd prevailed upon some friend to get the money Bertram and . . . William wanted, and that we would soon have peace once again."

CHAPTER 23

Bachelor Rooms

Rosalind was not the only one who found it necessary to be out early that morning. Adam Harkness risked his mother's ire by insisting on limiting his breakfast to some cold mutton and bread eaten out of hand while he made his way through the streets with the rest of the workers, carters, street hawkers, and barrow men. Sir David had granted them only a single day's grace to learn all they could about the immediate circumstances surrounding the death of Fletcher Cavendish. Given what they already knew, Harkness did not think it was going to be enough.

Regardless, Harkness determined his first step should be to find out more about the weapon. Had it been a more ordinary knife, he would have consulted Sam Tauton, or another of his fellow officers, but for this delicate and decorative object, he needed a different sort of expert.

Bond Street was just waking up for the day. Boys were folding back the shutters on the windows, and shopkeepers moved behind the glass, setting out various glittering objects to tempt passersby. The shop Adam knocked on had the words "Isaacs & Sons" painted in gilded letters over its window. A neat, dark woman Harkness knew to be Mr. Isaacs's daughter-in-law paused in her work of setting out a garnet necklace to unlock the door and let him in.

Mr. Isaacs himself stood behind his shop counter. He was a tall man, his broad shoulders slightly stooped beneath his coat of good black cloth. His salt-and-pepper beard was trimmed close to his chin and his gray hair covered with a plain black cap.

"Good morning, Mr. Harkness!" Isaacs said as Adam stepped inside. "How can I be of service today?" Mr. Isaacs was among those businessmen who regularly subscribed to *Hue & Cry*, to better help keep themselves abreast of any valuables that had gone missing, and might be presented under false colors for sale at their shops.

"You can tell me about this, if you please." Harkness laid the knife on the counter and unwrapped it. He had consulted Mr. Isaacs in the past, and valued him for his strict honesty. Isaacs took up the knife delicately and turned it over to examine it from all sides. He laid it across the edge of his hand to test its balance. He drew his narrow fingers across the chased handle. Finally, he walked over to the window, took out a jeweler's loup, screwed it into his eye, and held the knife up to the light.

"Well, sir," he said, turning back to Harkness and removing the loup. "I believe you have here a genuine article. It is an Italian stiletto, probably from Florence, probably from the period of the Renaissance."

"Not something that would likely be used in a theater or a play then?"

"I assure you, no. Not only is this far too precious, it isn't something you'd want waved about on stage day after day. Have you tried the point? Someone would lose an eye. Or his life," Mr. Isaacs added, touching one fingertip to the dark stains on the blade. "I would need to consult with some colleagues of mine, but my initial guess would be it was meant as a weapon for a lady. Perhaps it was owned by one of the Borgias or the Medici clan, who occasionally had need to defend themselves, usually from their own relatives."

So not something the murderer was likely to have picked up on the spur of the moment. Unless Cavendish had it in his dressing room, the man or woman who killed him must have brought the knife along.

There was one answer, at least. Harkness didn't like it, but at least he had it.

"Have you ever seen a knife like it?" Harkness asked Mr. Isaacs.

Isaacs shrugged and laid the dainty weapon back onto Harkness's kerchief. "Like it, most certainly. This particular one? Not to my knowledge. Again, I can ask my colleagues in the trade if anything of the kind has been sold recently, but I would not hold out hope of a positive answer. When Napoleon conquered the peninsula, his armies looted Italy of thousands of such trinkets. Now the British Army and all the others are busy looting Paris. Therefore, it's probable that rather than having been purchased at a shop, this pretty toy came direct from someone's hand."

Like the hand of a ship's commander recently returned from the wars.

"Thank you for your help, Mr. Isaacs."

"I am only sorry I could not have been of more assistance, Mr. Harkness. You will please let me know if there's anything else I can do for Bow Street?"

"I will, sir," replied Harkness. "You may be sure of it."

Harkness's next port of call was the King's Arms Hotel. The management, the waiters, the porters, and the footmen were all eager to talk, but none of them had much new to say. Mr. Cavendish had ordered a private dinner. Mr. Cavendish had come and gone in ways that matched the story Harkness had heard from Miss Thorne, and again from Alice Littlefield when he spoke to her. Captain Seymore had arrived and had to be removed.

"It was not," the manager confessed, "the first time."

The manager was likewise perfectly willing to let Adam into the suite of rooms that Mr. Cavendish occupied whenever he was in London.

"He always wrote to us to make sure we set these aside for him," Harkness was told when the manager unlocked the door. "He was very particular."

He was also very neat, or else the rooms had been cleaned. All evidence of personal occupancy had been tidied away. Adam walked through the rooms once without touching anything. The apartments were not large, but they were comfortable. There was a sitting room with a hearth, a dining room, a dressing room, and a boudoir. All were well furnished though not elaborately so. But there were no ornaments or keepsakes on display, only some books that proved to be bound plays.

Harkness found himself wondering if the staff had been helping themselves to souvenirs.

He returned to the sitting room, where he'd seen a plain, covered desk. It was unlocked and he raised the lid. There he found writing paper, pen, and ink, all laid out and ready for use.

When he opened the side drawer, however, the stale scent of a dozen different perfumes wafted up. It wasn't difficult to see where it came from. Harkness reached in and removed bundle after bundle of letters. Well, if he'd needed any proof as to Cavendish's propensities, here it was. The letters were on all shades of paper—pink and blue and even violet. They'd been sorted by color and tied in matching ribbons.

Which puts paid to the idea that the staff has been picking up stray objects. No one would leave these. The papers would pay out hefty sums to get their hands on Fletcher Cavendish's love letters. And probably at least some of their authors would pay hefty sums to get them back.

Harkness riffled through the letters. They were written in any number of different hands and inks. Some looked barely literate. Were there any from Mrs. Seymore? He pocketed the packets, and he needed every last one of his pockets to do it. He'd go over them later, preferably where none of his fellow officers would see, or he'd never hear the end of it.

A second drawer was stuffed just as full, but these were bills—tailor, cobbler, provisioner, wine shop. All were asking, in a range of polite and businesslike language, to be paid at Mr. Cavendish's earliest convenience. Courts were mentioned with increasing frequency the farther he dug down.

Harkness closed that drawer and moved to the dressing room. The wardrobe and the dresser's drawers were well filled with good clothing. There were plenty of shirts and coats and collars, all in excellent repair. His tailor might want to be paid, but not to the point where he'd cut Mr. Cavendish off.

There was an inlaid box on the top of the dresser. Harkness lifted its lid, and he froze.

The box was filled to the brim with jewels. There were rings and stick pins, bracelets, chains, and brooches. Men's and women's ornaments of all styles were jumbled together. Some were brand-new but some were obviously antique. Harkness lifted up a ring mounted with a red carbuncle the size of his thumbnail and held it to the light. He'd seen enough jewelry to tell the genuine from the fake, in most cases. This was most decidedly genuine.

He picked up a pearl stick pin and ran his thumb across it, testing for the telltale roughness that was the indication of a genuine pearl, and felt none. A fake then, but a fairly good one.

There was a rattle of a key in the door, and click of a latch. Harkness closed the lid on the box immediately and turned smoothly around.

A pale man in a black coat and waistcoat walked through the door. His high crowned hat was battered and his neck and shoulders were crooked. He had a walking stick under one arm, a sheaf of papers under the other, and a ring of keys in his hand.

If he wasn't an attorney of some variety, Adam would eat his own boots.

"Who are you, sir?" the man demanded. "And what is your business here?"

"Adam Harkness of Bow Street," Adam answered. "Who are you?"

Hearing this, the man bowed, albeit awkwardly, since his hands were so full. "Mr. Fetch, of Inner Temple. I am the late Mr. Cavendish's attorney. I suppose you are looking for evidence among the wreckage?"

"After a fashion," said Adam. "I suppose you are here to take charge of his possessions?"

"For the moment. What there is." Fetch dropped papers, stick, and hat on the sideboard and gazed about the hotel room with a kind of weary distaste.

"Did Mr. Cavendish leave a will?" Adam asked.

"No, curse the man. I begged him to put his affairs in order. I don't know how many times I told him what a comfort it would be to his friends and his heirs and assigns, but he just laughed at me. 'It'll only be a comfort to my creditors, Mr. Fetch, and when I'm gone, I don't care what trouble I give them.'" Fetch sighed heavily. "I could not make him understand how much trouble it would be to me personally. Not that he would have cared much."

"So you know of no family?"

"None," said Mr. Fetch flatly. "I mean, I assume there must once have been a mother and one of course presumes also a father of some sort. But I've done his business for ten years now, and Mr. Cavendish never mentioned a single relation who still walked the earth."

"Are there many creditors?" asked Harkness.

"Only half of Bond Street," said Mr. Fetch. "And a good portion of Jermyn Street as well." He opened the wardrobe. "We'll be selling most of these back to their makers." He lifted the lid on the jewel box with one finger and his gray brows shot up in surprise. "Well, it seems I owe Fletcher an apology. He was keeping some kind of savings."

"Not really. At least some of them are fakes."

"I should have known." Fetch let the lid fall with another sigh. "Never put your faith in actors, Mr. Harkness. You are doomed to disappointment."

"Had you seen Mr. Cavendish lately?"

"Not since he returned from France. He wanted some money, of course, and wanted me to convince his banker to advance him something against his salary at the theater."

"Did he get his advance?"

"Oh yes. Mr. Cavendish usually found a way to get what he wanted." Fetch opened the central desk drawer to reveal a purse tossed among the papers. He undid the laces. "Empty," he said, and sighed again. "Well, the inventory will be a simple matter at least."

Harkness retrieved his own hat. "I will leave you to your work then, Mr. Fetch."

"Thank you. If there is anything I can do to assist, please call upon me. Cavendish was a rogue and a wastrel, but as far as I know, he'd done nothing worth his dying for."

"Thank you, Mr. Fetch." Adam bowed.

Adam also thanked the hotel manager and left the man with a card, and a few shillings for his time and trouble. The Littlefields' major was not the only one who kept a fund. That done, Adam stepped out into the sunshine. It was a clear, warm day with only a few clouds scudding across the sky. The streets were filled and all the city was going about its business.

And here am I, doing little better than wandering aimlessly about.

Unless the correspondence Harkness had appropriated offered up something new, Cavendish's apartments had been as much of a disappointment as Cavendish's dressing room in the theater. Harkness had taken the letters as a matter of form. He didn't think they'd yield much. If there had been an especially attached or distressed female hanging about Mr. Cavendish, someone would have mentioned it by now. In fact, someone would have mentioned it within five minutes of Bow Street being called. It was the sort of thing that came up quickly. But thus far, the only distressed female who figured prominently enough in Fletcher Cavendish's life to merit special comment was Mrs. Seymore. While she might be a poetess, Harkness did not believe her the sort to send perfumed love notes on pink paper.

Despite this, the matter was looking increasingly simple and increasingly sordid. A jealous husband, and a dead lover, or suspected lover. Seymore's wife had lied to try to protect her husband and possibly herself, but that was not a crime.

If Captain Seymore was smart, he'd find a lawyer who would

lead the jury to believe the captain had caught Cavendish and his wife in the act. If that were so, then by killing him, Seymore had simply been defending his property and his honor. They'd acquit without a second thought.

And yet something about this conclusion bothered Harkness. It was not that it was sordid, or too simple. It felt wrong. And, if he was forced to admit it, part of the reason it felt wrong was the presence of Miss Thorne. Harkness remembered Rosalind's contention that Mrs. Seymore had complicated the matter with her actions. He had not had the chance then to point out to her that persons involved in criminal actions frequently made the mistake of saying too much in an attempt to disguise what had really happened. Yes, he had raised the possibility it might not be her husband that Mrs. Seymore was attempting to shield, but there was no word of such person in any of the stories he'd heard yet.

He wondered how Miss Thorne was faring among the Seymore clan today, and if she had learned anything that would point to a different conclusion. He wondered when he would have a chance to talk to her again.

Be careful there, Harkness. Be very careful.

The situation was ludicrous. When he looked at Miss Thorne, or spoke with her, or stood near her, he was fine. He was, in fact, entirely himself and glad to be so. But when they parted, he had to walk, or perform some other vigorous exercise, for an hour or more before he felt he could settle into his own skin again.

Harkness wasn't a raw schoolboy. He knew the signs and symptoms of a serious attraction. He'd lost his heart, and reclaimed it, several times. But Rosalind was fundamentally different, not only in her character, but in her station. He had no way to court her. He could not offer to walk her to church on a Sunday. He was not going to meet her at a country dance, or a public assembly, or the panorama in Hyde Park. Except for the Littlefields, they knew no one in common. What he did know about her family had to be kept secret, but otherwise he knew nothing of her past or of her present for that matter, unless she was engaged in some matter such as the one that had taken Fletcher Cavendish to his end. The courtesies she had been raised to forbade him from calling at her house. The only way he had to spend any time with her was in the role of a glorified tradesman.

And then there was Devon Winterbourne, Duke of Casselmain, if you please, who took her to the theater and looked at her like it was his heart she held in her hand.

And yet, Adam was carrying the note she'd written in his breast pocket, and he had no intention of removing it, even though it was currently weighted down under a wealth of perfumed letters.

And please God, never let Tauton, Townsend, or Mother find out, he prayed as he crossed the cobbles toward Drury Lane. *I really never will hear the end of it.*

CHAPTER 24

Together on the Straight and Narrow

He was introduced into the plaintiff's family; He soon
became pleased and deeply interested in the charms, and
the beauties of her person.
—*The Trial of William Henry Hall vs. Major George Barrow*
for Criminal Conversation

When Rosalind returned home from the Seymores', it was to find a stack of fresh correspondence on her desk, but there were three letters in particular that she sorted from the others.

The first was from Alice.

On the trail of Margaretta's wedding to the captain. Why
couldn't she have been famous when she got married? I'm
coming to dinner in hopes you have a date and a church!

The second was much longer, and sealed not only in wax, but in official red ribbons. It instructed Miss Rosalind Thorne to present herself at the coroner's court to be held at Bow Street Police Office on the named date to give evidence concerning the death of one Mr. Fletcher Cavendish, actor. It happened to be the same night she was invited to dine with Mrs. Broadhurst's friend, who also invited Sir and Lady Bertram, and Lord Adolphus. Rosalind wrote a polite note to Mrs. Broadhurst saying that she must cancel. Since her name was already in the papers, she needed to give the hostess a chance to avoid the potential for disconcerting her guests, who might find the inclusion of such a woman at the table uncomfortable.

The third letter was short, shorter even than Alice's.

Will you meet me? Rotten Row, after the fashionable hour.

   D.

Rosalind sat at her desk and considered her correspondence and her visiting book. Eventually, she pulled out a fresh sheet of paper and trimmed her quill. Her conversation with the widowed Mrs. Seymore had raised several possibilities in her mind, but she would need to call on specific connections to find out if they could be fulfilled. Rosalind wrote three letters to likely candidates to send with the second post. After that there was little to do but wait, and hope a satisfactory answer would come in time.

That's true of so very many things.

Rosalind set her two short letters in front of her, along with two fresh sheets of paper. First, she addressed Alice.

St. Margaret's Church, seventeen ninety-eight. A very small wedding by all accounts. I am sorry I cannot do better yet.

   What can you find out about Lord Adolphus Greaves, younger brother of the current Marquis of Weyland?

   R.

This sealed and laid aside, she turned her attention to the other note.

Will you meet me?

Rosalind picked up her quill again and allowed herself a moment of hesitation. She had plenty of worries and plenty to do. Only one full day remained to her before the inquest, and for all her tortuous morning in the house of Sir and Lady Bertram, she had discovered very little that did not lead to yet more confusion. Indeed, she now had one great question to crown the whole matter.

Why did Mrs. Seymore tell Virginia their money troubles were at an end?

She could easily put Devon off. Given the curious state of her emotions since this matter began in earnest, she probably should.

Rosalind dipped the pen in the ink and wrote down a reply consisting of a single word.

Yes.

Hyde Park was famous in song and story, not to mention Sunday serial and romantic novel. Deer and milk cows together roamed its broad green lawns and were equally startled by the dogs, horses, and children of those who sought in the city meadows some semblance of the healthy countryside. Vendors hawked sweetmeats and corsages. Small tearooms offered rest and refreshment.

But the park was perhaps most noted for the broad avenue called Rotten Row. Every day during the season, at a set hour of the afternoon, the aristocratic and the fashionable paraded up and down its length. Horses and carriages were admired, or not. New gowns, new rings, and new gossip were all displayed for general comment. Lovers and hopefuls caught glimpses of one another. Rivalries were formed and proposals accepted.

During that time, one could barely move for the traffic. But by five o'clock, the whole crowd vanished back to their houses to dress for dinner and whatever other entertainments the night might hold, leaving Rotten Row entirely empty.

Therefore, it was easy for Rosalind to see Devon standing beside a roan mare that nosed idly at the lawns. Devon bowed as Rosalind reached him, and she curtsied in return.

"Will you sit?" He gestured to the stone bench.

"Would you mind walking?" she answered. "I've been sitting a great deal today."

"As you choose." He took the horse's bridle, and with only a little coaxing, he convinced the animal to leave the grass and follow along peaceably.

They walked along in silence until it became evident to Rosalind that Devon was going to leave it to her to start their conversation. She cast about for a neutral topic.

"How is Louisa?" she asked finally.

"Not speaking to you, I'm afraid," Devon told her. "She won't forgive you for being in the company of her departed hero and not telling her about it."

The papers had come out, and with them, the news that Fletcher Cavendish's last act had been to dine in the company of Alice Littlefield, a lady journalist for *The London Chronicle*, and one Miss Rosalind Thorne, gentlewoman.

"Please send her my deepest apologies."

"As soon as she comes out, I will. When I left, she was locked into the sitting room with four or five of her bosom-beaus, a stack of plays, a tray of cakes, and more handkerchiefs than I was aware we possessed."

"I think bosom-beaus would be gentlemen."

"Bosom-belles then. Anyway, there was a great deal of

sighing and declaiming and I think they may be committing poetry. I fled the house before I had to find out."

"Probably wise," Rosalind said solemnly.

Rotten Row ran straight as a ruler. Gravel crunched under their shoes and the horse's hooves. A dog barked in the distance and a cow bellowed its annoyance.

"Is there anything I can do to help, Rosalind?" asked Devon.

"I don't think so."

"Then why did you write me?"

"So you wouldn't worry. So . . . you wouldn't think I was avoiding you."

"Are you?"

Rosalind had to pause for a long time before she answered. Not because she did not know what she wanted to say, but because she wanted to be absolutely certain her voice would be under her control when she said it. "A little, I think. Seeing you again . . . It has not been easy for me, Devon."

"Or for me," he admitted. "And yet here we are again, and you are . . . what is it you are doing, Rosalind?"

She felt herself smile, and a little bitterly. "Getting in over my head."

Devon chuckled. "I suspect that's not going to stop anytime soon."

Rosalind made no answer, but tipped her face toward the long rays of the evening sun. After the day indoors and in carriages and among all the assorted Seymores and their verbal daggers, the heat and fresh air felt wonderful.

Devon watched her. She could feel his gaze against her skin. It had always been like that with him, since the first time she'd seen him across a crowded country ballroom. She wondered if it would ever fade.

She waited for him to tell her to stop this. To say that she was walking into all kinds of danger, socially, morally, perhaps even physically. He would surely ask if she had been spending any time with Adam Harkness, and what was the nature of their conversation.

But he did not.

"I'm thinking of giving a dinner," Devon said casually.

"You are?"

Devon nodded. "It's Mrs. Showell's idea, really. You know she's chaperoning Louisa? Well, she wants to parade a few eligibles in front of her one last time before everyone heads off to the country. Leaves a good impression on all sides, she says. For myself, I need to think about the elections coming up, so it's worth it to feed some of those concerned. It'll mostly be political men and their wives, nothing rarified. Your friend Mrs. Norton will be there. Should Mrs. Showell write you out an invitation?"

"Whatever will Louisa say?"

Devon smiled, just a little. "If you accept, we will find out."

Rosalind stopped and faced him fully.

"I know what you're doing, sir."

"What am I doing?"

"You're subtly and slyly trying to bring me into company, specifically mutual company, where we might see more of each other."

"Am I?" Devon's brows rose in mock surprise. "How deceitful and underhanded of me." He paused. "Will it work?"

"I don't know."

"Then there's at least a chance it might."

Now that she was looking straight at him, Rosalind could see the concern on Devon's face, the humor, and yes, that boyish hope that she had missed before. Devon's succession to the title of Duke of Casselmain had been as hard on him in its way as her fall from social grace had been on her. They had both been forced to change to suit their new part, and both had lost something in so doing.

But perhaps Devon had gained as well. There was a strength about him, a confidence. She looked at him as a stranger might, and saw the poise, the assurance with which he moved. And yet, and yet, she could see the essential self that was Devon beneath it all.

But beneath it all, who was this lady who stood in front of him? Rosalind didn't know. She moistened her lips and tried to find a teasing answer to give him.

Devon, though, spoke first. "It was Charlotte, wasn't it?"

Rosalind's mind went utterly and completely blank. "I don't . . ." she stammered.

"That's who you were chasing after when you ran out of the theater box the night Cavendish was killed," said Devon. "You saw your sister."

Rosalind turned abruptly. She walked two or three steps, before she could force herself to stop again. She was running away. It was ridiculous. She squeezed her eyes shut. She was running away and suddenly about to dissolve into tears.

Stop this. Stop it at once.

"Rosalind?" Devon had come up beside her again. Something nudged her bonnet, and she put her hand up to push the mare's ridiculous and very wet nose aside.

"Behave," said Devon.

"I hope you're talking to the horse," murmured Rosalind.

"I promise," he answered. "But the question stands. Was it Charlotte?"

Rosalind sighed. "I thought so. Maybe. I don't know."

Devon patted his horse's side, trying to keep her calm, and

distract her from the culinary possibilities represented by Rosalind's best straw bonnet. "I do," he said. "I saw her as well."

Rosalind felt her shoulders curl in on themselves, felt herself huddling, shrinking. "I knew it," she murmured. "I didn't want to really, but . . . It wasn't the first time I'd seen her recently."

Devon frowned. "Where else?"

"You must promise not to ask how I got there."

"I promise."

"It was in Graham's Club."

Devon looked at her for a long time, but he honored his promise and asked no questions. He also did not fail to understand what finding her sister in such a place might mean. "In that case," he said, "it might be better for you both if you simply let her remain lost."

"Could you let your sister remain lost?"

"I'm ashamed to say I probably could."

"I don't believe you," Rosalind said.

Devon smiled at this, but it was quite unlike his usual expression. This smile was bitter and tight. Rosalind felt cold disquiet stir inside her. But then the smile was gone, and it was only the familiar and comfortable Devon beside her.

Familiar, comfortable, and kind. "I could make some inquiries if you wanted," he said.

She did want inquiries. But Rosalind found she didn't want Devon to be the one to make them. She wanted to hide the shame that would surely come with the discovery of Charlotte's location. But Devon had already guessed that her sister must have fallen into some sort of disgrace, so any desire for concealment was pointless. And who else could she trust as much as she trusted Devon? Who else, indeed, would know Charlotte on sight, like she did?

"I think she's using the name 'Cynthia.'"

Devon nodded once more. "I'll let you know if I hear anything."

"Thank you."

They had reached the park gates by now. The church bells began their ragged tolling. *Dinnertime*, they said. *Evening is approaching, time for all to lay aside their sensible daytime selves and prepare for the gay, giddy, and fashionable night.*

"Rosalind?"

"Yes?"

"I'm planning on taking Louisa for a drive to see the new Waterloo Bridge on Sunday. It has nothing to do with the theater and actors so she might just find it bearable. Will you join us?"

Rosalind allowed herself a moment's hesitation. There were so many reasons not to do this, and at least a dozen of them referenced the emotions that stirred in her each time she came near Adam Harkness. And yet here was Devon, and he was familiar and close and trying so hard to come back while she was trying so very hard to run away. And to what exactly?

"Yes," she said. "Thank you. I'd like that."

CHAPTER 25

The Events Backstage

Her wit electrified all the fashionable world, and her
dancing and acting made the fortune of the entrepreneur.
—Captain Rees Howell Gronow,
Anecdotes of the Camp, the Court, and the Clubs

The crowd around the Theatre Royal had not thinned at all in
the hours since Mr. Cavendish's death had become known, but
its nature had changed. Now, instead of the honest laboring
classes and other passersby who had been there at the spur of
the moment, it was composed of prosperously dressed girls and
youths. Many wore black and clutched white lilies or red roses
in their hands. These blossoms were laid reverently in front of
the theater door. Those inclined to less dramatic display simply
lingered on the cobbles, exclaiming over the murder and the
mourners and the probable outcome of tomorrow's inquest.

Of course, there were the inevitable broadsheet and play
book peddlers rubbing shoulders with the sellers of commemo-
rative miniatures, penny portraits, and engravings. The print
shops must have had their people awake all night to create the
supply.

But for all this assorted activity, the gathering was entirely
peaceable. The mourners might weep, and one girl collapsed into

the arms of her friends, but no one approached the constables stationed at the theater doors, or made any untoward disturbance in the lane, or in the alley or the yard.

Having satisfied himself that the peace was being adequately kept, Adam made his way inside to Dr. Arnold's office.

"Ah, Mr. Harkness." The theater manager shook his hand. "Thank you for coming. We've gotten the notice from the coroner." He held up the letter. "Tomorrow then?"

"Yes. The coroner's decided it's more important to get the verdict in than it is to grant us an extra day to gather some last bits of information," Harkness told him, leaving out mention of the long meeting with Mr. Townsend that had preceded this decision. "I gather from your letter that you've determined no money's gone missing from the strong room?"

"None, and all the drafts were likewise accounted for. Is it ridiculous I should be feeling disappointed at that?"

"No," said Harkness. "I'd be glad of such a simple motive as burglary. But as it is, there's nothing for it but to keep looking. I appreciate you arranging for Mr. Kean and Mrs. West to speak with me."

Dr. Arnold waved this away. "They are actors, sir. They will not deny themselves an audience, however small. We should have them with us momentarily. In fact!" Arnold paused and held up his hand. "I hear their delicate tread in the passage even now."

Proving he also did not mind the occasional dramatic gesture, Dr. Arnold got to his feet and flung open the door. Edmund Kean, who had discarded his borrowed cloak and doublet in favor of a precisely tailored pea green coat and buff breeches, laughed in surprise. He bowed deeply to the woman who stood beside him and gestured that she should enter the office first.

As she did, the woman lifted her lace veil to reveal an oval face of pure and clean lines, but what riveted Harkness were her eyes. Large, shining, and a brilliant green, they slanted catlike above her cheekbones. She wore no cosmetics, which surprised Harkness a little. She also saw he was staring, and she smiled as if she and Mr. Harkness were sharing an entirely private joke.

"Mr. Adam Harkness," said Dr. Arnold. "May I present Mrs. Frederic West. Mrs. West, Adam Harkness, principal officer of Bow Street."

Harkness bowed, and tried to remember how to speak without stammering.

"It is very good to meet you, Mr. Harkness," she said. Her voice was light and clear, not dulcet, not sultry, but entirely matter-of-fact, which made it comfortable to listen to her. "You will forgive the drama of the veil. I thought with the crowds still about, it might be better to proceed incognito." She smiled, again giving the impression of the two having shared a joke. "You are surprised an actress would not seek publicity?"

"I'd expect a true actress to know how to time her entrance," replied Harkness.

Kean threw back his head and laughed. "Oh, very good, Harkness." He settled himself into one of the chairs set out. Dr. Arnold pushed one forward for Mrs. West, who accepted with thanks.

"Well, Mr. Harkness, I daresay you know your business, and don't need my interference," said Dr. Arnold as he turned to set a tray with a brandy bottle and three glasses on his desk. "I must go speak with my director about the remainder of our season. Yes, yes, Mr. Kean," Arnold added soothingly as the other man seemed prepared to interrupt. "The moment Mr. Harkness releases you, we will want you to join us so we may hear your thoughts on this important matter."

Mrs. West turned just a little toward Harkness, and winked. Harkness could not keep from grinning. If Mr. Kean noticed, he gave no sign. He did, however, pull out a very large handkerchief and press it against his nose.

"Forgive me, my dear Mrs. West, but that is an unusually persistent scent you have applied."

Mrs. West lifted her chin. "I shall be more careful next time," she said.

Harkness coughed and settled into the remaining chair. Kean also coughed, but he did put the kerchief away. "Now, sir, you see we are entirely at your disposal. How may we be of assistance to the legendary Bow Street runners in unmasking the villain who robbed us of so great a talent as Fletcher Cavendish?"

Mrs. West laughed. Like her face, the sound was pleasant and open. "I see the eulogy is progressing nicely, Edmund. Forgive him, Mr. Harkness. He is one of us who is never truly offstage. How can we help?"

"Mrs. West, I understand you were delayed at the theater the night Mr. Cavendish died."

"I was. There was a problem with my carriage, and so I had to wait an extra hour before I could return home."

"Did you see Mr. Cavendish during that time? Or hear, quite accidentally, any sounds from his dressing room?"

"Mr. Harkness, I have been on the stage for ten years now. If you wish me to be insulted, you will have to accuse me of something far worse than eavesdropping. Yes, as a matter of fact, I did hear voices. Loud ones, coming from Fletcher's dressing room."

"Man's or woman's?"

"I recognized Fletcher's, of course. He bellowed at me onstage on a nightly basis. The other . . . I believe it was a woman." She turned to Mr. Kean. "But you were there, Edmund. Did you know who it was?"

Mr. Kean went dead white. "But I was not there."

"Edmund, don't be ridiculous," said Mrs. West, but all levity had vanished from her tone. "I saw you leaving, just before I went down for my carriage."

"I was not there!" cried Mr. Kean. "What on earth would I be doing there? It was not even my night to perform."

"I saw you," insisted Mrs. West. "Do not ask me to lie for you."

Kean leapt to his feet, rattling the tray of glasses. "I say you did not see me! How dare you, woman that you are . . ."

Slowly, Mr. Harkness climbed to his feet. "Mr. Kean, I'll thank you to sit down," he said. The actor opened his mouth to draw breath, but then took a second look at the man in front of him, and the way he held himself. Kean sat down.

Harkness turned to the actress. "Mrs. West, are you sure it was Mr. Kean? Could it have been someone wearing his clothes?"

She stopped. "Someone in *costume?* Oh, good heavens! I had not thought of it." She paused for a long moment, her bewitching eyes flickering back and forth as she attempted to recall the scene. "I . . . I do not think I saw his . . . their face. I cannot be sure."

Adam nodded. "Mr. Kean," he said. "Do you keep a change of clothing in your dressing room?"

"Several. I . . . Great God!" he cried. "I assumed my man had taken them away for cleaning."

Harkness let out a long breath. There. That was how the murderer had left the theater without the blood on his (or her) clothes being seen. Simple. Neat. Practical.

It was becoming increasingly likely that Fletcher Cavendish's murderer had planned out his crime well ahead of time. And that he, or she, was familiar with the ways of the theater, as well as the contents of the dressing room.

"Thank you," Harkness said. "That is very helpful."

"It is terrible!" cried Mr. Kean. "Impersonating me! The coward! The filth! That suit cost me fifty pounds!"

"Edmund, if you don't behave, I shall tell Dr. Arnold to send you to bed without supper," said Mrs. West wearily. "What else, Mr. Harkness?"

Harkness suppressed a smile. "The voices you heard arguing in Mr. Cavendish's dressing room. You said you heard some of what they said?"

"It wasn't much, I'm afraid. I heard the word 'money' repeated several times, and I assumed one of Cavendish's creditors had caught up with him."

"You said you thought it was a woman, though."

Mrs. West leveled her eyes at him, and her formerly warm gaze was very direct and very cold. "A woman may not be a creditor, Mr. Harkness? She may not keep a shop, wash laundry, or sew a coat?"

"I beg your pardon," said Adam at once. "It has come to light, however, that Mrs. Seymore may have been asking Mr. Cavendish for money."

Again the two actors looked at each other, and this time they both burst out laughing.

Adam waited until their mutual merriment faded. "I take it Mr. Cavendish had none?"

"Money ran through that man's hands like water," said Kean. "We are all profligates, but Cavendish was positively childlike. The man had no thought at all for the future." Kean sobered abruptly. "As if he believed he did not have one."

"There's no need to be morbid, Edmund," said Mrs. West.

"Fletcher simply lived in the moment, which is fine while one's looks hold. Eventually, it would have got him into trouble. But as it stood, he was as bad as any schoolgirl. A diamond this, a ruby that, and then give it all away to some friend, or at the gaming table."

"Oh yes, that. He loved that."

"I don't understand," said Harkness.

"Cavendish enjoyed gambling, Mr. Harkness," said Kean. "Along with the drink and the ladies. But nothing was more enjoyable to him than to take some jewel from his finger or his breast and toss it into the middle of the highest stakes table that would have him and exclaim, 'There! That should suffice!'"

Harkness thought about the jewel box he'd found in Cavendish's rooms. He also looked at Mrs. West for confirmation of this story, and she nodded. "I saw him do it more than once."

"I have a feeling he did not tend to win these items back?"

"Oh no, that was never the point," said Mrs. West. "The point was to make the grand gesture, in front of the audience. He loved the looks on their faces."

"But anyone who knew him even a little knew he lived on credit," said Kean. "He even tried to borrow from *me*."

"Poor naive lamb," murmured Mrs. West.

"Then why would Mrs. Seymore come to him for money?"

"Perhaps it was the other way around," suggested Mrs. West. "Perhaps he was asking her for money?"

Harkness shook his head but did not elaborate. "Is there anything else you can say about that night? We know that Mrs. Seymore was at the theater, not once but twice."

"Ah!" sighed Mr. Kean. "The divine Mrs. Seymore. Now there's a woman who was meant to be on the stage."

"No," said Mrs. West. "It would not suit her at all."

"Jealous, my dear?" asked Mr. Kean.

"Don't be ridiculous," said Mrs. West again. "But I've met the divine Margaretta. She's very good at flirting with her gentlemen friends, and she is a wonder with a sentimental ballad, but she's brittle. Her character was flawed in the firing somehow. I think she knows this, but she doesn't want anyone else to. That means she spends all her time trying to cover up something no one is looking for, and she gets very afraid when someone might just be examining her too closely."

"Did Cavendish love her?" Harkness asked. "Is it possible he had been hectoring her into leaving her husband for him?"

Mrs. West gave a small bark of laughter and at once pressed her hand against her mouth. "Oh, I do beg your pardon, Mr. Harkness, but that is simply unimaginable. Cavendish was not a predator, much less a tragic hero. He did not chase women nor fall begging at their feet. He was a serpent. He stood still and fascinated the pretty birds until they came to him."

"Did he fascinate you?"

As soon as the question was out of his mouth, Harkness expected Mrs. West to take offense. But she did not. "No. He never took up with his lead lady while the play was running. It was bad for the show, he said. But he did inform me that he fully intended to let me come to him as soon as our run was finished." She glanced owlishly at Adam. "Now you intend to ask if I agreed to it."

"No," said Harkness. He kept his attention on Mrs. West, because he had a feeling if he had a clear look at that grin Mr. Kean was leveling at him, he'd be tempted to wipe it off the man's face.

"I will tell you anyway," said Mrs. West mildly. "I did consider it, briefly. But I decided it was probably not worth the trouble."

"What would that trouble have been for you?"

"When a man lives as Cavendish lived, he is apt to leave some broken hearts and other such complications behind him. When choosing my particular friends, I prefer to select from among those less encumbered."

Do not stare, Adam, Harkness instructed himself. *That thoughtful look is not for you.* Except perhaps it was. It certainly was not for Mr. Kean, who was grinning again, damn his insolence.

"What of the criminal conversation suit?" Harkness asked. "Did that worry him at all?"

Kean and Mrs. West looked at each other, questioning. At the same time, they shook their heads.

"He never even mentioned it. Usually he did not mention them unless he found the gentleman particularly amusing or annoying."

"And there was no one else who came regularly to his dressing room? No one he owed a particularly large sum to? No woman with whom he was particularly entangled?"

They both denied this, then each mentioned a name for the other's consideration, only to have it promptly voted down.

Damn, thought Harkness. "Thank you. There is just one other thing. I am going to show you both something, and I need to ask if you recognize it."

He unwrapped the knife and held it up for them to inspect.

"'Is this a dagger which I see before me?'" murmured Kean.

"Not now, Edmund," said Mrs. West. "It is in very poor taste. To answer your question, Mr. Harkness, no, I have never seen that thing before in my life. Mr. Kean?"

But Mr. Kean just shook his head. "I'm sorry to say it, but no."

"Then it did not belong to Mr. Cavendish?"

Kean shrugged. "That I could not swear to. I do know he

didn't keep it about the dressing room. I would say, however, it doesn't look like his style."

"How so?"

Kean examined his fingertips, and quite possibly that portion of himself where some last bit of discretion lodged. Fortunately, from Harkness's point of view, the actor's hesitation was short-lived. "Cavendish came from nothing, Mr. Harkness. His mother whelped him in the ditches of darkest Yorkshire. His education was from the vicarage Sunday school, his talent one of those jokes that Nature likes to play on the world. Now, we were not intimates, but I'd drunk with him, and I saw him in a brawl once. My God, it was the closest I'd ever been to witnessing one man actually murder another. The other fellow crawled away a bloody mess, and there in the ruin stood Cavendish, without a mark on him." Kean clearly didn't know whether to be awed or appalled. "And that was just with his fists. If Cavendish was going to take a weapon to himself or anyone else, he'd get hold of a good butcher's knife or a straight razor. A lady's toy like this"—he gestured toward the blade—"it would only make him laugh."

CHAPTER 26

Charitable Errands

*No one was more rigorously disposed to maintain the
quarantine laws of fashionable life, and reject all contact
with infected persons.*

—Catherine Gore, *Pin Money*

After Rosalind had parted from Devon in the park, she walked
home, oblivious to the fading light and the lowering clouds. All
she could think of was Devon's invitation. No, his invitations,
and his frank admission that he was trying to move their orbits
closer together.

And yet what would he find when he did come to her orbit?
This mass of deceit that was the business of the Seymore family.

She did not know what to think about that. She did not know
what she wanted to think. She did know, however, that she must
see the matter through. There were innocent people caught in this
tangle. With the exception of Alice, she might not have sorted all
of them out yet, but they were there. She could not leave them
friendless. When she had spoken to Mrs. Kendricks about the
feeling that she might do some good, she meant it. For the first
time in her life, she felt she had some genuine power to change
lives for the better. Yes, Mr. Harkness would do his best, but Mr.
Harkness might be sent away at any moment on other business.

And if she admitted it to herself, she was a little angry.

People were lying to her. People were attempting to use and deceive her. The idea of walking away and letting those persons believe they had gotten away with it rankled her. That might be selfish, and petty, but it was nonetheless true.

What was also true was that Rosalind knew she could not make a decision about Devon and the life he offered if she believed she had gone to him because she could not manage the life she made for herself. She must finish this thing and be free to go to him, or to stay as she was. She could not give herself reason to believe that she had turned to Devon out of failure.

Thankfully, that morning when the early post arrived, there was a letter in it from Virginia.

Dear Miss Thorne,

I have good news. I have secured you an invitation to the dowager marchioness. She is not at home in the usual way, but she is expecting you at one o'clock.

Mrs. Cecil Seymore

Rosalind allowed herself the luxury of sleeping late, eating a good breakfast, and attending to her home, her accounts, and the correspondence. Of course, it was not entirely an ordinary morning. Ordinary mornings did not begin with a knock on the door from a Bow Street patrolman.

"Ned Barstow, Miss Thorne." The man touched the brim of his hat in salute. "Sent on express orders from Mr. Harkness. I'm to keep an eye on the door for you . . . an' here they come."

A trio of men in stovepipe trousers, coats and waistcoats hanging open, and ungloved hands did indeed come hustling down the street, waving hands and pencils at the house numbers.

The newspapers had arrived. Ned Barstow stationed himself squarely on the first step of Rosalind's stoop, and pushed back his own coat to display the scarlet waistcoat marking him as a "Robin Redbreast" patrolman of Bow Street.

"Morning, Tom, morning, Lewis," Ned said amiably. "Come to see the sights, have you? Theater's that way." He pointed, with his truncheon.

I will have to write a thank-you note to Mr. Harkness, thought Rosalind as she retired indoors. She also sent for Mrs. Kendricks to make up an extra cup of coffee and a sandwich for Mr. Barstow.

Thus guarded, Rosalind had a peaceable morning, but she found herself glancing at the door, looking for Alice, or Mr. Harkness. When neither of them arrived, she found herself frowning, and wondering if something might possibly have gone wrong.

You're becoming morbid, Rosalind, she told herself. *If there was bad news, you would have heard it already. Nothing travels faster, except maybe gossip.*

Holding firmly to this sensible thought, Rosalind changed into her best and most respectable gray walking costume. She gathered her letters and lists and unearthed an old subscription book from the few weeks when she really had helped Mrs. Lindsay take contributions for her various charities.

Her first stop, however, was Mr. Clements's library.

"Ah! Good morning, Miss Thorne! You are returned already?" cried Mr. Clements as she entered. He also glanced from side to side, the better to ascertain, Rosalind thought, whether the reading room of his library remained empty. "I hope you were not too disappointed in the work of Mrs. Seymore?"

Rosalind found herself peering closely at the little man's face to make sure there was no hidden *entendre* in his remark. If there was, however, it was hidden very well indeed.

"I could not say, yet, Mr. Clements," she replied. "I find I need more time to judge."

"Then how is it I may help you today?"

"I am in need of a particular favor, Mr. Clements. I believe you have mentioned that you sometimes acquire books and manuscripts for scholars of antiquities."

The librarian laid his hand on his breast. "I have the honor."

"I have some letters in my possession. I need to know if they were all written by the same hand. Is there anyone you know who might be able to tell me? I know it is frequently done in novels and plays, but I need more than a rough guess. I need an expert's word."

Mr. Clements cocked his head toward her. For a moment she thought he was going to refuse her, but he just gave a small smile. "I think I know the person. You may have to travel a little, just past the edge of Westminster. The scholar I have in mind is elderly, but is an acknowledged expert on the study of modern manuscripts. She—"

"She?" said Rosalind.

"She," Mr. Clements replied, nodding. "Miss Elizabeth Onslow is her name. She is particularly noted for her authentication of modern manuscripts and her exposure of several prominent fakes. You have perhaps heard of the Orlando deception? She was instrumental in its disruption."

Rosalind hesitated. The inquest was tomorrow. There would be no time to make the journey before then. "I admit I was hoping to find someone closer."

Mr. Clements shook his head firmly. "If you require a match made of different handwritings, Miss Onslow is the person you

need. And you will, I think, like her. Truth be told, I have several times thought I should find a way to introduce you to each
other. You are both, in your way, unique, and I feel you would
understand each other very well. I can write immediately if you
wish, and lay your question before her."

It was a risk, but being wrong about the authorship of the
accusatory letter would have ruinous consequences. The delay
also might have an advantage in that it would open a window
during which more of the letters might be discovered.

"Please do write Miss Onslow, Mr. Clements. It is a matter
of some urgency, so I hope we may hear from her soon."

"I will make sure she understands this." He bowed, then he
paused. "It is a very sad thing about Mr. Cavendish, is it not?"

"Very sad," Rosalind agreed.

"I should be very glad to know the one who killed so fine a
talent was brought before the authorities. I personally would be
glad to assist in such a matter, if the opportunity arose."

"I wish you good day, Mr. Clements," said Rosalind.

"And a very good day to you, Miss Thorne," he replied.

Rosalind's decision to try to meet Lady Weyland had less to do
with gathering information regarding the Seymores and more to
do with ascertaining how the Weylands felt about their beleaguered cousins. Lord Adolphus had come as a surprise to Rosalind. He seemed firm, quiet, and competent. He was also a
welcome guest in a household that openly resented his brother,
the marquis. It was possible the murder of Fletcher Cavendish
had nothing to do with the tortured line to the Weyland title. It
was equally possible the two events were intimately connected.
But to judge, Rosalind needed to fully understand both sides of

the family. She had met the Seymores. It was time she met the Weylands as well.

The Weylands, according to Virginia's letter, resided in the venerable Holbrook Square. The house itself was broad and white and well cared for. The youthful footman who let Rosalind in wore gold-braided livery and a curled and powdered wig. A maid in sober gray who spoke with a soft Russian accent took Rosalind's card in to her ladyship and then returned to say Rosalind was expected. She helped Rosalind off with her coat and led the way down a carpeted passageway to a private office.

"Miss Thorne." Lady Weyland did not rise when Rosalind entered her room. "How do you do?"

"I am well, thank you, Lady Weyland. It was very good of you to agree to see me."

Rosalind's first impression of the dowager Lady Weyland was that she was very young. In part, that was because she was petite and slender, and her hair beneath her matron's cap was still quite fair and fine. Her black gown set off her pale skin, and her wide brown eyes seemed fixed in an expression of perpetual astonishment. It was only the lines around her eyes and the creping beneath her chin that gave away her age.

"Do please come in and sit down." Lady Weyland waved Rosalind toward a tapestry-backed chair. "I confess, I see very few visitors these days. My health is not what it was, and of course, my time is very bound up in caring for my son. But Virginia wrote in such glowing terms about your charity, I felt I had to make the effort. Tell me, how was Virginia when you saw her?"

"She was well, although, you may understand, the whole house is a little distressed at the moment."

"Ah, yes. I confess I was wondering if you would mention

that so unpleasant business. But then," she said, "that is what brought you here, is it not?"

Rosalind dipped her gaze, and did her best to raise a blush. "I confess that it is. I am sorry to have tested your hospitality in this way."

"I think you have more nerve than I should, entering the house of an enemy."

Rosalind managed to keep the expression of her astonishment to a slight lift of her eyebrows. "I had no notion that you were my enemy, Lady Weyland."

"I feel that perhaps I should be, as you are a friend to Mrs. Seymore and *that* branch of the family."

So. Despite Lord Adolphus's amiability, the ill-feeling was not entirely on the side of the Seymores. That was very much worth noting, as was the fact the dowager felt no need to hide it.

"I understand there is some bad feeling," said Rosalind. "And I am very sorry for it, but it is not my purpose to increase the difficulty."

"I'm sure it is not, but perhaps I may be forgiven if I press you to indulge in at least a little gossip. As I told you, I do not get out beyond my own circle much. What are people saying about . . . about Mrs. Seymore? Do they make much connection between her name and Fletcher Cavendish?"

"There is some low and idle speculation. I do not pay it any attention."

"Then you do not believe it?" Lady Weyland asked.

"No. I do not."

There passed across that tender and doll-like face a look of supreme calculation, and Rosalind had the sudden realization that, for once, she might have been completely mistaken in the character of the woman in front of her. For all her youthful countenance, Lady Weyland was not at all a simple soul.

"You are speaking the truth," Lady Weyland murmured. "That is interesting. Lady Bertram may have been right to worry about you."

"Lady Bertram spoke to you about me?" asked Rosalind, surprised.

"She wrote"—Lady Weyland waved her handkerchief toward the desk—"to warn me that you might make an appearance, that you were Margaretta's creature, and that I should refuse to admit you." She smiled sadly. "Johanna believes that if she demonstrates sufficient worry and care for my delicate person, I will strive to influence my son in her favor."

"Lady Bertram has some ambition."

"Lady Bertram should learn to take matters into her own hands rather than waiting for others to die," snapped Lady Weyland. Rosalind knew she should drop her gaze to her hands again, which was the universal parlor signal for polite discomfort with an indecorous statement.

She did not. "That is a difficult lesson for some women to learn. We are taught, are we not, that it is for others to act for us? But not all of us have had that luxury," Rosalind said.

"You have some understanding, Miss Thorne. No. It has always been my burden to act for my son, the marquis. I shoulder that weight willingly, although it has meant that I must retire from the society I used to so delight in." Lady Weyland sighed. "But we make these sacrifices and we make them freely, otherwise what are we for?" She waved her kerchief again.

Rosalind's brow wanted to furrow. Something stirred in her memory as she watched Lady Weyland, but Rosalind could not put her finger on what it was. There was something familiar in her elegant movements and in the ring to her voice. One thing Rosalind was certain of, however, was that Lady Weyland wore her fragility as a mask. The dowager marchioness knew people mistook her, and she used it.

"But I do not mind so much," Lady Weyland was saying. "These modern gatherings—with their crushing crowds and waltzes and *gallopes*—they are nothing like those we knew in the old days. They are giddy but not daring. There is no adventure, no heart to them . . ." She smiled fondly at her own memories. "But you are a daughter of the modern age. Perhaps I shock you?"

"Not at all, Lady Weyland," said Rosalind. "It is something I would have liked to have seen." Which was not true, but this time Lady Weyland did not seem to notice. That look of calculation flickered across her features again.

"Will you come meet my son, Miss Thorne?" She stood, her stiff black skirts rustling. "He says he is very dull this morning, and I know he would welcome some fresh conversation."

"I would be very glad to," Rosalind said at once. She hoped that her relief did not show. Sir and Lady Bertram's fortunes rested entirely on the marquis's health and attitude toward them. If Rosalind could meet him face-to-face, it would be of great assistance to her inquiries, and her understanding of these unhappy families.

Lady Weyland led Rosalind down a long, graceful gallery hung with all manner of paintings in the Dutch and Italian styles. Some were portraits, but many were landscapes or classical scenes. Rosalind kept her eyes on her hostess as she moved, trying as hard as she might to discern what point made the woman seem so familiar.

When they reached the door at the end of the gallery, Lady Weyland knocked softly. "Darius? Darius, my dear, I've brought a visitor."

"Come in," answered a wavering voice.

Lady Weyland opened the door softly, as if she was afraid to let out too much air, or perhaps let in too much light.

The curtains had been tightly drawn so the room was shrouded in twilight. Despite the warmth of the day, a huge fire blazed in the marble hearth. Rosalind remembered what Lord Adolphus had said about his brother's love of antiquities, and the room bore him out. The walls were lined with cabinets, and in each cabinet stood collections of precious objects. In one stood dozens of china figurines; in another they were bronze or copper. In yet another were painted miniatures, and in another, an array of knives and short swords that ranged from the crude to the breathtakingly elegant.

In the midst of this grand collection, a thin young man lay on a *chaise longue*. The skin of his face was drawn tight across his bones. His eyes were huge and clear and his mouth was very red in his pale face. The whole effect was so striking, Rosalind felt like she were looking on an elf knight from an ancient ballad rather than a flesh-and-blood man. A round table with a shapely alabaster vessel had been set before him, where his eyes might easily take in the sight of it.

"Who is this, Mother?" he asked. His high, light voice held a ragged edge. It was that edge that reminded Rosalind that the marquis's illness was real. The rest of this place was so dramatic, she had for an unworthy moment wondered if the invalid was exaggerating his malady for effect.

"Darius, this is Miss Rosalind Thorne. Miss Thorne, my son, Darius, Lord Weyland."

Rosalind made her curtsy and the marquis nodded in reply. "Pray excuse me for failing to rise, Miss Thorne. I am not having one of my better days." He waved toward the chairs situated on either side of the round table. "Will you sit and stay awhile? I so seldom see anyone beyond my family."

"Thank you, Your Grace." Rosalind took the chair indicated.

Lord Weyland shifted uneasily. "I'm sorry, Mother . . . the pillow . . ."

"Oh, yes, of course dear." She ran to the couch and adjusted the awkward cushion. "Is that better? Do you need anything else? I can send the girl for a cool cloth . . ."

"No, no, there's nothing. Except a little wine and water, and surely we should send for some tea for Miss Thorne . . ."

"Please, do not trouble yourself," Rosalind said.

"Oh no, it's no trouble at all," the dowager replied. "I should have thought of it at once."

Darius smiled weakly as his mother darted for the bell to summon the maid and relay his requirements.

"I am quite spoiled, Miss Thorne," he rasped. "It is true there is no love like a mother's love."

"You are fortunate," murmured Rosalind politely as she watched Lady Weyland direct the maid to move a chair closer to her son so that she could sit by his head.

"I am." Lord Weyland raised his huge eyes to the dowager marchioness and gave her a fond smile. "Now, tell me, what do you think of this amphora? It is my latest acquisition."

The alabaster vase in question was tall with a long, slender neck and two curved handles. Rosalind's boarding school education had included some study of ancient history, and she thought this to be a reasonable specimen of Grecian work, but she simply smiled. "I am not an expert in antiquities," she said truthfully. "Perhaps you could tell me about it?"

As she expected he would, the marquis launched into a minute and energetic description of the amphora. He detailed its provenance and its rarity and exquisite perfection. The tea was brought, but this created only a brief pause in his monologue. He described exhausting himself in the letters he had to send, in the men he interviewed, the bidding he endured, despite his weakness, to bring it "safe home to me."

"My health does not permit me much excitement, Miss Thorne," he said. "What energy I have, I spend in the acquisition and admiration of beauty." He reached out and caressed the side of the amphora. But his hand soon fell away. "I'm sorry," he said. "I find I am suddenly quite exhausted. But . . ." He turned his huge eyes on her. He raised a single finger to trace a line in the air between them, and Rosalind found it necessary to suppress a shudder. "I think I would be glad to see you again, Miss Thorne."

"That is very kind of you, Lord Weyland." Rosalind stood and curtsied and tried not to hurry as she followed Lady Weyland out the door.

"Well, Miss Thorne," said Lady Weyland as they traversed the gallery to the stairs. "How lovely. I have seldom seen Darius take so immediately to a new face. But then, my son has an eye for the unique and the precious." She smiled, and again, that surge of familiarity struck Rosalind. She was almost glad for it, because it covered over the other, far less pleasant sensations left by her conversation with the marquis.

Lady Weyland cocked her head toward Rosalind. "A word of advice, if you will hear it, Miss Thorne? Do not have *too* much to do with the Seymores. My sister, rest her soul, did not marry judiciously, and her folly has left its predictable stain on the character of her sons. My Adolphus cares for them because he sees it as his Christian duty, but . . ." Lady Weyland shook her head sadly. "Blood will tell, Miss Thorne. Blood will tell."

"I hear you, Lady Weyland," replied Rosalind. "And you may be sure I will think over all you have said, most carefully."

"I know that you will." The dowager smiled easily. "And I look forward to seeing you again."

Rosalind reclaimed her bonnet and her coat. She spoke by rote, delivering up the expected pleasantries, commonplaces, and thanks. She could not concentrate; she could not think of anything except the sudden lightning bolt of understanding. She knew why Lady Weyland looked so familiar.

In her smile, in her movements and the way she carried herself, Lady Weyland reminded Rosalind exactly of Margaretta.

CHAPTER 27

The Implications of the Past

The public . . . welcomed the tale which represented him as governed by deadly malice growing out of the more impassioned and noble rivalry for the favor of a woman.
—Thomas De Quincey,
On Murder Considered as One of the Fine Arts

Rosalind did not want to go home after her encounter with the marchioness. The atmosphere of Weyland House clung to her like a miasma, and somehow, she did not want to bring it into her personal environs.

There is no time for such ridiculousness, she told herself firmly. *You have only a few hours before you must dress for dinner, and if nothing else, you must write Alice, and tell her . . .*

But what will I tell her? What did I actually see? Rosalind frowned at the swinging curtains that covered over the cab's windows, trying to decide exactly what of the dowager had reminded her of Margaretta, and what she truly thought it meant.

Blood will tell. Lady Weyland's voice rang in her ears.

Do I believe this is a matter of blood?

Oh, Alice, you need to find that church.

But when Rosalind arrived in Little Russell Street, she saw at once she was not going to have the luxury of attending to her correspondence, at least for a little while, because Mr. Harkness was standing in her parlor.

"Mrs. Kendricks tried her best to turn me away," he confessed as she entered. "So you can't blame her for this."

"I'm sure it is not in any way her fault," answered Rosalind, a little testily. Of course, Mr. Harkness noticed.

"Is something wrong?"

Rosalind thought of the marquis's eyes, measuring her exactly as he had measured the alabaster vase. "Nothing new," she said and gestured Adam to a chair. If she was not prepared to disclose her new suspicions to Alice, she was certainly not going to hold them up to Mr. Harkness for scrutiny. "What can I do for you?"

"I came, Miss Thorne," began Mr. Harkness but he stopped. "I came, I think, to warn you."

"Of what?"

"I've just completed an interview with a pair of actors from Theatre Royal. What they said will come out at the inquest tomorrow and . . ." He stopped again. Rosalind felt her spirits, already depressed, begin to sink further. It was most unlike Mr. Harkness to be unable to finish his sentences. "It begins to look like Mrs. Seymore did indeed kill Mr. Cavendish."

Rosalind felt her eyes try to start out of her head. "What could make you say that?" she croaked.

"Because it's the simplest answer, and most of the time, Miss Thorne, the simplest answer is the truest. Mrs. Seymore wanted to be rid of a husband who had grown intolerable. She wanted to be rid of a lover who had become a burden, and a danger to the future of the child she carried. If she kills the one and hangs the other, her problems are at an end."

"No. Her problems are just beginning."

"How so?"

"She will become a scandal. She will not be able to earn a living, and the rumors of what she has done will haunt her all her days."

"All her days in London, Miss Thorne. All she needs to do once the men are taken care of, is leave."

Rosalind paused.

"She could go to Paris, or the Continent. Italy. America. She is a clever woman, and she is used to making her own way. If she can write, she can hope to earn a living just about anywhere."

"Change her name, live quietly, leave the title and the disaster that is the Weyland marquisate to Sir and Lady Bertram and wish them the joy of it," Rosalind mused aloud. "Then why not just leave? Why risk not just one murder, but two?"

"Because the captain, or Cavendish, might have followed," he said.

Rosalind turned her face away. She was very tempted to ask him to leave now, but that was simple cowardice. She could not run from what he said, or from its implications.

"Can you tell me what these actors said that has set your sights so clearly on Mrs. Seymore?" she asked.

He did tell her. He laid it out in a simple straight line, organizing the dramatic words of Mr. Kean and Mrs. West, and Rosalind listened.

And Rosalind frowned. "Is this the way it went?" she interrupted. "Mrs. Seymore goes to beg Cavendish, not to stop him from killing himself but to ask for money. Cavendish has no money, but promises to get her what she needs."

"Yes." Mr. Harkness nodded. "And she returns later that night to collect it and kills him, either in a fit of rage because he does not have the money, or because that was her plan all along. Then she changes into Mr. Kean's clothing and—"

"No," Rosalind interrupted him. "She doesn't. She couldn't have."

"Why not?" demanded Mr. Harkness.

"I saw her dress, you will remember. There were stains about the hem, but nowhere else. If she had taken the time to change to men's clothes to get out of the theater, assuming she could undress without the help of a maid, why would she get back into the ruined dress?"

"To complete the disguise," Harkness answered. "It was part of her plan to get you on her side."

"But the servants would have noticed such a change, even that little girl who lives in . . ." *Who had showed up at the door half asleep and unable to think even to light a lamp or a fire . . .*

Mr. Harkness nodded. "Did the servants say anything about finding men's clothing? Or about her changing?"

"I have not asked about it," admitted Rosalind.

"Then there is the matter of this accusatory letter," said Harkness. "The one she said she showed you when she came to engage your help, and Alice's. Have you actually been able to find any others?" said Mr. Harkness.

Rosalind opened her mouth. She closed it again. She was tired, she was disturbed, and not one thing Mr. Harkness had said was helping clear her mind. "I have not had the opportunity to make a thorough search."

"You must face the fact that Mrs. Seymore may have fooled you as well, Miss Thorne. She is very good at it."

"This is not about my pride, Mr. Harkness," said Rosalind tartly. "There are still other avenues of inquiry. Alice is helping look into Mrs. Seymore's background . . ." As soon as she said it, she realized she had made a mistake. Harkness leaned forward, just a little.

"Why Mrs. Seymore's background, Miss Thorne?"

She looked at him, but she saw the dowager, and Lord

Weyland. "Because there might be some fresh thread leading from the past."

He nodded, and dropped his gaze to the carpet. Rosalind felt her shoulders tense. Whatever he was going to say next, she knew she did not want to hear it.

"I need to ask you a question, Miss Thorne. I do not want to, but it has become necessary."

Because I am defending the woman you believe to be guilty. Because we both know her to be a liar, and you need to know if I am involving myself deliberately in those lies. Rosalind understood all this, and she did not blame him for any of it, but at the same time, her heart and her hands trembled, just a little.

"You know you may ask me anything," she said, but it took more effort than it should.

"The night Fletcher Cavendish died, I saw you run from the theater."

"Yes." Her voice would not rise above a whisper. "I did."

"Why?"

"You may believe me when I say, Mr. Harkness, that it had nothing to do with this."

"I want to believe you, but I also need an answer." He held up his hand. "And please, do not ask if I trust you. You know that I do."

"I do. I . . . It is not something I can tell you."

"Is it something to do with Mrs. Seymore?"

"No."

"Then Lord Casselmain?"

"No!" she cried. "It is entirely personal."

"Miss Thorne . . ." said Mr. Harkness quietly. "You must see that with this new evidence, Mrs. Seymore's tale of suicide may not hold with a jury. The matter may well go to trial. When it becomes known you were assisting Mrs. Seymore, your movements will be scrutinized, especially since you dined with Cavendish that evening. I may be forced to say that I saw you. Please," he said softly. "Let me help you. Tell me what I saw."

Rosalind bowed her head. She should have known this could not remain secret. Not now. *I walked into this*, she thought bitterly. *I had the chance to say no, and I did not.*

"I have a sister, Mr. Harkness," she said. "I have not seen her since I was seventeen when she left home with my father."

"I'm sorry."

"Thank you. Recently, I thought I had seen her, when I was looking into a matter that took me to, well, a club in St. James. That night at the theater, I thought I saw her again. I ran after her, but I lost her."

She waited for him to look away. She waited for him to ask the next questions, the ones that would force her to admit that she suspected her sister was on her own in London and surviving by her wits and her looks.

But he did not. "Thank you for your honesty," he told her instead. "I am sorry I had to do this."

She shook her head. "There's no part of this that's been easy."

"No," Mr. Harkness agreed. He also got to his feet. "I can tell you wish me gone, Miss Thorne." He bowed. "Thank you for everything you have told me. I'll show myself out."

He turned and he walked toward the door.

Will I be a coward? Rosalind thought to herself. *No. I will not.*

"She may have already fled her past once before."

"I'm sorry?" Mr. Harkness stopped with his hand on the door.

"Margaretta," said Rosalind. "Mrs. Seymore. She does not talk about her past. She tells people she is an orphan and that she had a small inheritance that paid for her education."

He quirked an eyebrow toward her. "From your tone, I take it you have your doubts?"

Rosalind gave a small laugh. "Mr. Harkness, I have been to boarding school. How on earth does an anonymous orphaned girl from such an enclosure manage to become intimate friends with a man like Fletcher Cavendish?"

CHAPTER 28

A Small, Private Supper

A female servant should never make friendships with or take the advice of milk people, butchers' or bakers' servants, &c. for mostly they seek their own interest and profit in everything.

—Samuel and Sarah Adams, *The Complete Servant*

"Mrs. Broadhurst! I am so glad to see you!"

Mrs. Oldman was a comfortable-looking matron who bustled forward to meet Admiral and Mrs. Broadhurst the moment they entered her airy front hall. "And this is Miss Thorne, about whom I have heard so much?" Mrs. Oldman curtsied and then, unexpectedly, threaded her arm cozily through Rosalind's. "I must claim her at once, because another of my guests has been asking about her."

Rosalind smiled at Admiral and Mrs. Broadhurst, who of course released her, and let herself be pulled gently along with their hostess.

The Oldman home was new and graceful. Not grand perhaps, but the rooms were well proportioned. One of the customs attached to the English dinner party decreed that guests should gather a half hour before the dinner, and Rosalind had been in many sitting rooms that were either so crammed with people that conversation became impossible, or were so empty as to lend a depressive hush and echo to the atmosphere. There was no such problem here. The guests circulated freely and Mrs. Oldman had no trouble steering Rosalind toward a familiar figure standing by the windows.

Lord Adolphus bowed as Rosalind approached. "Good evening, Miss Thorne. How very good to see you again."

Lord Adolphus was immaculately dressed in the black coat and white breeches mandated by a formal dinner. He wore the fussy attire easily and comfortably. She found herself wondering how a man raised in such an environment as she had seen in Weyland House had managed to acquire the air of quiet distinction that Lord Adolphus seemed to carry with him.

"Lord Adolphus." Rosalind made her curtsy. "I am glad to see you. I had understood Sir and Lady Bertram were to be here as well?"

"Yes," he said distantly. "They were invited, but unfortunately, they had to excuse themselves."

Rosalind followed Lord Adolphus's gaze as it drifted casually about the room. Faces turned quickly away from them both, and the tenor of the conversation shifted. This signaled that the guests were talking about the Seymores, and the murder, and the inquest. They did not, however, want Lord Adolphus to hear them doing so.

"Yes, of course," said Rosalind. "It is understandable, considering the circumstances."

"I am worried about tomorrow, Miss Thorne," Lord Adolphus murmured. "Not just because of the scandal. That's already breaking, but I'm worried for my cousins. All of them," he added, in acknowledgment of the question he saw in her eyes. "Is there nothing you can tell me? No way in which I can help?" His gaze swept the room again, looking, Rosalind thought, for anyone who might be listening just a little too closely. "I have a particular role in my family, Miss Thorne. I do what I can to keep my family name sound in the face of . . . many challenges. I have learned to be patient, to work quietly, and I hope, to work well. But my ability to do so depends on my knowing what is going on."

He works selflessly for his family, Lady Bertram had said, and now it seemed she was correct. Rosalind found herself more than a little surprised at this. There were very few saints in the world and she had never met one among the *haut ton.*

"I sympathize, Lord Adolphus," Rosalind told him. "I would help if I could, but the matter is a difficult one, and there are . . . contradictions." She thought again of Lady Weyland, of Mrs. Seymore, the marquis, and Sir Bertram. "There are also confidences I may not betray."

"I understand." Lord Adolphus inclined his head once. "Well. We will just all have to pray that the Almighty will see justice done here below. Now." He drew in a great breath. "I need to ask you a very great favor."

"What is it I can do, Lord Adolphus?"

He smiled, and somewhat to Rosalind's surprise, and the smallest bit of alarm, the mild man began to blush. "You can permit me to introduce you to someone very dear to me."

Rosalind hoped he did not see how she relaxed. "I would be delighted to meet any friend of yours, Lord Adolphus."

With a bow, Lord Adolphus led her to a corner of the room. There, standing quite on her own, a small crystal glass of sherry in her hand, was a tall, thin girl, her sharp face surmounted by a large, beaky nose.

"Miss Vaughn, may I introduce Miss Rosalind Thorne, who is a friend of my cousin, Mrs. Seymore. Miss Thorne, please allow me to present Miss Penelope Vaughn."

Miss Vaughn smiled, but much more at Lord Adolphus, Rosalind noticed, than at her.

"H-how d-do you do, M-miss Th-orne?" said Miss Vaughn as they made their curtsies.

"I am very well, thank you, Miss Vaughn."

"L-lord Adolphus p-promised to introduce you tonight. He s-s-s-says you are an avid reader of history."

Rosalind had thought the stammer was the bashfulness of a plain girl, but now it was clear it was a chronic condition and may have helped explain why she was standing alone. Persons who stuttered, especially women, were frequently considered to be mentally deficient. But a lively intelligence shone behind Miss Vaughn's eyes and Rosalind soon found herself settling into a conversation of both history and politics that caused the waiting hour to positively fly past. She could not help but notice, however, how frequently Miss Vaughn's gaze strayed restlessly about the room, until she saw where Lord Adolphus had gone, at which point she would smile and relax again.

"Have you known Lord Adolphus long?" Rosalind inquired.

Miss Vaughn blushed. "W-w-we met last year. A-a-at a book auction my father took me to. Th-they were bidding against one another, and Father went to congratulate him wh-when Lord Adolphus out-bid him." She smiled. "H-h-hardly romantic, I know."

"Any meeting that results in a friendship is a good one."

"Just s-so. Lord Adolphus b-began coming frequently to m-my father's house to talk with him about books and read in his library, a-and we b-b-became correspondents. It is easier for me." She made a small gesture toward her own mouth. "B-but we became friends as well."

The gong sounded for dinner and Mrs. Oldman began moving among her guests, directing the gentlemen to lead in the assorted ladies. Lord Adolphus came at once to stand by Miss Vaughn's side, and would not be moved. Rosalind could not help but notice how Miss Vaughn's eyes shone as his lordship held his arm out to her.

Well, Rosalind thought as she let herself be taken to dinner by Admiral Broadhurst, his wife being given over to Mr. Coombs. Another ritual of the dinner party was that, for reasons lost to antiquity, husbands and wives did not go in together.

Rosalind wondered if Lady Bertram knew about even the existence of Miss Vaughn, let alone the smiling warmth with which Lord Adolphus helped her to her chair before he took his own place. What would she think if she did? If Lord Weyland were as close to death as everyone believed, it was Lord Adolphus who would succeed him. If he married and produced a son, or two, or three, the title and all its privileges and appurtenances would slide entirely out of reach to Sir Bertram and his branch of the family.

Inside her mind, Rosalind frowned. Not only at the memory of Lord Weyland, pale and wan on his sofa, speaking with such elegant covetousness of his collection, but at the fact of Lord Adolphus and how he stood between his brother and Sir Bertram. While Lord Adolphus remained unmarried, Sir and Lady Bertram's attempt to keep the captain from having a legitimate son made some sort of sense. But if Lord Adolphus planned to make an offer to Miss Vaughn, or anyone else, such maneuvers seemed not only malicious, but laughable.

Once again, Rosalind thought that if Sir Bertram, or Lady Bertram, had been inclined to murder anyone, it ought to have been Lord Adolphus. Captain Seymore was the only member of the family who had reason to murder Cavendish.

What a strange and callous creature I am becoming, she thought ruefully as she helped herself to the white sauce for the fish that was placed in front of her. *To sit musing over who is most likely to consider killing some member of their own family.*

It might all still prove pure coincidence—the story of drama and possible suicide, the death of the actor, the pathetic chasing after the remote possibility of a title. Mr. Cavendish's death could have been over money, and the malice or disappointment confined to the house of Captain Seymore. But no matter which way she turned them, Rosalind's thoughts refused to settle quietly on this conclusion. Something was still missing in her understanding.

She thought again of Lady Weyland, and her resemblance to Mrs. Seymore, and how Mrs. Seymore claimed to be an orphan, and yet came so easily and quickly into the sphere of that family.

Rosalind wished she had Alice to talk to, or Mr. Harkness. But as it was, she ate her fish, and smiled at the conversation around her, and continued to wonder.

The dinner passed smoothly, as did that time afterward when the ladies retired to take tea together so the gentlemen could enjoy their port in masculine privacy. A few hints were put forward about the Cavendish murder and the inquest, but Mrs. Oldman squashed them with ruthless politeness. Miss Vaughn sat next to Rosalind and drank her tea, and smiled. The young woman was clearly used to saying as little as possible, and ignoring the pitying glances that were cast in her direction.

But as Rosalind passed her a fresh cup of tea from Mrs. Broadhurst, she saw a different look in Miss Vaughn's eyes. It was not quite anger, but it was a promise, and a cold one. Miss Vaughn looked out on this host of pitying ladies, and Rosalind knew she was thinking of Lord Adolphus and the day she would outrank the entire gathering. What, she imagined Miss Vaughn was thinking, would they do with their condescension then?

Rosalind drank her tea and wondered that as well.

The gentlemen rejoined the ladies to talk for a while of the season that was drawing to a close, of plans for retiring to country houses, the state of the roads, and the difficulties in packing up a household. Mrs. Oldman proposed that Miss Tully play for the gathering and that young lady leapt up at once. Somewhat to Rosalind's surprise, she proved to be very good, working her way through a Bach prelude with accuracy, if not inspiration.

Rosalind took advantage of the moment provided by the applause to get to her feet and walk to the window to stretch her legs just a little. A moment later, Lord Adolphus joined her.

"Well, Miss Thorne," he said. "How goes your acquaintance with Miss Vaughn?"

"I like her," said Rosalind at once. "She is a very intelligent and perceptive young lady."

"She is, very much so." Lord Adolphus smiled fondly at Miss Vaughn. She must have felt his regard, because she glanced in their direction and instantly blushed.

His lordship dropped his gaze. He also changed the subject. "There was something I wanted to bring up with you, Miss Thorne," he said. "I understand you went to visit my mother today?"

"Yes. I am helping a friend canvas for her charity, and Mrs. Seymore, Virginia, mentioned your mother was particularly interested in causes related to the relief of consumption patients."

"I see." Lord Adolphus touched the lapel on his coat. "And did Mother agree to assist?"

"I'm afraid I was unsuccessful in that regard."

"Well, Miss Thorne, some days my mother can be a little prickly. Perhaps I could be of assistance?"

"That is very generous of you, Lord Adolphus," she said. "But I would not care to impose . . ."

"It is no imposition. I believe very firmly in the importance of charitable works." He pulled a folded letter from his coat pocket and passed it to her. Rosalind took it in the hand that held her fan, so that the exchange might be shielded from the gathering.

"Miss Thorne," said Lord Adolphus softly but firmly. "I am aware you are my cousin Margaretta's friend. I see that you are also a woman of sense and discretion. You want to help her. I am glad she has help. But I ask you to understand this. My mother's care for my brother has taken a toll on her. She may sigh after the adventures of her youth, but she is no longer strong, or worldly. I must ask you to see that she is not disturbed any further with this business. If you have questions, you can ask me, and I promise I will do my best to answer."

Lord Adolphus walked away then to stand behind Miss Vaughn's chair and to smile at the music, and at that particular young woman.

Rosalind looked at the paper in her hand. Making sure her back was to the gathering, she unfolded it quickly. It was a bank draft, made out in her name.

It was for one hundred pounds.

CHAPTER 29

The Inquest Is Opened

When the coroner receives news of violent death . . . he is then to issue a precept or warrant to summon a jury to appear at a particular time and place, named, to inquire when, how, and by what means the deceased came by his death.

—John Impey of the Inner Temple,
The Practice of the Office of Coroner

"I hope you had a good breakfast," Alice said when she and George arrived at Rosalind's door. "It's going to be a very long day."

That had been four hours ago, and only now was the clerk of the court ringing his great bell and calling the inquest into the death of Fletcher Cavendish to order.

"Oyez! Oyez! Oyez!" the old man hollered over their heads. "You good men of this county summoned to appear on this day to inquire for our sovereign lord the king when, how, and by what means Fletcher Cavendish came to his death, answer to your names as you shall be called!"

The magistrate's court at Bow Street took up one end of a surprisingly plain room. Its unadorned blue-gray walls had been dimmed with ash and soot from all the usual sources. There was only one inadequate window for air, and so the chamber remained hot, close, and stale. The officials who took the statements and testimonies sat behind a broad table covered with papers, pens, candles, and ledger books. A short set of stairs led to the witness stand, which was little more than a raised landing fenced by a carved rail.

The court itself was bounded by an openwork iron fence. The rest of the room was used as a gallery where any who wanted to watch the proceedings could stand. Today, they jostled shoulder to shoulder. The clash and rumble of their voices had begun to feel like a ragged drumbeat against Rosalind's ears.

According to George and Alice, in a more ordinary case, the hearing would have been held at the public house across the street. Today, however, the crowd was expected to be so large, and so potentially unruly, it was decided to give over the magistrate's court to the inquest. That way there would be a better chance of keeping the proceedings from becoming a complete mob scene. Rosalind was glad. The partial mob scene around them was enough to make her unexpectedly grateful that she and Alice were to be called to give evidence. The status of witness earned them a place in the actual court, where there were benches, and some relief from the immediate press of the crowd.

Captain and Mrs. Seymore sat at the end of one of the benches, he in his blue coat with its gold braid, and his hat held on the knees of his white breeches. She wore a lace veil, and she was not the only one. Adam Harkness stood talking with another veiled woman, who sat with a horse-faced man Rosalind realized with a start was the actor Edmund Kean.

Adam saw her watching him, and he nodded to her, but did not approach. Rosalind looked away and tried not to think about how she had missed him yesterday. There was so much else to concentrate on, beginning and ending with Mrs. Seymore.

What was Margaretta going to say when she was called? Would she still be wielding the sword and shield of that suicide tale? It was beginning to make the rounds in the papers. Even Alice had been obliged to write something about it, although, Rosalind noted, A. E. Littlefield's comments were much more ambiguous than the lush and lurid speculations in a number of papers.

"I don't want to have to retract too much," Alice said. "In case Margaretta changes her mind."

"Have you had any luck finding out about her marriage?"

"None!" shouted Alice. "Do you have any idea how many St. Margaret's there are in London? At least four! There's Margaret's-by-the-Lane, by-the-Field, and by-the-Water, and that's not counting the three variations on St. Margaret and St. Mary's. You'd almost think she didn't *want* anyone to know where she'd actually got married." She glowered over at Margaretta. Something, Rosalind realized, was wrong.

"I was expecting you for dinner the other night," Rosalind said.

"Yes, I'm sorry about that."

"What happened?"

Alice's mouth tightened.

"Oh, tell her," said George. "You're going to have to anyway."

"I went to see Margaretta," said Alice. "We had a lovely little quarrel and I'm not sure I'm speaking to her again, even if she comes out of today unscathed."

"A quarrel? Why? Over what?"

"Over the fact that everybody knows she's lying!" shot back Alice. "Over the fact that it's a stupid lie and it's going to get somebody hanged!"

Heads were beginning to turn in her direction. George whistled and made a lowering gesture. For her part, Alice glowered at the staring men and women, until every last one of them looked away.

"Did Margaretta listen?" asked Rosalind as softly as she could and still be heard. She very much wanted to tell her friend about the resemblance she'd found between Lady Weyland and Mrs. Seymore, but now was not the time or the place.

"I don't know," said Alice. "That's why I don't know if I'm speaking to her again." But Rosalind heard her friend's voice break.

Because you don't know if you're going to get the chance. Oh, Alice.

The coroner's clerk worked his steady way through the business of calling up and swearing in each of the twelve men of the jury. Now, much to Rosalind's surprise, they seemed to be filing out of the court.

"What's going on?" she bawled at George.

"Going to see the body!" he shouted in answer. "I hear they've brought it down to the cells."

Rosalind tried not to shudder at the thought of the elegant Mr. Cavendish being carted about in such a manner, and failed.

"Courage, Rosalind!" Alice patted her arm. "Whatever Margaretta decides . . . Oh, look! Isn't that Lord Adolphus?"

"Where?" Rosalind craned her neck to try to see through the jostling crowd. Alice caught her shoulders and turned her toward the front left corner of the room.

Lord Adolphus had sensibly secured himself a place by the wall, which meant he was only squeezed on three sides. She couldn't see Sir Bertram or anyone else with him. It seemed once again, Lord Adolphus was acting as his family's representative. She found herself wondering if his lordship had instructed them to stay away.

"I need to speak with him!" Rosalind cried to Alice. "I'll be back directly!"

Alice looked at her as if she'd declared she needed to part the Red Sea. However, as no divine intervention seemed forthcoming to ease her passage, Rosalind resorted to the use of her elbows and the judicious application of the heel of her half boot on several sets of toes. By these indecorous but effective means, she managed to maneuver herself to stand in front of the younger of the Seymores' aristocratic cousins.

Lord Adolphus tried to bow, but there was not enough space.

"Miss Thorne!" he cried. "How may I be of service?"

"I came to return your property, Lord Adolphus." Rosalind pulled a sealed packet from her reticule. "I am unable to use it."

She'd sat up late with the bank draft lying on her desk in front of her. She'd written a half-dozen necessary letters, and several unnecessary ones, while she tried to decide what it meant and what to do. The conclusion she reached was the same one she'd held at the beginning.

Lord Adolphus, the bookish and considerate peacemaking brother of a dying marquis, had offered her a bribe.

"I do not ask for it," he said to her now.

"And yet here it is."

"Oh, take it, man!" bawled the stranger at his shoulder. "Got anything for me, sweetheart, eh?"

"Have a care, sir!" snapped Lord Adolphus. "This is a lady!"

"Oh, aye, and can't you just tell by looking?" sniggered another fellow.

"Your property, Lord Adolphus?" said Rosalind calmly.

Lord Adolphus stared at the packet, and slowly, reluctantly took it from her hand. Rosalind nodded, and turned and began to make her way back toward Alice and George, stepping a little more decidedly on some toes than others.

When she returned to her place on the bench, Rosalind saw that Mrs. Seymore was watching her. But Margaretta did not rise, or speak, or even gesture, except to rest her hand on her husband's arm.

The jury had reassembled in front of the benches set by the court's front wall for their use. The clerk was ringing his great bell once more. Both Alice and George pulled out their notebooks and began scribbling furiously. Alice, Rosalind noted, was applying her old drawing lessons and sketching the faces of the persons around them, and not always in a complimentary fashion.

"Oyez! Oyez! Oyez!" the clerk cried and a relative hush spread through the sweltering room. "If anyone can give evidence on behalf of our sovereign lord the king, when, how, and by what means Fletcher Cavendish came to his death, let them come forth and they shall be heard!" The clerk paused for a deep breath. "The court does call one Adam Harkness. Adam Harkness! Draw near and give your attention to this court!"

Because of the crowd, the process of drawing near took a little time, but eventually, Adam was able to mount the stairs to the witness stand. He was, Rosalind saw, formally arrayed for the occasion, wearing his red waistcoat and carrying his white staff of office. His badge was clearly visible on his coat.

She was staring at him, and it took her a moment to realize why. It was because Rosalind had never seen Mr. Harkness so at home. This jostling crowd, this stifling room where fates and secrets would be laid bare before the law was as comfortable to him as a quiet drawing room might be to her.

The clerk gave Adam a Bible, which he held up in his right hand.

"Do you swear that the evidence you shall give to this inquest, on behalf of our sovereign lord the king, touching the death of Fletcher Cavendish, shall be the truth, the whole truth, and nothing but the truth?"

"So help me God," said Adam, and he kissed the book.

The coroner at the table shuffled several of the papers in front of him. He wore an ordinary black coat and buff breeches. The grand accoutrements of robes, wigs, sashes, and high benches were reserved for those judges who presided over formal trials and convictions. Such as the trial that would come if it was decided that some specific person or persons had "committed murder against Fletcher Cavendish."

"Coroner's Sir David Royce," said George to Rosalind. "We call him Sir Dead Reckoning, because he's so good at finding his way around a corpse."

Sir David found his paper, and picked up a pencil. "You are Adam Harkness, principal officer of the Bow Street Police Office?" he asked Adam.

"I am," replied Mr. Harkness.

"How is it you were called in the matter of the death of Fletcher Cavendish?"

Mr. Harkness described how he met the constable outside the police office (omitting the fact that they collided violently). He told about entering the dressing room and finding Cavendish dead on the floor.

Sir David ticked off the points on his paper one by one.

"Mr. Harkness, were you able to ascertain the cause or nature of the death?" he asked.

"He was stabbed once through the heart with a knife, later identified by one Mr. Abraham Isaacs as a stiletto, probably antique and of Italian origins."

This caused considerable crying out and consternation on the part of the assembly, until the clerk had to ring his hand bell again to quiet them.

Adam continued on, unperturbed. He described how he questioned the night porter, the theater manager, and the manager of the King's Arms Hotel as well as Mr. Kean and Mrs. West, and from them he had both learned and confirmed the order of events that occurred that evening, including how Mr. Cavendish had dined in the presence of a Miss Alice Little-field and a Miss Rosalind Thorne and how those persons, each questioned separately, all told him that Captain Seymore had interrupted that meal, an interruption he had also confirmed with the hotel manager, two footmen, and the waiters who served the dinner.

Captain Seymore bowed his head while the crowd whispered and pointed. George made a note and elbowed Alice. She read it and shook her head and added a word of her own. Mrs. Seymore, sheltered by her veil, kept her face fixed straight ahead.

"What is the significance of this interruption, as regards this inquest, Mr. Harkness?" asked Sir David, ticking off three more points on his page.

"Captain Seymore had been seen earlier at the Theatre Royal, attempting to gain entry. At that time Captain Seymore was looking for his wife, Mrs. Seymore, whom he believed was engaged in illicit conduct with Mr. Cavendish."

The crowd gasped and the crowd shouted. The clerk clanged his bell, but was ignored for a very long time. The captain mopped at his forehead with his sleeve. Mrs. Seymore didn't move. Rosalind felt her fists clench.

"The court does call one Miss Rosalind Thorne. Miss Rosalind Thorne! Draw near and give your attention to this court!"

CHAPTER 30

You Shall Tell the Truth

*Upon view of the dead body [he] shall inquire of the
persons that hath done the death or murder; also of their
abettors, and consenters, and who were present when it
was done.*

—John Impey of the Inner Temple,
The Practice of the Office of Coroner

Rosalind stood. She focused carefully on each movement. The
entire room was looking at her. They must see a woman of
breeding and dignity. They would stare, they would talk, but she
would not give them extra food for their gossip.

She climbed the three steps to the witness stand. The heavy,
worn Bible was placed in her hand. She heard the oath, gave her
affirmative reply, and kissed the book.

When she lowered it, she looked across the court and saw
Adam standing by the door, perfectly calm and assured. He
nodded to her once, and Rosalind found herself able to breathe
that much more easily.

Sir David asked her to confirm her name, her address, and
the fact that she was an unmarried gentlewoman. She did so.

"Now, Miss Thorne," said Sir David. "How was it you came
to dine with Mr. Cavendish the night of his death?"

"Mr. Cavendish had sent myself and my friend a pair of tickets for the performance," she replied. "We were invited to dine together at his hotel afterwards."

Sir David looked at his list while the crowd whispered and sniggered. Rosalind made herself keep still, with her hands folded neatly before her. Adam was watching her. She would not give him reason to worry.

"What was the reason for this gift of tickets?" asked Sir David.

"I was fortunate enough to be able to assist a lady of Mr. Cavendish's acquaintance with some social matters," she answered. She had, somewhat to her shame, practiced several versions of this speech in front of her glass before settling on this one in particular. "Mr. Cavendish caused me to be presented with a pair of tickets by way of a thank-you."

The mutters rose up from the crowd, and the laughter and the sniggers. Rosalind's jaw clenched.

"Where did you dine?"

"It was in the parlor dining room of the King's Arms Hotel, as Miss Littlefield, my maid, Mr. Cavendish's valet, and the hotel manager can attest, if it should become necessary."

"I'm sure no one is suggesting any impropriety on your part, Miss Thorne," said Sir David with a long and meaningful look at the crowd. "Your manners bear you out. It is deeply unfortunate that a respectable woman such as yourself should become involved in such a matter."

Rosalind lifted her chin and made sure to keep her breath even. Another ragged laugh drifted through the court. Her gaze darted left, then right, and came to rest on Adam. He had not moved. He betrayed no hint at being perturbed by any stray sound or jest.

Showing me I have nothing to fear.

"Now, Miss Thorne, you will please say what happened during this dinner?"

"There was some conversation," she said. "Miss Littlefield, being a newspaperwoman, was interested in theatrical and social matters. Mr. Cavendish spoke pleasantly and impersonally. And then we were interrupted."

"Describe the interruption."

Rosalind felt her shoulders relax just a little. She was not to be asked for particulars of the conversation. Adam nodded minutely.

Rosalind described how the captain burst in. She told them how Seymore had tried to get Mr. Cavendish to admit to an infidelity with Mrs. Seymore, but that Cavendish would not. She told how the captain had retreated, and Mr. Cavendish had closed the door.

"Did Mr. Cavendish seem unduly upset or angered by this interruption?"

"He did not," she said. She wanted very badly to look at Mrs. Seymore to see how she received this statement, but she forced herself to keep her attention on Sir David.

"Did he say anything regarding the cause or merit of the accusation? This," he added to the jury, "is of importance, as you gentlemen may be asked to determine if the blow in question was dealt with malice and premeditation or in the heat of a moment's passion."

The men all nodded earnestly.

The commonplace sins of a commonplace life. Rosalind heard that sonorous voice again in her mind. *I wish I could have put on a better show for you, Miss Thorne.*

"Mr. Cavendish only remarked that he was used to such accusations and they meant little to him," said Rosalind. "He did not own the particular accusation in any fashion."

Sir David nodded, and he looked at his papers. He lifted up the one in front of him and moved it aside.

With that, Rosalind was excused. She felt strangely light-headed as she walked down the steps. The whole room had taken on a dreamlike quality and she seemed to be drifting through it.

"Sit down, sit down," said George quickly. "Breathe, Rosalind. You're going to faint."

"Of course I'm not," snapped Rosalind. But she did take several deep breaths, just in case.

Alice was called next, and she delivered her statement in short, rapping sentences and retreated, Rosalind thought, rather quickly. She also needed several deep breaths before she reclaimed her notebook from George.

"Honestly," she muttered as she began to write again.

Then, the court did call Stanislas Ulbrecht, who gave his profession as night porter at the Theatre Royal. Alice sketched the man, and drew a question mark over his head, which she showed to George, who nodded again. The night porter, with much scratching of his face and tugging at his ears, told about getting to his post in time for the evening's performance, and how Mr. Cavendish arrived shortly afterward.

He told how Captain Seymore had arrived sometime after that, and been turned away.

Sir David ticked off another of his points. "Now, Mr. Ulbrecht," he said. "With the clear understanding that no one is accusing you of negligence in your duties, is it possible that after this, Captain Seymore could have gone round to another entrance and gotten into the theater without you seeing him?"

Captain Seymore started to his feet, but his wife pulled him back down. She leaned close and whispered in his ear, and he subsided, but just a little.

Ulbrecht tugged his ear and scratched his corded throat. He shifted from foot to foot.

"Well, I've only one pair of eyes, haven't I?" he said at last.

George underlined his note. Alice added an exclamation point. Sir David made another mark, and moved on.

Ulbrecht swore that Mr. Cavendish left after the curtain had fallen, but that he returned. He further swore that Mrs. Seymore had arrived, but not until some hours later and had seemed much agitated at that time.

"You saw her?" pressed Sir David.

"I did that, sir," agreed Ulbrecht.

"With his one pair of eyes," murmured Alice.

"And aside from her agitation, you noticed nothing unusual about her person or demeanor?"

He had not. He had not known anything serious was wrong until Mrs. Seymore came down the stairs to find him to open Mr. Cavendish's dressing room door, which then revealed the dead man with the stiletto still in his chest.

Someone screamed. Someone fainted. The proceedings paused while the prostrate personage was taken away. George and Alice compared descriptions. Rosalind looked toward the corner where she'd spoken with Lord Adolphus, but Lord Adolphus was gone.

"The court does call one Captain William Seymore!" cried the clerk. "William Seymore! Draw near and give your attention to this court!"

A great chorus of hisses and booing erupted from the crowd. The clerk rang his bell to no effect at all. Captain Seymore, his face utterly impassive, climbed to the stand and set his hat on the railing.

"Quiet!" bellowed Sir David. "Quiet! Or I'll clear this room!"

The threat worked, eventually. Captain Seymore stood before

them all as he might on a ship's deck, his feet spread wide for balance and his hands behind him. His spotless uniform lent him a dignity beyond what Rosalind had seen in him yet. The captain was sworn in. He gave his name, his address, and his occupation, or rather, his former occupation as an officer in the King's Navy, now retired.

Mrs. Seymore turned her veiled face toward her husband. Her gray gloved hands were folded decorously in front of her.

What will you do? Before she dressed for the dinner party yesterday, Rosalind had written to Mrs. Seymore, detailing her visit with the dowager. The reply she'd received with the early post had been brief.

You must *find the one who did this.*

Sir David shuffled his papers again. He read the one in front of him, and laid his finger on a particular point.

"Did you, Captain William Seymore, go to the Theatre Royal on the night in question to try to see Fletcher Cavendish?"

"I might have," answered the captain shortly. He did not look at Sir David. He did not look at anybody. He kept his eyes fixed on the court's far wall, as if it were the horizon. "I don't remember."

"Why don't you remember?"

"Because I was the worse for drink."

The murmurs and the gasps and the barks of laughter rose. Alice and George wrote. The captain stood at attention and he waited for his questions. Rosalind wished she were anywhere but there. She wondered where Lord Adolphus had gone and what it meant.

"Then you don't remember breaking in on him at his dinner?" asked Sir David.

"No, sir, I do not."

"Because you were the worse for drink?"

"Yes, sir."

"Can you think of any reason you might have done these things? Aside, sir, from the fact you were the worse for drink?"

The court chuckled.

"I did at the time believe my wife . . . that Cavendish had seduced my wife."

Shock. Outrage. The rattle of laughter. Mrs. Seymore bowed her head. Because of the veil, Rosalind could see nothing of her expression.

Sir David considered the written page in front of him, and at last laid it aside.

"Captain Seymore, do you still believe Cavendish seduced your wife?"

The court held its breath. Rosalind found she was holding hers as well. Captain Seymore looked toward his wife. She raised her chin.

Admit your shame. Rosalind heard the captain's plea echo in her mind. *Own it.*

I will not lie, replied Mrs. Seymore. Except she would and she had, repeatedly. But the one lie her husband demanded was the one lie she would not and could not tell, because it would condemn not just her, but her child.

Or so she said.

"No, sir," said the captain. "I do not believe my wife deceived me with that man."

A murmur spread through the court, and a few chuckles, which were abruptly silenced. Alice's pencil stilled, but just for a moment.

"What has changed your mind?" asked the coroner.

"My own better judgment," the captain croaked. "My under-standing of my wife's honest nature and her loyalty to me. I want . . . I wish it to be known, I had decided not to go forward with the suit."

Sir David frowned. So did Rosalind. Did Sir Bertram know about this change of heart? she wondered. Did Lady Bertram?

Did Lord Adolphus, who still had not returned to the court?

"The captain's just paid for Margaretta's suicide story," murmured Alice. "He's figured out that if he accuses her in public, she could change her mind, and condemn him."

"Maybe," answered Rosalind. "Maybe." Because there remained Mrs. Seymore's determination to protect the child she carried. And there also remained the unknown question of what the other witnesses would say. What Rosalind did know was that what the captain said now was entirely at odds with what he'd said before.

"Thank you, Captain Seymore. You may step down," said Sir David.

"The court does call one Mrs. William Seymore!" cried the clerk. "Mrs. William Seymore!"

Amid the gasps and the murmurs, the jeers and the slurs, Mrs. Seymore moved with the grace of a queen. She mounted the stand without hesitation and lifted her veil. The sight of her pale and beautiful face elicited a fresh round of murmurs. She kissed the book with reverence.

Sir David laid a new sheaf of papers in front of him.

"Mrs. Seymore, I have here a sworn statement from you, signed in the presence of Mr. John Townsend of Bow Street, that Mr. Cavendish did in your hearing threaten to kill himself." He laid his finger on one point of the page. "Is this true?"

CHAPTER 31

Lies and Refutations

But it is only by circumstances that you will infer the criminal connection between the parties.
—The Trial of Birch vs. Neal for Criminal Conversation

Rosalind's fists clenched. Alice and George poised their pencils and together leaned forward.

On the stand, Mrs. Seymore dropped her gaze, delicate and decorous, and turned her face away.

"Yes," she breathed.

Again, the court erupted into tumult. There were wails of grief and wordless cries.

"Liar!" someone shouted. "Liar! You did this!"

"Throw that man out!" bellowed Sir David. Adam gestured over all their heads, and a pair of patrolmen waded into the crowd. Mrs. Seymore clutched at the rail, and swayed on her feet. Rosalind wondered if she planned to faint.

Eventually, however, the crowd calmed and Sir David was able to continue.

"Mrs. Seymore, in your statement, you affirm that it was because of this threat of suicide that you went to the theater not once but twice, and that your intention was to remonstrate with Mr. Cavendish."

"Yes," said Mrs. Seymore again. "He told me he was in love with me, and I went to beg him to break off all connection with me, because I did not love him. I loved my husband."

"Your statement further says he showed you the stiletto, which he then had in his possession."

"Yes."

"And you later recognized it as the weapon that killed him."

She gripped the railing with both hands. "Yes, sir," she breathed.

When the uproar occasioned by this latest assertion died away, Sir David picked up a page and read it, and laid it down again.

"Thank you, Mrs. Seymore," he said. "You will keep yourself ready. You may be recalled later."

"Well, well, well," murmured George. "She is sticking to her story after all. What do you suppose that means?"

"I have no idea," said Alice. "But I think Mrs. Seymore should be worried." She laid a hand on Rosalind's. "How are you doing?"

"I don't know." Rosalind watched the Seymores sit stiffly and uncertainly beside each other. "And I don't think Mrs. Seymore does either." Because how could a woman be doing when on the one hand she told a tale of suicide when with the other she was writing to Rosalind to find a murderer?

Next, Edmund Kean was called, to cheers and adoring sighs from the assembly. He mounted the stand to declaim with grand feeling and dignity of his friend (the great man!), and he had to swear that he did share a dressing room with Fletcher Cavendish, but at the hour of his death he had not been there. Upon hearing this, he dissolved into tears and was barely able to choke out that this was so before he had to be led away.

"Bravo," breathed George as he wrote.

Mrs. West, for her part, mounted the stairs to the dock like she was taking center stage. She drew back her veil to great applause. Unlike Mr. Kean, the actress shed no tears, but gave her statement calmly and clearly. The court hung on her words, rapt and silent, until she spoke of overhearing the argument coming from Mr. Cavendish's dressing room, and the word "money."

There was something happening at the front of the court. Mr. Townsend had stepped in from somewhere Rosalind did not see. Now he was leaning close to Sir David, and handing him a piece of paper. The two men read it together, and conferred in close whispers.

"This cannot mean any good," said George.

"Thank you, dear brother, that's most helpful," Alice muttered.

"Is your pencil still sharp, dear sister?" he answered. "I think somebody's in for it."

Sir David was nodding. Mr. Townsend patted his shoulder and stepped away, but did not leave. He stationed himself behind the coroner's chair, and folded his hands behind his back. Rosalind looked around for Mr. Harkness, but did not find him. Mrs. Seymore's face was turning, from Mrs. West in the stand, to Sir David, and back again.

Rosalind's fingers knotted in her skirt.

"Mrs. West," said Sir David. "You heard this argument through a closed door, did you not?"

"I did, sir."

"So you did not see with whom Mr. Cavendish spoke?"

"No, sir, I did not."

"Can you say on your oath whether it was a man's or a woman's voice you heard speaking with him at that particular time?"

Mrs. West paused. She frowned, and Rosalind bit her lip.

"I thought it was a woman, but I could not swear to it."

The excited jumble of voices rose again. This was new and entirely unexpected. Rosalind found her gaze riveted on the fresh piece of paper Sir David held in his hands, as if she thought she could discern its contents if she simply stared hard enough.

"So it might have been either a man or a woman?"

For the first time, Mrs. West's poise wavered. Rosalind looked at Mr. Townsend, who stood at the coroner's shoulder and watched, and smiled, just a little.

"I . . . yes, it might," said Mrs. West.

"Oh, good lord," breathed Alice. "Oh, no. This cannot be happening."

"What?" whispered Rosalind.

"They're getting set to hang the captain," said George. "Townsend is standing there to make sure the right questions are asked."

"No. It cannot be." The room was sweltering, but despite this, Rosalind felt herself go suddenly and completely cold. She looked frantically around for Mr. Harkness, but he had not reappeared. Neither had Lord Adolphus.

What does it mean?

Sir David gestured to the clerk and said something, which Rosalind could not hear. That man bowed his assent, and raised his voice once more.

"The court does call one Lord Adolphus Greaves. Lord Adolphus Greaves! Draw near and give your attention to this court!"

"Lord Adolphus!" Rosalind exclaimed. "What could Lord Adolphus have to say!"

"I don't know," replied Alice. "But I think Margaretta is wondering the same thing."

Although Mrs. Seymore had drawn her veil back over her

face, she had not regained her former composure. As Lord Adolphus climbed into the stand to be sworn in, Margaretta clutched at her husband's arm, but Rosalind could not tell whether it was to reassure herself, or to hold him in place. Mrs. Seymore leaned close to the captain. Was she whispering to him? What was she saying?

"Now, your lordship," said Sir David to this new and unanticipated witness. "I have here a statement that you were also at the Theatre Royal the night Fletcher Cavendish died."

Rosalind clapped her hand over her mouth. Lord Adolphus was at the theater? All the conversation they'd held, all the times he'd protested he wanted to help, and he'd said nothing of it.

"I was there, sir," Lord Adolphus was saying. "I arrived about the hour of one, after the performance, when I felt there was less chance of being seen or recognized."

"What was your purpose in going there?"

"I had something of a personal nature to communicate to Mr. Cavendish."

"And that was?"

Lord Adolphus hesitated. His shoulders under his well-tailored brown coat hunched in, and he folded his hands together on the rail in front of him, an attitude that made him look younger than he was.

"Captain Seymore is my cousin, sir," said his lordship at last. "I knew he was in want of money, but because he is proud, he would not accept a gift from me. I suspected that want was the true cause behind the criminal conversation suit he threatened against Mr. Cavendish. It had occurred to me I might be able to strike a bargain with Mr. Cavendish. I told him I would pay over the sum the captain had named as damages in his suit. All Cavendish would have to do was represent the money as his, and

say that he was paying it to end the suit before it came to court."
Lord Adolphus paused and lifted his clutched hands and lowered them again. "This would not save the Seymores from all unpleasantness, but it would at least keep Mrs. Seymore from being dragged before the public."

"So this bargain you proposed to Mr. Cavendish was for Mrs. Seymore's sake?" asked Sir David.

Somebody sniggered and somebody muttered. Sir David glared across the court. "For the whole of the family's sake," said Lord Adolphus. "My mother, Lady Weyland, is a reclusive woman, sir, and my brother, the marquis, is in poor health. The threat of scandal even at a remove is painful to them."

"And what was Mr. Cavendish's response to your proposal?"

"He refused me," said Lord Adolphus. He coughed and he cleared his throat. "He . . . laughed at me. I remonstrated with him, and he told me . . ." Lord Adolphus stopped. "He ordered me out of his rooms."

Sir David drummed his fingers against the table. "What, specifically, did he tell you?"

Alice leaned forward, so did George, pencils poised, eyes shining with suspense and anxiety. Rosalind looked at Mrs. Seymore. She was holding the captain's shoulder.

"I reminded him of my rank and station. He told me he would laugh in the face of any man who made himself ridiculous. He would laugh at me and he would laugh at Captain Seymore when he came, because he was such an absurd little man."

"Then," said Sir David slowly. "Lord Adolphus, it is your testimony that at the time you spoke with him, Mr. Cavendish was expecting Captain Seymore?"

"Yes, sir," said Lord Adolphus. "It is."

The captain shot at once to his feet. "You lie!" he bellowed. "You lie!"

Mrs. Seymore was on her feet, too, but whatever she said was lost in the commotion raised by the crowd. She clutched at the captain's coat, but he shook her off. "Liar!"

Rosalind pressed her hands against her mouth. It was not possible. It could not be happening. She was pushed and jostled and deafened and she sat as she was, her eyes wide and staring, as if at a new murder.

It was beautiful. It was in its way perfect. Nothing Lord Adolphus said directly contradicted what Margaretta said, so Margaretta could not be accused of lying, just in the way that nothing Margaretta said contradicted anything Rosalind had seen.

Around her the tumult continued. Alice lost her pencil. George had to take a swing at a man who tried to grope his sister's bottom as she bent over to try to retrieve it.

Somewhere in the midst of it, Sir David dismissed Lord Adolphus from the stand. He bellowed to the jury that they had heard the testimony and they were to consider the verdict. Mrs. Seymore stared at Sir David, or maybe it was at Mr. Townsend, because Mr. Townsend was still smiling slightly in satisfaction.

Mr. Harkness, where are you?

But Mr. Harkness did not reappear. The jury, clustered on their benches, murmured and gesticulated, and at last turned to face Sir David. One man stood up from among the twelve.

"Mr. Foreman," said Sir David. "How do you find Fletcher Cavendish came to his death and by what means?"

"No!" cried Mrs. Seymore. "This is not the way! This is not what happened! I *told* you . . ."

Mr. Townsend moved. He hurried from his place beside the coroner, to take her shoulders. He murmured something to her, but she tore herself away and clutched at her husband's coat.

The foreman looked on with something like pity in his eyes.

"We find Fletcher Cavendish murdered, by William Seymore, late of His Majesty's Navy."

The room erupted; screams of horror and outrage filled the air. Captain Seymore dropped back into his chair as if his strings had been cut. Mrs. Seymore sat down slowly beside her husband, her hand pressed over her mouth. Mr. Townsend touched her, and she jerked away.

Seymore stared down at his wife, and then threw back his head and roared with laughter.

"Oh, well done, Margaretta!" he boomed. "Very well done indeed!"

CHAPTER 32

While the World's in Mourning

Nothing is so satisfactory and gratifying to the public as a genuine protracted mystery.

—Percy Hetherington Fitzgerald,
Chronicles of the Bow Street Police-Office

The day of Fletcher Cavendish's funeral, London ground to a halt. Crowds of mourners blocked the streets before the watery sun rose over the rooftops. Landlords lucky enough to have rooms along the route of the procession reaped astounding profits from those who wished to have a view above the common crowd.

The church could not contain one tenth of the people who tried to gain a seat.

In the end, it was the Theatre Royal itself that took charge of the lavish arrangements required to take Fletcher Cavendish's mortal remains from the church to the graveyard. Dr. Arnold, conscious that this might be the most important spectacle he ever staged, did not stint on the cost, or neglect a single detail. The finest funeral furnishers in London were engaged. The coffin was teakwood and silver. The shining black hearse was decorated with bundles of white plumes and lilies. There was a feather man to lead the procession, and no fewer than eight mutes in black livery and powdered wigs. Flowers were show-ered from every direction, and it was only the skill of the driver that kept the plumed horses (all of them coal black) from shying away. Mounted constables rode alongside the hearse to deter women and girls, and not a few boys, from throwing themselves in its path. This was mostly effective.

Sampson Goutier later declared he would be deaf for a week from the crowd's wailing. Ned Barstow swore he'd seen an entire boarding school class worth of girls collapse in a dead faint.

Rosalind did not attend. There was no time. Mr. Harkness had made that very clear as they stood together in the Bow Street court room while the crowd around them drained away.

"Seymore will go before the magistrate either today or tomorrow," Adam had told Rosalind when she asked what would happen next. "He will be charged. Causing the violent death of another is a breach of the king's peace and so it doesn't require someone to make a specific complaint. If the Seymores do not already have an attorney, they should engage one. Judges may still say that no lawyer is needed and an innocent man should be able to explain himself simply and clearly, but . . ."

"But we all know that innocence is rarely so simply stated," Rosalind finished for him, and Adam nodded.

"The magistrate will then decide whether the captain is to be held for trial and if bail is to be allowed. Which I doubt it will under the circumstances."

"So he will be left in jail," said Rosalind. "For how long?"

"Three days, maybe four. Possibly as long as a week, but I wouldn't count on it. There is no set schedule of trials. When his case comes up will depend on the existing docket and on the attorneys. And I will warn you, since there is already a guilty verdict from the coroner, the trial, when it comes, will not take more than an hour or two at most."

"Will you . . . remain involved?" Rosalind asked.

"Not unless I'm called for. The deed is done, the suspect is in custody. It's for the courts to take things in hand now." He looked at her with his patient, penetrating eyes. "And you?"

"My charge has not changed," she told him. "Although I think the reasons for it may have."

For all her doubts about Margaretta and the reasons behind her conduct, Rosalind was certain of one thing. Captain Seymore had not killed Fletcher Cavendish. She did not like the captain. He was a drunk and a boor. She did not pretend even to begin to understand the nature of his marriage. But these were not crimes for which he should be hanged.

It was possible there was nothing Rosalind could do. Time was fast running out and powerful persons were determined to see the captain hang. But she had to try, if not for Margaretta's sake, then for her own, so that in days to come when she had cause to examine her conscience, this stain was not too dark.

"Mr. Harkness, why did you leave the court?" she asked softly.

Adam's face grew cold. "I was sent on an errand," he said, but as Rosalind looked in his eyes, she knew he meant something quite different. He meant: *I was gotten out of the way.* Because Adam Harkness might have objected to the questions, or to their abrupt ending. He might have had something to say that prevented the inquest from being tied up in a bow and saving Mr. Townsend from embarrassment.

"For what it is worth, Miss Thorne," said Adam quietly. "I do not think this attempt to obscure the truth around Cavendish's death began with Mr. Townsend, and I do not think it should end there."

Rosalind found herself very much in agreement with this.

Now Rosalind sat at her writing desk with a list of necessary letters, including the one she realized she must send to Lady Bertram. She dashed them off with haste, crossing the names on her list off as each missive was sanded and sealed. She had three days, according to Mr. Harkness, perhaps four. A week at the longest. It was not enough time. There was too much she didn't know.

She did know that, except for the captain, every person associated with the Seymores had lied to Bow Street and the coroners. Even Lord Adolphus had lied. Those lies had together buried one pathetic truth. The night Fletcher Cavendish died, Captain Seymore had been too drunk and too confused to have killed a strong and sober man.

She must find out who wrote those insinuating letters, and why. Surely, once she did that, she would have a thread she could follow to—to what exactly? Somewhere. Anywhere. As long as it led an innocent man away from the gallows.

Therefore, while the rest of the city donned its best mourning, Rosalind was out before dawn with Mrs. Kendricks following determinedly behind. They walked as far past the funeral route detailed by A. E. Littlefield as they could before finding a cab stand with an optimistic and miraculously sober driver to drive the rest of the way to the Seymores.

Even though Rosalind had left before full light, she still had to shoulder her way through the crowd that had gathered in front of the Seymores' house, and then give a letter to one of the four constables on guard there to take to Mrs. Seymore to see if she would be allowed inside.

This assumed that Mrs. Seymore was even home, or awake. The sun had barely touched the rooftops. The service at the church would be starting. Was Mrs. Seymore in attendance there?

No. The door opened and the little maid, Margie, leaned out and beckoned to her. Rosalind hurried inside and Margie slammed the door and locked it.

"The mistress is in her study. I'm sure you know the way?" Margie curtsied, and bolted. Clearly the day was proving far too much for her. Rosalind found she could easily sympathize. She turned to Mrs. Kendricks.

"I'll go see if I can be of use," the housekeeper said, and disappeared through the green baize door to the kitchen.

In Mrs. Seymore's study, the drapes were still drawn, and although the lamps were lit, the room still felt close and gloomy. Mrs. Seymore sat at her desk, as disheveled as Rosalind had ever seen her. She still wore her silk wrapper over a saque gown of undyed muslin. A single teacup was perched carelessly on a pile of books.

"You must forgive me, Miss Thorne," Margaretta said, waving Rosalind to a chair. "None of our servants has arrived yet. I suspect they are staying away deliberately. We've only Margie and Mrs. Nott, and Margie has been near hysterical all morning."

"It is going to be a difficult day," said Rosalind.

"It is. And I was not expecting visitors, at least, not any I'd be prepared to admit." Mrs. Seymore glanced toward the closed windows. "Mrs. Nott informs me there's already been some stones thrown. We are lucky the mob has a bad aim."

"I am very sorry, Mrs. Seymore."

"I was tempted to put on black." She adjusted her plain skirts. "I wasn't sure it would be appropriate, though. But what on earth is appropriate when one's supposed lover has been murdered, and one's husband is in jail for it? I don't suppose you've come with any news?" she added hopefully. "I've written the lawyers. As a wife, I cannot . . . I cannot engage an attorney to save my husband," she added in a whisper. "Ridiculous, is it not? But I do not have the authority. I must hope my brother-in-law will make some effort. Until then, I'm dependent on you."

Rosalind took a deep breath. "And I am dependent on you,

Mrs. Seymore," she said. "Have you searched for the accusing letters yet?"

Margaretta blinked at her, confused for a moment. Was it possible she'd been drinking?

"And people call me hard-hearted," Mrs. Seymore murmured. "My husband has gone to jail, Miss Thorne, after doing all he could to keep me and . . . our family safe. I have not had the strength nor the heart to go riffling through his things."

Her exhaustion was genuine. Rosalind could read it in every line of her face and her form. But Rosalind could not let her rest. "Mrs. Seymore, regardless of your husband's guilt or innocence in this matter, your friendship with Fletcher Cavendish and your husband's intent to file for criminal conversation are now public knowledge."

"William was going to withdraw the suit! He said so!" she cried. "He stood up and said so!"

"That doesn't matter and you well know it," replied Rosalind firmly. "He is going to his trial. The attorneys for the crown will be at their work. You must have those letters in your hands. Once they leave this house, they leave your control and we cannot in any way predict what use will be made of them, especially as we do not know what's in them."

And I do not know if these letters are real, or another lie made up to get me on your side.

"How could they leave this house?" asked Mrs. Seymore. "The doors are locked, Mrs. Nott is on the watch . . ."

"Attorneys, Mrs. Seymore, bribe servants. They do it to get evidence or speculation that they can make use of at the trial. Your servants will be offered money and drink and whatever else men can think of, and these men will be after souvenirs at best, evidence at worst."

The silence of the room seemed to press more closely against them. The servants were not there. They were in their own homes, or at the funeral procession, or in the public houses, where the loyal and watchful Mrs. Nott would never see them.

They might have already taken what they could with them. The temptations would be extraordinary.

"You must also consider that the author of those letters may know something about Mr. Cavendish's death."

Clearly, Margaretta had not thought of it. Her view had been narrowed by the press of the circumstances around her in the past few days. "Of course, of course," she murmured. "You are right."

Moving with more energy than she had since Rosalind had entered the house, Mrs. Seymore pulled a ring of keys from the desk drawer. "We'll begin with his study."

And so they did. The study and the desk, and the bookroom and its other desk, as well as the captain's separate dressing room. Rosalind had not had a chance to see so much of the house before. It was all as elegant as those few rooms she had already been admitted to. The bookroom was especially well furnished. Spanish wood carvings and vases of Italian glass stood on the shelves alongside the books. There was a map case surmounted by a globe, and an elaborate framed chart of the Mediterranean on the wall.

On the desk lay two slender letter openers with silver and enamel handles.

Mrs. Seymore saw Rosalind looking at them.

"They are copies," she said. "I bought them myself in Jermyn Street, a year ago. No, two, I think. William likes pretty things. I can probably show you the receipt, if you give me time to find it."

"There is no need," said Rosalind. But as she turned away, she could not help but wonder who else had seen those copies.

Mrs. Seymore searched the drawers and the boxes. She unlocked the closets to pull open those drawers and move the shirts and coats to search for possible hiding places. Rosalind watched her. Margaretta's face was drawn tight and her movements were sharp, nearing frantic at some points. Her mouth moved silently as she whispered angrily to herself.

If the letter she had given Rosalind was a fake, she would be acting now, and if she was acting, it was an extremely skilled performance. But then, Rosalind knew the woman was very good at this sort of show.

When nothing was found, they agreed they should return to the study and search again. Like the bookroom, the study was decorated with maps and charts and globes. But there were no ledgers such as Rosalind was used to seeing in the private room of a man with a household to keep. The only letters they found were from Sir Bertram, or from bill collectors.

Mrs. Seymore unearthed a final stack of these from the bottom drawer of the mahogany desk. She flipped quickly through them, only to throw them down on the desk in disgust.

"Nothing," she declared. She was looking around as she spoke, for the letters or for some inspiration, Rosalind could not say.

"Could he have kept them with his brother?" Rosalind asked. "Or at his club?"

"Possibly, but there's no way to find out, is there?" Margaretta threw out her hands. "Oh, leave it to William to help hang himself!"

The frustration was genuine. Mrs. Seymore stood with her hands on her hips and her mouth compressed as she glowered at the room around them. The pose was unguarded. Rosalind wanted to believe that Mrs. Seymore truly did not know where the letters were. But she did not know if she dared.

"Mrs. Seymore, tell me, have you seen Lord Adolphus since the trial?"

"Lord Adolphus? No. He's written, of course, but he's needed at home today. Why do you ask?"

"The night before the inquest, Lord Adolphus gave me a hundred pounds," Rosalind told her. It was a risk, because Mrs. Seymore was an accomplished liar and because of that resemblance to Lady Weyland that Rosalind still did not understand. "At the time, he said it was for a charity I was collecting for, but he made the draft out to me personally. I gave the money back to him at the trial, because I was uncertain as to his real reasons for offering it. It was after that he gave his testimony."

"Well, surely it was no surprise Lord Adolphus was called as a witness," said Mrs. Seymore slowly.

"Yes, it was. A great surprise. Mr. Harkness had not mentioned him once. If Ada . . . If he had known Lord Adolphus had been at the theater that night, he would have said something, even if only during his testimony."

"You think Lord Adolphus gave his testimony because you gave him back his money? That is a significant assumption, Miss Thorne."

"I know it. That's why I'm telling you about it. I'm wondering if you can offer any other explanation."

"None whatsoever. But you have your suspicions, I can tell."

"I believe Lord Adolphus was bribing me to prevent me from looking too closely at his mother and his brother in regards to Mr. Cavendish's murder."

Mrs. Seymore's cheeks grew pale. "What has that to do with the letters?"

"I wonder if Lord Adolphus might have convinced Captain Seymore to give them over for safekeeping."

"Why would he do that?" whispered Mrs. Seymore. "No. Never mind. I know why."

Rosalind pictured Miss Vaughn. She pictured Lady Weyland

and the marquis, and she remembered Lord Adolphus's face as he spoke of working so long and so quietly to keep the family name above reproach.

From the grim lines on Mrs. Seymore's face, Rosalind could tell she was thinking of something similar. Margaretta crossed the room and rang the bell.

"Mrs. Nott," said Margaretta as soon as the housekeeper entered and made her curtsy. "Has Lord Adolphus been to the house in the past three days?"

Mrs. Nott's eyes shifted left to Rosalind and then back to her mistress. "Yes, madam. He was here just before the—the inquest. You were napping and he did not like to disturb you. He said he wished to make sure the captain was all right, and that he was ready to face the court. He had, I think, some notion the captain might try to run away."

"Did you see Captain Seymore give him anything?" asked Rosalind. "Or notice him carrying anything away?"

This was a mistake. She'd been too hasty. Mrs. Nott drew herself up. "What happens between his lordship and my master is not my concern."

"But it is mine," snapped Mrs. Seymore. "Please, Mrs. Nott. Did you see anything?"

Mrs. Nott's thin mouth twitched. She wanted to speak, but in the end, she shook her head. "I'm truly sorry, madam," she said. "I saw nothing."

Mrs. Seymore's eyes glistened with anger and tears. For a moment Rosalind thought she would shout at her servant, but she just turned away, pressing her hands against her belly.

"Thank you, Mrs. Nott," said Rosalind.

Mrs. Nott's jaw worked itself back and forth for a moment, but she kept her silence, curtsied once, and took her leave.

As soon as the door closed, Mrs. Seymore started for the

desk. "I will write to Adolphus," she said. "I'll ask him about the letters."

Rosalind put a hand on Margaretta's arm. "I think perhaps you should not."

"Why?"

"The letters have become the loose thread in this entire knotted problem," Rosalind told her. "At the beginning, they appeared to be driving the events. But the longer we have gone on, the more they have appeared out of place." She stopped and marshaled her nerves.

"Mrs. Seymore, is there anything you want to tell me about these letters? Or about your relationship with Lord Adolphus or Lady Weyland?"

Rosalind waited. Mrs. Seymore searched her face, looking for hints or cracks or flaws that she might work upon. Rosalind made very certain she would see none.

But she did see the moment Margaretta made her decision.

"I think we should leave it," Mrs. Seymore said. "What good will bringing these letters to the attention of Bow Street or the attorneys do for the captain? I did not recognize the handwriting in the one I found. Without knowing the author, their contents will just become fodder for the case against William."

"But we might still discover who wrote them," said Rosalind. "You said yourself that you are not in regular correspondence with most of Captain Seymore's relatives, and they are the ones with the greatest interest in disrupting your marriage. It is also possible that the handwriting has been disguised. There are, however, persons who can detect such disguises and accurately discern one hand from another. I am going to meet such an expert shortly."

Rosalind watched Mrs. Seymore's face as she turned away.

She watched how Margaretta pressed her palm against her forehead and against her mouth.

"Forgive me," Margaretta said. "I keep hoping this will get simpler, but it does not."

"Lies never do, Mrs. Seymore."

"You still believe I am the one lying to you?"

Rosalind didn't answer that. She couldn't. Because Mrs. Seymore was right. Because Rosalind could not turn away from the possibility that Mrs. Seymore herself had written the defamatory letter Rosalind carried.

CHAPTER 33

The Guilty Man

*And how many soever be found culpable by inquisition,
in any manners aforesaid, they shall be taken and delivered to the sheriff and shall be committed to the gaol.*

—John Impey of the Inner Temple,
The Practice of the Office of Coroner

The smell was the first thing anyone noticed about a prison. It coiled out of the doorway as soon as the keeper unlocked the portal. Next was the damp that slid over the skin as if it were a property of the darkness itself.

Harkness followed the jailer, a squat little man with dirty pores and one tooth left to him, down into the cell where they'd taken Captain Seymore after the verdict had been pronounced.

He did not do this thing. Harkness had stood in front of Townsend in his private office. The inquest had finished and the station was all but empty of men, most of whom were out trying to clear the crowds from the street and from in front of the theater.

That's a matter for the courts now, Mr. Harkness, said Mr. Townsend. *Don't you worry. If he's innocent, he's only to explain himself. Not a man on that jury doesn't know what it's like to be blind drunk.*

Despite this, when Harkness left the house this morning, he

pointed his steps not to Bow Street, but to Newgate Prison. Now he stepped past the jailer into the foul little basement cell where Captain Seymore had spent the night.

No one had paid for the captain's comforts. The barred room was empty of blankets, bedding, or baskets of food, such as were often found among prisoners who had family to care for them or the means to buy extra privileges.

Captain Seymore lay on the bare mattress, his burly arms wrapped around himself, blinking up at the ceiling. He did not get up as Harkness walked into the cell.

If it was not suicide, it was either the captain or Mrs. Seymore, Townsend had told Harkness. *They were the only ones there at the time. And even your Miss Thorne does not truly believe it was Mrs. Seymore.*

They were the only ones seen, Harkness had shot back. *Have you been inside that place? You could hide Napoleon and his whole army in there!*

Then find me the little corporal, replied Townsend. *And I will cheerfully arrest him. But I will not see a lady dragged into the mire when it is not necessary.*

"I've been in worse, you know," Captain Seymore said finally, more to the ceiling than to Harkness. "The *Leopard*, now that was a foul, stinking ship. At least I know this berth will not drown me."

"I've come to talk to you about what happened at the inquest," said Harkness. He should not be here. He had no reason to come talk with this man. His part in this business was at an end. And if Townsend found out . . . he'd have to sit through a reprimand at best. At the worst he'd be posted to Bath or somewhere like it for the winter.

But Harkness could not let the thing go. Not yet.

There was nowhere to sit except for the bed, so Harkness

kept his feet. "What you said to your wife in parting—'Well done, Margaretta'—what did you mean by it?"

"Just what I said." There was a grated slit of a window in the far wall. Seymore stared out at the falling rain, watching the pools collect on the sill and trickle down the wall.

"Do you believe Mrs. Seymore wanted to throw the blame on you?"

Seymore made no answer. He showed no effect of the cold, reminding Harkness yet again that this was a sailor in front of him.

"Mrs. Seymore has said you'd been receiving anonymous letters, supposedly detailing her affair."

"Yes."

"Did you keep them? Where are they?"

A tight smile formed on the captain's face. "Those letters were burnt."

"Why? If you were planning on filing for criminal conversation, they would have been evidence."

"Because I changed my mind about the suit, as I told you, and so they became meaningless. I burnt them," he repeated firmly. "The night before the inquest."

Harkness stared at the man, who in his turn stared at the rain with dull eyes. "You are telling me you believe your wife might be a murderess, but not an adulteress?"

"I don't know what I believe anymore," the captain replied, and in his voice Harkness heard that flat despair that was worse than any rage. "Perhaps that's what makes it so easy to simply choose to hang."

"I cannot believe, sir, that such a man as you would want to see his enemy escape."

Seymore swung his legs off the bed. Grime smeared his white breeches. His queue had come loose and his fringe of hair hung loose about his ears. No man looked good in the jail's gloom, but the captain looked flushed. Harkness wondered if he had a fever.

Seymore's hard eyes raked Harkness up and down. "You never loved beyond your station, did you, Harkness? You never looked up and saw the moon and wanted it for yourself."

Harkness made no answer to this.

"Well, let me tell you, sir, it's all well and good, until the moon comes and offers herself to you. Then you've got to keep her, and give her all she wants, and you've got to keep giving it. You know that if you falter, if you fail, she'll just launch herself right back into the sky. And there you'll be, with your arms empty and no way to call her back. You may take it from me, sir, that is when you simply . . . give up."

"So you want to hang?" demanded Harkness.

The captain shrugged. "Doesn't matter, does it? Career's done. Wife's what she is. My brother's actually rubbing his hands at the thought of having me out of the way, and if there ever was a person who did . . . who could . . . it's too late. Why not hang and be done?"

"Only one reason. So they all know in the end you wouldn't be beaten by their tricks."

Swinging at a man's pride was low, but it tended to work. Not this time, though. Captain Seymore just raised his eyes back to the grating, and the falling rain.

"There is one other thing you should know, sir," said Adam. "Mrs. Seymore is still trying to find out who killed Fletcher Cavendish."

That turned the captain around. "Is she?"

"She's written to Mr. Townsend about posting a reward and she is . . . employing certain agents to assist in the matter."

Seymore stared at him blankly. "Well, good luck to her

then," he said harshly. "If you'll excuse me, I'm tired." With that, the captain lay back down on his bed, wrapped his arms around himself, and closed his eyes.

Harkness wanted to shake the man, to beat him about his fool head until he woke up and made some effort to save his own life. But in the end all Adam could do was pound on the door for the jailer. The man arrived, clanking his keys to let Harkness out and lock the iron-banded door after him.

But experience and intuition struck Harkness, and instead of moving away, he leaned back to the door.

"I wonder, Mr. High and Mighty Harkness." The captain's voice drifted softly through the grating. "If you had to choose between your wife and your brother, sir, could you bring yourself to do it?" Harkness heard the captain say to the rain and the darkness. "And which would it be?"

With these words whispering in his thoughts, Harkness followed the jailer out into the air.

Could I bring myself to do it? he asked himself as he turned up his coat collar and pulled his hat down against the rain. *Which would it be?*

"Ah, Mr. Harkness!"

Harkness turned to see a stout little man puffing toward him, waving his walking stick and clutching a sheaf of papers close to his body. "I was told I might run into you here." Harkness frowned at him. Who knew he was here? Not Townsend. Harkness hadn't told him.

The man touched his dripping hat brim. "Hiram Close, Esquire. A word with you while we walk, sir?" he asked. "Preferably to someplace dry?"

Harkness shrugged and started up the street and toward the coffee house on the corner. He didn't have much time. Townsend had already listed three new assignments for him since the inquest. To keep him busy, he knew, and away from this exact spot.

"What can I do for you, Mr. Close?" Harkness asked.

"I'm engaged to act on behalf of Captain Seymore, sir," Close answered, and surprise stopped Harkness in his tracks.

"You are?"

"Indeed, sir," huffed the lawyer. "And we were to go somewhere dry?"

Mrs. Morton's Coffee Rooms were both dry and crowded, but Close and Harkness managed to find themselves a spot at the long table. They had to lean close together to hear each other over the students arguing politics and the stock jobbers arguing trade.

"There are those most anxious that the captain be cleared of these scurrilous charges," bawled Mr. Close.

Harkness frowned. "You surprise me, sir. The captain is under the impression that his brother wishes him dead."

"But it is not his brother who engaged me. It is Mrs. Cecil Seymore."

Harkness drew back and stared at the lawyer, who had hunched himself over to the mug of steaming coffee. "Mrs. Cecil Seymore? His sister-in-law? Does anyone else in that house know what she's done?" If Sir Bertram really wanted the captain dead, he would not be glad to know his dependents were acting counter to his wishes.

Mr. Close shrugged in a ripple of rusty black cloth. "That I could not say. My point is that I wish to engage you on the matter, sir. I've the fee, and the permission of your superior." He patted the sheaf of papers on the bench beside him. "So far all the inquiries have centered on Captain and Mrs. Seymore. But we've plenty of other persons to look at. For instance, I'll want to know what can you tell me about this Miss Rosalind Thorne . . ."

"You will not trouble Miss Thorne, sir," said Harkness. "I'll talk with her."

Close's high forehead furrowed in surprise. "Then you will take the job, sir?"

"Yes."

"Excellent!" Close heaved a sigh of relief, and took a mighty swig of coffee. "Now I feel sure we'll find the guilty party. Have you any objection to my interviewing Lord Adolphus? No? Good. We've not much time, sir. I'm expecting the matter to go before the bench in three days at the most."

Harkness got to his feet and reclaimed his hat. "Then, I'll begin right away."

Find me the little corporal, Townsend had said. And now Harkness had reason to look, and he knew exactly where to begin. But even as he strode once more out into the rain, Seymore's words followed him.

If you had to choose between your wife and your brother, could you bring yourself to do it?

But it is not his brother who engaged me, said the lawyer. *It is Mrs. Cecil Seymore.*

Harkness stopped in the middle of the street and began cursing himself for ten times worse than a fool. He'd been busy with the movements of Mrs. Seymore, of Captain Seymore and Cavendish, on that night. But the captain had dined with his brother. His brother who, if Miss Thorne was right, was keenly interested in inheriting that damned title. So much so, he was urging the captain to get a divorce, and declare the child his wife carried illegitimate.

Had anyone in this mess stopped to ask themselves where Sir

Bertram Seymore had gotten himself to while Fletcher Cavendish was being murdered?

Or for that matter, Adam added, because he knew what Miss Thorne would say if she were there, *has anyone asked about* Lady Bertram?

Harkness drew his hat down farther on his head, and set out at a run.

But when he reached Little Russell Street, it was only the housekeeper, Mrs. Kendricks, who answered the door.

"Miss Thorne is not at home, sir," Mrs. Kendricks said, frowning at the water that dripped from his hat brim and the hems of his coat.

"When will she return?" he asked, puffing at least as badly as Mr. Close. "I have something urgent to ask her."

"I could not say, sir," answered Mrs. Kendricks. "She left quite early this morning."

"Where did she go?"

"Someplace called Woolcombe Hall," replied the housekeeper. "She seemed to think she'd be able to find herself a lady scholar there."

CHAPTER 34

The Spreading Ripples of the Past

But it is chiefly in fashionable society that the art of quiz-
zing forms so important an accomplishment.
— Catherine Gore, *The Sketchbook of Fashion*

Mr. Clements's guidebooks declared the village of Woolcombe to be picturesque but unremarkable, with the exception of its singularly fine and dramatic old hall that belonged to the Onslow family. For the coach ride, Rosalind had brought with her a small basket with some sandwiches and a bottle of barley water that Mrs. Kendricks insisted she take, and a muffler, in case it turned cold. She also tucked a stack of letters in her reticule, including the one from the woman Mr. Clements called the most respected scholar of modern manuscripts in the United Kingdom.

It had been written in the tidiest, and tiniest, hand Rosalind had ever seen.

Dear Miss Thorne,

I was most interested to receive your letter and would be glad to look over the correspondence you mention.

I regret that it is not possible for me to travel as far as

London. If you do not wish to trust your business to the vagaries
of the daily post, you are welcome at Woolcombe Hall on any
day. If you cannot come direct to the hall, the landlord at The
White Swan will be able to arrange for you to be brought to us.

Sincerely yours,
Elizabeth Onslow
Woolcombe Hall, Woolcombe

All the while, Rosalind felt the passage of time beating like
wings against her mind. *Three days. Maybe four*, Mr. Harkness
had told her after the inquest. Only now it was two days, maybe
three.

And she knew nothing at all, except that Captain Seymore
had not killed Mr. Cavendish, and Mrs. Seymore could not
have. But Mrs. Seymore might know who did commit the murder, and she might have planned the crime.

Two days, perhaps three, before the trial, and then one or
two hours that would clear Captain Seymore or condemn him
absolutely. Rosalind had to know the truth before then, to save
the captain, and protect herself and those around her.

Yesterday, when Rosalind returned from her exhausting and
disheartening trip to see Mrs. Seymore, she found Louisa's aunt
and chaperone, Mrs. Showell, sitting in her parlor.

"How is Louisa bearing her loss?" Rosalind asked, once the
polite preliminary greetings had been exchanged.

"Oh, Louisa." Mrs. Showell sighed. "Louisa went out with a
group of her silliest friends, all of them in heavy mourning for
Mr. Cavendish, with veils, which she spent three quarters of her
pin money on. The rest was spent on white roses so they could
gather on Mrs. Sullivan's balcony for the express purpose of
tossing them down onto the hearse, or the heads of passersby."

"I wonder that you allowed it."

"Oh, I knew Mrs. Sullivan would not let them do anything too foolish, and it is better she exorcise it from her system. Now. It is not Louisa's behavior I'm here to talk about. It is yours."

"Mrs. Showell—"

"Oh no," Mrs. Showell interrupted firmly. "I see you getting on your dignity, my girl, and I will not have it. Your name is now painted all across the newspapers alongside the ridiculous stories about that actor's murder. While it is titillating, it is hardly the sort of notice a gentlewoman hopes for. We must therefore rally our resources to make sure it is well and widely understood that although the situation is not at all respectable, you yourself are merely a victim and a bystander and none of us hold you to be in any way touched or spoiled by the situation."

It took all Rosalind's training in deportment not to let her jaw drop.

"A full frontal assault is our only option," Mrs. Showell went on. "I've let it be known I'm calling here to invite you to our supper party, and of course, you will be seen with Louisa as soon as I can persuade the ridiculous girl to come out of mourning. Then, there is the Thompkins ball and concert being given to close out the season. I have already spoken to Lady Thompkins about your invitation. You will make up one of our party."

"Mrs. Showell, I appreciate your concern, but it is truly unnecessary."

"It is highly necessary. There is still a chance my nephew will bring you around to his way of thinking. If you are to become the Duchess of Casselmain, you must do so without this cloud hanging over your head."

Rosalind felt her cheeks begin to heat.

"None of that, Miss Thorne, if you please. You are angry at me, I can bear that. You are proud. I approve. I also know your family, and your circumstances. Frankly, I admire the way you've handled a situation that would have crushed many of us. It is my opinion, Devon could do far worse than you for his wife."

His wife? The words repeated themselves in Rosalind's mind. *No. You cannot think it. It is not possible. I cannot.* He *cannot . . .*

"Devon has made no declaration to me," she said.

"I know that as well," replied Mrs. Showell. "But you and I both know he has lost a considerable portion of his heart to you. But set all that aside and curse me as an interfering old woman after I leave. Now we must be practical. If you and Devon reach an understanding, you know that you must demonstrate that you are still accepted by society. If no understanding occurs, you still need that acceptance to be able to continue your current mode of living." The canny old dame smiled triumphantly. "There now, I've surprised you. Well, you are not the only one who understands the order of things. So I may assure Lady Thompkins and Louisa of your acceptance?"

Rosalind paused, searching for the flaw in Mrs. Showell's argument, but not for long, because there was none. "Yes, of course you may tell them."

"Excellent." Mrs. Showell heaved herself to her feet. "Sensible girl. I don't suppose I can convince you it would be to your benefit to drop the poetess entirely?"

"It might be, but I cannot. I have made promises." That, of course, was not the only reason to continue her association with Mrs. Seymore, but it was the only reason Rosalind could give which Mrs. Showell was likely to accept.

"Well, I would not have you break your word, but you do understand that I cannot have her about until the matter is cleared? After that, we can wait a decent interval and I will receive her and we will see what can be done."

Despite her troubles and amazement, Rosalind felt a sudden rush of sympathy for this direct and practical woman, who had come here for the sole and simple reason of helping those she cared for. After the Seymores and the Weylands, it was a breath of sweet air to Rosalind's weary, worried heart.

"Mrs. Showell," she said. "I imagine you know that I agreed to accompany Lord Casselmain and Louisa to walk on the new bridge on Sunday?"

"Oh, yes. Where is my head? Devon did mention that. I will make sure Louisa is sensibly dressed."

"If you'll permit me, Mrs. Showell, I think it would be better if she was allowed to keep her mourning for the outing."

Mrs. Showell arched her brows and then she chuckled. "I spy your plan, Miss Thorne! You may be right at that. Now, chin up, and for heaven's sake, put some sort of end to this sorry affair! We all need some rest."

And with that, she sailed out, leaving Rosalind alone, and barely able to breathe.

As the letter had promised, the landlord at The White Swan was perfectly ready to arrange for a pony trap to take Rosalind from the post coach up to "the hall."

"We's used to Miss Onslow's people traipsing through here," he said cheerfully. "Never can tell who'll be along next."

Now Rosalind stood at the door of a sprawling squared-off structure that looked more like it had been built to hold off invading armies than to house a family. The windows were entirely blank, and the walkway and the garden were both overgrown and deserted. The bell out front clanged harshly. The first reply was the squawking of the infuriated chickens in the courtyard.

The second was the huge, heavy *woof* of an annoyed hound.

At last the door opened with a long, pained creak. Rosalind clutched her basket to her side and told herself not to be ridiculous.

"Miss Thorne? How do you do?"

Rosalind found herself face-to-face with the most beautiful girl she had ever seen. She was the embodiment of the English rose. Her hair was the true, pure, pale blond, her cheeks perfect pink, her eyes wide and clear blue. Her peaches and cream skin was marred only by several black smears on her delicate fingertips.

Dressed for the evening, she would have caused exclamations in any ballroom. As it was, she wore a plain blue housedress and a gray smock. A great, gray wolfhound stood beside her, wagging its tail slowly.

"Miss Onslow is expecting you," the girl continued. "If you will follow me, please?"

With the feeling of stepping into one of Mrs. Cuthbertson's novels, Rosalind stepped into the dim hall. The beautiful girl and her great hound led Rosalind through cool, and entirely empty, corridors. Time and neglect had dimmed the linenfold panels and the grand tapestries. There was no sound except for their footfalls against the stone.

"We are rather isolated here," said the girl. "All Miss Onslow's time and resources are dedicated to the library. And here we are." She stopped before a great carved door that was a match for the hall's entranceway. But this one opened smoothly on well-oiled hinges, and Rosalind stepped into another world.

It was indeed a library, but Rosalind had never seen its like in a private home. This was the result of generations of careful and patient collecting. It was a great long hall, two stories high. The walls of the main floor were lined in bookshelves. Above that, an elaborate catwalk circled the whole of the hall, with yet more shelves above. Long slanted reading tables stretched down the center. Iron chandeliers (none of them lit) hung from the vaulted ceiling. The only windows were those set near the ceiling, and Rosalind could discern the individual sunbeams as they streamed through.

Rosalind became aware her mouth had fallen open. Her guide smiled. "Yes, it does have that effect on people who see it for the first time. Miss Onslow is in the back."

The hound had already trotted ahead, and Rosalind and the young lady followed him to the far end of the hall. A broad desk waited there, with two lamps burning on it. The woman who sat there looked up at Rosalind's approach and stood to welcome her.

"Here is Miss Thorne to see you, Grandmother."

Grandmother? But she's Miss . . . Rosalind shoved her shock quickly into the back of her brain.

Miss Onslow proved to be a wispy cobweb of a woman. The top of her head barely reached Rosalind's chin. Her white hair had been neatly braided beneath her cap, but a few locks had slipped free to float around her forehead and ears. Her eyes were almost lost in the wrinkles, but they nonetheless sparkled bright and keen as she took Rosalind in.

"Miss Thorne, how delightful!" she cried, her voice surprisingly mellow and smooth for so ancient a dame. "No, now, none of that," she said as Rosalind made her curtsy. "We do not stand on such ceremonies here. I had enough of them when I was a girl. Come and sit down and let us talk about your problem."

"Miss Thorne must be hungry," said the granddaughter. "I'll go see if Gemma has anything to eat." She left, with the wolfhound trotting hopefully behind her.

Rosalind was staring again.

"Rebecca is beautiful, is she not?" said Miss Onslow calmly.

"I, ah, yes. She is your granddaughter . . . Miss Onslow?"

"The youngest of them, and the only one who chooses to make a home with me." Miss Onslow settled herself once more behind her desk and waved Rosalind to the chair that had been set beside it. "Now, Miss Thorne, tell me of yourself. How is it these letters and their attendant problems have fallen to you?"

Rosalind forced her thoughts away from this extraordinary home and its inhabitants back to the matter that had brought her here. "I have a friend who has entered into some difficulties . . ." she began.

"No," said Miss Onslow abruptly. "No. It will not do. I cannot help you, Miss Thorne."

"Perhaps if you were to look at the letter . . ."

Miss Onslow waved her hand. "I do not need to. I already know I can be of no use."

"May I ask why not?"

"Because you are not prepared to be forthcoming about your reasons for being here. I will not help someone who will not be honest with me."

Rosalind felt her cheeks begin to burn. "I beg your pardon. It was not my intent to deceive."

"Of course not. But I recognize drawing room diplomacy when I hear it." Miss Onslow leaned forward, and Rosalind smelled dust and jasmine. "Such temporizing can hide so very much, Miss Thorne. For all I know, you intend to cause harm to some petty rival."

For a moment, Rosalind did not know whether to be delighted or offended. As neither reaction would serve very well, she settled for direct. "Very well, Miss Onslow. I make my living by assisting women with problems of various kinds and degrees. I was recently engaged to prove a gentlewoman's innocence against a charge of adultery. Shortly thereafter, her supposed lover was murdered and her husband is to be tried for the crime. I believe him to be innocent. I also believe that proving the identity of the person who wrote the letter I have may shed light on the reasons behind the false charge, and show me how to flush out the murderer."

Miss Onslow's bright eyes glittered with something very close to greed.

"Ah! Now, that is a story with heart and life's blood, not to mention the ring of truth. I will be very glad to help you. If, that is, I have not now offended you by my behavior."

"I confess, Miss Onslow, I do not know quite what to make of you," Rosalind told her. "But I will gladly accept any help you are willing to give. I do not have much time left to me."

Rosalind retrieved her basket and lifted the cloth that covered it. "Here is the letter, and here are two written by my leading candidates I have for its authorship." She laid down the blackmail letter, followed by the letter from Sir Bertram that Mrs. Nott had given her, and (with a slight hesitation) the one she had received from Mrs. Seymore with the fee for her assistance.

There was still another in the bottom of her basket, but she would wait to bring that out.

Miss Onslow unfolded all three documents and smoothed them out side by side on her desk. "If you could move the lamp a little closer, Miss Thorne. Thank you." She picked up a large brass-rimmed magnifying glass and peered at each letter in turn. She took her time, looking from one to the other, touching a word here, and another there, her mouth moving soundlessly the entire time.

Rosalind had seldom found it so difficult to compose herself to patience. The fire crackled in its hearth. The dog settled at its mistress's feet, resting its shaggy head on its paws. Rebecca came in with a tray bearing cold pigeon pie, rock cakes, and a bottle of what proved to be dandelion cordial.

At long last, Miss Onslow straightened her shoulders and laid the glass down. "I am sorry, Miss Thorne. I must disappoint. None of these letters were written by the same person."

Rosalind's spirits plummeted. "You are certain?"

"I am. If you'll look here." Miss Onslow took up the glass again. "Both are well tutored, possibly even by the same tutor. But the shape of the *A* here, and here, it is almost indistinguishable from the *E*, here. You see? Whereas in this, the letter *A* is quite distinct from *E*. Also, the way in which the *T* is crossed, is different in each. I expect this person"—she lifted Mrs. Seymore's letter—"might have a dominant left hand, but has been taught, as so many are, to write with the right." She looked again at Rosalind. "I'm afraid this is not what you wanted to hear."

"It . . . complicates matters," replied Rosalind. "But that is hardly your fault."

"Perhaps you could tell me of your problem," suggested Miss Onslow as she poured out two glasses of cordial. "Whatever it might be. I spent my time in the grand salons of the previous generation before I retired from the world. Now, I spend it surrounded with the blood and gore and scandal of history. You will find I am not easily shocked."

The salons of the previous generation . . . Rosalind paused with her glass of cordial halfway to her mouth. "I . . . Is it possible, Miss Onslow, during that time, you might have been acquainted with the Marchioness of Weyland?"

"Weyland?" Miss Onslow knit her thin, pale brows. "You don't mean old Lord Weyland's child bride by any chance? Little Agnes Donville?"

"Yes," said Rosalind, her heart turning over in a kind of uneasy hope. "That is who I mean."

"Is that what business brings you here? Goodness. I should have realized."

"I have been attempting to find out more about her," said Rosalind. "I've tried all my acquaintances, but no one knows anything." She'd been through letter after letter, reaching out through every connection she could think to use. But while everyone spoke of Lord Adolphus and his charity and his competence and his devotion to his ailing brother, not one would admit to knowing the dowager marchioness.

"She told me she once entertained quite a bit," Rosalind said to Miss Onslow. "And confesses to an adventurous girlhood . . ."

"Ha!" laughed Miss Onslow sharply. "'Adventurous' is one word for it. Oh, Miss Thorne, that girl was a scandal." She grinned. "Have some pie, Miss Thorne. This may take a bit."

CHAPTER 35

Pleasing Reminiscences

But alas! The friendship was fleeting and delusive.
—*The Trial of William Henry Hall vs. Major George Barrow
for Criminal Conversation*

Rosalind restrained her impatience and let her hostess help her
to some pie and cakes and more cordial. A plate was arranged
for the grateful hound and Rosalind felt close to screaming,
until she saw the gleam in Miss Onslow's eye, and realized she
was being teased, and quite possibly tested.

"Well, Miss Thorne," said Miss Onslow as she pushed her
chair back from her desk and picked up her own plate. "Hear
you now the tale of Agnes Donville. The youngest hanger-on of
what was, back in the nineties, a most notorious clique."

"What made them notorious?"

"Their salons, chiefly," said Miss Onslow. "Gatherings of the
great, the near great, and the would-be great."

"Were they political?"

"Oh, no, good heavens. They were gamblers."

Rosalind's throat closed.

"I know," said Miss Onslow over the rim of her cordial glass.
"It was scandalous even then, before we all became so prim and
proper. What would happen is that one of these ladies would

send out invitations to a private party at one or another of their grand houses—and they were universally grand. The guests who accepted would find every game they could ask for—cards of all descriptions, a faro bank, hazard, all of it. There would even be a cashier on hand to change notes, and always a man of business who could be counted on for a loan, if one was in need."

Rosalind's thoughts darted instantly to Mr. Fullerton and his drawer of jewelry and letters.

"Of course the lady hostess took her share of the winnings," said Miss Onslow. "And by this means did these fine ladies greatly increase their individual incomes."

"Is this how the dowager made her fortune?" Rosalind remembered the icy calculation tightening Lady Weyland's doll-like face, and found she could believe it very easily.

"I expect it became impolite to remember, let alone talk about it," said Miss Onslow. "Especially once Agnes married a marquis. There was at the time, however, a great deal of speculation about her relationship with old Lord Weyland, especially since she allowed him to fleece her guests, as long as he handed over her share of the extra."

Rosalind opened her mouth, remembered her manners, and closed it again. Miss Onslow smiled.

"Ask your question, Miss Thorne. I do not mind."

"Were you one of these notorious ladies?"

"I flitted about the edges for a time." For a moment, sorrow clouded her bright eyes. "You know how it is, Miss Thorne. We gentlewomen are frequently forced into shapes that are not natural to us, and it can take a great deal of hard experience to break us free." Miss Onslow set her glass down. "Is any of this of use to you?"

"It is," said Rosalind. "It changes a number of my assumptions, and I think for the better." Rosalind finished her own draft of the bitter cordial. "There is one other question—well, perhaps two."

"I am entirely at your disposal." Miss Onslow inclined her head graciously.

"You said, I think, that the old Lord Weyland was involved in his wife's gaming. Did that continue after they were married?"

"I believe it did."

"And . . . do you know what became of him and how it was he died?" she asked. "No one seems to ever speak of his late lordship at all."

"I'm afraid I don't know," said Miss Onslow. "I had already left town at that point, but I believe it was sudden, and I believe that it may have been . . . not entirely savory." She shook her head at her own distant memories. "Appearances are everything, Miss Thorne. Especially to those who are breaking proprieties." The old woman pulled herself back to the present. "We should, I assume, treat this as one question. Is there another?"

Rosalind reached into her basket again. "I've one more letter here, Miss Onslow. Will you look at it?"

"Certainly." She set her plate and glass on the tray and accepted the fresh letter Rosalind handed her. As before, Miss Onslow smoothed out the paper and applied her glass. Again, she did not hurry, but used the same time and care as she had with the others.

"Yes," she said. "I am certain of it. The hand that wrote this"—she lifted the defamatory letter—"wrote this."

She lifted the letter Rosalind had so recently received from Virginia, paving the way for her audience with the dowager marchioness.

"Thank you," said Rosalind. "The truth is, I had my suspicions. I just didn't like them very much."

Rosalind, who bore her own share of heartbreak, had recognized regret and sorrow in Mrs. Cecil Seymore. She had guessed easily that Virginia felt she had married the wrong brother. From there it was not too much of a stretch to imagine that Virginia in a fit of weakness might try to break Captain Seymore's unhappy marriage apart.

That was why Virginia had been so startled when Rosalind suggested that she and Margaretta might be friends.

"You didn't like your suspicions?" said Miss Onslow. "Or you didn't like yourself for having them?"

"A bit of both," admitted Rosalind. "You must forgive me, Miss Onslow, but my time is very short. I must get back to town at once."

"Of course." Miss Onslow got to her feet, slowly, but smoothly. "Now, since this is a legal matter, I will write to my friend Dr. Montressor on your behalf. He can confirm my findings and give evidence in court if required. I know how the law, like scholarship, prefers to receive its truths from a thoroughly masculine source."

"Thank you." Rosalind also stood. "I am very glad to have met you, Miss Onslow."

"And I you, Miss Thorne," she replied warmly. "Now let us find Herbert and the pony trap and get you back to town."

It was quite dark by the time Rosalind returned to London, nonetheless the streets were full of life and traffic. The carriages of the rich and fashionable traversed the avenues, taking them to and from the dinners and dances that would close out the season. Rosalind found herself looking at the lighted windows and wondering what was happening on the other side. Who was falling into love and who was falling into hate? What was being said in haste, and what would the people all find themselves waking up to when the cold, gray dawn came again?

She was tired, not to mention dusty and disheveled from her day's travel, and much depleted in her purse. Nonetheless, when she reached the coaching house, she immediately asked the man there to help her hire a carriage to take her to Sir and Lady Bertram's home. The day was done. Tomorrow was Sunday. There could be no trial. But Monday, Monday there could very well be.

The cab pulled into Soho Square. It was late enough that any crowd that had been gathered around it had cleared off for home or bed, or at least a warm drink, which was yet another reason for coming directly here.

The lamp beside Sir Bertram's door had been lit, and firelight slipped from between the tightly drawn drapes on the front window. Someone was home, and awake.

Nonetheless, Rosalind asked her driver to wait. Her reception would entirely depend on who waited sleepless on the other side of those draperies.

The liviried footman was smothering a yawn when he answered the door.

"May I help you?"

"Is Mrs. Cecil Seymore still awake?" Rosalind asked. "I need to speak with her. The matter is most urgent."

The man looked Rosalind up and down in such a way as to make it clear he was doing her a great favor by not simply ordering her to be about her business. At last, however, he stood aside to let her in, instructed her to wait here, and took himself into the parlor. He returned a moment later, and Rosalind followed him into Sir Bertram's elegant and antique-filled parlor.

Virginia was already on her feet.

"Miss Thorne!" she cried. "Whatever is the matter? Is . . . is it William? Or Margaretta?" she added quickly. "Sir and Lady Bertram have gone out . . ."

"That is just as well," said Rosalind. In fact, she'd been hoping for it. "I think you do not want them to hear what I have come to say."

Virginia's cheeks turned pale, and she sank back down onto the sofa beside her embroidery hoop.

Rosalind reached into her basket and brought out the defamatory letter. She handed it to Virginia, who glanced at it, and immediately laid it aside.

"I do not recognize this," she said, to the curtained window.

"Virginia," said Rosalind sternly. "I know that you wrote this. Please do not compound the problem. We do not have much time if we are to save William."

Virginia bit her lip.

"Why did you send that letter?" asked Rosalind.

Virginia picked up the paper and stared at it. With one savage gesture, she crumpled it into a ball, and threw it directly to the fire. Rosalind gave a cry and dodged forward, knocking the paper out of the air with her palm so it fell unharmed to the carpet.

Virginia watched her retrieve it, tears shimmering in her eyes.

"This house," said the widow. "This *family*. I have been inside it too long. If you live surrounded by envy, it warps your perspectives and makes you think that you deserve . . . something. Anything. Just because you want it."

"What did you want?" Rosalind returned the crumpled letter to her basket.

Virginia looked up in mute surprise. "You are such a perceptive woman, Miss Thorne. How is it you've missed this?"

"I don't think I have." Rosalind moved the embroidery hoop

so she could sit down beside Virginia. "You wanted Captain Seymore. You're in love with him."

Virginia nodded. "He comes here often, you know. Usually on his own, when Margaretta is out . . . somewhere. We talk. He . . . he is not a bad man, Miss Thorne. He just . . . he was dazzled, and he realized too late that enchantment is not love, or the kind of partnership marriage can be, and should be."

You felt sorry for him, and you were lonely and unhappy, and all that blossomed into something brighter. But Rosalind kept this to herself. "And because you loved him, and you did not wish to see him continue in his unhappy marriage, you decided to help matters along."

Virginia nodded miserably. "I managed to convince myself that Margaretta had indeed betrayed him. That her child was not his." She swallowed hard. "It is as if I'd contracted the infection from Bertram. You have no idea how much time he and Johanna spend brooding on the title. They are like children staring in the window of a cake shop. Bertram will always maunder on, asking why an invalid and an obsequious fool should have so much when he had so little, through a simple accident of birth." She twisted her fingers together. "When you hear a thought repeated so often, you begin to believe. And when that thought leads you to a way to help someone . . ."

"Margaretta thinks you are her friend," Rosalind said.

"I am. After a fashion. None of this is Margaretta's fault. I've seen her sort before, a lot, actually. She learned early that a certain kind of charm can open the grandest doors. Can I blame her for using her power? Especially when I know perfectly well I would have done the same, had I been able to." Virginia traced a circle in the air around her plain face.

"So, you convinced yourself Margaretta had made a cuckold of her husband. You wrote the letters so he would divorce her."

Virginia smiled weakly. "He was vacillating. Some days he was sure she was guilty, other days he tried so hard to convince himself she was innocent." A tear slid down from the corner of her eye. "I thought the letters would make it easier for him to get the divorce, and leave him with fewer regrets. It quickly became obvious, though, that I had only made things worse, so I stopped. But the damage was done. And now . . ." She shook her head. "Now he's going to the gallows and it's my fault."

"It has not happened yet," Rosalind said quickly, because Virginia's hands had begun to tremble. "And it may not happen at all, if we keep our heads. I need you to tell me though, what happened that night? Sir Bertram dined at Captain Seymore's house. We know that. Then Margaretta left to go to the Hoffmans'. Were you at home here? Did you see what Lady Bertram did?"

"Johanna did nothing," said Virginia. "She was home all evening. I dined with the girls in the nursery. Johanna had a tray in her room and then came down to do some sewing. I was writing some letters, of my own, not . . . well." She gestured toward Rosalind's basket. "Sir Bertram came home and sat for a time with Lady Bertram. They had their usual conversation about the unfairness of life in general and how the wrong people lived or died. Then, they went to bed, and I stayed up to finish my letters, and to think about my situation, about my girls, about . . ."

"William," said Rosalind for her.

"Yes. Then, the maid came and told me that William was at the door. He wanted Sir Bertram, but he'd gone to bed, so what should she do? He was not in very good shape, she said.

"Of course he was drunk. I had him brought into the sitting room and got a pot of strong coffee made up for him and sat with him while he drank it. We talked and . . . I was tired. I was sad. I saw how Sir Bertram was playing on the worst of his weaknesses and how the struggle between trying to do what his family wanted and what he knew to be right was killing him."

"You told him you loved him."

"Yes, as it happens. I did." Virginia picked up her embroidery hoop and stared at its bouquet of spring flowers. "I told him I expected nothing. I would make no trouble. I know I am a plain woman. I've no gift for attraction and no money and . . . well, set that aside. I also told him he should know that Margaretta was loyal to him, that Bertram was just trying to get him to declare her child a bastard because of the title. I knew this would mean an end to any thought of divorce, but I wanted him to know the truth."

"Did you tell him you wrote the letters?"

"Yes," she said softly. "And I told him I was sorry I had done so."

"Why?"

She laid her needlework back down and met Rosalind's gaze. This time, her eyes were dry and quite clear. "Because, Miss Thorne, after much reflection and many tears, I decided I would rather be able to live with myself than gain William's hand by such low deception."

"What did he do?"

Virginia laughed a little. "He stared, for a long time. He . . . took my hand and he held it. We were both shaking. I was on the point of tears. Then he kissed my hand and he left."

Left and went to his club to drink, because he didn't know what else to do. Left to stagger around town looking for the wife whom he did not love and who did not love him. He left to become dizzy and drunk, trying to understand what had happened, and who he should believe and what it all meant. He had thought his wife had betrayed him, and then learned to his shame that it was his brother who had truly done so, and he didn't know what to do.

"And you are sure that Sir and Lady Bertram were home all night?" Rosalind asked. "Neither one of them went out?"

"I am sure," said Virginia firmly. "I did not go to bed at all. I sat up with my tears. You can ask the servants if you need to."

"No. I believe you."

Virginia nodded. "Miss Thorne, you should probably know this. I have hired an attorney for William. He didn't want me to, but I did anyway." She smiled at the surprise on Rosalind's face. "I'm a widow, Miss Thorne, it gives me certain freedoms. William also told me to keep silent about . . . my feelings and what I have seen. But if it means I will save his life, I will say and do whatever is necessary."

"I know it," Rosalind told her. "Give me a day or two more. If no other way can be found, then I will go with you to speak with the attorneys."

"Thank you." Virginia reached out and the two women clasped hands and for a moment, held on tightly. "What will you do now?" she asked.

"I will do my best to try to find that other way." Rosalind stood up but as she reached for her basket, she paused. "Virginia? Where are Sir and Lady Bertram now?"

"Oh," she sighed. "The dowager marchioness is having what she calls a little entertainment for her particular set, and Sir and Lady Bertram have decided, of course, they cannot neglect her."

"Why aren't you there?"

Virginia smiled. "Great heavens, what would I do at one of the marchioness's gatherings? I have no money to lose at cards."

CHAPTER 36

Matters Overseen and Overheard

*During the summer months, it is much frequented as a
promenade, but there is not at present sufficient traffic to
afford the prospect of much profit to the proprietors.*
—Samuel Leigh, *Leigh's New Picture of London*

Sunday dawned bright and clear, and hot. Rosalind took herself
to church and sat in the pew.

What do I do? she asked as she stood and knelt and sang and kept
her eyes on the priest without hearing a single word of his sermon.

Because now that she knew about the dowager marchioness's
card parties, about her past and something of the nature of her
"particular set," she knew of whom she could ask the last few
questions that just might tie the remaining threads together.

The problem was, it would mean tugging on the one connection she had privately sworn she would never use.

What do I do?

She was still asking that question when she returned home
and changed into her lightest walking costume. The brooding
slowed her usual efficient manner of dressing, so Rosalind came
down the stairs only a few minutes before Mrs. Kendricks
announced that Lord Casselmain had arrived.

"Miss Thorne, I'm hoping you can convince Louisa to talk,"

said Devon as he waited for Mrs. Kendricks to help Rosalind on with her pelisse and bonnet. "We've got her out of her room, but it took both myself and Mrs. Showell to do it, and she's done nothing since but sit and pout. Truth be told, I'm a little worried about her."

"Don't be," Rosalind told him. "It's only two days since the funeral. She and her friends will calm down, especially once she realizes how deeply uncomfortable black bombazine is during a hot spell."

"Hmm. I had not thought about that. As usual, Miss Thorne, you are a step ahead." Devon offered her his arm and she took it, grateful for her bonnet's full sides so he could not see the uneasy expression on her face.

What am I going to do?

Mrs. Showell had not been exaggerating. Louisa had indeed put on full mourning, complete with a black lace veil and net gloves. Devon helped Rosalind into the phaeton beside her.

"I'm so very sorry for your loss, Louisa," said Rosalind.

Louisa made no answer, except to pull out her black hand-kerchief and lift her veil just enough to apply it to her nose.

Devon climbed onto the box and touched up his matched chestnut bays. The horses set off at an even trot.

"How is Mrs. Showell today?" she asked Louisa.

Louisa turned her veiled face away. Rosalind bit her tongue, and reminded herself of her resolve to let time and the summer sun do their work. Despite this, she had a momentary and utterly uncharitable urge to shout at the girl and shake her for her ridiculous theatrics.

He would have laughed at you! He cared for no one!

Except that was not entirely true. He had, in his way, cared for Mrs. Seymore. But why? What was Margaretta to him?

And what was she to the dowager marchioness?

The Waterloo Bridge had opened earlier in the season to great pomp and ceremony. The Prince Regent himself had been there. Bands had played and the lifeguards had marched on parade. No such ceremony was occurring today, but because the bridge was new and interesting it was a popular promenade. On a hot and sunny day such as today, the fashionable enjoyed driving or walking along its shining white span and telling each other various facts about its construction.

Louisa, of course, declined to get out of the carriage. Devon rolled his eyes, but impatiently agreed she could stay in the company of his man and the horses. He gave Rosalind his arm and they walked away to join the other promenaders. As they did, Rosalind nodded back behind them, so Devon could turn to see Louisa in the carriage, itching and fidgeting and tugging at the shoulders of her dress.

Devon smiled and they walked on. The breeze off the Thames was most refreshing and they watched the sailing ships and the rowboats and nodded to the people they knew, and Rosalind could not think of anything to say beyond the simplest of small talk.

It was not long before Devon, evidently, had had enough.

"How goes the matter of Mrs. Seymore?" he asked.

Rosalind stared straight ahead, keeping the shield of her slanting bonnet sides between them. "Not as quickly as it needs to, I'm afraid. I thought yesterday I had made some progress, but it turned out to be nothing at all and . . . Devon, I need to ask you about something. I don't want to. I never would except there's no time . . ." Her sentence, and her determination, trailed away.

He walked in silence for a long time, swinging his stick. But when he spoke again, it was softly and seriously. "How can I help?"

Rosalind took a deep breath. She could still pull back. She did not have to make use of this man in this way.

Why? Why am I doing this?

Because I want to see what he will do. I want to see how far he will go. I need to know . . .

I need to . . .

But Rosalind found she could not finish the thought.

So instead, she told Devon about her trip to Woolcombe, about the threads of money and blackmail that ran through all the events surrounding the murder of Fletcher Cavendish. She told him that Sir and Lady Bertram had most certainly not done this thing. She told him that Mrs. Cecil Seymore had fallen in love with her brother-in-law and had tried to interfere with his marriage.

She also told him of the dowager marchioness and her illicit gambling, and how Fletcher had been sure he could get the money he needed, from somewhere close at hand.

"Do you think Cavendish meant to get it from the marchioness?"

"Yes. I think he threatened to reveal her secrets if she did not give him what he needed."

"But in order for Bow Street or an attorney to take this idea at all seriously, you need proof that she has secrets to be revealed."

"Yes," admitted Rosalind. *And it has to be better proof than just Lord Adolphus's hundred pounds and his desire for his mother not to be troubled any further.*

Devon sighed. "I'm sorry to have to disappoint you, Rosalind. The dowager marchioness may have secrets, and they may be dark ones, but giving private gambling parties is not going to be among them. It is not entirely legal, but you may trust me when I say that there would not be more than a fine attached, and next to no scandal at all."

"It's not the parties I'm wondering about," she said. "But . . . it's what they might relate to in regards to the marchioness's conduct. Miss Onslow said the late marquis was older than she was. She also said that the dowager was notorious in her youth. She . . ." Rosalind stopped. She swallowed. "There is something about her that bears a striking resemblance to Mrs. Seymore."

Devon stopped them. He turned to face her. "Do you think that Mrs. Seymore is the dowager marchioness's natural daughter?"

"I think it's possible," Rosalind said. "I think that all this talk of Mrs. Seymore and the legitimacy of her child may have its origins not only in Mrs. Seymore's behavior, but her background. I wanted to know—"

"M-miss Thorne!" called a woman's voice. "I th-thought that was you!"

Rosalind stopped and turned so abruptly, she and Devon collided with the couple behind them, and had to spend the next several moments apologizing and ascertaining that no one was hurt. When the other couple moved on, Rosalind was able to see a man and a woman standing arm and arm by the bridge rail.

It was Penelope Vaughn who hailed them, and with her stood Lord Adolphus.

Rosalind pasted a smile over the shock on her face. Hoping she did not look anything like as awkward as she felt, she led Devon over to them.

"H-h-h-how nice to see you," said Miss Vaughn. "How are you t-t-today?"

"Very well, Miss Vaughn." Rosalind made her curtsy. "Lord Adolphus Greaves, allow me to introduce Devon Winterbourne, Lord Casselmain."

The men bowed and agreed it was very good to meet each other. Fortunately, like Rosalind, Devon had a lifetime's worth of practice keeping his thoughts out of his face and he betrayed no hint that he and Rosalind had just been discussing murder and Lord Adolphus's family in the same breath.

"A very fine day, is it n-n-not?" said Penelope. Her hands remained looped around Lord Adolphus's arm. "Are you enjoying the v-view?"

Rosalind agreed it was and said that they were. Devon spoke lightly to Adolphus, asking where his lands were, what he thought of the prospects of the shooting for the coming autumn, a bill in Parliament, all the commonplaces. But Rosalind had to fight to keep her gaze from drifting to Miss Vaughn's hands. Penelope was not wearing gloves, which was unusual, and a little improper. But what she was wearing was a ring of sapphires and diamonds.

And she wore it on her left hand.

Penelope caught the direction of her gaze. She lifted one finger to her lips and smiled. Rosalind nodded once and smiled to indicate her congratulations.

"As delightful as this is, I'm afraid you must excuse us," said Lord Adolphus. "I promised to have Miss Vaughn home to her father before four o'clock. You will excuse us, Miss Thorne? Lord Casselmain?"

They all said their farewells and strolled away in their separate directions. But Rosalind could not help thinking to herself, *Lady Bertram is going to be devastated. What will they do now?*

"Rosalind," said Devon, lifting her out of her private, and not entirely pleasant, thoughts. "Before we met your friends, you were going to ask me another question. What is it?"

For a moment, Rosalind considered letting the matter rest where it was. Prying information out of Devon was distasteful in the extreme, and her spirits were already depressed. But Rosalind found herself looking over her shoulder at Lord Adolphus and Miss Vaughn, as they strolled arm-in-arm down the bridge. She also thought about Virginia sitting alone in her workroom, determined to do the right thing even when it meant the ruin of all her hopes. Rosalind felt her hesitations fall away. The captain's life was at stake, and so were the other lives around him. If she turned delicate, they might all be lost. Rosalind found she was not ready to take that risk. If Devon could not understand . . .

Well, perhaps it is better if we both know that now.

"I wanted to know if your brother Hugh ever attended any of Lady Weyland's parties, and if, perhaps, there were any rumors about her having had an affair, or affairs."

"Is that why you agreed to come out with me? Because you needed to ask this question?" Devon's voice was light, conversational. Rosalind did not look to see his expression. She did not want to know.

"No," she told him, and tried not to be irked at the question. *He has every right to ask under the circumstances.* "I came out because I wanted to see you, and Louisa."

She did not look. She would not look. She did not want to watch Devon's face while he tried to decide if he believed her.

"Yes," he said finally. "My brother did go to some of Lady Weyland's parties. They were famous once upon a time and . . . there was always somebody there willing to let him play on credit or for things such as a watch or a stick pin or such."

Rosalind bit her lip and tried not to feel she had betrayed them both by making him speak of this.

"As to whether or not she ever had an affair, or an outside child, I don't know. But if you ask it of me, I may be able to find out." He paused. "Are you going to ask it of me?"

"I don't want to," she told him again, and did not bother to disguise the pleading in her voice. "I would not, only there is no time. The trial could be as early as tomorrow."

"Yes, of course," Devon murmured. He also stopped and gazed upstream at the crowd of boats and barges. Rosalind tried to breathe and hold her peace. Devon would make up his own mind. Or not.

But all he said was, "We should probably get back. I'm sure Louisa has roasted long enough. If I bring her home in a faint, Mrs. Showell will never forgive me."

"Yes, of course," said Rosalind, and inside, her heart cracked, just a little.

CHAPTER 37

Venturing into the Past

He smiled but to deceive: He courted but to destroy: and by
his studied and disguised reserve prevented suspicion.
—*The Trial of William Henry Hall vs. Major George Barrow*
for Criminal Conversation

. .

Rosalind and Devon did not bother with polite chatter as they returned to the phaeton. Devon helped her in next to Louisa and closed the door. Their eyes met, and still they said nothing.

I'm sorry, Devon. I'm sorry, Mrs. Kendricks, she added ruefully. *I'm sorry, Mrs. Showell.*

I'm sorry.

Fortunately, the drive back to Little Russell Street was a short one and not without its bright moments.

"I have decided to put off mourning." Louisa threw back her veil. "I know Mr. Cavendish would want us to carry forward in our lives with grace and dignity, just as he would."

"I'm certain of it," said Rosalind solemnly. She also handed Louisa a fresh handkerchief so the girl could mop her indecorously streaming brow.

The clots and clusters of newspapermen on the walk beside Rosalind's door had all but cleared. This, Rosalind knew, was a temporary reprieve, and the moment the trial was announced, they would all be back in force. She tried not to blush as she saw them taking note of who she was with and scribbling it all down in their books.

"You could come stay at the house until this is over," murmured Devon as he helped her from his carriage. "With Mrs. Showell and Louisa . . ."

But Rosalind shook her head. "No," she said. "I'm fine. Bow Street has put all of them on notice."

And we both have too much thinking to do. She kept her eyes straight ahead, because she did not know if she would see some trace of relief on Devon's face.

I will deal with it all in its place, thought Rosalind as she said her farewells and closed the door behind her. *I must keep my mind on the matters immediately in front of me. On the death of Fletcher Cavendish and its ties to the Seymore branch of the family.*

Rosalind thought again of Lord Adolphus and Miss Vaughn. What would Lady Bertram do when she found out? Was she the reason the engagement, as it seemed, must be kept a secret?

Or was it Lady Weyland who would object? Rosalind frowned at this idea as she unknotted her bonnet ribbon.

"Oh, I am sorry, miss!" Mrs. Kendricks exclaimed as she hurried up the passage from the kitchen. "I was just putting supper in the oven and did not hear you."

"That's quite all right, Mrs. Kendricks," said Rosalind. "I am still capable of taking off my own hat."

Her housekeeper looked skeptical, and despite everything, Rosalind smiled. "Did anything noteworthy happen while I was out?"

Mrs. Kendricks's face tightened. "Mr. Harkness stopped by, but I told him you were out."

Their eyes met and Rosalind did not have to ask the question poised on her lips. *You told him I was with Devon. Because you're worried . . . because you think . . .*

"He left you a note," said Mrs. Kendricks. "I put it on your desk."

"Thank you, Mrs. Kendricks."

But when Rosalind picked up the note in question, she frowned. She had seen Mr. Harkness's writing. She was no expert in the analysis of such things like Miss Onslow, but she would swear on her life that Adam was incapable of writing her name in such exaggerated copperplate script.

Neither would he ever use a seal that particular shade of rose pink.

Rosalind broke the seal and unfolded the letter and read it. Her knees shook, and failed her, and she sat down hard in the chair.

The note was a short one, written in the same elaborate slanted writing as her name had been.

Miss Thorne, it said.

You may call if you choose. Tomorrow at noon.

Cynthia Sharps

Cynthia. There was an address. It was in a fashionable square, not too distant from where Rosalind sat. Barely half a mile, in fact. Half a mile and a world away.

Charlotte.

My sister.

Devon had made inquiries, but it was Mr. Harkness who had found her. Of course it was, because it was what he was trained to do.

Her hands were shaking. Tears pressed behind her eyes, but she could not tell whether they were for relief or shame. Or fear.

"Are you all right, miss?" Mrs. Kendricks had come in without Rosalind hearing.

"Yes," she lied without turning around. "I just . . ."

But at that moment the doorbell rang. Rosalind looked up with an attitude very close to despair. Was there not to be a moment's peace?

Mrs. Kendricks set her jaw and marched out into the foyer. A heartbeat later, Rosalind heard the exclamations of a familiar voice. She rose, trembling, to her feet and turned just as Alice burst through the door.

"Rosalind!" Alice cried, darting forward to grab Rosalind's hands. "It's a Sunday miracle!"

"What's happened?"

"I've found her!" Alice bounced up and down on her toes like a schoolgirl.

"Who?"

"Margaretta's mother!" Alice shouted triumphantly. At the same time, she noticed the crumpled paper in Rosalind's hand. "What's that?"

"Nothing," replied Rosalind. "Nothing at all."

"The wedding was at St. Margaret's-by-the-Lane," Alice told her as they climbed into the hackney cab she had kept waiting. "The church register gives the bride's name as Margaret Coyningham, with her parents listed as John and Mary Coyningham, formerly of Number 16, Simonds Lane, but now both deceased."

"Margaretta said she was an orphan."

"Margaretta has said a large number of things," Alice reminded her. "Now, I talked with the curate, and he was able to point me to Simonds Lane and there . . ." Alice stopped, her eyes sparkling.

"There, what?" demanded Rosalind.

"You'll see," said Alice.

"Alice!"

"Oh, no. For this once, Rosalind Thorne, I'm going to be the one with the mystery."

As it happened, it was easy to see what led Alice to believe she'd found the right place. In fact, it appeared in the form of a large written notice affixed to the freshly painted door of an otherwise unremarkable house:

HOME OF THE LATE FLETCHER CAVENDISH,
OF THE ROYAL THEATER
ALL PERSONS WISHING TO SEE THE ACTUAL ROOMS
MAY APPLY TO
MRS. COYNINGHAM, NO. 16
FOR ADMISSION
3D.

"Oh, dear," murmured Rosalind.

"Actually, it's very encouraging," said Alice. "Some people do not like to talk to the newspapers. This tells us she will be more than willing to spread the word of her connection, to Mr. Cavendish at least."

"Will she be giving tours on a Sunday, though?" asked Rosalind.

Alice gave her a pitying look. "Perhaps, though, it would be best if we did not mention Margaretta right away."

"Because if the daughter has disavowed the mother, the mother may not be in any hurry to acknowledge the daughter?"

"Exactly."

Rosalind nodded. "I shall stand back and let you lead us."

Alice curtsied in acknowledgment and together they hurried across the rutted street.

Number 16 proved to be a brick and timber residence with deep eaves. Its door was also freshly painted, but was very much dented and chipped underneath the brass knocker. Alice plied that knocker smartly enough to leave a few new scars on the wood. A slightly grubby boy opened the door and peered out at them.

"Is another party, Mrs. Coynin'ham!" he shouted back into the house.

"Now what have I told you? No shouting! You come and get me!" A woman, presumably Mrs. Coyningham, hurried up the dim passage. She cuffed the boy, but turned a broad smile on Rosalind and Alice. "Good morning, ladies. Come to see the rooms of our very dear late lamented Mr. Cavendish?"

Mrs. Coyningham was a plain, stout woman. Her hands had been hardened by years of work. Rosalind found herself looking closely at her. She had dark hair, now mostly iron gray, and large, dark eyes. But there was nothing of Margaretta's beauty about her, and nothing of her sophistication. For a moment, though, Rosalind thought she saw the same flash of calculating intelligence in this woman's eyes that she had spotted in Mrs. Seymore's.

Did this woman give birth to Margaretta? Or was it Lady Weyland? Rosalind tried to compare in her mind this woman with the beautiful, sophisticated, calculating dowager, and found she could not tell.

"Yes, of course, we are here to see the rooms," Alice was saying. "But we were hoping to speak with you as well, Mrs. Coyningham. I am Alice Littlefield, and I write for *The London Chronicle*."

"Them papers," sneered Mrs. Coyningham. "Tramping up and down my stairs, wanting a look for free. You can take your papers and—"

"We would not expect you to waste your time," said Alice immediately. "I cannot speak for other establishments, but the *Chronicle* will of course pay the admission, and compensate you for any additional time."

This may or may not have been true before the landlady opened the door, but it hardly mattered. Rosalind, to prove she and Alice were there in partnership, opened her reticule and drew out a coin. Mrs. Coyningham squinted at it and, apparently satisfied, tucked it into the pocket hanging from her apron. "If you ladies will wait here one moment, I'll go and get the keys."

Good as her word, Mrs. Coyningham returned with a bunch of keys in her hand a moment later and led them both back toward Number 20.

"It was in the good old days that Mr. Cavendish came to us," Mrs. Coyningham said with the air of someone beginning a familiar recitation. "I remember it like it was yesterday. It was summer then, like it is now, and just as hot as ever could be. 'Madam,' he said to me, 'I have worn out three pairs of shoes searching for a place where I might lay my weary head, and nowhere throughout the city have I heard more praised than the rooms of Mrs. Coyningham.'"

Having heard Mr. Cavendish speak, Rosalind found herself believing he might actually have said this, or something close to it.

Mrs. Coyningham led them up a set of fresh-scrubbed stairs, which creaked badly under their shoes, to a passage that smelled of damp and coal smoke. A black and slightly wilted funeral wreath hung on the door at their right.

"Here we are, dears." Mrs. Coyningham opened the door and stood back so Alice and Rosalind could walk in. The flat

they entered was notable for being scrupulously clean. Otherwise, these were of the plainest possible kind of rooms, sparsely
furnished with whitewashed walls and bare, splintered boards.

"This is the very front parlor to which Mr. Cavendish returned every day after another success on the boards. 'The
boards,' you see, is what a professional actor calls the stage or
the theater," Mrs. Coyningham added. Alice nodded vigorously.
She also brought out her notebook and pencil and began taking
notes in rapid shorthand.

"He wore a blue cloak in them days, and he always hung it
here on this peg." Mrs. Coyningham touched the peg in question. "Always in a rush, was our Mr. Cavendish. I cannot count
the number of times I had to fly after him to take him his hat."
She fondly smiled at the pegs, and the memory. "I always kept
a good fire going for him." She moved to stand by the hearth.
"And lor' what it did cost in coals. 'Never mind that, Mrs.
Coyningham,' he'd tell me. 'Just you keep my room good and
warm.' 'Twas for his voice, you see. He couldn't risk taking a
chill or a cold, bless him, or he'd be out a night's wages for the
performance."

From here she went on to point out the very chair, the very
stool, the very table, the very window, the very washstand and
basin, and the very table where Mr. Cavendish performed such
remarkable feats as sitting, lacing his boots, washing his face,
and eating his supper.

"It always had to be piping hot, he was that particular. But he
was ever such a gentleman, it was a real pleasure to see him enjoy
a good meal. Nothing fancy for Mr. Cavendish, not like some.
'Mrs. Coyningham,' he said. 'A good plain joint of English beef
gives me more pleasure than all the feasts of the emperors!'
Roasted was his preference. He did not care for boiled."

Rosalind looked about the room and tried to imagine Fletcher

Cavendish as a young man in these bare rooms, running in and out at odd hours, returning with friends, male and female. Dreaming of the future, hoping for a part and a decent payday.

Then, she tried to picture the dazzling Margaretta here as a little girl, and she failed utterly.

"Did you ever get to see him perform?" Alice was asking Mrs. Coyningham.

"Oh, you couldn't stop him performing!" the landlady laughed. "Many's the evening he'd come down to my little kitchen and recite his new speeches."

"A private performance by Fletcher Cavendish!" gasped Alice. "Thousands would envy you!"

"He always asked my opinion, too. 'Now, Mrs. Coyningham, you've a sharp eye,' he'd say. 'Tell me what you think and be honest now.' Always so anxious to improve, he was." She sighed. "I knew it was only a matter of time before he'd leave us for the wider world. You cannot hide such a light under a bushel, no indeed, you cannot."

"I imagine Margaret enjoyed his readings?"

"It was more like her reading to h—" Mrs. Coyningham stopped, and Mrs. Coyningham turned. "Who is Margaret?" Mrs. Coyningham's dark eyes narrowed at Alice. "I don't know any Margaret."

"I was referring to your daughter, Margaret," said Alice calmly. "Now Mrs. William Seymore, the noted poetess."

"You're wrong," said Mrs. Coyningham flatly. "And you've had your look. You'll be leaving now."

Alice did not budge. "I'd be sorry to have to leave so soon, Mrs. Coyningham. Because you see . . ." Alice opened her reticule and pulled out two gold sovereigns. She held them up for the woman who gave three-penny tours to admire. "I've brought these for the mother of the celebrated poetess, Mrs. William

Seymore. I have two more if she's willing to talk with me about her daughter."

The internal war that was waged behind Mrs. Coyningham's eyes was fierce, but it was brief. She held out her palm. "I didn't realize you was talking about my girl," she muttered.

Alice laid one of the coins in her palm. "Then you do have a daughter named Margaret and she is now Mrs. William Seymore?"

"That's right. Not that she ever cared to let me know it." The woman pocketed the sovereign. "I didn't find out she was married until Mrs. Cheetham up the way showed me a notice in the paper."

"What happened? Did she run away from home?" asked Rosalind.

"'S right." Mrs. Coyningham folded her arms. "I was away helping my brother, and put her in charge of the houses. I came home, and she was gone. Left me ten pounds on the kitchen table. Ten pounds! For nineteen years of raising her and teaching her and making sure she had everything I could give!" For a moment Rosalind thought the woman was going to spit. "Now she's a fine lady with her books and her poetry and all the upper crust singing her praises, and she tells them she's an orphan." Mrs. Coyningham glowered at Alice. "You write that, if you please! You write and you tell the whole world she's an ungrateful daughter!"

"When did this happen?" asked Alice.

Mrs. Coyningham shrugged. "Fifteen years ago, twenty maybe. She was eighteen or nineteen, I think."

"Why have you never told anyone?" asked Alice.

"Did Mr. Cavendish leave at the same time?" asked Rosalind.

Mrs. Coyningham's jaw tightened, and that was all the answer either woman needed.

"They did leave together," Rosalind said.

"And you assumed she disgraced herself," added Alice.

"An' what was I supposed to ass-ooom?" drawled the landlady. "I saw the way 'e was with women. I thought my Margaret was too smart for that, but 'e got her in the end. That's why the tours. Figured I should get something back for all he took from me. She was always a good girl, a hard worker, very good at her lessons. Mr. Elliott lent her poetry books and told 'er she should go out and sell 'er writing . . . a girl can only be flattered so long before it gets under her skin."

Elliott? thought Rosalind. *Who is Elliott?* Then, of course, she knew.

Alice, in the meantime, had contrived to look entirely shocked. "I'm sure there was nothing improper between them, Mrs. Coyningham. But genius does recognize genius. You said it yourself, a light cannot be hidden under a bushel."

Mrs. Coyningham snorted. "A light doesn't deny the candle, does it? A light doesn't say the candle's dead and forget that candle slaved for years and never send a coin or a bit of anything to help get her through the winter."

"Perhaps she will now," said Alice. "Perhaps with all the troubles she's been through, she'll have a change of heart."

"She may do as she pleases." Mrs. Coyningham sniffed. She lifted her chin and turned her head, and the light from the window caught her profile, and Rosalind saw it. Under the weight of years and hard work and strain, she finally saw the resemblance. It was in the shape of her eyes as well as their color, the rounded line of her jaw.

This was Margaretta's mother. Rosalind's hope that she had uncovered the core of the troubles crumbled away.

But then why does the dowager remind me so strongly of

Margaretta? Rosalind asked herself as she struggled to resettle her thoughts and pay attention to what was going on in front of her. *There must be some reason behind so marked a resemblence.*

"Now, I've answered your questions," Mrs. Coyningham was saying. "You give over what you promised and you take yourselves out of here."

"Of course." Alice brought out the remaining sovereign. Mrs. Coyningham snatched it off her palm and stuffed it into her pocket.

"Do you have any message for Margaret should we see her?" asked Rosalind.

From the anger in Mrs. Coyningham's features, Rosalind feared the message would be unrepeatable, even for Alice. But that anger faded slowly. "You tell her I have never forgotten her," she said. "You tell her I have never stopped praying . . ." She hesitated. "You just tell her I'm still here."

Oh, yes. This woman was indeed a mother, and she was pining for her missing child, whether she wanted it known or not.

"We will tell her, Mrs. Coyningham," said Rosalind. "And thank you."

Rosalind and Alice curtsied to the landlady and moved to take their leave, but Rosalind stopped when she reached the door.

"Mrs. Coyningham, a moment ago you used the name *Elliott* to refer to Mr. Cavendish."

"Well, that's the name he gave back then, isn't it? Malcolm Elliott. I expect he thought *Cavendish* would sound better from the stage or some such."

"I expect so. Thank you, Mrs. Coyningham."

The only answer she gave was to raise her chin.

Rosalind and Alice left her there and closed the door behind themselves. But as they walked down the creaking stairs, they did both pause, to look to each other and silently acknowledge the sound of weeping from the room at the top of the stairs.

"Well," sighed Alice as they emerged into the muddy lane once more. "It looks like it was your common or garden-variety scandal after all," said Alice. "Young Mr. Cavendish ran off with young Miss Coyningham, and after a while, they both went their separate ways. It's nothing to do with the Seymores or the dowager marchioness."

"No," said Rosalind. "That doesn't fit. Even if Margaretta was a naive young girl at the time, she isn't now. She understood the man she was dealing with. She would know he could not be expected to help her simply because they'd once been in love. There's something else."

"What could it be?" Alice peered at her friend. "Rosalind, you've got that look in your eye. What are you thinking?"

"I'm wondering how a starving young actor and the daughter of a woman who keeps a boardinghouse get ten pounds to leave her mother and still have enough money left to successfully vanish," she said slowly. "I'm thinking about scandal, Alice, and how it can affect low as well as high."

Alice considered this. "Except when scandal affects the middling classes," she said slowly, "sometimes it's not called a scandal, is it?"

"No," said Rosalind. "It's called a crime."

CHAPTER 38

As We Shall All Be Reunited

Servants of other *families ought not to be told the peculiar habits and conduct of your own.*
——Samuel and Sarah Adams, *The Complete Servant*

Naturally, Alice wanted to proceed at once to Bow Street.

"It's Sunday," Rosalind reminded her. "None of the principal officers will be there."

"Tomorrow morning then. The major wants me in the office but he will excuse me for—"

"I can't," said Rosalind. "I have . . . an appointment."

Alice narrowed her too shrewd eyes. "What could possibly be more important than this?"

"I . . . I'll tell you afterwards," said Rosalind. She had to repeat variations of this several times before Alice finally accepted it.

"If you hear the trial is happening, send word," Rosalind told her friend as they parted on the doorstep of Little Russell Street. "I will come at once."

Alice frowned, and promised, and frowned again.

Now Rosalind stood in front of a new residence in a quiet neighborhood, with the pink letter in her hand. The house was terraced brick and very fine. The square in which it was situated was neat and respectable. Rosalind would not have blushed to be seen there at any time of day.

I don't need to do this, she said to herself. *I can turn and go. I can come again. What if the trial is being held today? What if it is happening this moment? A man could die because . . . because . . .*

Because I want to see my sister. Because I want to know why she left me. Because, may God help me, I want to know that she's all right.

She just had to hope the world was kind enough not to hang a man because of it.

Rosalind rang the house bell and was admitted by a plain-faced, plain-dressed maid, who took her up the stairs and let her into a parlor and asked her to please wait.

Rosalind stood in the middle of the room and tried to breathe calmly. She tried to tell herself that she was wrong in her assumptions about Charlotte's mode of living. Surely, she had been mistaken somehow, somewhere.

But the room around her told the tale, with its stylized French furniture and its silks and gilding. It was too rich, and too luxurious. In fact, what it reminded Rosalind of most was Mr. Fullerton's apartments at Graham's.

The door opened behind her. Rosalind drew in one more breath.

"Hello, Rosalind."

Rosalind turned. "Hello, Charlotte. Or do you prefer Cynthia?"

Her sister smiled. "From you, I think I'd rather Charlotte. I don't get to hear my name much these days."

She hasn't changed all that much, Rosalind realized. Charlotte still carried herself with her confident, sophisticated air. Her face still held the beauty that had marked her out when they were young—clear and fair, yet with something of an edge to her, a hint that this was not simply another pretty girl to be taken for granted. Or perhaps that was just the memory of all her tart teasing from the days they'd shared a bedroom. And a home. And . . . and . . . and . . .

"Would you care to sit down?" Charlotte gestured her toward a pair of round-backed, gold silk chairs.

"Thank you."

Charlotte settled herself on the sofa, lounging against its curved arm, the skirts of her peony pink dress spreading around her.

"You look well," said Rosalind.

"I am well," replied Charlotte. "How are you?"

Rosalind found she had no answer. "Where . . . How is our father?"

Charlotte sighed, clearly just a little disappointed. Rosalind felt a ridiculous pinprick of irritation.

"Father is in his rooms," her sister answered. "I kept him with me for a while, but after a certain point, that proved . . . awkward. I pay for a couple of manservants to wait on him and keep him out of the worst of trouble."

"And he is well?"

"I will not insult you by saying I am surprised that you care. Yes, he is relatively well. I cannot always be there, but I receive regular reports."

Silence fell again. The Baroque clock on the mantelpiece ticked loudly. Rosalind glanced toward it and saw how the mantel was crowded with china figurines, mostly cavorting shepherds and shepherdesses, in, she noticed, various states of decorous *dishabille*.

"Why, Charlotte?" she asked the clock, and the figurines.

"That is a question that covers a lot of ground, Rosalind."

She made herself turn her gaze back toward her sister. *I will look at her*, she told herself. *I will see who she was and who she is and who I am as I stand near her. I am her sister. She is mine.*

"Why did you leave with him? Why didn't you *tell* me?"

Charlotte looked down at her perfectly kept hands. "You were seventeen, Rosalind. And a very silly seventeen, may I add. Soppy in love with Devon Winterbourne and thinking no one had noticed. I didn't believe you knew what a state our mother was in, or our father. And when he told me . . . he spun such a beautiful story. You know how he could do that."

Rosalind nodded.

"I wanted very badly to believe the things he told me about how he had been cheated by false friends, and about how desperately he needed me. When I compared a life of being father's helpmeet, and staying in our mother's house with her constant hectoring and nervous spasms and criticism . . . I didn't see it as any kind of choice at all really." Charlotte paused. "It was less than a year before I found out I had been the silly one."

"You could have come back," said Rosalind. "You could have written."

"No," her sister replied. "I couldn't. Not by then."

"Was it father's idea that you join the *demimonde?*"

"No," Charlotte said again, just as flatly and just as firmly. "That is one sin you cannot lay at his door. I set my own feet on this particular road. He did take the money, though."

Old anger surged up in Rosalind's veins. "You don't have to do this, Charlotte," she said earnestly.

"What else am I to do?"

"I have a house. You could come live with me."

But Charlotte only spread her pretty hands. "And then what would I be? Your housekeeper? Or just the fallen woman you so charitably took in because she now repents her sins and learns to make lace and knit caps for poor orphans?"

The retort stung, but Rosalind did not let it stop her. "We'd work something out. I've made my own life now and—"

"Yes, I've heard something about that." Rosalind looked up sharply and Charlotte smiled archly. "You're surprised? It's a small world, Rosalind, and society is far more permeable than it likes to believe. I've kept an ear out for word of you, and I've heard how you've made yourself into a useful woman. Working for your living. Mother would have fallen into despair at the two of us."

"Yes," Rosalind admitted. "She would." Because Mother would have seen little difference between what Rosalind did and what Charlotte did.

Charlotte's expression softened, and when she spoke again, she at least tried to be gentle. "If I came to stay with you, word of who I am and what I have been would get out soon enough, and there would go your reputation among the ladies you depend on."

"Perhaps I would not care."

"Perhaps I would." Charlotte smoothed down her pink skirts and rubbed her white hands together. For the first time since she'd entered the room, she seemed ill at ease.

"It is not so very bad, Rosalind," she said. "I am not romantic about any of it. I have money in the bank. In fact, there were times I was considering sending you some. I have a steady protector now, and he *is* very romantic. He has said he wants to marry me. I think I will turn him down. He'd have to divorce his wife to do it, and what a man will do to one, he will soon do to another."

Rosalind knew she should be appalled. Horrified, even. She should flee from this fallen woman and forget she ever existed. Charlotte Thorne should be thought dead.

And yet, when Rosalind thought of Captain Seymore in prison and his brother and sister-in-law so busy with their ambitions that they were willing to see him falsely condemned, the level of outrage she was meant to show simply would not come to her heart, or her tongue.

"You should probably go now," Charlotte said softly. "I expect my gentleman soon."

"Of course." Rosalind got to her feet. "I . . ." She stopped and swallowed and started again. "Thank you for agreeing to see me."

"I am glad you came, Rosalind."

Rosalind reached out. She grabbed her sister's hand and felt how it was slender and delicate and warm. And familiar. So very wonderfully, sadly familiar. "I'm glad I came, too," she said, and she looked directly into Charlotte's eyes. They were bright with the tears she was holding back.

"May I . . . write to you?" her sister asked.

"I'd like that," said Rosalind.

Charlotte's eyes slipped sideways to the clock. She pulled away, smoothing her skirts and running a palm across her brow. "You have to go, Rosalind. But I am truly glad you came. You will take care?"

"I will. Will you?"

Charlotte smiled, and Rosalind again saw that sharp edge that had always belonged to her sister. "I have been for ten years."

The maid showed Rosalind out. She walked across the cobbled square, passing the perfectly respectable tradesmen and the perfectly respectable matrons. A few men who might have been anything from clerks to shop owners stood talking on the corner. It was as normal a day as when Rosalind had mounted the stairs. Nothing had changed in the world at all.

On the far side of the square Rosalind stopped, and she turned. A well-dressed gentleman in buff and blue came sauntering down the walk, swinging his stick and whistling. He tipped his hat to a pair of women walking past and trotted up the steps to the house and let himself in.

She did not know him.

Rosalind turned and walked away.

CHAPTER 39

The Memory of Samuel Tauton

Encouraged by hopes of discovery . . . officers, newspaper men, and ingenious speculators all work together, and pursue a common track.

—Percy Hetherington Fitzgerald,
Chronicles of the Bow Street Police-Office

In the normal course of events, Bow Street's principal officers were discouraged from working on Sundays. As good, upstanding family men, they should be spending that day at church and at rest. This particular Sunday, Harkness found himself not only working, but thrown out of his own home.

"You get those things out of here, Adam Harkness!" His mother waved her dishrag at the piles of Cavendish's letters. "I'll not have my Sunday kitchen smelling like a bawdy house!"

Saturday had been spent entirely in the warren of the Theatre Royal, talking to everyone and anyone he could get to stand still long enough—from the tired and brassy young women of the chorus; to the old sailors who took the skills they gained working in the rigging and turned them to working the ropes that flew the scenery in and out; to the seamstresses and the mantua makers. No one could remember any untoward person coming or going from the principal dressing room. No one could remember any disturbance at any time that night, except when Captain Seymore had tried to get past "Old Knobby" Ulbrecht.

"Now, sir," they all said, "can I get on with my work?" That is, when they weren't damning his eyes and other portions of his anatomy, and ordering him out of the way.

From the theater, Adam had gone to the home of Sir and Lady Bertram, only to be turned away before he could even set foot in the door.

"My master says the matter is closed," the footman told him. "He says he will not have the peace of his home interfered with by Bow Street or the papers or any others."

"May I speak with Mrs. Cecil Seymore then?" Adam tried.

"My orders are to refuse all callers," said the footman. "So take yourself off, right?"

"Do you have any orders about taking a note?"

He didn't, and Harkness scribbled a few lines on a leaf from his notebook and gave it to the man along with a half crown, and took himself off, sour and discouraged.

"It's enough to make a man turn republican," he said to Sam Tauton as they took a meal together at Regent's Oyster House. "Sir Bertram's so set on finding a way to that title, he's willing to hang his brother."

"I don't suppose it could be he knows his brother's guilty?" suggested Tauton.

"No," replied Harkness firmly. "I'll grant that somebody in that family may have stabbed Cavendish, but it wasn't the man I saw in Newgate." Something haunted Seymore. Harkness was sure of it. But he was equally sure it was not a guilty conscience. With enough time, he might have been able to find the answer, but nothing like that much time remained.

"Well, if not Captain Seymore, then who?" asked Tauton.

But Harkness shook his head and drank his beer, and went

back out. There was an answer, and if it would not come to him, he would go and get it. So Sunday found him not at church, nor enjoying the roast at his family table, but in the patrol room with Mr. Cavendish's collection of love letters spread out in front of him. With them, he had another note, this one from Mr. Fetch.

Docket's moving fast. Several matters dropped. Our man could come up before the judge Monday.

Adam could hear the clock tick in Townsend's private office. He could hear the bells ringing out from the churches. Every sound of the passage of time reminded him that the day was waning. The trial would come up, whether or not he or Seymore's attorney was prepared. He would be called to give testimony and explain his evidence, and he had none. So the judge and the jury would look to the obvious suspect, the jealous husband.

"There is an answer," Adam growled. "Where is it?" he demanded of the useless flowery pages of his notebook, his worn patience, and his taxed memory. "Where is it?"

He was still asking himself that question when he woke late on Monday and, cursing himself for a sluggard and a fool, raced back to the station, to find Stafford had a note for him. He tore it open, and sagged against the wall in relief.

Not today, Mr. Fetch had written.

"One more day," muttered Harkness. "One more day and I've still not a clue in the world."

And so he went to the prison to try once more to talk to Seymore, who shut his mouth and turned his face to the wall.

And he went to Soho Square, and was once more turned away from the door. He stood beside the square's famous fountain of Charles II and stared at the windows like a frustrated suitor, but the drapes remained closed, and if Mrs. Cecil Seymore even knew that he was there, she was not coming out.

And he went back to the theater and questioned Dr. Arnold again, and Mr. Kean again, and Mrs. West again.

"I'm sorry," they told him. "Truly. I wish there was more."

And here he sat again, with the afternoon turning to evening outside, and the clock in Tauton's office making its damned incessant ticking, and he could not do the one thing he wanted so much to do.

He could not go find Rosalind.

It was ridiculous. He should not be afraid, but since he'd left the letter he'd gotten from her sister, he could not make himself return to her house, or write her, or make any other approach, because he could not stand the possibility that she might turn him away.

She never would. She wanted this. She wanted to know.

Except when people got what they wanted, sometimes they found it was more than they could stand. Harkness stared at the scented letters, all from women who had gotten what they wanted of Mr. Cavendish, and found it had done them no good at all.

"Mr. Harkness?" called Tommy from the doorway. "Mr. Harkness, there's a couple of ladies here . . ."

Harkness spun about to see Miss Thorne and Alice Littlefield.

"I am beginning, sir, to believe you have fabricated your mother and family," said Rosalind. "I think you live here."

Adam rose to his feet and bowed. "There are days my mother would agree with you."

"We've news for you, Mr. Harkness." Alice wrinkled her nose. "Good lord, what is that smell?"

"That is the scent of infatuation." Harkness grimaced. "And not a certain amount of disappointment."

Rosalind touched the piles of letters. "Oh, dear. From Mr. Cavendish's admirers, I assume?"

Alice lifted two of the pink letters and scanned them, and set them down immediately. "If I die suddenly, I am ordering George to burn all my correspondence."

"Which is what the captain says he did with those letters defaming Mrs. Seymore that he was sent," Harkness told them. "And so we're left with this." He waved his hand over the scented piles. "I can only hope, Miss Thorne, Miss Littlefield, you have found something more useful."

"Have we!" cried Alice. "George is pea green with envy!"

But Harkness was looking at Miss Thorne. "You seem rather less enthusiastic than Miss Littlefield."

Rosalind turned her back on the table, and the letters. "Perhaps when I know for certain what it means, I will be able to muster a better feeling," she said. "But right now, Mr. Harkness, we are still dealing in speculation and possibility."

"What sort of possibility?"

"That of a very old crime."

Harkness felt himself smile. "In that case, Miss Thorne, I know exactly the man we need."

"Harkness," said Tauton an hour later when he strode into Townsend's private office. "I'm not sure what's put you in more danger. Using this office without our superior's gracious permission, or pulling me away from Mrs. Tauton's supper."

Harkness, finding himself in the unusual position of having to play host to Miss Thorne, had decided to appropriate Mr. Townsend's office. He also sent Tommy across to the Brown Bear for coffee and whatever was hot on the fire, for Alice and

Miss Thorne had admitted they had not stopped for their own suppers.

Alice, though, had left before the food arrived.

"Rosalind will give you the news," she said. "I have to get home. I've been chasing about London the past several days, and it's left George to write *Society Notes*, and I cannot tell you what a mess he's making of it." She pulled a face. "Come find me tomorrow, Rose."

Rosalind agreed that she would.

"Miss Thorne." Harkness got to his feet as Tauton marched into the office. "Allow me to introduce Samuel Hercules Tauton, principal officer of the Bow Street Police Office. Mr. Tauton, Miss Rosalind Thorne."

"At last!" Tauton swept his hat off and gave his most theatrical bow. "I am delighted to meet you, Miss Thorne."

"As am I, Mr. Tauton. As we've removed you from your supper, perhaps you'll join ours?" She gestured to the remains of the meal on the table—bread and cheese and a roast duck with potatoes.

Tauton smiled, and slapped his paunch. "Never been known to turn down a bit of bread in all my born days. Especially not in good company." He drew a chair up to the table. "A man in my position never knows when his next meal might be his last."

"Mr. Tauton exaggerates," said Adam as he resumed his seat.

"Mr. Harkness is too modest." Tauton helped himself to the food in front of them. "I'd tell you tales of our young hero of the horse patrol, but"—he pointed his knife at Rosalind—"I'd hate to see the blush fade from those pretty cheeks."

"I assure you, Mr. Tauton, I am not easily shocked."

"No, I can see that about you. Well, now, I think you two have more on your minds than potatoes." He held up a forkful of the vegetable in question.

"We were hoping to tax that famous memory of yours, Tauton," Adam told him.

"I am entirely at your disposal," he said. He also slurped down a prodigious draft of the coffee that had arrived with the meal.

"It's the matter of Fletcher Cavendish," Miss Thorne said.

"Rather thought it might be." Mr. Tauton set the mug down with such a bang. "What have you found?"

Rosalind repeated the story she had already told Adam— how Alice had found Mrs. Coyningham and her lodging houses and how they learned that young Margaret Coyningham had run away with Fletcher Cavendish, but had changed her mind and somehow, somewhere, become married to Captain Seymore instead.

"Mr. Cavendish was born under the name of Malcolm Elliott," Rosalind said to Tauton. "And we were wondering if you recalled that name ever coming before the magistrate's court? Or into an investigation?"

"May I take it, Miss Thorne, you also do not believe that Fletcher Cavendish died at the hands of a jealous husband?"

"No, sir. I will believe many things of Captain Seymore, but not that he killed because of outraged honor."

"Well." Tauton scratched his chin. "I say you're both reaching a good long way, but let me think a minute here."

Sam laced his fingers together across his stomach. His small eyes stared into the distance, flickering back and forth as if he were reading in some ledger that he alone could see.

"What was the woman's name?" he asked finally. "The landlady?"

"Mary Coyningham," Harkness told him.

"Coyningham, is it?" Back and forth, back and forth, turning over the pages of the mental ledger. "Something . . . no. I'm sorry. If they were up to something between them, it's not something I've heard about."

Harkness resisted the urge to curse at length. Miss Thorne might not be easily shocked, but he'd no wish to test that statement.

Rosalind's jaw clenched, and he knew she was suppressing her own disappointment. He thought about the other piece of paper he carried in his pocket. He'd been tracing more than one lead in the past few days, but this one . . . Looking at her now, angry and disappointed, he once again considered the wisdom of being the one to deliver this particular news.

Tauton was getting to his feet. "I am sorry I could not be of more help to you, Miss Thorne. But I will keep thinking on it. If anything does turn up"—he tapped his forehead—"I'll be sure to let Harkness know at once."

"Thank you, Mr. Tauton," she murmured.

There has to be something. No business like this comes out of nowhere. There's too much at stake, too much . . .

"Miss Thorne," Adam said suddenly. "Where did you say Mrs. Coyningham kept her houses?"

"Simonds Lane," she answered.

"Let's have a look at the map," he said to Tauton. "Maybe that will joggle something loose."

Tauton sighed and waved his hand for Harkness and Miss Thorne to go first out into the patrol room. Rosalind went at once to the great map of London and Westminster that had been tacked to the wall. She frowned at it for a long moment, tracing the tangle of streets, alleys, and yards with one finger. "Here," she said.

Tauton leaned so close his nose almost touched the wall. Miss Thorne stepped back to stand beside Harkness. He tried not to think about how in the middle of all his worries, he had enjoyed these few hours playing host to Rosalind, listening to her talk, watching her animated features. He tried not to breathe too deep, to take in the clean scent of her.

Get hold of yourself.

Because she'd also told him she'd been in the company of the Duke of Casselmain just today. Harkness was not a man to ignore such a fact, no matter how much he might want to.

"That's it!" cried Tauton, shocking Harkness out of his distracted reverie. He turned around, beaming all over his broad face. "Harkness, you've gone over the death of the old marquis in this business, haven't you?"

"Oh, *blast!*" cried Rosalind.

Harkness felt his jaw drop.

"I knew I was missing something obvious!" she said. "Tell us quickly, Mr. Tauton!"

Tauton knew better than to smile, at Miss Thorne at least. "Not your fault. I imagine no one's spoken of it. A family so concerned about blood and dignity and so on would be less than eager to explain how his lordship had been found dead in the gutter in a rather mean neighborhood."

"But I knew he was not above reproach," said Rosalind. "I'd been told he was not only a gambler, but probably a card sharp. And possibly regularly cheating other gentlemen."

Both men stared blankly at her. Rosalind told them about her visit to Woolcombe and all she had learned from an extraordinary old lady named Miss Onslow.

When she finished, Tauton shook his head. "I hate to tell you this, Miss Thorne, but you may have just cut the legs out from under your own hopes there."

Her brow furrowed. "Why, Mr. Tauton?"

"I remember it clear as day. Old Lord Weyland was found here." Tauton laid a finger on the map. "Now, that's two streets from Simonds Lane. At the time, his death was put down to robbery and indiscretion. Many's the gentleman who thinks more highly of his ability to defend himself than he's reason to."

"But there was something more there?" said Harkness.

Tauton nodded and rubbed his finger along the side of his nose. "He still had his purse on him, and it was full."

Both Adam and Rosalind stared.

"You see the problem there?" Tauton gazed owlishly at them. "How does a man die from a hooligan's blow, or even, you should forgive me, Miss Thorne, an altercation with the keeper of a particular sort of house, and not lose his purse? Or his watch and his silk coat? But I remember," he murmured. "He was as intact as if he'd died at home."

"Could it have been an apoplexy?" asked Harkness.

"No. His face was entirely smashed in."

"An accident?" suggested Miss Thorne. "A bad fall?"

"Maybe. Or, from what Miss Thorne just said, maybe one of those gentlemen he cheated caught up with him and decided not to bother with the business of the dueling ground." He looked to the map again. "I was a young man then, green as grass, but I do remember seeing him on his back like he was, with that sorry, broken face, and thinking that perhaps our Lord Weyland had died elsewhere, and been moved."

CHAPTER 40

For the Sins of the Past

*The public, too much shocked at the idea . . . welcomed the
tale which represented him as governed by deadly malice
growing out of the more impassioned and noble rivalry.*

—Thomas De Quincey,
On Murder Considered as One of the Fine Arts

"I should not let you go alone," said Mr. Harkness as they both hurried from the Bow Street Office.

"We have no time," she said. "Mrs. Coyningham will not talk to me again, and the Seymores and Weylands will not talk to you. We must divide and conquer. Will you send word to Little Russell Street as soon as you can?"

"I will," he said. "You may depend upon it."

There was something under those words that Rosalind did not choose to put a name to. She turned away and climbed into the carriage that was waiting for her.

Before Rosalind ordered the driver to take her to Margaretta, however, she told him to stop at her house.

"Mr. Barstow." Rosalind called the startled patrolman. She also, most improperly, opened the carriage door and leaned out. "Will you come with me?"

"Where to, miss?"

"Mrs. Seymore's house," she told him. "I'm going to need your help gaining admission."

Ned, who was clearly used to circumstances that could change in a heartbeat, smartly touched the brim of his hat. "Quite right, Miss Thorne. Very happy."

The crowd of newspapermen in front of the Seymores' house had thinned somewhat, but there were still a good dozen or so lounging against the railings, talking together, shouting at the prettiest of the maids passing by and casting the occasional hard looks at the constables flanking the door.

"Now then, lads," said Barstow as he ushered Rosalind up the steps. "No need to bother yourselves, this is Bow Street business here." He rapped smartly on the door. Eustace, who looked like he hadn't slept in the past month, opened it.

"No one . . ." he began.

"That cannot possibly apply to me, Eustace." Rosalind smiled as she blatantly barged past him, leaving him to sort out the matter and manner of her entry with Ned Barstow.

The timid little maid squeaked as Rosalind barged down her passageway and almost dropped the vase she was polishing.

"Never mind, Margie, I know my way." Rosalind breezed by. "Your mistress is in her study, is she not?"

"She's up . . . upstairs, miss, but . . ."

"Thank you, Margie." Rosalind gathered her hems and mounted the stairs, looking for all the world like she belonged there. She did not even pause before opening the door to Mrs. Seymore's apartments. But once inside, Rosalind stopped dead.

Mrs. Seymore's pretty boudoir was a sea of trunks. Her lady's maid was in the process of removing a walking costume from the wardrobe to the bed to pile with a half-dozen others.

Mrs. Seymore turned to see Rosalind, and anger blazed in

her eyes, but only for a moment before it was smothered up by her usual *sangfroid*.

"Miss Thorne. I was not expecting you," she said. "May I take it you have some news?"

"Yes," replied Rosalind. "I know that Fletcher Cavendish killed the old Marquis of Weyland."

"What!" cried the maid before either of the ladies could speak or move. "*C'est impossible!*"

"You may go now, Josephine," said Mrs. Seymore. "And you will keep your mouth shut."

Josephine all but dropped the gown she carried. "*Oui, madame.*" She curtsied, and fled.

Margaretta closed the door behind her and turned the key in the lock. She stood there, with her hand on the door for a long time, composing herself.

"How did you find out?" she asked finally.

"Alice and I spoke with your mother," Rosalind told her. "And with what she told us, the officers at Bow Street were able to piece together the rest."

"Alice told me you were perceptive, and enterprising." Margaretta crossed to the chair in front of her mirrored dressing table and sat down, both hands laid across her belly. "Very well. The former marquis died in my mother's house. It was an accident, and it cannot possibly matter to anyone now."

"It does matter," said Rosalind. "You know that it does. If for no other reason than it matters whether or not you had anything to do with it." Rosalind touched her hand. "If I found this out, Margaretta, others will as well. It will be used at the trial. So will the fact that you are preparing to leave." She nodded toward the trunks and the clothing.

"I planned to leave *after* the trial," said Mrs. Seymore. "Therefore, I needed to be ready at a moment's notice."

"You can say that, but will you be believed?" asked Rosalind. "At the moment, it looks like you are getting ready to flee from justice."

"Justice," sneered Mrs. Seymore. "Justice has nothing to do with any of this."

Privately, Rosalind felt inclined to agree with that pronouncement, but she kept this to herself. "Then think on this," she said. "The man who died in your mother's house all those years ago was a marquis. You are married into that family, and that family is playing for the title. You write poems and dramas, Mrs. Seymore. What conclusion does your story crafter's instinct tell is going to be reached?"

Mrs. Seymore's beautiful features twisted tightly. "He was a vile creature!" she cried. "He was a sharp and a blackmailer and had the gall to play the outraged husband! He tried to kill Malcolm!" The force of her words brought her to her feet and Rosalind fell back a step. Margaretta's breath heaved. She was flushed, raw, and angry, and entirely herself. For the first time, Rosalind saw the girl she had been, the daughter of Simonds Lane, who had left herself behind so long ago.

But that, too, was only for an instant. The discipline of long years caused Mrs. Seymore to pull herself back, to gain control over breath and speech. "What happened was entirely an accident," she said, her low, musical voice ringing through the boudoir as clearly as her shouts had. "Malcolm—Fletcher—was only defending himself."

"You know that? You saw it?"

She's going to lie, thought Rosalind as she watched the uncertain shifting of Mrs. Seymore's face.

"No." Margaretta sat back down, heavily and gracelessly. "I only came into the room afterwards."

Rosalind moved to stand beside her. "Tell me what happened."

She set her jaw. "Malcolm . . . that was the name I knew Fletcher by in those days. He took rooms in my mother's house. Oh, you should have seen him then, Miss Thorne," she whispered. "He burned like a fire at midnight. He was poor and ragged and he could charm anyone and anything. I'm not sure he ever actually paid his rent," she added. "And as you've met my mother, I'm sure you realize what an amazing thing that was."

"I can imagine," said Rosalind.

"We were nearly the same age. I was my mother's helper and I expected I would inherit her houses and be a landlady, but, well . . ." She ran her hand once over her stomach. Her corsets had been loosened, Rosalind saw. "I will say this for my mother. She wanted to do as well as she could by me. We'd had a pair of schoolmasters as tenants once, and she'd talked them into giving me lessons for their room and board. They taught me to read, and read me poetry. I fell in love with it. I even started writing. A little. In secret. I never showed anyone my work, though."

"Until Mr. Cavendish . . . Mr. Elliott came."

Margaretta smiled, but only a little. "He didn't just read to me. He talked to me, about dreams and ambitions. He told me how he'd come from nothing at all, and now he was walking among the finest people. He told me how they were so easy to fool. Put on the right dress, he told me. Say your aitches. Make your curtsy, tell them a story that entertains them, and they never look further. He showed my poems to the newspapermen he knew and spun stories about the genteel orphan girl who was an unheralded poetess of great genius. Some of them began to pay me for them."

"Were you lovers?"

Margaretta laughed once, coldly. "Girls raised in boarding-houses lose their innocence quite young, Miss Thorne. I knew all about men and their honeyed words, and I'd seen too much of Malcolm's ways to tumble that easily. Women threw themselves at him, and he never once thought to get out of the way." She paused and that fond and distant smile grew hard as glass. "He liked to tell me about them, as a friend. It amused him, I think, to debauch me by proxy," she added. "But he knew I'd never say anything to anyone, especially my mother. If she'd gotten wind of the number of women he brought back to rumple her clean sheets, she would have pitched him out on his ear, charm or no, and then I'd lose my friend.

"He liked to take me to the gaming houses for similar reasons. He loved to see the aristocrats at their worst and laugh at their follies. They were greater actors than any on the stage, he said. He borrowed dresses for me from the theaters he played at, and added paste diamonds and taught me how to talk, and either no one noticed or no one cared that I was not what I seemed." She spread her hands. "You wondered, I know, how I learned to comport myself as a lady? That was the result of Malcolm's little jokes."

Mrs. Seymore was a keen observer. Young Margaretta Coyningham would have been the same. Rosalind could imagine her standing by the wall at the salons, watching the grand ladies charm the gentlemen, and watching how the gentlemen competed for their favors. How they spent more freely, boasted more wildly. Promised more outrageously.

And that explained the resemblance between Margaretta and the dowager marchioness. It had never been a blood relationship. It was a similarity of mannerism. Because Margaretta had learned how to behave by watching Lady Weyland.

"And that was how Fletcher . . . Malcolm . . . knew Lady Weyland?" asked Rosalind. "He was invited to the private parties given by her and her friends?"

Mrs. Seymore nodded.

"And that's how you started getting some money?"

"I'm a good gambler, and I was able to hold on to what I won, at least sometimes," she added ruefully. "Enough times. This was also, as you've realized by now, where I met the captain. He and Sir Bertram used to go and drink and gamble and"—she waved her hand—"so forth. I don't think Sir Bertram enjoyed them much, but it helped keep him close to the marchioness, which was all-important to him. William loved the pomp and the lights, and of course, ever the sailor, he never missed a chance to throw his money away."

"You were not in love with him then?"

"I didn't even think much of him. But he was asking to marry me. I was grateful to Malcolm for the story of my orphaned state, since it meant he would not try to speak to my father, or my mother. Malcolm used to abuse William terribly when we were alone. He said I was made for far greater things. He even promised to marry me himself if William wouldn't leave off. I didn't believe him, but I liked hearing it."

"Did you know Lady Weyland was one of his lovers?"

Margaretta shrugged. "Probably. There was such a parade, I didn't pay much attention to who they were as individuals. Until, of course, the one night." She began straightening the items on her table, lining up the perfume bottles and silver and ivory cosmetic boxes neatly beneath the mirror.

"What happened?" asked Rosalind.

"My mother was gone for a few days to help her brother. His wife had a fever. That left me to mind the houses." This matched what Mrs. Coyningham had said. Rosalind nodded in encouragement. "Malcolm, Fletcher, knew I was alone there, and he . . . decided to take advantage.

"One night, Fletcher came back from the theater with not just a woman but a lady. Lady Weyland, as it turned out. I knew her from the parties. He was, I think, giving her a thrill. What do they call it when the wealthy go down into the poor neighborhoods to drink and gawk? Slumming, isn't it? He was taking her slumming in my mother's house." She lifted the silver hairbrush and laid it down next to the hand mirror. "Well, I was in the kitchen with my notebooks when I saw a gaudily dressed man ride past the window. I don't know how he knew where to find them. I suppose somebody must have overheard their plans or paid a footman. Some such. At any rate, I assumed he was after Malcolm, and whoever he was with. I ran out the back door to make my way around to the house so I could warn them, and help bundle whoever the lady was out."

"That was . . . remarkable of you."

She lifted her eyes to their reflection in the mirror. She was tired. The glow that was supposed to accompany the quickening of her child was absent from her worn face. "I know it is difficult to understand, Miss Thorne, but Malcolm was the only real friend I'd ever known. When I was with him, there was a chance I might become something more than myself. That meant more to me than any of his faults, or affairs."

"I do understand."

The look Mrs. Seymore shot her was skeptical, but she said nothing. "But I was too late. Just as I was about to pull open the door . . . I saw the man fall from the window."

"And no one else saw?"

"It was three in the morning, and our house stood apart from the neighbors then. I was stunned beyond speech or movement and then Malcolm came barreling out. He grabbed me, shook me . . . convinced me to help him remove the body, and say nothing." She sighed. "And before you say it, I know now that was foolish. But we were young, and we were nobodies, and there was a peer of the realm dead at our feet. Who would believe we didn't deliberately do him harm?"

"So you knew who it was?"

"I'd seen him on Lady Weyland's arm, and even if I hadn't, well"—Mrs. Seymore shrugged—"there she was standing at the window, her hands clapped over her mouth to try to keep from screaming."

Rosalind's breath caught in her throat. "It was Lady Weyland? You saw her? You could swear to it?"

"The lamp was lit. I saw her clearly."

"When was this? What year?"

Margaretta paused. "Seventeen eighty-seven. I remember, because I'd just turned nineteen."

Events and conclusions tumbled together in Rosalind's mind. Her heart constricted and her throat went dry. Was it possible . . . Could it be . . .

"Stay where you are, Mrs. Seymore," Rosalind said urgently. "Remain at home. See no one. Speak to no one. Keep your nerve steady."

"But where will you go?"

"The circulating library. There is something I need to look up."

Mrs. Seymore hadn't seen it. She wasn't looking from the right angle. To her, that night was about so many overwhelming things. It was about herself as a girl, moving a corpse, saving a friend, about denying that Malcom—Fletcher—could have deliberately harmed this old, vicious man. It was about taking her money and running away, about deciding to make a bargain with a man she'd fascinated, about the rest of her own life.

Margaretta hadn't truly stopped to think about what she had done, and exactly what it might mean for the sons of the lady who had stood at that window and tried not to scream.

CHAPTER 41

The Importance of Careful Research

I desire to point out the grotesque anamoly which ordains
that a married woman shall be "non-existant."
—The Honorable Mrs. Caroline Norton, *A Letter to the Queen*

There was, Rosalind knew, quite literally not a moment to waste. The evening was growing late. She ran down the stairs, past a startled Mrs. Nott, and out into the street. The crowd of newspapermen fell back as she darted between them.

They also may have laughed. Rosalind decided she would not worry about that.

"Mr. Barstow," she gasped. The patrolman was standing by the hired carriage, keeping one eye on the newsmen and one eye on the driver. "I need you to go find Mr. Harkness and tell him to meet me at Little Russell Street as soon as possible." She tore open the carriage door and climbed inside before he could move to help her. "Where to, miss?" called her driver with a laugh. Clearly this was more fun than he'd had in a long time.

"Mr. Clements's Circulating Library," she called back. "As quick as you can!"

The driver did his best. Indeed, he took several corners so sharply, Rosalind feared the carriage would overturn. She clutched the squabs and clenched her jaw, and reminded herself that she'd asked for this.

Despite all these efforts, it was full dark by the time the driver drew the horse to a halt in front of Mr. Clements's library. The shutters had been closed over the windows, and the curtains drawn on the door, but lamplight still gleamed on the other side.

Rosalind, defying a lifetime's training, ran to the door and hammered on it.

"Mr. Clements!" she cried. "Mr. Clements!"

`There was a moment's shuffling and thumping but then the shade over the door was drawn back and Mr. Clements's face peered out through the glass.

When he saw who it was, his eyes flew open wide and he at once unlocked the door.

"*Madre de Dios!*" he cried as she barged past him into the dim reading room. "Miss Thorne! What is the matter?"

"I am so very sorry, Mr. Clements," Rosalind told him. "But I need . . ." She stopped and drew in a long, shuddering breath. "This is most extraordinary, I know, but have you a peerage list here?"

"Yes, of course," he answered reflexively. "What is the matter, Miss Thorne?"

"Something has gone very wrong, Mr. Clements, and I've need of this information at once."

The librarian's face hardened into grim and soldierly lines. He vanished into his back room, just long enough for Rosalind to pace once between the counter and the door. When he reappeared, it was to lay a heavy volume on the counter beside the lamp and the cash box.

Rosalind murmured her thanks and leafed quickly through the fat volume until she found the pages dedicated to the Marquis of Weyland.

It was clearly an older edition, because the first name read:

Greaves, Arthur Septimus Maxwell Finch, Marquis of Weyland.

Rosalind slid her finger down the article, past the date of birth, the title, the schooling, and the marriage, until she came to the bottom.

Sons:

Greaves, Darius Septimus Maxwell Headly Finch, Earl of Hadworth . . . She skimmed past the other titles and the names of his parents.

Born, she read, *1784.*

Too early. Her hands had gone cold. Rosalind grit her teeth, and turned the page.

Greaves, Adolphus James Hector George Finch, she read.

Born, she read, *1787.*

There it was. Lord Adolphus had been born while Lady Weyland was having an affair with Fletcher Cavendish. Rosalind pressed her hand against her mouth. If anyone wanted to, they could call his paternity into question. If illegitimacy could be proved, or at least proved enough, then Adolphus could no longer inherit the marquisate.

Rosalind closed the book.

"Thank you, Mr. Clements," she whispered as she handed it back.

"Are you well, Miss Thorne?" the librarian asked her anxiously. "Do you need to sit down?"

Rosalind laid her palm against her cheek and was not

surprised to find it quite cold. "No," she said. "But I do need to go home. Don't worry. A friend is waiting for me."

These words and a small smile were enough to placate Mr. Clements. He did, however, insist on walking her to the door, and handing her into the carriage.

"Little Russell Street," he told the driver as he handed the man a fresh coin. She did not protest either the instructions or the gesture.

The possibilities and problems rattled through Rosalind's mind as her carriage jostled across the ruts and cobbles. If Sir Bertram ever found out the things she had, he could take Lord Adolphus to court. It would be an uphill battle, and an expensive one, but it could be done. That envious, impractical, stubborn man could file suit and strike Adolphus from the succession for the marquisate.

And Lord Adolphus had to know this was the case. And so did Mrs. Seymore.

And so did Fletcher Cavendish.

Lord Adolphus had money, or at least he could get it. Fletcher needed money to give to Mrs. Seymore. Fletcher had known Adolphus could be his son. He'd held this information back, saving the secret like the last jewel in his case to throw down on the table in a grand gesture.

Lord Adolphus admitted he'd gone to the theater that night. He was a small man, a much better fit for Mr. Kean's clothing than Mr. Cavendish's. He had ready access to all his brother's lovely antiques, including the cabinet filled with all manner of knives and swords.

"Here we are, miss."

Rosalind blinked. The driver was undoing the carriage door. She hadn't even realized she'd closed her eyes, or that the carriage had stopped. She climbed out slowly. She remembered to thank the driver and, stiff and shaking, climbed up the steps to her house.

She fumbled for her keys and let herself inside. There was a light burning in the hall, and another in the parlor. Rosalind frowned.

"Mrs. Kendricks?" she called as she pushed open the parlor door.

A woman rose from the chair by the hearth, but it was not Mrs. Kendricks.

"Miss Th-th-thorne," said Penelope Vaughn. "I've c-come to ask you. P-please. Stop this."

CHAPTER 42

The Many Victims
of a Misspent Life

Love may vacillate. Hate knows its own mind.
—Catherine Gore, *The Debutante*

"Miss Vaughn!" Rosalind exclaimed. "What brings—"

But Penelope cut across her words with a curt gesture. "You already know," she said. "I—I am here to stop you before you h-harm the best man alive."

"That is not what I want," said Rosalind softly. "Sit down, please. We are both upset. Let me ring for my housekeeper to bring us some tea."

"She is not here," said Miss Vaughn.

Rosalind froze in the act of reaching for the bell. "She is not?"

"No. I'm afraid I told her you and I had been at dinner together because you had wanted to talk to me about the m-m-matter of C-captain Seymore, and you had taken ill. She is now somewhere between here and m-m-my father's house," Penelope added. "I w-will have to think o-of something to tell h-him later." She smiled wanly. "Sh-she is v-very devoted."

"Yes. She is." Rosalind let out the breath she'd been holding.

"Miss Vaughn, if you have come all this way, you must know that Lord Adolphus has done a great wrong."

"I know everything," said Penelope. "And it does n-n-not matter."

Rosalind looked at the plain, intelligent young woman, standing so tall and dignified in the shadowed room.

"Perhaps not today," Rosalind said. "But it will. Miss Vaughn, I know what it is to live with secrets. You cannot bury them deep enough. They will be resurrected."

"I-is it m-m-money you want?" Miss Vaughn countered. "I—I have enough of my own and will pay."

"I do not want money."

"Th-then l-let me implore you, Miss Thorne." Penelope paced restlessly in front of the hearth. "What good does this do? To whom does it really matter? Cavendish is dead and the only persons who mourn him are a lot of silly schoolgirls. Adolphus is alive, and he is a good man. He is spending life and fortune to make this society of ours a better one."

But Rosalind shook her head. "Do you want to know why it matters? Come with me to meet the woman who is getting ready to flee the city for the sake of her child. Come to the prison and meet the innocent man who will hang for no greater crime than being a fool. Come with me . . ."

"He—he loves me, Miss Thorne," said Miss Vaughn. "He is all that I have."

"I am sorry," Rosalind told her. She moved forward, her hand out, but Penelope shrank back.

"I thought you understood," Penelope whispered. "Y-you *know*. Th-those of us who must live in the *haut ton* are living in a straitened jacket. If we do not fit the shape and expectations imposed on us, we suffer. I am an ugly girl, Miss Thorne, and my stutter makes people think I am a deficient in my senses. I have my fortune, and that's all, and if you knew . . . if you knew the kind of men who have offered to take me off my parents' hands . . . I never for a moment thought I would find a man who would respect my mind, my character, as Adolphus has done. He wants a helpmeet. He wants me. His title, my money, the way we fit together, we could be great and show the whole world what might be done.

"His family is a bad one. That is not his fault. But if you open their weaknesses to public gossip, he will be ruined along with them."

And so will all your hopes for a future where you can snap your fingers in the face of society, where you are not pitied anymore, where you are free and strong and sought after.

Rosalind remembered standing in the darkened garden as a young girl. She remembered seeing her father through the carriage window as he turned away. She remembered her godfather explaining, in detail, all her father's crimes, and what they meant to her, and would mean for the rest of her life.

She remembered folding Devon's letters away, unable even to read them.

It wasn't fair. It was never fair. And all Penelope was asking was that Rosalind help her as Rosalind herself had been helped. Penelope only needed a few secrets to be kept, so that she could have a good life.

Except those secrets will not be kept. Rosalind remembered Miss Onslow, and Samuel Tauton, and Mrs. Coyningham, and even Mr. Clements.

And Charlotte. And Father. And me.

One day, someone would come to this woman. It would be when she was Lady Weyland, and had money and power. They would need something—something that was so important to them that they did not care who they broke to get it. They would tell Penelope a story of the sins of the past, and she would have to decide whether to pay or to fight, not just once, but again, and again.

That was the life Adolphus was leading Penelope to—one that need and love would make, but could not hope to save.

"Where is Lord Adolphus, Penelope?" she asked. "What is he doing while you're delaying me here?"

Her mouth twitched. "A-a-actually, he is enduring another of his mother's foul parties. H-he thinks I—don't know, but I do. He w-wanted to protect me from all of this. Th-that's why he insisted we keep our engagement secret until he inherits the title. Th-then we are free."

"He does not know you've come to me?"

She shook her head. "Again, I ask you, Miss Thorne, to leave him alone." She reached up to the mantelpiece and brought down a folded paper. "Y-you spoke of secrets a moment ago. Miss Thorne, I have here one of y-yours."

Rosalind's heart stopped.

"Th-this is the address of a certain house where you were seen visiting a w-woman of the demimonde kn-known commonly as Cynthia Sharps, but when you were girls, you knew her by another name."

Rosalind's first reaction was to shout. Her second was to snatch the paper from Penelope's fingertips.

She did neither. "You had me followed."

"Easy enough to do," Penelope said quietly. "There are men who may be hired and they b-b-blend in so very easily when there are al-r-ready newspapermen hanging about." She held the paper a little higher. "I do not want to use this. I do not want to tell Lord Casselmain about your sister. Adolphus would not want that. He wants to make things right. To fix them. T-to show the world th-that he is the one who deserves the title."

"What a hard life he had," murmured Rosalind. She could

not imagine what it must have been like for that small, younger brother. To be neglected and ignored while the whole world waited for his brother to die. To watch his mother spend her life lurching between smothering care of his spoiled elder sibling and pointless dissipation. With such examples in front of him, it was a wonder that some spark of conscience kept him from committing fratricide.

Or maybe it was cold, hard practicality. Why go through the trouble to do what the disease would do, soon or late? It was clear the one thing Adolphus had learned to do in his life was wait.

I have learned to work quietly and well, he had told her. But that had not been enough when faced with the double threat of Fletcher Cavendish and Sir Bertram.

Rosalind frowned.

"W-we will do as Adolphus would wish," Penelope was saying. "W-we will hire a b-better attorney for the captain. We will find a way to save his sorry life, since that is what c-concerns you so."

"What concerns me," said Rosalind slowly, "is the truth."

"The truth." Penelope laughed bitterly. "The truth is F-Fletcher Cavendish w-was a rude, foul man who l-lived to laugh at his b-betters. Th-that is the truth!"

"And for this he had to die?" whispered Rosalind. "For the fault of . . ."

She took a step forward and Penelope took a step back, so she was pressed against the cold hearth.

And Rosalind stopped and Rosalind stared, and Rosalind took the time to curse herself for a fool.

Because Fletcher Cavendish did not have to die because he was foul and small-minded and all the other things Penelope Vaughn accused him of.

He had to die because he threatened Lord Adolphus.

Because Penelope saw a road to freedom and consequence at

the side of a good man. Perhaps he had even given her the beautiful knife, a lady's weapon.

Ulbrecht would let a lady into the theater. It didn't matter when. She could have hidden in the warren and waited until she could have slipped through unseen. She could have argued and shouted and offered to pay.

Mrs. West could have heard a woman's voice, just as she thought.

And in that moment, Rosalind understood she had been too slow and too late. Because Penelope had reached up onto the mantle and now she held a pistol in her hand, and despite the shadows, Rosalind could see that the hammer was cocked.

"I will not let you do this," she said, and her hand was absolutely steady. "I will not let you take my husband from me."

"Will you shoot us both?" asked Adam Harkness.

The door opened at her back. Rosalind threw herself flat onto the floor, arms stretched out. Penelope screamed and straightened her arm.

Rosalind grabbed great fistfuls of Penelope's dark skirts, and yanked down with all her strength.

Penelope screamed and toppled and Mr. Harkness lunged forward and the world turned over and everyone was screaming and shouting, including Rosalind. The next thing she knew clearly was that Adam wrapped his arms around her, half pulling, half shoving her aside. Penelope was at her feet, choking on her tears.

Adam lunged forward once again, grabbed up the pistol, and backed away, keeping himself between Rosalind and the fallen Miss Vaughn.

"I'm sorry." Rosalind pressed her hand against her mouth. "Oh, Penelope, I am so very, very sorry."

And then she was shaking and she was weeping, and Adam pulled her close and held her for a very long time.

CHAPTER 43

A Brief Pause, a Deeper Breath

And if we shadows have offended, think but this, and all is mended.
— William Shakespeare, *A Midsummer Night's Dream*

"How was Mr. Barstow able to find you in time?" Rosalind asked Adam, much later, when the sun had risen and Miss Vaughn had been taken away to be charged with a breach of the king's peace in the death of Fletcher Cavendish.

"He didn't," Mr. Harkness told her with a smile. "It was Mrs. Kendricks. She smelled a rat as soon as Miss Vaughn walked into your house and had the whole of the emergency patrol out scouring the city for me." He chuckled. "I hope you intend to say your thanks."

"Oh, I do," Rosalind whispered weakly. "I most certainly do."

Rosalind said thanks, and many other things, to Mrs. Kendricks, who had many a tart reply and a few firm suggestions, all of which Rosalind swore she would consider with the utmost attention.

But that would have to wait until Alice and George finally agreed to vacate her parlor, which did not happen until after she told them the whole story several times over so they could make sure they had all the details. The major, Rosalind was informed, was talking about putting her on the staff, since she was such an excellent source of material.

The trial of Penelope Vaughn was a sensation. The crowd that gathered outside the Old Bailey almost rivaled the size of the crowd for Fletcher Cavendish's funeral. No fewer than six barristers managed that woman's defense, and the testimony of one Miss Rosalind Thorne took a full hour because there were so many questions and counterquestions and points to be gone over.

It was to no avail. Miss Vaughn was found guilty, and her fainting father had to be carried from the court.

The next day, Lord Adolphus, younger brother of the Marquis of Weyland, disappeared entirely.

The day after, his body was found, washed downstream from the new Waterloo Bridge.

Two days after this, Rosalind Thorne put on her best black dress, and took a cab to Weyland House. There, the footman, because no one had thought to give orders to the contrary, conducted her to Lady Weyland's sitting room. That lady sat on her white sofa, with the curtains drawn. There was no fire in the grate and no lamp or candle lit. The room's twilight turned all the pale furniture gray, and Lady Weyland was colorless as any ghost in her black bombazine dress.

"Miss Thorne." Lady Weyland lifted her head and her eyes glittered, but whether it was with tears or anger, Rosalind could not tell. "What could bring you here?"

"Lady Weyland, I am well aware you have lost one son and must soon lose another." Uninvited, Rosalind moved farther into the room. "I would not grieve you further. But there is something that must be said."

"As you can see, I am otherwise unoccupied." Lady Weyland waved her hand to indicate the dark and empty room. No one sat with her. Not one friend had braved the threshold of this house that was sinking so quickly under its accumulated scandals. "What is it you wish to discuss?"

"It took me a long time to realize what your connection with Mr. Cavendish truly rested on. Fletcher Cavendish, then Malcolm Elliott, did not kill your husband." Rosalind paused. She need not have. She had, she saw, the dowager's absolute and undivided attention.

"You killed him," Rosalind said.

A white line appeared around the dowager's pale mouth.

"You were a passionate and adventurous young woman. He was an old man," Rosalind went on. "You both enjoyed the tables and he gave you considerable latitude in your behavior, but there were things he was not prepared to tolerate. He caught you *in flagrante* with Fletcher Cavendish, and you pushed him out the window. He fell and that was the end of it."

"How dare you! You cannot . . . you indecent thing!"

"It may have been an accident," Rosalind added, but there was no change in the mask of fury on Lady Weyland's doll-like face. "Mr. Cavendish got you out of the house, then took care of things afterwards." *With Margaretta's help, thus tying the two of them together, for better or for worse, and leading us all to where we are now.* "Perhaps it was an act of chivalry, or possibly because he did not trust you not to turn on him. Did you tell him you'd borne his child, or did he guess it?"

"I cannot think why you would find it necessary to say such things to me, Miss Thorne."

This was not true, but it did not matter. Rosalind expected the denial and had come prepared to explain as much as proved necessary. "Because I do not wish for there to be any misunderstandings between us in the future. I am, in the general run of things, beneath your notice. I wish to remain that way, and for all my friends to remain that way. It would be a sad thing if some stray word from so highly placed and respected a woman were to be misunderstood by idle persons who might be guilty of the careless talk so frequently heard in drawing rooms."

"You cannot possibly hope to prove anything that you say." Lady Weyland rose. It took all Rosalind's strength to deny her training and keep her seat.

"Such stories do not need to be proved," Rosalind reminded her patiently. "They only need to be circulated. Perhaps you were immune to such a rumor before, but not now." Lady Weyland's name was in the papers. Her past was linked irrevocably to the current scandals, and it was being crowed over by pens far sharper than Alice and George's.

Slowly, stiffly, Lady Weyland sank back onto her sofa. For the first time since they'd met, Rosalind thought she looked old.

"Have I not lost enough?" the dowager whispered.

"Yes," said Rosalind. "More than enough. You have lost your life and the lives of your children. You have seen the title pass from your line to that of a woman of no family or breeding whatsoever. It would be my most sincere hope that nothing more need be taken from you."

Lady Weyland looked at the shadows again and the shadows did not so much as shift.

"I assure you, Miss Thorne," she said finally. "You need not concern yourself with me. I have never socialized much outside my own circle. I expect now I shall do even less."

"Then I shall trouble you no further, Lady Weyland. Thank you for your time." Rosalind stood. "You may not believe this, but I truly am very sorry for your loss. I took the liberty of writing on your behalf to an old acquaintance." Rosalind removed a letter from her reticule and placed it on the table. "I had reason to meet her during these past days. She says she would welcome your correspondence, when you are ready."

With that, Rosalind took her leave, walking from the dark house into the open air. She took in as deep a breath as her corsets would allow. But even the sunlight failed to lighten her heart. There was still one more call to pay.

This time when Eustace showed Rosalind up to Mrs. Seymore's boudoir, the trunks were stacked in neat piles, bound with cordage and labeled in the poetess's precise hand.

"Where will you go?" Rosalind asked.

"Paris," Margaretta answered. "It is an excellent place to be a woman of letters, and far fewer people ask, or care, about who one's parents may be, or what they may have got up to." She put her hand over her belly and smiled. "It is what I should have done in the beginning, but . . ."

"It is difficult to leave a life you have striven so hard to maintain," Rosalind finished for her.

"We worked well together," said Margaretta. "William and I. He kept his promises to me when he said he'd keep me safe. I never wanted to hurt him. Truly, I did not. But the money ran out and his brother . . ." She waved both hands like the balances of a scale. "It was too much and it fell apart."

Rosalind nodded. "So you will remain married?"

"Oh, no. That was a false hope." Margaretta smiled weakly. "We've had a very long talk, Virginia and I. She's quite intelligent. She's also right about a number of things, including how greed can be contagious." She touched her belly once more. "I wanted so much for this one to have everything."

"He will," said Rosalind. "Because he will have you."

Mrs. Seymore smiled. "Oh dear. I may have to borrow that from you for my next poem. Mother love is always a popular subject."

"What will happen next?"

She sighed. "It's in the hands of the attorneys. There will be a deed of separation, which will include a private agreement for the maintenance of a household for me and specifying that I may keep my own earnings so I can support myself and my child."

"I think that would be wise."

"Then it's a petition for divorce and . . . after that . . ." She spread her hands. "I wish Virginia the joy of him."

"I know that you do," said Rosalind.

To Rosalind's surprise, Mrs. Seymore took both of her hands and pressed them warmly. "Thank you for your assistance, Miss Thorne."

"I'm sorry I could not do more."

Margaretta shook her head. "You have done enough. I have a chance to make a future now, which was more than I had when I came to you. And don't worry," she added. "Before I go, I will apologize to Alice."

Rosalind smiled and squeezed the poetess's fingers in return. "I wish you the very best of luck."

"And I you."

The two women stood with their hands clasped for a long moment. Then, Rosalind took her leave and walked out into the rain-washed summer day. The crowd of newsmen had been chased from the walk. There was only one man left there, in fact.

"May I have the honor of seeing you home, Miss Thorne?" Adam Harkness bowed, straight and compact as was his way.

"Thank you, Mr. Harkness," she answered. "I would be most glad of the company."

They fell into step together, and began the long walk back to Little Russell Street.

Rosalind knew there would be decisions to make. There would be truths and emotions to face, and she would face them.

But not today. Today she would walk in the sunlight, and be glad for the simple facts of her life. Perhaps she would stop for tea and cakes, and to pick up that new biography from Mr. Clements.

And that would be quite enough for today, thank you.

Photo by © Barbara Tozier

Darcie Wilde is the author of the Regency Makeover Trilogy of eNovellas as well as *A Useful Woman*, the first novel in a Regency-set historical mystery series inspired by the novels of Jane Austen. Her book *Lord of the Rakes* was a 2014 *Romantic Times* nominee for Best First Historical Romance.

Visit her online at darciewilderomance.com.